SOUTH CHINA MORNING BLUES

South China Morning Blues

Ray Hecht

BLACKSMITH BOOKS

South China Morning Blues
ISBN 978-988-13764-5-9

Published by Blacksmith Books
Unit 26, 19/F, Block B, Wah Lok Industrial Centre,
37-41 Shan Mei St, Fo Tan, Hong Kong
Tel: (+852) 2877 7899
www.blacksmithbooks.com

Copyright © 2015 Ray Hecht
www.rayhecht.com

Editorial assistance:
John Cairns • Samuel Rossiter

First printing 2015

Also by Ray Hecht:
Pearl River Drama
The Ghost of Lotus Mountain Brothel
Loser Parade

子＊丑＊寅＊卯＊辰＊巳＊午＊未＊申＊酉＊戌＊亥

DRAMATIS PERSONAE

Character	Sign	Translation
Jackie	鼠	Rat
Danny	牛	Ox
Marco	虎	Tiger
Sheila	兔	Hare
Ting Ting	龍	Dragon
Eric	蛇	Snake
Steven Lee	馬	Horse
Kyla	羊	Goat
Terry	猴	Monkey
Lu Lu	雞	Chicken
John	狗	Dog
Amber	豬	Pig

BOOK I
深圳
Shenzhen

Prologue: 1, 2, 3, 4, 5

Danny Boy
Sheila's Clan
Marco Polo in China
New Term
Always a Bridesmaid…
Betrayed!
Travel, Breakup
Good Life
Times Change

Epilogue I: Tears, A Few
Epilogue II: A Blessed Thing
Epilogue III: Gloriously Rich

1
虎

I think it's very important to judge people based on appearances.

This comes from my background in sales and marketing. It's a simple matter of cost-benefit analysis. My time is too fucking precious to give every idiot in the world the time of day. Impress me fast, or get out of my way.

This especially goes for women. Damn right!

So I walk into the club with arms around my awkward co-worker (I've read that Chinese guys are more touchy-feely, and y'know, when in Rome…), and I feel that I'm the real alpha male of the venue. Any girl here I want, she's mine. All that's left is that I need to make a choice. Who will I impress?

But something feels off. I've been in this city four consecutive months already and yet can't say that I'm able to read these people. Blank and bored looks occupy the women's faces. There are some damn hot ones here, to be sure, but how do I know they aren't working girls? I need some big and obvious signal, or else my time just isn't worth investing.

Here at the Santa Maria club is the place to be on a Saturday night. I've needed this all week, and it's the culmination of my entire day. I spent the afternoon trying to pick out a perfect tie. Plus I napped for three-and-a-half hours so that I can stay up late and remain full of energy. The air around me holds just a hint of the cologne that I picked up from the airport Duty Free. If only I knew where to get some coke in this country, I'd have done that too.

I yell over the hip-hop music and order three glasses of red wine. *Pinot Noir*. It's a South American blend, the best I can get here.

Taking a sip, I realize that I was wrong. The wine's terrible. I should have ordered rum and coke. How do you say rum in Mandarin? I can't be bothered to remember these things.

"Jackie", my workmate (Chinese people and their English names, am I right?), bobs his head up and down. Looking so damn out of place, he wears the same white dress shirt, with the outline of a wife-beater underneath, which he wears every day. Badly in need of a haircut and with long pinky nails, he looks like he couldn't get a job here serving drinks, and yet I know that he makes a salary four times the national average.

Me, I'm in my element.

It's getting harder to order a drink in this place, grown significantly more crowded in only the last 20 minutes. The air turns thick and hot, and I hate the smell of male sweat. It's different from a woman's sweat, which I can accept.

I step outside for a minute. There isn't much action out there, and it's just as sweaty. Blame the weather. In the dead of night, I've stepped out from an overcrowded nightclub with faulty air conditioning, and it's still as humid as a sauna. The so-called fresh air feels polluted, like the cigarette smoke inside the venue. I'm still not used to it, and I hate the feeling of that bead of sweat almost always rolling down from my brow to my nose. Nothing I can do, but wipe at it with the back of a shirtsleeve and try to ignore it.

Santa Maria's halfway an open-air club, with seats outside too in sort of a park setting surrounded by potted trees. Out here can get just as densely populated on a Saturday night. Bunches of cliques form. Beautiful women linger, but they're all with men. One plays pool. Another laughs while looking at a young Turk's camera pictures. What the hell? I don't see anybody I know and don't want to stare too much, so I go back inside.

The music's loud. The DJ, a hot Chinese girl, literally unapproachable, waves her hands up, and the dancing crowd reacts. All of us on the edges can't be bothered to wave our hands in unison. The white guys mostly look around for girls, although one guy approaches me and asks, "What's your industry?" I'm about to tell him that I make six figures, but instead just ignore him. And the Chinese at tables play dice games.

Some of the girls are short, some skinny, some tall and some fat. Almost all have straight black hair and almond eyes. Aside from a few Russian models and overweight Europeans, the majority here is Chinese, and that's okay for me these days. I'm learning to like it. They come from all over China, I'm told. Cute-wifey chicks from Sichuan. Slender leggy babes from the *Dongbei* North. Cantonese with bad teeth. There may even be a few Japanese or Koreans here, but I wouldn't know. All I know is that the clock keeps ticking, and I'd better make my choice.

Ah! There she is. I see her, but don't approach just yet. She's dancing. I don't dance. But she suddenly stops when noticing me. Eye contact. Here she comes. It's easier this way. I judge her by her looks. I'm pretty sure that I can read this situation just fine, cultural differences aside.

"DO YOU SPEAK ENGLISH?"

Yeah, I know. Is that a great opening line or what?

兔

I've never slept with a foreign man. But I've been preparing for a while and feel almost ready.

Truthfully, I was an English major at Huizhou Normal, but I cheated all the time. We only had fun and watched movies. I miss those simpler days. Oh, I did have a crush on my foreign professor, but felt too shy to talk to him. He was so young and came from Ireland. I used to wonder where he is now. More recently, I don't care much. I meet *laowai* every day, and it's no big deal.

I dislike my job. It's very boring. I don't think that I'm the office-lady type. But I do appreciate the free time to spend on the Internet. I can flirt on the WeWa application, but I never meet most of those people. While I like talking on the telephone and making conference calls, I hate the business meetings. When the management watches over me, I'm so nervous. I don't like meeting the customers in person, especially the Taiwanese ones.

Tonight gives me my respite from the workweek. I wear my sexiest outfit, exposing almost my whole bare back. Strapless bra. High pump shoes. I tweezed my armpits and even tried shaving my legs, something that my friends would never do.

It all should be worth it, and I sincerely enjoy dancing. More than that, I crave a new experience. Everyone says this is the city's best club.

My roommate gets even more into this than I do. She dances, but isn't looking at any of the men.

I choose "him" because I know that we never will have any deep relationship. He's an arrogant rich man, and I hope that he buys me many presents. Name-brand ones, maybe Louis Vuitton! Bags, shoes and diamonds. Then when I meet the next man, and the one after that, I hope that the previous men – like the one I meet now – will kindly leave me alone. Then one day when I'm rich, married and have my own home, I will never even remember his name.

I need this now. Already I'm fantasizing. I want him to take me to his elegant hotel room and fuck the hell out of me.

"HELLO. WHERE ARE YOU FROM?"

虎

She's mine. I ditch Jackie, wink at her and squeeze in past the crowd, carefully maneuvering my wineglass between the bodies. She's looking straight at me. Sweat gathers on my forehead, but I ignore it. I'm unsure if she's answering me. She says something to me, but it's as if a mute button has been pressed and her mouth forms the words "I speak

English" or "I don't speak English". I'm not sure which, but I get that sense of interest and go with it.

When she says something more, I still don't understand, so I just nod. That appears to work.

Carefully I make it into place right next to her, and the crowd squeezes our chests together. When I place my glass of wine to her lips, she takes a brief sip.

兔

He's mine. The red grape wine tastes good. I wish that he'd buy me a glass of it. Not because I don't have the money to buy my own, but because I want to know for sure that he wants me.

But I can't be too easy, so I stare right at him as I back away into the center stage where everyone dances, and I carry on moving my hips and waving my arms. I don't know this song, but I like the beat. Just as with this man, I know nothing, but so far I like it.

I hope that he likes me too. This guy's too cool to dance with me properly just yet, but that doesn't stop him from staring.

虎

Watching her dance, I smile and then laugh. But this can't go on for much longer without progress. I need a change of scenery, and so I jerk my neck to motion that I'm going outside. Then I play it cool, turning away and not looking back.

This usually works, and sure enough, once I've taken a breath of fresher air, I find that she's standing right next to me. Game on.

"It's so hot in there."

"Yes." She speaks English.

"New York weather isn't like this," I say.

Talking about the weather? I know, lame, right? At least I say where I'm from, and that's a good topic. It gives her all the information about me that she needs. I put my arm around her, and she doesn't resist. Then I make a joke that she doesn't get, but she laughs anyway. I take her hand, and she squeezes mine back. Very good sign.

She's tall, I realize. Her shoulder almost reaches mine. She's slim too, the shape of her backside as thin as a child's.

We barely talk. If only all women were like this.

"Let's go back inside. I'll buy you a drink."

"Okay…"

Again we play the game of me watching her dance and she watching me watching her dance. We do this for at least an hour. I don't know where my co-worker has gone. Sometimes the girl talks to her friend, but most of the time she stays in my zone. Between us, we've had three cocktails. I'm rather buzzed while she just nurses her gin and tonic.

"Let's get out of here."

"Okay…"

One annoying factor is that I can't check into a hotel without a passport. They always crack down on laws for foreigners these days, and I've been rejected at a few hotels lately. It wasn't like this back in '05 when I first came to the province on business. Damn, ever since the Beijing Olympics. Well, I won't carry my passport around with me everywhere, but I do need it in situations like this.

We keep walking. The music grows softer, the air becomes fresher, and out beyond the palm trees, a line of taxis await.

"My place it is."

Back home in the United States, unless I'm really at the top of my game, it usually isn't so easy to convince a woman like this. Here, I can't say it's much of a problem.

I'd open the taxi door for her, but she hurriedly lets herself in and sits. Nervous much? I hope not.

She talks to the driver for a few moments, discussing Lord knows what. Meanwhile, I sift through my phone for my apartment address. This is the taxi routine.

I show the saved Chinese characters on my phone to the driver. He nods. The two of them talk some more before he flips down the meter and off we go.

Even yet, I don't know what these streets are. In my wallet, I keep business cards, a pile of them half-an-inch thick, that tell me how to get around in this city. Almost always by taxi. Rarely by subway. Never by bus.

While I have my phone out, something occurs to me. "What's your number?" I ask. "I'll save it in my phone."

She punches it in and then calls herself as we play with our cell phones. Next I need to type in a name.

Wait. What's her name again?

兔

The sex feels okay. I like the style of his home. It's very big and neat. I suppose that a cleaning lady must come here every day. What did he say his job is? I didn't understand.

"Yes, I like you do that."

I'd just expected more, but what exactly? Maybe never-ending, rolling orgasms? A bigger penis? He's just a man. A bit taller. Wider. Hairier chest. Sharper nose.

"YEAH, YEAH, YEAH."

Just 30 minutes ago, we got out of the taxi, walked through the gate, kissed in the elevator and then he gave me the tour: living room, kitchen and toilet. He suggested that I should cook for him someday. Okay, sounds nice. We went into the bedroom last. He lit a candle and took off my clothes.

Two months have passed since I broke up with my boyfriend, two months since I last made love. Well, I think I'm still good at it.

"FASTER, FASTER."

Our clothes lie heaped in a pile next to the king-sized bed, together with a condom wrapper. He sprawls on his back as I sit up and ride him backward and forward. I like the feeling of this. We've only just begun this thing. I'm sure the endless pleasure will begin soon enough. He had better last long enough for me.

虎

The sex feels awesome. I'm so turned on that I'm going to cum any second. She's skinny, no ounce of fat on her. I love that flat stomach. She didn't put up any resistance. Totally into it! Goddamn, I still have the charm!

I grab her ass, and she moans, liking it so damn much. Cowgirl style, just like porn! I lay back, comfortable like, and let her do all of the work. I fondle her tits. Not a bad size for her nationality. Not the biggest I've had, but they fit her frame. She loves it when I give them a hard pinch.

Right away, it's too much, and I know that I'm on the verge of exploding. Squeezing near her hips where her love handles would be if she had any, I loudly release. Then I pull her down next to me, and I think that she wants to cuddle. She caresses my balls for a second, lets out a deep breath and then crawls over me to get something from her purse. I don't care because I'm totally relaxed.

She walks to the bathroom, returns and lights a cigarette. So clichéd. I'm slightly surprised; I don't think she smoked at the club, but I don't mind.

Damn. She looks sexy standing nude in my bedroom and smoking in the dim light. It's like art.

I do enjoy China. So far, this place has worked out well for me.

2
牛

"Shenzhen is a modern developed city."

I listen to the kid's rehearsed monotone speech, and my ears perk up at the mention of Shenzhen, where I plan to move as soon as possible. Eight months in middle-of-nowhere Hunan is enough.

"Now I live in Futian District," the child continues. "My hobbies are playing football and computer games."

As the speech continues, I feign attention, getting lost in my own thoughts about where I've been and where I'm going. Four months ago, I went to Hong Kong. It was Mid-Autumn Festival. Damn good time. Now it's Chinese New Year, and it's damn cold. At the border to Hong Kong, you pass through a train station called Lo Wu, or Luohu, that being the Mandarin-influenced Shenzhen side. Cross the border, and there you are, suddenly gone from the Chinese mainland into a British-built, kinda-sorta China pseudo-sovereign nation-state or something like that. I still have a lot to learn.

"My family is my mother and father and country-brother."

At this point, I'm just tuning out the poor kid, hardly listening at all. I pretend to write some notes.

Today I'm working at an English summer camp in Conghua, Guangdong Province, a few hours north of Guangzhou. In fact, I'm judging an English competition. Dozens of counselors and countless primary school students are in attendance. They gave me a hotel room, and I get to entertain the kids.

It's not snowy weather here in southern China, but the humid wetness entails a biting cold. Not as bad as where I came from, but goddamn chilly for what had been promised to me as a tropical zone. And this campus/hot-spring resort is low on central heating.

As you may have guessed, I'm an English teacher.

"Eighty points," I say.

Everyone claps, and I begin pretending to listen to the next kid's speech.

Truly, I'm looking forward to the real world. Quaint village China is charming in its own right, but I need some time in a real first-tier city. Sometimes I need to eat tacos, pizza, or hummus. I need less McDonald's and street food (McDonald's and KFC do exist in Hunan, but that's all there is for your international palate). I can't eat white rice without even soy sauce in every single work-approved meal. While I need to practice Mandarin, I need to speak English with grown adults even more. I need to find a bookstore with English paperbacks beyond Victorian literature and textbooks. I need a faster Internet connection, places to catch taxis, a decent bar for hanging out and chances to hear live music and sing karaoke in a language I understand. I need a social scene and a group of friends I can relate to.

Most of all, I need a girlfriend. A smart girlfriend, a cool one not just studying broken English and using me to pass her TOEFL exams. I need a modern, worldly, middle-class Chinese woman who I can watch movies and drink beer with.

"Thank you, Teacher Danny."

I stand up and step onto the stage. Three kids wait for me. With all the points tallied, their scores are tied. Arbitrarily I choose first and second-prize winners, and everyone claps. Hundreds of pairs of eyes focus on me. If I ever suffered from stage fright, then this kind of job cured me of it long ago.

Today's the last day. An enormous suitcase waits in my hotel room, and tomorrow morning I'm taking the bus to my new place. I got this job online and they pay double compared to the college. I'll teach middle school kids. They'll give me a furnished apartment in the middle of a "garden", one of those big, luxury Chinese apartment complexes.

This should be great. First thing, I'm going to eat spaghetti at the mall. Then I'm going to enjoy a massage. Then I'm going to get very drunk and try my luck at the clubs.

The day ends, and my time with this summer camp gig has concluded. I give a farewell speech and wave goodbye to my students. In return, I receive tearful waves back. They get so attached. It's only been a week.

I take a shower at my hotel. I watch some TV, and most of it I don't understand. One Hong Kong channel shows a lame Australian reality show about cooking. Here, I'll take what I can get. The Cantonese commercials bore me, and I turn off the TV. I watch a downloaded sitcom on my laptop, have a rest and then nod off for several hours.

I wake up early, have breakfast (buns and eggs) and wait in line to collect my 5,000 *kuai*. Not bad pay for a week's work.

Half-heartedly, I say goodbye to the counselors, who are young college students, English majors working as teaching assistants during the summer for credit. I give an even less-hearted goodbye to the other *waijiao* teachers, the foreigners. I didn't really want to get too close to them. Call me a snob, but wow, what a bunch of losers. Most of them are Germans or Eastern Europeans, with assorted accents, qualified for their jobs only because of their white faces. A few of my fellow Americans are here too, the worst of the lot, being red-state high-school dropouts, half of them sexual predators only in it to deflower those naive little counselors.

Look, I'm hardly the most qualified professor-type teacher. Still, I got my bachelor's degree and the TEFL certificate before moving halfway around the world, and here I naively thought that teaching was a serious thing.

Little did I know before coming to China that nothing here is serious, especially not with expats. Endless miscreants end up here as so called "English teachers". I don't know if they are running away from ex-wives, child support and warrants, or if they're actual registered sex offenders back home. All sorts of scenarios make sense, but really I just don't want to know.

We've only just started this tale, and already I'm getting negative. Someday I'll backtrack and tell you my stories and about my experiences. You'll see how such cynicism can spew from a young guy like me. Or maybe soon everything will get better, and I'll totally forget. I can be moody.

First, let me relax. I want to settle into my new home. Shenzhen, that legendary, overnight city sits right beside Westernized Hong Kong. I don't know for sure if living there will be better or worse. But it should be damn interesting.

* * *

It's still me. I still have a story to tell, and I'm not finished. Now I'm going back to the beginning, back to when I first came to China. I'd never even been to another country before. Well, I had been to Canada. A short drive from Ann Arbor. That doesn't really count. Until I flew in last year, I never had a single stamp in my passport.

Now, I've been to Thailand, Vietnam, Laos, Hong Kong and the mainland…

As I had prepared to graduate from the University of Michigan, my final lame-duck semester primarily defined by watching action movies in my apartment while the roomies were on-campus, I looked into working in Asia. I applied for a TEFL program (Teaching English as a Foreign Language) that set up recent graduates to work at Chinese universities, even paying for their flights. I'm sure glad that I did.

Hunan province was an amazing experience, and basically what I expected. Moderate economic development. Ancient temples and beautiful sights. Easy job. New culture. Bad English.

Hong Kong, on the other hand, was a bit different from what I anticipated. And Shenzhen was a complete shock to my system. You might say that I was pleasantly surprised. This is not China rising, per se, but rather this is China *surpassing*. Beyond the First World, this is Zero World 2.0 or something. Like Las Vegas or Manhattan times ten spread out to the size of the whole tri-county area. I don't know if it's all some superficial cheap-plastic model, and maybe it's going to crumble next year, but I still think that the superficiality of Shenzhen trumps the substance of Ann Arbor by quite a bit.

Suffice to say, I need to stay in China for a while.

I remember my first night in Hunan province, feeling jet-lagged and culture-shocked. That's when I met Charles, my roommate for just one weekend. The school gave the foreign teachers off-campus apartments, beating the dormitory where the Chinese professors lived. For Charles, his contract had ended, and mine was just beginning. We had a few days of overlap, and I slept on the couch until he fully moved out. He gave me his brief introduction to the teaching profession.

"Dude, you will be getting so much pussy."

"Um…"

"Don't be shy, man. Those coeds will be ripe for the picking."

Not that I wasn't looking forward to meeting a nice girl, but did he need to be such a wretch about it?

Charles told me how he got a fake degree on Khao San Road in Bangkok last summer. He had been here ever since and learned all the essential Mandarin phrases for picking up 19-year-old girls.

"First thing you do is get a WeWa account. Message them and invite them over here to study. You got to get them drunk. Say that drinking wine is part of the Western cultural experience. Ha!"

"Okay. I'm on Facebook."

"No way! You can't use Facebook, at least not without a VPN. These girls won't even be able to log on there."

"I've read that quite a lot of Chinese students these days use software to sidestep the Great Firewall thing. Young people are more open-minded about getting information from abroad, and such."

"Maybe, but those aren't the chicks you want to bang. Chicks who can email in English are probably all snobby and shit. You want to meet students who suck at the language and who've never left the province before. They're all super-impressed that you're a white guy talking to them. It's awesome!"

"Well, that is higher standards…"

"And the brilliant thing is that they will never, ever tell their friends. You can dump one and go on to the next every bloody week. Dude, you're gonna love it here."

Later that day, I surfed around online on the ESL (English as a Second Language) forums and read several articles about teachers getting fired for blogging about fucking students. I vowed not to take my lead from those people...

* * *

My first week in Shenzhen goes well. I have experience and a system. Everything comes down to learning the new names and smiling to a few parents.

While opening day can be tricky, I made it through at the middle school with much less incident than on my first day when young. These days, the kids are more fashionable and surprisingly rich, a few of them even fluent in English. Every other student has the newest iPhone and isn't above playing video games in class.

I received a tour from the assistant principal and met some of my co-workers. A math teacher. A PE teacher. Most can't speak English, and my Mandarin definitely isn't up to speed. (People here seem to have an accent different from up north. I've been assured, though, that the main dialect in Shenzhen is Mandarin, not Cantonese, because of the whole Special Economic Zone economic-miracle-history thing.) The campus looks surprisingly impressive and upper class. The halls shine with fresh white paint, and the green school uniforms look like they were designed by someone from a famous label. I think I chose this job well.

My morning classes consist of two one-hour sessions with 20-some kids per room. So I use the textbook for 30 minutes and play tic-tac-toe or hangman on the whiteboard for another 30. I try to remember a few names, but mostly just make jokes and lecture from the textbook.

So many differently-sized kids sit in front of me. At this age there's a major gap between pre and post-growth spurts. The short skinny ones, the tall fat ones and all the other combinations in between – they all flow through the sea of classrooms.

The morning goes by fast, and soon I take a three-hour lunch break in which I walk across the street to my home, make instant noodles, eat them, and then take a nap. The Chinese teachers always invite me for smelly lunch in the cafeteria, but I politely decline. Three more hours, repeat the pattern. Not a bad schedule at all.

Before I know it, the routine has me on autopilot. Suddenly it's Friday, and the week's over, done. Contractually speaking, I only have 42 weeks left.

One of my co-workers is Amber, another foreign teacher, in her case from Canada. She lives next door to me. Bleached blonde hair and a bit of an attitude. Overall, I'm happy to meet someone with the same general background. Altogether, the school has four non-Chinese teachers, but the graying Mrs. Hartford and Mister Schumann are probably not as much fun. Twenty-something Canadians are basically my culture, right? I exchange greetings with the staff every morning, but Amber is the only one worth being friends with.

We met on the first day and introduced ourselves. It always starts with, "Where are you from?" Then we talked about movies, and she told me about the neighborhood's best bootleg-DVD shop.

We both live in Qian Shi Tou Garden, beneath the luxurious high-rises of Luohu District. "That's Luohu," she explains, "the oldest business district with lots of Hong Kong investment."

Next time, I see her on the morning walk, and after that I always wave hello. In the evenings, we're busier, but a few times she waves first. She has worked at the Qian Shi Tou Middle School for the past year, and her Mandarin is better than mine. The students aren't shy to tell me that they like her more than me. She seems nice.

"Futian District," she continues, "is in the middle where the government offices are."

"Where's the hip district with the clubs?" I ask.

"They're all like that."

When Friday evening comes, she catches up with me, and weekend plans come up for discussion.

"Danny, you've got to check out Blank Slate with us."

"Blank Slate?" I say. "Sounds very cool."

"Exactly."

"So where is that?"

"Nanshan District. The newest one, my favorite. It has lots of tech companies, maybe like the Silicon Valley of the south. Very chill, I like it. And it's the farthest from here."

We exchange numbers and WeWa IDs, making a plan. By 10 p.m., four of us meet outside the front gate of Qian Shi Tou Garden. There's me, Amber, her Hong Konger boyfriend Steven Lee, and his mainland work colleague who doesn't have an English name and whose Chinese name I didn't catch. After introductions all around, we squeeze into the backseat of a taxi. Steven Lee seems to be the leader of the group and tells the driver where to go.

I'm surprised to see that the taxi meter starts at 13 *kuai* here. It keeps going, past 40, 50 and 60. Is this the cheap, affordable living standard of China I've heard so much about?

The meter stops at 72, plus three as a surcharge for gas. Although splitting the fare four ways amounts to about 18.5 each (less than US$3), there's a cheap Chinese part of me that nags, having been conditioned after all these months, and I can't believe a taxi ride could cost so much.

Blank Slate is cool. Steven Lee (I'll refer to him that way because he keeps calling himself the full "Steven Lee") says that it's the original rock club of Shenzhen. Some famous Chinese star I'd never heard of played here last month.

"Take a look at the photos on the wall," Steven Lee tells me.

"I'm impressed," I say, looking at a puzzle of photographs hanging there. They depict endless bands and pretty-girl singers posing on the stage, and I don't know any of them.

I do like the décor. It's a crowded dive bar. Lots of ironic Communist decorations. The stage, indicated by an empty, lonely drum set, sits at the same level as the chairs. There's no band playing tonight, just everyone hanging out and smoking cigarettes. They have tables out front too.

Apparently, this is Shenzhen's bohemian district. I didn't know they had one here. It's Overseas Chinese Town (OCT), modern and scenic, slightly off the beaten path.

"Where are you from?"

"How long have you been in China?"

"What do you do?"

"What brought you to Shenzhen?"

"What do you think of the weather?"

All the usual conversation.

The turnout is about half foreigner and half Chinese. I hear Australian accents, German speeches, British cheering, French conversations, Cantonese, Mandarin and what I can only assume to be Swahili.

When I'm handed a small pill, I don't even know whose palm dropped it to me. I think it's Ecstasy. Cue a flashback to my college freshman year.

Steven Lee mouths the letters M-D-M-A under the music, smiles, swallows a similar pill and washes it down with Tsingtao beer.

I think *what the hell* and swallow mine too. It tastes as bitter and mediciney as anything I've ever ingested. Before it kicks in, a Chinese girl sitting beside me at the bar starts talking. Immediately, she introduces herself.

"My name is Cherry."

She's looking right at me. She wears a cute beret and a stylish sweater and she asks me all the usual questions. I struggle to keep my composure and to impress. I talk about how I love to travel and how I'm new to the area, and won't you please show me around?

But soon the feeling kicks in, and I stare out in front of me in a meaningless daze. She says something or laughs. I don't know. It's so loud that I can't hear the quiet.

Um, I don't think that was Ecstasy. But didn't Steven Lee specifically tell me? Where is he? Where's Amber? Suddenly I feel very paranoid and self-conscious. The girl walked away a long time ago. Or is it that she walked away one minute ago? How long have I been here? Time has no meaning. What am I doing in this place? Where am I?

WHAT THE HELL AM I DOING IN THIS PLACE?

I walk outside in a way that must look comical to anyone watching. Somehow I feel like I'm underwater, under moon-gravity or something. Big careful steps lest I fall into the earth. Leaning against a palm tree, I try not to look at anyone entering or exiting. Everything's spinning. I'm a bit nauseous and trying to play it cool.

"I'm, uh, I feel, uh… highly inebriated?" I say to no one in particular. What is this?

I sit down on a space between the sidewalk and dirt to wait it out. Hopefully no one's looking at me.

It's so weird. I'm in China and in this place. Is it real? I'd be very surprised if this was real.

These are the thoughts that come to me with my eyes closed in the cool night air, shivering as gravel crawls up my pants.

An hour later I'm breathing heavily, and the sensation of oxygen molecules in my lungs feels more abstract and less lumpy. Well, I don't exactly sense that it's an hour later because time isn't something that I can judge right now, but my cell phone does flash to me: 2:18 a.m.

I rub my eyes and go inside and pee a very long pee. I order a beer. It's dark, but I wish that I had sunglasses. The bar is emptier than it was an hour ago. I hope that girl is gone.

Steven Lee approaches from the side of the bar, looking just as disheveled as I feel, and says, "Sorry, mate. That was definitely ketamine. Always happens these days. Never know what you're going to get."

He says this very casually with no effort at discretion. Always happens indeed. His tie is undone. His hair gel's all out of shape. Amber is leaning on his arm, and she looks the worst of all. She has a small bruise on her chin. The easy consensus is that it's time to share a taxi ride home.

That was K?

And that was my first weekend in Shenzhen, and my first of many new experiences.

3
牛

After living here six months, I still have no girlfriend. I've had wild experiences, gotten drunk on beaches and high on rooftops, and taught more than I ever imagined possible to adolescent children of various levels. But mostly, I just wish that I had a girlfriend.

Meanwhile, I watch all of my new friends bounce from relationship to relationship. Steven Lee jokes with me about how he cheats on Amber, and I wish that he wouldn't. All the Americans and Europeans I've met at Blank Slate and Santa Maria have a new Chinese girl on their arm every Saturday night.

Maybe I shouldn't complain. In fact, I have gotten laid four times (mostly due to dating websites), a pretty good rate for me. But as soon as I start talking about kung fu movies, Taoism or how I never want to get married, they stop calling me back. All of the girls I've met want either a one-night stand or immediate marriage. Where's the middle ground in the Middle Kingdom?

I tried to date some foreigners, and that's even worse luck, especially with South Americans, Russians, and that crazy girl from Florida who stole my shoes.

Nobody respects English teachers in this town. I miss Hunan.

Today I'm with some people I met through a WeWa travel group. It's a Saturday. We're bowling, and I have my sights set on a thin Cantonese girl with great hair. There are 12 of us, six per lane, and I reckon that I'm doing pretty well with my flirting.

"Nice shot!" I yell as the bowling ball rolls down a gutter lane.

"You're so mean," she snaps and sticks out her tongue.

Yeah, I think this will work out.

Her name is Sheila, and she seems very elegant. Her accented English sounds more European than Asian. I admire the way that she curves her back when standing up and holding the ball. I really hope she likes me.

Later we sit on the benches, weary and perspired. The game has ended, and people are discussing what to do next.

"Let me ask you something," I begin.

"Go ahead," she says.

"I'm thinking about my contract for next year. I'm halfway through now. Do you think that I should stay in Shenzhen, or live in another part of China?"

"Well. Shanghai is nice. But people are mean there."

"What about Beijing?"

"I've never been there!"

"You're Chinese, and you've never been to Beijing?"

She shakes her head no.

"Never been to the Great Wall?"

She shakes her head faster. It's so cute.

"Oh, what are we going to do with you, Sheila?"

She giggles, and we conclude that the economic development makes Shenzhen the best place to be. That's the answer I wanted.

We go outside. Several of our fellow bowlers discuss taxis. Some of them are due to go north and some west. I lead Sheila away to a vacant part of the street, and there we exchange numbers (that part's always easy). Now I'm trying to convince her to share a cab with me.

"I think it's the same way."

"Where do you live again?"

"You know. The same way you're going."

"I don't know," she says with a mischievous smile that I take as a sign.

I put my hand on her hip. She doesn't back away.

"Come to my place," I tell her, trying to sound confident.

Gently she steps back and says, "No, I'm going with my friends. Nice to meet you, Danny."

Abruptly she leaves, returning to the group of girls with whom she'd arrived. I wave goodbye and then take a taxi by myself, looking at my cell phone during the whole ride and thinking about what message to send. Using the pinyin option, I text the characters for goodnight, *wan'an*. She replies with a happy face emoji.

So many things I could have said.

"I want to show you something on my computer."

"Come to my place. I insist."

"No? I won't take no for an answer."

"Give me a kiss goodbye."

"A kiss on the cheek, then."

"Plan for a date."

Never mind. I blew it again. What in the fuck is wrong with me?

兔

Work is dull, and so I often just play on the computer or send messages to my friends. Usually I talk to my Chinese friends on QQ and to my *laowai* friends by WeWa app.

Danny, the English teacher, sends me a message every day. He's so nice. I hope we can be good friends and he'll teach me more English.

I am halfway through writing the report and I get up to make coffee. Unless I'm careful, I'll fall asleep, and it's only Tuesday with many days still to go until the fun weekend.

By next month I'll have worked at this company for one year. I believe I deserve a promotion, but I'm so nervous. How to ask that sort of thing? My manager's nice, but he is from Hong Kong and I can't be open with him.

Tonight I want to go to the bookshop and buy a book about sales or a self-help book. There's so much to learn.

What's that English idiom that Danny taught me? Ah yes, "work sucks".

虎

Work is awesome. Every time I make a sale, it's like I feel my cock growing by the inch, tearing against the tightening fabric. The factories here can't make underwear to deal with my shit! Thirty per cent growth this year, and I mean that in more ways than one. China is the motherfucking Holy Land!

"Marco," says Jackie, raising his hand for a high-five.

I play along and slap him hard. "Yeah! We just got out of a conference call and faxed over the contracts for *two overseas clients*."

"I think we celebrate tonight with martinis," he says.

"I like the way you think."

One of my projects has been to civilize Jackie. Take him shopping for designer clothes. Get him up-to-date on international pop music. I need someone to play wingman for me at the clubs, and that's the least he can do. Once I had personally approved his salary and commission raise, I knew he was ready. It's still pitiful compared to North American levels, but for him he really feels like an up-and-comer.

We make plans to meet after work, and I declare I'm going to get him laid.

Later I shower again, for the third time today. You've got to do that in this heat. I floss, brush my teeth with a Colgate electric toothbrush, and pack fresh Doublemint strips in my back pocket.

I crank up the rapper Chamillionaire and spend a good hour picking out the right outfit. Tonight I want flash, but casual. I decide against a tie, but choose a purple shirt to peacock a little. Finally, I bling it up with my most glittering watch to let the ladies know this is a guy with money. They'd never guess what I really paid for it in Kowloon.

I try to go for brand names, but in southern China you just can't help yourself with the imitators.

After some last-minute tweezes on my eyebrows, I run outside to catch a taxi. Jackie's texting me using the WeWa hookup app, and I know *it's on.*

Friday night, and as I pull up into the crowded bar street district, I think to myself, *I hope I don't bump into any women I know.* Guys are okay, I am the social man about town and everyone needs to see that. But the most unappealing part of going to the club is seeing women you've slept with. Sometimes I can't even remember their names. Unless you're trying to hit that ass a second time, it doesn't do any damn bit of good to see them again. Every time you move to a new city, got to get used to it. There's no smooth way around it. Polite nod, slight wave, just enough to impress anyone who may be watching but not enough to rekindle what is ultimately a waste of time. You know what you're here for, and that's *new pussy.*

You don't even have any liquor in you yet and already the routine begins.

What was the name of that movie again? *Brightly Lit, Big Metro.*

兔

"What do you think?"

"Huh?"

I talk to my friend Duli, but our eyes don't connect. We sit at a table outside. I face the street, and she faces a television screen. The dance floor's behind us. Not only is it noisy, but I am distracted…

I see a familiar man, and it was so long ago that I almost forget. I'm a different person since then, and I have no need for him. What will he do?

His eyes flash at me, and it seems like he almost makes some kind of a gesture. So do I, but then he walks away before I can do anything more. Quickly I try to forget about him amid all the stimulation around me at this place.

I look back to my friend. "Duli, yesterday was my salary. I can't decide if I should buy shoes or one of the new smartphones."

"Oh, whatever you like."

I stand up and decide to refill our drinks. "I'll be right back," I say.

Going to the bar, I order two gin and tonics and bring them over. I should be nice to Duli because I make more money than she does. With all this talk about expensive shopping, I'd be rude not to treat her.

I try to be a good friend, but return to see that she has wandered away from the table, talking to a fashionable local man dressed in designer jeans and slick glasses. He's short, but still a little taller than her. He shows her a joke on his cell phone, and she laughs.

I finish the first glass and I'm already a bit drunk when I reach for my phone. I'm asking myself: *Should I wait until Duli returns, or should I drink hers?*

I am also asking myself: *Who can I text now?*

Both of my problems soon disappear. Duli quickly returns, giggles at me, grabs her drink, and then rushes back to talk to the man with glasses. Then my phone vibrates, and I open WeWa to see that boy Danny has sent me a text message.

Hi Sheila, what's up!

I am curious, bored and anxious for something different, yet I'm not in the mood to meet strange men here, especially not by myself. So I enter into a conversation with Danny.

I'm at Santa Maria, so busy here.

Nice. I'm at the cinema in Choco Mall across the street. About to watch the new superhero movie…

Okay.

So…

Why not? *I like those kinds of movies,* I write.

I await his invitation. Come on already!

Come over, and say hello!

After saying goodbye to Duli which I think comes as a relief to her, I walk the short distance to the mall. It's just downstairs to the metro station and then upstairs to the cinema on the third floor. Although it's not so easy in high heels, there are escalators and the journey is quick.

I find Danny waiting for me in the coffee shop. This is our second time to meet in person, and something seems different. He sits alone, sipping an iced coffee. He just wears jeans and a white T-shirt. He looks so young, almost like a student, and I know he's two years older than me but from looking at him I can hardly believe he is a teacher.

"Wow, you look great," he says.

"Thank you. I was at the club before, dancing. It's the style."

"Sorry to interrupt, but it's so cool that you came here. Thanks!"

"It's okay. I'm happy to meet."

He wants to buy the movie tickets, but I insist on paying for myself. We pick our seats on a computer screen at the register. He wants to buy popcorn, and I'm still a little drunk, although not really hungry.

Honestly, I don't understand this movie. It has too much fighting and only a little bit of a love story. The superhero can fly in the air and fight villains, but I think it's a little ridiculous. Still, Danny appears to enjoy it very much. He laughs at jokes that I do not get and smiles the whole time.

The movie ends, and I stand up. I'm ready to go, but Danny stops me.

"No, wait," he says.

"It's over."

"Wait."

Everyone leaves, and after the movie credits, there's another scene that lasts for one minute. Danny really likes watching this part. We're the only ones left, alone in the theater.

We return the 3D glasses and visit the toilets. Danny doesn't even ask me to go with him for a drink at the bar street across the way.

It's late. We take a walk outside. The streets, though still busy, are emptier than two hours ago when I last walked this path.

"What did you think of the movie?" he asks.

"I think it was very exciting."

"Reminded me of Stephen Chow," he says. He likes to make Hong Kong cinema references.

"Oh, I see."

"Um, do you know about Stephen Chow?"

"No, who is he?"

We have a confusing few minutes as he struggles to explain clearly about this movie star, supposedly from Hong Kong. I check on my phone and see that Chow Sing Chi's English name is Stephen…

"How to say?" Danny asks me.

"*Zhou Xingchi*," I say in Mandarin.

"I'll totally forget that."

"I didn't know… I'll try to remember his English name. *Stephen Chow*. He's popular in America?"

"Sure, lots of fans of Hong Kong movies know him. I like *Shaolin Soccer*."

"I know that one too. It's great!"

"*CJ7* wasn't as good."

"You can watch more Hong Kong movies in Shenzhen these days."

"Well," Danny says and takes a breath. "That's one problem of living in China for me. I love buying cheap movies at the copy-DVD shops, but I can only get English-language American movies."

"Why?" I ask.

"Because Chinese movies, or European ones for that matter, have no English subtitles. Sometimes they do, but it's a poor-quality copy, so the subtitles make no sense. Sometime I'll show you the weird translations. It can be really funny!"

"Sure, let's watch another movie together sometime," I say slowly. Of course, I'm hinting that we should watch the movie at his place.

"Yeah, Sheila, you can tell me when the next Hong Kong flick with English subtitles comes out in a cinema here or whatever. Do they really have English on the screen?"

"Yes, all the time, but usually for the Cantonese movies from Hong Kong. Not so often with the Chinese-mainland movies."

"That's cool," he says.

"I'll invite you," I say.

He smiles and we walk to the corner with all the taxis waiting, and he hails the first one and opens the door for me. I don't know if he wants us to go together or not. I'm waiting for some signal.

Very nervously, he approaches me. He's so nice. I give him a hug and a kiss on the cheek. He doesn't kiss me back. I get into the taxi and look at him, just standing there waving. He's such a nice boy.

I tell the driver where to take me. Soon I'm home and going to sleep.

牛

I'm so stupid. What's wrong with me? I haven't felt this much self-loathing since I was 16 and listening to industrial music alone in my bedroom. This is quite the nostalgic depression setting in.

I vow to do nothing tomorrow but stay at home and masturbate to Asian porn on the Internet. All day. I don't want to see anyone.

I think about how I should have done this and how I should have done that.

I think about how I wish I could visit a prostitute. I hear there are so many in this town. From walking around, I wouldn't know. To me, this place is still an alien planet. I have no idea what all of these Chinese characters around me mean. I've been here fourteen months now, and I usually tune most of it out. All I can speak are a few set phrases that I tell the taxi drivers to get me home. I couldn't do any depraved, immoral things if I tried.

I drag myself the long distance from the taxi to the front gate of the residential complex and then to my apartment. Everything's so damn lonely. Living on the 28th floor means an excruciatingly long elevator ride. I plan to sleep in until after 1 p.m. tomorrow.

It occurs to me that I need a new social scene. Amber never introduces me to girls. Sheila doesn't like me in the right way. I'm not into getting high, I'm too old for that, and Steven Lee's of no use. Even on the dating websites, I keep striking out.

What am I doing in this stupid country? There must be a reason. I contemplate this and my lack of communication here. Finished moping through the hallways, I take out my key and open my door.

Suddenly it hits me. Looking at my apartment, I make a momentous decision. I know the solution. I'll go to one of those Mandarin-language schools. I see those ads everywhere, and there must be one nearby. Finally, I could learn something. I know that I can afford it, and I have plenty of free time. It'll be good for me, one hell of a vocational training! Who knows? Years from now when China runs the world, it could be very useful indeed. I decide to plan for my future, study, be productive and make myself proud. And, most of all, I hope it will be a good place to meet girls.

4
虎

On occasion, I like to celebrate by going to see whores. It's so damn easy in this town. Don't even need to learn the language.

But today I don't need to celebrate that badly, so I opt for a massage.

Well, I could probably convince the masseuse to do full-service. Okay, I admit it, maybe learning the language would be a bit useful.

After a long Tuesday, there's no sense rushing out to a club, but I do need to relax so I go to this spa just down the street from my loft. The door-girl out front wears a tacky purple dress, smiles, and lets me inside. Everyone smiles when they see me. They start speaking to me in Chinese, and I just shrug my shoulders. I hear the word "*massagee*", and that's good enough. They see my expensive clothes and briefcase and they get the picture. I want the *VIP deal*.

I'm led to the locker room, where I put my clothes away. They lock up my possessions and give me that wrist-key thing. I shower, and the guy hands me pajamas. My hair smells good, and my feet feel clean all the way down to my toes.

They lead me to a private room, one with a TV, and I take off my shirt and watch some Hong Kong drama for a minute. Then the girl enters. She's short, cute, and if I was in Thailand or somewhere like that I'd choose a more classically beautiful look, but she'll do.

The massage feels good, and she's brushing her hands against my sack. I'm getting hard. She puts oil all over my back and goes lower, lower and lower...

Awesome. It's that moment when she slides off my pants. I love that moment. I'd be ready to pop if I was short on time, but I got plenty, so I try to make it worthwhile.

Eventually I'm turned over, and her hands are on my balls. She takes my shaft and the oil. Everything feels so good, and oh, yeah...

For a second I think about all the guys she serviced today and whether she likes her job. It's almost like a dream. I'm in another place. I could be high.

I wonder what I'm doing in this place and what I'm doing to these people. Who am I to be doing this thing?

Then I refocus on my education, on economic incentives and on free markets and realize that I don't give a damn. We're all out for ourselves. I have a sweet orgasm that lasts like 20 seconds and then she cleans up after me. I'm sleepy, but I make it through the rest of the hand-and-shoulder massage. She dresses me, and once the time's up, I sign something, and she leaves.

I take a brief nap. I have a nightmare, but immediately forget it when I wake up. I get up and stretch, and go shower and change back to my clothes. I pay and the guy smiles and laughs at me and I wink at him. Tip included, this is nothing. I never want to go back to New York; I want to live here forever and ever. I walk outside in the still darkness and return home, and have a real nice sleep. After walking outside into the still-darkness, I return home and dive into a really nice sleep.

Next week, I'll do it all again. I need it to celebrate. I need it to deal with the stress of a bad day. The worse my day or the greater my celebration, the more I'll pay. I can return to the same place or find another one with hotter girls. I can pick up sluts at a club, where I flash my money and they flock to me. I can search online for a girl who speaks English, book a hotel in Dongguan for a weekend or fly to Southeast Asia on a holiday and pay for three girls at once.

I can do whatever I want because I'm a Westerner in this country, and I rule. No consequences! It's my right, a matter of economic incentives.

5
牛

"*Wo shi Meiguo ren.*"
   "*Wo shi Yingguo ren.*"
   "*Wo shi Yindu ren.*"
   "*Wo shi Meiguo ren.*"
   "*Ah? Ta ye shi Meiguo ren?*"

Each of us was asked where we come from. Well, a more direct translation would be, "Which country-people are you?", but that's Chinese for you. Being first, I said that I'm an American. My classmates come from all over… British, Mexican, Indian and then I realize that the girl across the room is an American too.

After class, I approach her. I'm kind of nervous, not having done this kind of thing with a white girl for a while. "*Ni cong nali lai?*" I ask.

"Um… Wait. What does that mean again?" she says.

"Where are you from?" I say. "Aren't you paying attention? We pay enough money here."

"Oh, California. Chinese is hard. Well, you're really good in this class."

"Thanks." I nearly blush. "I don't know. I've already been in China for fifteen months, but I think that I still have a lot to learn."

"Okay, let me try!"

She's so cute and bubbly.

"*Ni jiao shenme mingzi?*"

For a second, I think about this. "My name is Danny," I say, and we shake hands.

"That's enough Chinese for now, don't you think? My name is Kyla."

She's a little short and slightly overweight (well, not really, just compared to Chinese girls). Her hips make a nice shape inside her jeans.

We decide to go to Starbucks after class (they're everywhere), and we find one right across the street.

This time in English, I ask her again where's she's from and what's her whole story. She gives it to me.

"I went to San Francisco State, but grew up in Orange County. No, I've never been to Michigan. I want to go. Really, I want to travel to so many different places. China's the first place I've ever gone. I think it's so cool. I really want to travel the world. I majored in design and like to draw, but my heart wasn't in it. I was in a rut living at home last year, so my friend recommended working as an ESL teacher to see the world. Why not, right? Yeah, I'm an English teacher too. I thought about going to Japan, but I hate the cold weather, being a SoCal girl, y'know, and its hella cheap here, so I decided to try this place. Hey, you should show me around. And so I figure that I'd better learn the language. I mean, China looks sure to take over the world, right? What could be a more useful job skill? So I went to Choco Mall, just looking at clothes, and this guy outside hands me a flyer. Usually I ignore guys like that, but the training-center thing looked good. No time for me to go to Shen Uni, right? I showed up, paid, and here I am! Now it's your turn to talk."

"I don't know what to say…" I clear my throat, stall for time and try to be witty. "How can I keep up with you?"

She laughs. I think it's a sign that she likes me.

Out of necessity, I give a brief summary of the life and times of Danny Benton. I keep it dull, maintaining an air of mystery. Mostly, I just don't want to come across as a loser. It turns out that we have quite a lot in common, from being fans of cinema to the serious practice of eating with chopsticks.

Our discussion leads to a suggestion of going out to eat together at a nearby Chinese restaurant. When the waiter gives us forks and knives, we just chuckle. That's our own inside joke. I feel like we're growing closer by the minute.

"I know, right?" she says, talking fast and full of energy. "I mean, I spend so much time learning how to say that I want to order chicken, and people just take for granted how hard it is to learn to say a damn sentence in Chinese. Then they assume that I don't even know how to eat with chopsticks. Argh!"

We revert to the subject of movies, and I mention my DVD collection. "If you've been in China for a while, especially in a place like Shenzhen, then you notice that everyone has these *flat* DVD collections, ones without plastic boxes. We all only buy those bootleg ones, which just don't look that good on a bookcase."

"I know!"

"However, I had my legitimate collection shipped in here. Real DVDs, I swear."

She laughs at this, so I proceed to a subject that I always seem to talk about, one that's important when watching foreign cinema, the fact that "you can't get professional English subtitles".

"I know. For me, I'm into anime, and I see that it's really popular here, but they only translate into Chinese. Even if something's supposed to be in English, it's always in this weird fucked-up scramble of letters."

"I hate those fake English things. They're ridiculous."

"Y'know," she says, "those fake subtitles can be pretty hilarious. Sometimes they're from like the wrong movie, from crappy Google Translate or something."

"I feel sorry for any poor English-major college student who needs to do the translating. What are people even thinking, bothering with pretending that DVDs should have all these language features when it's just for show on pirated bullshit?"

"It's just so China."

We share a good laugh, and eventually I convince her to come to my place to take a look. The taxi ride feels awkward, but for a moment she leaves her hand on my thigh, and I'm unsure what to do. We aren't even drunk.

Upon arrival, I open a bottle of wine. I had saved it for something, and this looks like as good a time as any. She seems really excited to be here. Her enthusiasm rubs off on me. The more she drinks, the more she turns touchy-feely, which I see as a very positive sign.

I talk about Hong Kong New Wave and pop a Herman Yau movie disc into my machine. My living room comes fully furnished, complete with a comfy couch, and we plop down next to each other. We don't even make it halfway through the film before we're making out.

"I like this movie so far," she says.

"Not enough to watch it through to the end?" I joke.

"I like you more."

"I like you too, Kyla."

We go into the bedroom, and somehow I remove her clothes. Lord, it's been so fucking long for me, and I didn't expect this today. I need to work tomorrow morning, I think, trying to maintain my composure. That means waking up early, and I'll need to shave. Now I don't even know what time it is and don't care to check.

My heart pounds and thumps and I'm nervous but I think I'm performing well.

"Shit," I say. At this point, we're both naked.

"What is it?"

"I don't have any condoms."

She goes to her purse, solving the problem. Then we pick up the pace.

I hope that I can make her cum. I kiss her neck and thrust as hard as I can. She wraps her legs around me, and suddenly I need to turn up the air conditioner because it's getting so moist in here. Most of all, I enjoy the kissing.

Soon Kyla sleeps beside me, and I think about how comfortable I feel. This might work for me. Kyla could become my girlfriend. We could watch movies and study together. On weekends, she could sleep here, or I could sleep at her place. We could travel across China together, and I'd always have a date when going out to the clubs. We could become a couple and make friends with other couples. For example, I wonder what Amber and Steven Lee are doing this weekend.

Yes, I could get into quite a comfortable routine. This year in China, it's me and Kyla. Who knows? I really could be okay with that.

Considering all that, it is truly unfortunate that I'm in love with my Chinese teacher.

牛
Danny Boy

I've shopped with Kyla at the Eastgate shopping center for two hours now. It's a big, crazy, congested market with bargains, deals and fake name-brand clothes, and Kyla loves it. I like the food, the energy of 10,000 Chinese shoppers and a few of the gift shops with sunglasses, watches and odd jewelry. But I can't say that I enjoy watching her pick out clothes. It's the typical frustrating male-female story.

"Which one do you like better?" Kyla asks me. She holds up a blue blouse, along with a yellow one, and I'm totally indifferent.

I'd need more daring than I can muster to say that she looks good in them both. That would sound like such a cliché, and I'd still be pressed to say more. So I reply, "The yellow one."

To my left, a linen shop plays disco music. To my right, '90s techno blazes into my right ear. I smell the aroma of barbecue coming from downstairs. Upstairs, the polluted smell of nail salons dominates.

It's impossible to stay still here, so I pace in a circle. A person could be pushed aside by the crowds, pick-pocketed and dumped in an alley before realizing it. But I can fit in well enough by moving like one of the locals. So I walk the border of this block a dozen times to make sure that I don't stand out from the crowd. I try to be patient, but I'm bored.

I tell Kyla that I'm going to the DVD shop while she tries on shoes. She knows the place, so I push my way downstairs to the underground caverns of the electronics section. Video game images of Marios and Gods of War jump out from every angle while air conditioners and LED lights pound at me from all directions.

At the shop, I face endless stands displaying the latest Hollywood blockbusters, all in flat paper cases scanned from movie posters. Each movie costs only the equivalent of US$1.50. Most aren't even out yet back home. Soon I hold a stack of DVDs three inches thick.

From the corner of my eye, I notice some appealing skin. In this spot, customers have become scarcer, but those who are there study the promised contents very closely. This is the porn section. A dozen-odd nude Japanese girls smile up at me from the movie covers, and I can't help smiling back. Slowly, I slip a few extra cases into my own stack, trying not to look obvious as I inspect the backs for summaries and screen shots.

One arousing film appears to feature a bathhouse. Another has lesbians. I eagerly add three more to my pile and hope that no one notices me as I anxiously navigate away into the new-releases section.

"Hi!"

My heart nearly jumps out of my chest. I don't know why I instinctively feel so shocked, exactly like when I was young and Mom caught me looking at Internet porn. I feel the hairs above my ears turning white.

"Hi, Kyla."

She carries another large bag, this one filled with jeans and scarves. I doubt if she even notices my surprise.

Taking a deep breath, I play it cool. "Have you seen this one yet?" I ask, showing her a new romantic-comedy flick.

She grabs it from my hand. I hope that she doesn't notice the porn disc directly under it on the pile. Slyly, I hide the stack behind my back and readjust it. Then I move the movies to my side, glancing down to see that a sci-fi action film now faces outwards.

"I've heard of this one, with that actress. Let's watch it tonight."

"Cool," I say.

I'm sweaty, but I blame it on the heat. Somehow I need to buy this stuff without her following me to the cashier. Think, man, think!

"Check out the new releases on the back wall over there," I suggest.

"You ready to go?" she asks.

"Yeah, but you just got here. We all love a good DVD browse so you should spend a few minutes looking."

I walk with her because it would seem suspicious otherwise. Once she picks up a movie and begins to read from the back, I immediately speed-walk toward the cashier. In line, two Chinese gentlemen stand in front of me. Kyla remains distracted, holding up another movie and reading the back. I move up one space in the line, my heart beating.

Then I watch as Kyla disposes of the disc and walks toward me. I smile at her.

Just as she's almost joined me, she does a double-take, veers, and gleefully examines a stack of products lined up against a wall. Squinting, I notice that they're figurines from anime cartoons.

Suddenly the man behind shoves me, and I realize it's been my turn to pay for a few seconds already. I break out my hundred, spending most of it, and the cashier girl fails to bat an eye at my sporadic adult choices.

Here, they call that genre "yellow". I've learned that much. *Huangse pian.*

"Whatch'you looking at there?" I ask Kyla, once my DVDs are safely concealed inside a black plastic bag.

"I love this one," she says, showing me a cute robot-girl. "But it sucks because I'm not caught up on the series. I'd feel like a poseur buying the toy."

"That's really a shame."

"Yeah, but I'll just download the shows later."

"So are you hungry? Let's go."

"Okay."

We walk through an exit to a pizza restaurant to meet Kyla's friends.

"So what did you buy, Danny?" she asks me.

"Oh, just the usual."

"Let me see later."

As soon as I get a chance, I need to run into a bathroom, throw away all of the porn covers and hide the discs somewhere dark and deep. Where the hell is the nearest bathroom?

Such is the drama of my daily life on a Shenzhen shopping weekend. Having fun yet? I ask myself.

* * *

We settle in at a little pizza restaurant between two cell-phone mega-shops. On her phone, Kyla sends texts to some colleagues who happen to be in the area. They're ESL teachers too. When she asks me if she can invite them to join us, I say, "Sure, no problem."

While she resumes silently texting, I think about when I can secure some privacy at home next to watch those particular DVDs.

"Hey, you." Two guys, both Kyla's workmates, arrive. I've met them a few times before, but I forget their names. The balding American fellow's name begins with a B. Maybe it's Bill, Benjamin or Barry. The taller, blonder one comes from Sweden, and I'm not even going to try guessing.

"I'm so glad that it's Sunday. No work!"

"Josh really gets on my nerves."

"Yeah, I know."

They rattle on, discussing work for the next 10 minutes. Our pizza arrives, and I try to change the subject. Talking about food usually goes well.

"That's great," I say. "I'm so craving pizza."

"It's not that good here," says B.

"Take what you can get in China," advises Swedish.

"In this country, Pizza Hut is considered fine dining," says Kyla. "So I'll take it alright."

"Have you ever been to New York Pizza at City Center? The pizza there was voted online as the best in Shenzhen."

"I love it there," they agree. "It's expensive though."

Taking a bite, I decide that what we have here isn't bad. Something's missing though. I raise my hand and say, "*Nihao*."

The waitress approaches.

"Um, wait…," I hesitate. "How to say… *Gei wo lajiao jiang*."

She rushes away and swiftly returns with a bottle of Tabasco sauce. The lingo really works!

"Danny and I met at a Chinese class," Kyla proudly announces.

Just to show me up, B beckons, calling another waitress and begins speaking to her in fluent Chinese that I can't follow. Soon she returns with two kinds of drinks.

"He's been here five years," Kyla informs me.

"This is great," I say. "I'm still much newer here, and I feel quite happy to find a good Western food joint."

"There are better ones," B says.

"Cheaper here though," Swedish adds.

"Hey, I'm all for cheaper when it comes to Chinese food," I say. "I hate to cook and go out all the time. But in a nice restaurant with things like pizza and hamburgers, I don't mind paying."

"Do you notice," Kyla says, "that so many foreigners always go to McDonald's and KFC, like constantly? Yuck!"

I almost make a joke about how fat a lot of white people are. Then I think of Kyla's sensitivity on weight issues and keep the remark to myself.

"Next time I'll recommend a great Middle Eastern place," says B. "We were just in the Muslim district. Delicious!"

Later we walk around outside. With the guys still hungry after the small portions, we decide to get some street food. The other men share octopus fritters, and then we all have ice teas.

For a while, Kyla disappears, ditching me and going off with her co-workers. Feeling almost jealous, I eyeball some cheap MP3 players. She returns with a mischievous look on her face.

"I scored something nice," she says. I know that look.

"Where did your friends go?" I ask.

"Oh, they took the metro back to their place. I think they're still kind of hungover. Last night was pretty crazy for them."

"I see. That's a typical Sunday-afternoon dilemma."

"Maybe we should enjoy a quiet night in too, don't you think?"

I know where she's going with this, so I ask, "Your place or mine?"

* * *

Kyla breaks out the bowl and stuffs it like an old hand. She pops an old '80s movie into her laptop, and we watch it while on her bed. We giggle and laugh. I'd prefer red wine over pot, but this is her place and her thing.

Sexually speaking, I don't perform very well on marijuana. But Kyla loves it. From life experience I've learned that stoner girls typically don't get horny without getting high first. I feel too old for this, almost like

I'm back in my freshmen year watching cartoons or something. I don't feel like an adult.

But Kyla presses and I get hard. I feel dizzy and hear dialogue in the background while realizing that my clothes have been taken off me. The room seems strange, almost fake like a movie set. I find it odd to inject pornographic nudity into the family-film atmosphere, but my horniness gets the best of me, and I'm entering her already. We don't even use condoms. I don't want to cum too fast. I keep going for a while, but later, losing track of time and space, I exit and have a rest.

Then Kyla smokes some more, and inevitably I inhale a bit extra. We do it again. Soon it is dawn, but I didn't even orgasm, and while Kyla moaned earlier, she's sleeping now. The sun rises and I hear birds chirping, and I never can fall asleep after that.

Kyla works at a training center, a private English school, the sort that's big business in China. A lot of people I know in ESL prefer such jobs for the part-time hours. Whether the students are children or adults, it means working the evenings on weekdays. So Kyla sleeps in every Monday.

Of course, I teach at a proper middle school, and the first morning of a new workweek has started. Holy fuck! I need to get to class.

* * *

What a horrible Monday-morning hangover! I admit that it's not my first and probably not my last, but this one's pretty bad. The morning classes were a daze, leaving me with no memory of what transpired. I'm smelly, unshowered, and unsure of how much money I paid the taxi driver, but somehow I make it to work just five minutes late.

During the lunch break, I try to take a power nap in the office, but everyone's chatter keeps me awake. I feel too tired to sleep and can hardly wait until this day ends. After one more hour of break and just two more hours after that, I can go home to crash and burn.

My blank eyes stare at my computer screen as I try to save a draft of an email to Kyla. I don't think that we should see each other anymore. I'm not sure how to express it. During the time that I've been with her, I could have done so much more to improve myself. Like yesterday, I should have worked out. Frankly, I could have read novels or studied. I could have taken the time to pursue someone I like much more, someone who isn't a train wreck insistent on keeping me down.

I feel just plain depressed.

Whatsup? That's all that I write. I've never been good at breakups, especially in the email format.

She's probably at home enjoying a nice sleep. By the time I get to my home to do the same, she'll be preparing for work. We'll keep in touch on WeWa, see each other on the weekend and then do it all again.

Somehow I must make it through the day, drink lots of coffee, and just try to repeat lines from the textbook as dryly as possible.

And I haven't even watched the porn yet.

* * *

I plow through the entire week and never update the email draft. For a while, it haunts me. Every time I'm on the computer, I'm reminded of how I felt on Monday morning. Then my anger subsides, I delete the draft, and don't really feel like breaking up. I catch up on sleep, watch my movies, and by the time it's Saturday, I'm recharged and anxious for the weekend. I'll proceed with the Mandarin lessons and then a night of socializing.

"Hi, Kyla," I say when meeting her in class, and we hug. "Did you get my text? What do you think?"

"It sounds cool," she says. "Can I invite my friends?"

"Sure, of course."

Tonight there's going to be a big party at Blank Slate. Amber forwarded me an invite, forwarded to her by Steven Lee, and I forwarded it hence.

Kyla will forward it to B and the Swedish guy. Like a spore of the natural world, the scene will grow and evolve.

I'd like to invite my Mandarin teacher, but wonder how to go about that.

After class, Kyla comes to my place. For a few minutes, we review our lessons, but mostly we talk about movies. We make out a little bit.

When the time comes, we share a taxi with Amber and Steven Lee. He sits in the front while the three of us crowd into the back. I wonder if anything's wrong with their relationship. Well, I guess someone must be the odd-one-out on taxi rides of four.

The indie band at Blank Slate plays to perfection. Shenzhen has lots of DJs, plenty of dubstep and the likes. Every second hipster I meet tells me that he's a DJ. But I adore a good live show. The band plays catchy tunes. The musicians come from Iowa, with Shenzhen as their first stop on a mainland Chinese tour (last night they gigged in Hong Kong). I dance like a fool, and everyone else joins me.

"Welcome to China!" I cheer. When we all drink outside, I'm mildly sweaty from the heat and movement. I'm slightly tipsy as well from the rum, but I'm not high and really enjoying myself.

We sit at a long table with all our friends. What a good post-dance drink! I feel like I know everyone here.

Even the band sits with us to unload after the show. I saw them unloading, and, confidence fueled by alcohol, I personally convinced them to join us, and then ordered more beers.

"You got to sit here. I'll buy a round of drinks to thank you for the awesome show."

"How do you like China?" Amber asks.

"Different than Hong Kong, right?" adds B.

We splash around all the usual fresh-off-the-boat questions and comments.

In my mind, I'm the center of attention. I'm the leader of the group, a guy who really made it big in Shenzhen, now surrounded by Iowans,

Canadians, Swedes, Hong Kongers and, of course, many of their lovely Chinese girlfriends.

Brazenly, I wrap an arm around the lead singer's shoulders. He tells me that the band will stay at a nearby hotel and will tomorrow continue to Guangzhou.

"What's it like there?" he asks me.

"I'm not sure," I reply. "I've never been there for longer than a few hours in passing. It can't be as good as this."

The musicians insist that they really must be going. Then the cliques regroup, and the couples pair off, everyone starting to dissipate. Amber and Steven linger at the bar, B and Swedish go for a walk together and the Chinese girls speak among themselves in Mandarin. That leaves Kyla and me alone out in the night air.

"Um, I want to talk about something weird," she says.

Uh-oh, here it comes, I think. For a horrible moment, I stay dead silent. Then I start blabbering. "I'm sorry that I've been a little flaky lately. It isn't you. Things get frustrating at work. Maybe I miss back home. I'm sorry, Kyla. But I really did have fun tonight. Thanks so much for coming."

"What?" She blinks, totally perplexed.

Maybe I read something wrong. "Nothing," I mutter.

"Huh?"

"What…" I look down, "did you want to talk about?"

Oh, fuck, I'm so embarrassed! But I'm drunk enough to get over it quickly.

Kyla peers at me with suspicious eyes. Even if she wasn't angry at me before, she may be soon. I force out a slight laugh and gesture for her to continue.

"I wanted to ask what you think of Brandon and Niklas," she says.

Oh, those are their names. "They're cool, I guess."

"Do you, uh, get a gay vibe from them?"

"*A gay vibe?*" I wasn't expecting that.

"Yeah, do you notice how they're always together? Never around girls. I don't care or anything. It's cool with me either way. I just wondered what you think, Danny."

Taking a moment, I sip my drink and think deeply. I'm not very good at this sort of thing. Then a response comes to me. "Since I moved to China, my gaydar doesn't work like before," I say. "Maybe it's the Cantonese accent, the nasally, whiney thing. Everyone sounds gay already. Plus the girls all hold hands, and most of the foreigners are weirdoes anyway. I've given up trying to guess."

This analysis gets a big laugh from Kyla, and I indulge too. Completely unforced, true spasms of happiness erupt from us.

"GOOD POINT!" we agree.

Tonight felt truly great. I don't know exactly what my problem was this past week. Everything goes well in my life, and I need to stop being so damn anxious. When life's good, just enjoy it.

"I dunno," I add between laughs. "Maybe they're gay, or maybe they just don't like Asian girls."

Wish I could say the same for me.

兔
Sheila's Clan

Today my mother rang me and begged me to come for dinner. It's not even festival time. I have to go, and so I cancelled plans to meet my friends. There's a big party at Santa Maria, and we wanted to drink cocktails together, but Mother would never understand that.

After work, I return to my apartment, shower, and pick something conservative to wear. I take my time, chat online, and read emails from my manager and customers. That makes me almost late, so I rush outside, hail a taxi, and follow the familiar route back to the Futian District.

That's not exactly where I grew up, but it's the same basic neighborhood. Since my childhood, I've seen so much of Shenzhen change and develop, often watching through the lens of my family's real-estate business. Vaguely, I remember being slightly poor when very small, but starting right after my kindergarten time, we kept moving every few years, always into nicer homes. For the last five years, my parents have lived in Blue Bay Gardens. Basically, that was my home for my Shen Uni study years. In fact, my uncle owns many of the apartments there.

We're local Shenzhen people, *waidiren*, and that's rare. Almost everyone I know comes from somewhere else. It's not just the foreign *laowai* because in Shenzhen almost all of the Chinese are internal migrants from other provinces. True locals form a tiny minority. Half of my friends don't even speak Cantonese. But at least Shenzhen is my true hometown, and I don't need to travel for the Spring Festival.

My grandparents, and going all the way back to their grandparents before that, always lived here, even back when it was only Bao'an County with just a few fishermen settled along the coast. The Chen family has kept a presence here for hundreds of years, ever since the *Hakka* people first arrived in the south. Who knew that this humble place would one day become China's most developed city?

Our family holds many investments in real estate simply because we were lucky enough to own local property. We don't need to work very hard. We have exquisite furniture, buy designer clothes in Hong Kong, and drive new cars. That gives us rich, full lives, and nobody even feels thankful. It's just our normal lifestyle.

Dwelling too much on the past, I nearly forget to tell the taxi driver where to stop. I pay, rush out, staggering in my high heels, and hope that I'm not too late. The security guards here all know me, and I take the familiar route to our building. I'm the last one to arrive, suddenly the center of attention because everyone has waited for me before starting to eat.

"Little Sister, welcome home!"

It's a typical Cantonese dinner with plenty of rice, pork, shrimp, and vegetables. The large living room holds everyone comfortably. I scan the room to see who else is here. Father sits quietly on the couch watching sports on television. At the table, my two pairs of uncles and aunts talk gossip, catching up on family affairs. My grandmother, the matriarch, surveys the scene. Only three people here are younger than me: my cousin, Lu Lu, who is several years my junior, but we get along because we're of the same generation, and the two children, my niece Mimi and nephew Little Fo.

Mimi is ten years old, and her brother, Little Fo, is only five. They pay no attention to the adults. When I came in, they didn't bat an eye. Mimi plays on a portable computer game console, enthralled in her virtual world, and Little Fo plays with toy cars. They're getting so big, and Little Fo always grows cuter.

Solemnly, I explain that I'm late because of work. Although not entirely true, it serves as an excuse. This fails to impress Mother, who never understands why I want to work. She doesn't believe that women should support themselves after age 25, and it's hardly necessary considering our economic advantages.

Truly, I like my independence. I believe that I've learned a lot from living in the real world and dealing with international issues in my job and personal life. My family doesn't see work as so noble, regarding it as a normal middle-class activity to own apartment complexes and to not work if you wish. If they ever visited a factory, read English newspapers or surfed banned websites, their minds might open a little to understand the real world. We're lucky, and I appreciate it, but I don't want to take it for granted.

Yet we rarely talk about politics or anything like that.

"Why don't you get married?" my mother asks me. It's the standard generational-gap conversation.

"Mother," I say, "don't you know how it is these days? I'm too young. I must think about my career."

"You should come live here."

"Mother, why don't you visit my place more often?"

"It's in such a dangerous neighborhood. You could live here. Then we'd cook for you every day, and you could relax until finding a husband."

"Right, Mother."

"You're my precious daughter, please."

"Oh, what's that on the television?" I politely excuse myself to sit beside Father and watch a basketball game.

The children stay near my feet on the floor, and I edge towards them. Mimi doesn't even respond to me as she stares intently into smashed candy puzzles. Little Fo comes to me in a very adorable manner, and we play cars together. He's so innocent and sweet.

Soon Mother and my aunt push the children to the dinner table. The youngsters scream that they don't want to go, and my mother screams back that she'll call the police unless they do. Eventually, we start to eat.

It's a delicious dinner. By the end, I feel very stuffed. My family encourages me to eat more and more, insisting that I'm too skinny. I think quite the opposite and remind myself that I should go to yoga tomorrow.

The uncles drink beer, which the girls are not allowed. I could use a drink, and when I wink at Lu Lu from across the table, I think that she completely understands.

Soon Auntie does her housekeeping chores, cleaning the dishes, and I sit with Lu Lu to catch up on things. She brought a fashion magazine, and she's bored as well, not wanting to discuss marriage either. Instead we talk about our favorite places to shop in Hong Kong.

"It's a shame that we never go there together."

"I know!"

We vow to spend more time together. Mother notices that we're getting along.

When Lu Lu goes to the toilet, Mother pulls me close and says, "Your cousin's parents told me that little Lu Lu has many problems."

"Is that true?" I ask.

"She doesn't want to go to college. She dropped out twice now. They're worried."

"That's a pity."

"Why don't you help her to find a job?" Mother asks.

"Me?"

* * *

I suggest to Lu Lu that we should sneak away. "It's still early enough, and there's much to do," I say.

She glances toward members of the older generation. Yet again, we overhear the word "marriage". Meanwhile, the uncles still watch basketball. Mimi and Little Fo play with blocks, and they make an endearing sight, but Auntie's here to care of them. I decide to bond with my niece and nephew another time.

"Yes, let's go," Lu Lu says.

"How can you leave so soon?" Mother suddenly asks, catching me by surprise. "That's such disrespect! In my day, women of your age never went out alone at this time of night. It's so strange. I don't understand."

"Please, Mother," I respond. "My manager from work needs me for a conference call."

"Why so late? Your job's terrible!"

"Because it isn't late in England," I say. "I often work late because of the time difference. Little Sister-Cousin Lu Lu will come along, and I can introduce her to my employers."

"Alright, I give in," Mother says, strutting away.

We say our goodbyes and leave. As the children wave back, I promise to bring gifts for them the next time. The men grumble, my grandmother looks at me very disappointedly, and I overhear the other ladies immediately begin to gossip the moment we're out of sight.

"Let's hurry," I suggest.

Outside, we hail a taxi. It's almost midnight, but I think it'll still be fun if we hurry. I'm texting friends, and so is Lu Lu. When we arrive at Santa Maria, she excuses herself to visit the bathroom.

"I'll be five minutes."

Ten minutes later, an uncanny transformation has happened. I know that Lu Lu has stripped off her vest and tucked it into her purse, exposing her shoulders in a spaghetti-strap top. She has hiked up her skirt, replaced her stockings with fishnet tights and put on jewelry, but the most amazing aspect of all is her face. She wears thick black eyeliner and bright red lipstick. Having her hair tied up reveals her whole face.

"You look… nice," I say.

"Thank you, Elder Sister-Cousin."

I hadn't realized that my little cousin could fit so well into this scene. She flirts with all the men. Soon two businessmen in suits invite us to their table, and we drink several rounds. Suggestively, Lu Lu touches one man's forearm.

I get up to talk to some American acquaintances, just saying "hello" and "how are you". When I return, Lu Lu's very impressed.

"Wow, you speak English so well."

"I do work for an international trading company, you know."

"I want to meet a foreigner man."

"Ha, ha, I could introduce you."

"Really?"

I had been joking, but the light in Lu Lu's eyes looks very real. She leans in close to my ear and speaks just loudly enough above the club music so that the two men can't hear. "Let's leave these stupid Chinese men."

With that, she stands, announces that we must go, and exchange numbers with the man beside her. I say nothing to the other guy. Then Lu Lu and I hastily put distance between us and them.

"Why didn't you take the other man's number?" Lu Lu asks me.

"I don't like that guy. How can you give away your information so easily?"

"Oh, I gave him a fake number. If I want a free dinner, I'll call him and say that I must have made a mistake," she coldly says. "It's always a good idea to memorize a number that you can give to men and then take their details. That way, you're the one in control."

"Amazing," I say. "You should teach me more."

* * *

By agreement, Lu Lu and I meet again at the big bookstore on our next day off. It's another Saturday, but still early, and my afternoon plans remain open.

"Do you have any dates lined up for tonight?" she asks me.

"Ha, ha, you're always so nosy. No, I don't. What about you?"

"Maybe," she sneers.

Book Plaza Mall, near the central city-government offices in Futian District, makes a nice place for relaxation. There's an open park, beautiful architecture, a children's community center, and perfect spots for picnics if the weather's not too hot. I treat my cousin to noodles from a small eatery stand on wheels.

"The bookstore here has many educational books," I say.

"This whole shopping mall sells books?" she asks. "Wow, I've never seen such a place."

"We've lived in Shenzhen our whole lives, and you never came here? I often hang out here, like I did when attending university. It gave me a nice place to study on weekends."

"I don't like to study," Lu Lu confesses.

"I heard something about that."

"I don't want to discuss it."

We eat our noodles quietly. Once we finish, I lead the way to the language-studies section. As a gift, I buy Lu Lu a beginner's textbook that comes with MP3s and an educational DVD sample of American television shows.

"Promise me that you'll study," I say.

"Yes, Elder Sister-Cousin."

Next we visit a shop selling imported books elsewhere in the mall. This entire separate store just for foreigners is small, very expensive, and contains all the bestsellers from North America and Britain. Sometimes within these walls I feel a little like I've traveled to a foreign country. I always like to look at the magazines. I can hardly read entire novels in a foreign language, but it's nice to skim through fashion magazines.

"I understand nothing here,' Lu Lu says, peering about in wonder. "Ha, look at all the *gwailo* men in here. They're so handsome."

"Quiet!" I whisper. "Many of them can understand Chinese."

"Even Cantonese?" she asks in disbelief.

"Maybe, yes."

As I look at some cute children's books, the Dr. Seuss variety, and wonder if I should buy them as presents for my niece and nephew, I'm interrupted by a tap on my shoulder.

"Sheila?" someone says.

"Oh, hello," I reply. It's that nice boy. I haven't seen him around for a while. He's with a western girl.

"How are you?"

He introduces me to the girl, and then we talk momentarily about bowling, work and a travel website. There isn't much to discuss. The girl's quite fat, also from America, and an English teacher. She browses among the cartoon books, and within a few minutes, they say it's time to go.

"I hope to see you around soon at the bowling alley," I say.

"Bye, bye."

Lu Lu had disappeared during the conversation. You need to talk quietly in bookstores, and the chat was brief anyhow, so I hardly even noticed her absence. When she slinks back, I realize she's been hiding.

"I didn't know you were so shy," I say.

"Just around foreigners," she laughs nervously. "Who is that man, an ex-boyfriend?"

"No, no, nothing like that," I say. "He's just a friend of mine."

"It's amazing, Elder Sister. You have many friends. What do you think of the girl?"

"I don't know her. Maybe she's the girlfriend."

"Do you feel jealous?"

"No, I tell you, it's nothing like that!"

Laughing, we walk outside. There we talk more loudly and openly.

"Do you think she's beautiful?" Lu Lu asks. "I can't distinguish if foreign women are beautiful or not."

"Um, she looks okay, but a little fat."

"Ha, ha, that's what I thought too!"

As we reach the bus stop, I realize that time has passed, and I want to prepare for the next part of my day.

After we board the crowded bus, Lu Lu asks me one more question. "What was the name that man called you?"

"Sheila. My English name is Sheila."

* * *

Another week passes. I've invited Lu Lu to meet with Duli and some of my co-workers for drinks at a new club opening in Shekou. We're near the bay at Sea World Park, and many foreigners are nearby for Lu Lu to meet.

"Have you been studying English?" I ask my cousin.

"Honestly, no. I'm just so busy."

"What do you do all day? You don't go to school. You just live with Aunt and Uncle. Too busy watching TV?"

"No, I have my own place. I'm busy with work. Please!"

"Huh?" This is the first I've heard about Lu Lu moving away from home and working. Then why did my mother ask me to find her a job? Is there some secret in my family? I want to ask more questions, but Lu Lu changes the subject and chats with my friends.

Late into the night, I notice a strange thing. A man with a mustache, glasses, and what looks like a very expensive suit stares at Lu Lu. She says nothing. His hand glistens with rings and a wristwatch. I'd guess that he's a Hong Kong or Taiwanese businessman, but can't be sure without hearing him talk. He already has a lady with him, but he watches my cousin very coldly. I doubt if she's oblivious. Usually she stays attuned to such things. I believe that she ignores him on purpose.

Lu Lu takes my hand and pulls me to the dance floor. After moving to several Gaga songs, we go outside to catch some air.

"Who's that man in there?" I ask.

"I don't know who you mean," she says.

Shrugging, I drop the subject. Later we drink, seeking to get drunker.

Eventually the man disappears. He's replaced by what seems like a thousand other men, all with sweaty brows and smelly breath, constantly buying more drinks.

One by one, my friends and acquaintances vanish, and the bar empties. People leave to go home. Some must work early on Sundays. Others feel hungry and go elsewhere for barbecue food.

Stubbornly, Lu Lu won't let me leave. By when the sun begins to rise, I check my tab, and it's unbelievable how much money I've spent. Finally the music stops, and I still don't need to go home, but we can't stay here.

Sadly, I have no one to go home to, I realize. I think about my money and how maybe I should accept more free drinks, like Lu Lu does.

Together we stumble outside. There, Lu Lu vomits, and I give her tissues to wipe at her chin. Then we share a taxi because I'm unsure if she can get home without me.

My ears drum, my throat feels sore from yelling and my eyes hurt from the rising sun. On outings like this, I always forget to bring sunglasses in my purse.

Even so, I look through my purse, searching for I-don't-know-what. It's always filled with birth-control pills, lipstick and gum, but never what I really need at any moment. I peek inside Lu Lu's purse too, as she also frantically searches, copying me, and I see some condoms. Finally she finds a packet of her own gum and shares some with me. The world tastes better.

We speed along Shennan Road, our city's central vein, trying to outrace the sun. As we pass a familiar marker for Gangxia Village, my cousin groggily points out something.

"That's my workplace," she slurs. It's a fancy KTV, a karaoke club, the very worst kind.

Feeling a little sick, I don't ask for any details about her hostess job, karaoke singing or the men she meets when working there.

Lu Lu directs the taxi driver to her home nearby. This is the first I've seen of it, a small apartment deep in the urban-village labyrinth. She leaves, slamming the car door behind her.

Being compassionate, I pay for the entire taxi ride. I tell the driver to take me home quickly.

Outside of the moving vehicle, I see street vendors selling breakfasts.

虎
Marco Polo in China

Five of us take the long drive up to the factory in Dongguan. My only real companion is Jackie. Then there's the driver and two aging government representatives. I'm unsure of their official title or even if it's something translatable. Municipal Something-Something. Does that even matter with these corrupt Communist Party member types?

Leaving Luohu, we drive along the highway in a minivan, and within two hours, we'll be there. This is profoundly boring. I sit in the middle, and Jackie talks over me to the two graying Reps. Why was I seated in the middle?

This morning we exchanged business cards. For cultural reasons in this country, you always must use two hands to pass name-cards Asian-style. I'm reading the cards and can't get anything out of them other than contact numbers.

I put a lot of design energy into my own business cards, which show the trading-company logo and my personal information. One side is

English and the other Chinese, which I think makes a good touch. My secretary chose my Chinese name. All in all, my card cost damn pitiful chump change, 10 times less than at a Kinkos back home. That's just one example of the many costs I've saved by relocating here.

Soon I'm thinking about undressing my secretary, not because she's hot, but because there's nothing else to do. I wonder if I could get away with slapping her ass, rubbing her tits. What the fuck, if I'm thinking it, then why not go all out? Like, what if I just whipped out my cock for her?! It isn't such a litigious culture here.

I laugh to myself, quietly enough that no one notices. Such thoughts entertain me on these long dull rides. I twiddle my thumbs and peer out a window. It's almost like I'm a kid again with Dad driving my sister and me to Jersey.

My travel companions keep talking.

"*Xie xie*," I can say. And "*Nihao*".

Right now, I can't listen to music. I can't even read a book or a newspaper. It'd be rude. So I just smile and nod, trying not to fade into sleep or go crazy from boredom.

Everyone else still talks to each other, and I have nothing to add. I'm beginning to think that I'm here just for show.

* * *

Chinese factories, like many things in China, look nicer and nicer every year, but upon further inspection it's like the whole thing's a showroom kitchen with leaky pipes. While everything appears very high-tech, closer looks show that the wiring's ripped, the walls are cracked, and everything's somehow vaguely unglued.

I try not to think about it. After all, I'm not even the quality control guy. He'll come along next week.

All I know is that this place converts chemicals into vital cell-phone battery parts, and we at the firm need to broker an agreement to sell to customers in Western Europe and North America. For the most part, I just want to sign documents, get my picture taken, and make sure the deal goes through.

Soon we're holed up in the middle of nowhere, surrounded only by factories and hotels. After the factory manager gives us a quick tour, we head to a restaurant in a hotel down the street. I don't really care about the factory. As long as it doesn't go up in flames, that's fine by me.

Real work happens at the dinners. Jackie does the talking, which is his job. That's when we pay the government representatives to eat with us. It's always at one of those big, round tables with endless side dishes of strange Chinese food. Not like Chinatown at all! Truthfully, I prefer the working-man square lunchboxes to this. But most importantly, I drink up the *baijiu*, and all the little Chinese guys sound very impressed by my ability to hold liquor. Then my work here's done.

Finally the driver takes Jackie and me to the hotel in the downtown Changping District. We're back in civilization. Bright lights, all that. Now this feels more like home.

In true Chinese style, the hotel's lavish. The bellhop takes my bag and gives me a key card. I slump down on my bed ready to channel surf.

"Have a good night, Marco," says Jackie from across the hall.

"*Wan'an*," I say, now having exhausted my entire vocabulary.

The bellhop shuts the door behind him. I take a quick shower and change into a casual blue polo shirt and slacks. To kill time, I check if there's anything available in English on the Hong Kong channels.

For about half an hour, I wait. When I'm sure that Jackie wouldn't be hanging around, I sneak off to explore. From the lobby, I rush outside and check the area in front of the hotel for a newsstand. After buying a pack of cigarettes and a disposable lighter for just one *kuai*, I go on my way.

If I remember correctly, Changping has a reputation as the red-light district of Dongguan, although an argument could be made that the whole damn country is one big red-light district. Whatever. I'm horny these days and need to do something about it. Work keeps me busy, leaving less time to pick up at the clubs, and for the sake of self-control, I try to limit myself to one massage per week.

Looking around, I see some of the beautiful girls of Dongguan. I know they're all pros. The concept turns me on. I don't see any bars here, just shining five-story KTV discos. Being out and about on my own, I don't feel like hiring one of those hostesses and then singing lame Michael Jackson songs.

So I'm on my fourth cigarette, just hanging around and looking at all the Chinese restaurants, when a thin girl in a short white skirt walks by me. She's texting on her phone, and as she passes, I follow.

I tap her on a shoulder, and she looks at me.

"Baby, do you speak English?"

She just shakes her head, giving me the impression that she understands.

"I just want to ask you a question. What kind of phone do you have? I want to buy a gift for my friend. Can I take a look?"

"No, sorry." She walks away.

As I once learned at a sales seminar upstate, "no" just means "I want more information".

This time I grab her by a shoulder and forcibly turn her around to face me. She complies. They always do.

"I'm staying at the hotel down the street, and I have one thousand *kuai*. How much?"

She chuckles, covers her face, embarrassed, and scampers off again. I shrug, let her go and chalk it up to experience.

Tired, I don't feel like repeating this pickup process. I decide to wander the back alleys, and immediately I spy the pink-light brothels. A peek inside of the first one to my left shows it filled to the brim with waiting sluts, all with faces bearing familiar looks of profound boredom.

"Hello," yells the Mama-san.

What the hell? I decide, going inside.

This is me settling for what I can find. Save some money at least, I think.

I've got one more night here. Tomorrow evening, we'll treat the clients to a KTV party, and my luck should improve then.

Sometimes I like these trips to Dongguan.

* * *

After all the meetings and paperwork, this party represents the payoff. It seals the deal. We're all damn drunk inside what must be the most lavish karaoke club in all of southern China.

I know that's a bold statement, claiming to have found the most lavish in this most lavish of lands. But seriously, this club has to rank in the top five. When we go inside, there's a lineup of 40 girls in skimpy outfits. All of them nines or tens! In half-bikinis or half-miniskirts, red like Chinese lanterns. Plus the buffet's tremendous. The champagne tastes a little cheap, but for Asia, I'm okay with it.

Four men, each of us with a companion, sit in the little box-room without windows. We're the same crew as on the minivan ride, *sans* the driver. The Party Reps sing a few corny propaganda songs. I don't understand the lyrics, but you can tell patriotic propaganda jingles when you hear them. The TV-screen video, often enough hilarious, looks especially great with soldiers marching and soap-opera clips. But mostly the girls sing various Cantopop tunes while we men watch the show, eat fruit, and drink.

I needed to beg Jackie to come along, for translation services, if nothing else. Now he's drunk, loving it and taking a real liking to his girl. She seems familiar somehow. Maybe I fucked her cousin. I don't know, but it's entirely possible. Ha!

By thinking these thoughts, I amuse myself. The language barrier's still tricky. As for the girls, with the amount of money we're paying, they'd better comply. I see Jackie's girl rubbing his belly. The two old men each have an arm around a girl. I'm rubbing an open thigh and being treated to smiles. But impatiently, I can't wait to get out of here and back to my hotel room.

First, we must keep up appearances. "Marco, please sing us an English song," Jackie urges me.

"No, no, I'm much too embarrassed."

He translates to the others, and they all laugh.

"They say you must sing," he says.

I know that I need to surrender. Approaching the computer monitor, I have no idea how to choose a song. To me, it's all hieroglyphics.

The girls come up and press buttons for me, but no English appears. Jackie's girl, the familiar one, practices some English on me. "Hello, how are you?" she says, sounding like a robot repeating a pre-recorded line. She neglects to look me in the eye.

"Um, I'm fine."

"Please, what song you like?"

"I don't know yet. What songs you got?"

She directs me to an alphabetical listing on the screen. It's good to see ABCs. But this isn't how karaoke should work. Damn! I can't remember the name of every song in history and choose from memory.

"Can't you go by artists?"

"Sorry. What?"

Jackie translates, and then she presses more buttons. Finally we reach a list of musical artists. What a pathetic selection! Under the letter A, I know only Aretha Franklin. Under B, we have the Beatles. Okay then.

I choose *Can't Buy Me Love*, music starts, and here we go.

"*CAN'T BUY ME LOVE! I'll buy you a diamond ring, my friend....*"

Everyone cheers: the clients, my co-worker and the four beautiful working girls. It's a nice feeling.

"Ha, Marco's so talented," Jackie congratulates.

"Thank you. Thank you." I bow.

"Cheers," we all say at once and clink glasses. It's the one English word that every single Chinese person I've ever met knows. They know it even better than "hello".

* * *

In front of me, I have two bare asses. They cost me only a grand each. That's in RMB.

Enthusiastically, I slap the one on the left and pound away against the other one. She insisted that I wear a rubber. That part never gets lost in translation. This experience would have felt better without, but whatever…

I wish that I could persuade these girls to perform some lesbian shit. I push their heads together. They kind of kiss for a second, but then smirk and turn away. Don't these bitches watch porn, or what?

My cock feels ready to explode out from under me, almost like I should call in a bomb threat to the hotel or something. Fucking right on!

I press their bodies against each other. I pull their hair. Next I raise their asses one by one from the side of the bed. Standing, I go in and out one at a time. I feel like this makes a good workout for my ass and hips.

Within a minute, I'm bored of this so I make them lie on top of each other. Then I climb onto the bed and do the same, in and out, working my thighs.

On TV, a game show plays out. The participants yell something in Mandarin, and I don't get it. Well, it keeps the girls entertained.

They perform the loud, exaggerated moaning thing that girls here always do. Maybe they expect me to cum and finish this. But I'm a businessman expecting to get every *jiao* worth from the hour that I purchased. I popped a Viagra, easy enough to procure in town, and I expect to keep going for quite a while. But it could be better.

Damn! I wish I could procure some coke right now. Some things about home I do miss.

牛
New Term

The new school term begins. I see a lot of faces this Monday morning, some vaguely familiar, some favored students, some new faces. One of the new faces belongs to a fresh teacher.

Now I've become more senior and will be a mentor to the new guy. Other than an occasional substitute teacher, we have only four *waijiao* (foreign teachers), including me, Amber, Mister Schumann (Mrs. Hartford went back to England) and the new kid.

"Hi, my name is Aidan," he says. He looks like he must be 18 years old. Should he even be working here?

"Nice to meet you," I say.

His accent's hard to place, but he claims to come from New Zealand. I doubt if he's ever gone far from his hometown before. He has wide eyes all the time, fascinated by the new surroundings, and appears to sincerely enjoy working with teenagers.

I explain a few games to him and how to go through the textbook on a chapter-by-week basis. "Just don't take it all too seriously," I advise. "We're here to make the school look worldly, to justify the high tuition by parading as part of an international faculty. Show up every day, sound a bit entertaining and you'll do great."

"Thanks, Danny. That's so nice of you."

We exchange email addresses. Later I'll link him into the ESL forums. He'll be fine.

"Danny, how long have you been here?" he asks me on Friday.

"Well," I say. "I've been in Shenzhen for a year now, but in China almost two years. Before here I lived in a town you've never heard of up north."

"Wow," he says, easily impressed.

I feel cool, sophisticated.

Then he continues. "What do you like to do for fun now that it's the weekend?"

"Partying, mostly. Shopping maybe. That's the national pastime."

"Do you like to play football?" he asks. I remember that means soccer.

"Sorry. Not really."

"Oh," he says, disappointed. "What else is there to do? It's such a big city, and I don't know where to start."

"Tell you what," I say. "I know a ton of bars and clubs. What kind of scene do you like?"

He twiddles his thumbs and considers what to say. "I don't really know, but I always like how things look in the hip-hop videos."

"We'll go to a party on Saturday. I know just the venue. Meanwhile, explore. Ride a bus to random places. Eastgate is good. That's very Chinese, very Shenzhen."

On Weekend One, I introduce him to all the right people. We go to a bar and then the after-party, nodding off on taxi rides at dawn. He's shy, even around the Chinese girls, and I feel like I have a sidekick. He texts me all the time.

It's Week Two, a Wednesday, and the vice-principal tells me that she's happy with Aidan's performance. I hope that they'll notice my training factor and give me a raise next term. As I walk through the halls thinking about this, some of my students high-five me, and then I see Aidan down the hall. He looks lost. Maybe I should say something.

"Uh, hi."

"Hey, man," he says, still awkward.

"So did you go to Eastgate yet?" I ask.

"No, I'm not sure how to get there. To be honest, I haven't even left this neighborhood, except when I hang out with you and Amber."

"Allow me." I have the address saved on my phone and show him the screen.

"Those characters say, '*Lao jie*'. That means '*old street*'."

"Wow, you can read Chinese?"

"Well, not really. I just take some lessons. That's fairly beginner."

"Wow," he adds, still impressed.

"I'll text you."

Whenever I have a chance after work, I go to the marketplace to eat street food and people-watch. Aidan and I agree to meet after class for a quick snack of Beijing-style egg pancakes and *baozi* buns with vegetables inside. In front of the tobacco shop, we sit on a small bench and drink beers when Amber walks over from an alley and joins us.

"So," I say, continuing our chat, "if you take the 205 bus around the corner, or just take any taxi to a metro stop, it's easy to get there."

"I really want to buy gifts for my mom and dad," says Aidan. "Can I get that kind of thing at this place? But not too expensive."

"Then Eastgate's the place," says Amber. "Take a cab anywhere and learn to say it, '*dongmen*'."

"Loads of gift shops," I promise.

"I love going to those," Amber enthuses. "You can buy little fans for like ten *kuai* each. There's DVDs, handbags and jeans. Do you know the novelty condom shop, the one in the mall on the second floor? They make like lollipops and stuff. Great gag gifts!"

Aidan blushes.

"Are you going there tonight?" he asks me.

"I'm meeting my girlfriend. Just text me if you need anything, whatever."

"Okay."

"And one more thing," I add. "This should be obvious, but be very careful of thieves. This is pickpocket city."

* * *

Kyla and I watch a YouTube video courtesy of MegaSurf Proxy Systems. It's the only way to get around censorship in this part of the world. Kyla snuggles under my shoulder as we lie on the bed with a laptop over my stomach.

We laugh. She's high. I'm not.

I receive a text message and hear my phone vibrate. For a few minutes, I ignore it. Later I get up to pee and notice it's from Aidan.

"*CAN YOU CALL ME BACK PLEASE?*"

Frankly, I never like the all-caps-to-grab-attention thing. Going into the kitchen, I get another beer. "You want one, babe?" I ask.

"Huh?"

"You want a beer?"

"Sure, cool!"

We hang out for a while longer. Then my phone informs me of another message. Taking my time, I finish my beer and casually look.

"*I HAVE KIND OF AN EMERGENCY. MY PASSPORT WAS STOLEN.*"

Oh, Jesus.

* * *

I'm too nice. Really, I am.

When I call Aidan back, Kyla overhears and convinces me to meet up with him. Quickly I get dressed, and she comes with me, speeding by taxi to the historic Lao Jie McDonald's restaurant.

We find Aidan slurping a Coca-Cola alone. The poor kid looks terrible, as if his pet cat had just gotten run over.

"You know," I say, "this is the first McDonald's in mainland China. In 1990, it began as part of the original Special Economic Zone experiment. It's a real historical testament to globalism."

"Wow," he says, not entirely interested, but struggling to be nice and to stay calm.

After a long pause, I get down to business. "Let's figure out what we're going to do."

"Okay."

"Exactly what happened?"

"I was trying on these shoes," he says, and shows us his footwear. They're Vans knockoffs, green and look nice. "I left my backpack and walked around. To test them out, you know. When I came back, my backpack wasn't there."

"I specifically told you to be careful," I say, sounding stern and condescending.

He hangs his head a little. "Yeah, I know."

"Live and learn," Kyla says compassionately. "Let's go find a cop."

"Do you think," he pauses for effect, "that the merchant was in on it?"

We walk around among the endless crowds of shoppers, and Kyla holds onto her purse very tightly. For several minutes, we don't say anything.

Finally I can't hold my tongue any longer. "Why the hell did you bring your passport to go shopping, man?"

"I don't know. I'm sorry."

Two cops stand on a nearby corner. I take out my phrasebook and try to convey what happened. Mostly I end up saying my classic line, "*Ting bu dong*", which means I don't understand.

"This isn't working," I say, taking out my cell phone. Embarrassed, I call Steven Lee and explain the situation. The perturbed police officer understands when I hand him the phone.

"I called my Chinese friend," I explain to Aidan.

"You can't translate?" he asks me.

"I can't speak much Chinese, dude."

The officer talks and then gives me back the phone. I raise it and listen.

"Mate," says Steven Lee. "It's like this. You need to make a robbery report at the nearest Public Security Bureau station. Then you can go to the consulate for his country. It's up to his country to issue a new emergency passport. The police officers will give you the address to go for the report."

The officer writes something on a notepad, smiles at us, and says something else.

"Fucking useless police," I say.

"What?" Aidan asks. Kyla just looks at me.

"Nothing," I mutter.

I can't stay angry. Really, I don't like conflict. Mostly I just hope that Aidan doesn't do this again one day and drag me around all over again.

We make our way to the main street and find taxis waiting at the corner of Shennan and Eastgate. From Aidan's face, I can see that he feels terrible. Poor guy. He'd just arrived in the big city, and out in the big world, for that matter, and it was too much for him.

"I'll take care of school for you tomorrow," I tell him.

"What? Why?"

"They have to know that you won't be there for at least the next two days. I'll explain what happened, and maybe they can find a substitute to cover your classes."

"Oh, I see."

"Just go to the address. It's the main police station, and I'm sure that someone there speaks English."

"And then?"

"Then you look up online where to find the nearest New Zealand consulate. I don't know. It should be in Guangzhou somewhere. That's the capital of the province."

"Canton," says Kyla, mentioning Guangzhou's other name. "Y'know? I've been to the American consulate too. Don't worry. Taxis are cheaper in Guangzhou."

"Can't I go to Hong Kong?" Aidan pleads.

"Think about it. How can you cross the border with no passport? So look it up, call those guys, make an appointment and bring all the police paperwork. See what happens."

"I don't even know how to get there."

"It's super easy," Kyla says, like a mother explaining a simple math problem. "You take the express train downtown. The big station there. From Luohu, only two stops from here, to Guangzhou East."

"Can you give me the address?"

"Maybe I can go with you, at least to the train station," my girlfriend offers. "I don't work until six in the evening. I'm free so we'll hang out and have brunch."

"Thanks, Kyla," he says.

More sympathetic than me, she places an arm on his shoulders.

"What do you think of Guangzhou?" he asks. That's his last question before we climb into a taxi and go home.

"At least I'll get to go sightseeing there," he adds, followed by nervous laughter.

"I never really liked Guangzhou that much," I say. "It's just some city. No special feeling."

"Oh. Well, I hope that I don't get kicked out of China. I just arrived here."

"I doubt that'll happen," I say. But I don't tell him that I'm sure because I'm not. Truthfully, I have no idea what transpires in such situations.

"Hey, don't worry so much. This probably happens to someone every day. It can't be that big of a deal."

* * *

Ultimately, Aidan needed to call his parents to wire him extra money. The school wasn't happy that he missed work, but there was no choice. It's part of the price of doing business with foreigners. They'll deduct the days and money from his paychecks later.

He got an emergency passport issued overnight, one with a 30-day emergency visa. I don't know how much that costs for New Zealanders. He had to miss another day of work to go to pick it up. Next month he'll have more paperwork to do back in Guangzhou and at least one more day away from the school. I think that he's less depressed about it since returning to Shenzhen. All in all, it worked out reasonably well.

Aidan learned a valuable lesson about the big bad world, and I acquired a warning-story to tell new visitors. Nothing like that ever happens to me, but truthfully, this place lies deep within the jungles of Southeast Asia, and the civilized veneer's only a thin mask. I know what goes on when no one's looking. Just on the periphery, from knowing Aidan, I witnessed a little bit, and so I feel slightly more street-smart.

兔
Always a Bridesmaid....

"Lu Lu is getting married!" When telling me this, my mother can't contain her excitement.

The news reaches me on a workday when I'm on lunch break with my colleagues. We're eating chicken at the fast-food place, a daily ritual, and I have excused myself to talk on the phone. The restaurant's very near a metro station, and at this time of day everything's even busier and noisier when I step outdoors. Still, I prefer some privacy for this conversation.

"Congratulations," I tell Mother.

"We'll have a big meal on Friday night. You'll be there." She tells me this, not asking.

"I'll see you on Friday." What amazing news! My, it's so sudden. I never even met Lu Lu's new boyfriend, but I have heard a lot about him.

"He comes from Taiwan, you know."

"I know."

"He's from a very rich family."

"Of course, I know."

I hear Mother sigh, and then comes this. "Oh, Little Dau-Dau, your cousin's so much younger than you, and this is such happy news, but when will you get married?"

Dau-Dau, meaning Bean-Bean, is my mother's nickname for me. She calls me that whenever emotion overwhelms her, whether she's angry or crying tears of joy. She gets increasingly emotional on the phone, and I hear her tears welling up. Before she can start to talk about other relatives and their marriages, I pretend that I have a work emergency and promise to call her back as soon as possible.

A few weeks pass, and the first of several formal wedding parties happens tonight. We'll eat dinner at an exquisite restaurant inside a five-star hotel in Huanggang Village. Another dinner, courtesy of the groom's family, will take place when they visit. Next month will be the official wedding celebration. After that, Lu Lu needs a visa to star in another wedding party, this one in Taipei. She's so lucky. Most people in our family will probably never find an opportunity to visit Taiwan.

By now, Lu Lu has told me much more about her fiancé. After changing jobs quite often, she had spent a month working in Dongguan. She met her future husband there and learned that he does a lot of business all across Guangdong Province, especially in Shenzhen, and in Hong Kong too. So when she moved back to Shenzhen, they continued the relationship.

Lu Lu says that he picked her up at a bar, but sometimes her story changes to suggest that they met in an office. So far, I never have dared, nor wanted, to press her about the true details. Mostly she speaks of the relationship by bragging about the gifts that he'll buy her, like a designer dress, pearl necklace, boots, and authentic French perfume.

After my mother's initial announcement, I'd immediately called Lu Lu to confirm the Friday plans and congratulate her on the news. She told me then that her husband will buy her a home, and I have no reason to doubt it. He will still travel for business, but whenever he comes to southern China, they will live together. She will cook and clean for him, or hire a housekeeper to do that, but even then, she'll be in charge of the household. She'll get to stay independent. It sounds like a part-time-wife job, and that's every Chinese girl's dream.

One thing that I like when talking to my cousin, Lu Lu, is that she never asks me when I'll get married.

I'm happily single now, and my work gets busy with the changing tides of seasons. Last month I received a promotion, and with each day, I have less and less time to myself. The weather turns cooler, and I can no longer wear short skirts. In a few weeks, I'll travel to Guangzhou for the Canton Fair. I feel the most fulfilled when I'm busy, and so there's no reason to feel anxious.

As a priority, I needed to save money for a wedding present. My workday ends, and I make a trip to the bank. Then a taxi drops me off at the hotel, and I check my purse for the tenth time to make sure that the present's still there. I feel nervous when carrying so much cash on me.

A hotel doorman opens my taxi door, and another graces me into the impressive building. I hope that I'm dressed well enough for the occasion. When walking up the stairs, I almost trip over my high heels. After I tell the restaurant hostess that I'm expected, she leads me into a private room.

"Hello!" members of my family yell to me.

"Nice to see you all," I reply.

I'm trying to process who has arrived and who has not (Mother's in a corner with many other relatives scattered elsewhere) when suddenly Lu Lu jumps up and gives me a big hug. I glance toward her and see her new husband nearby. He looks just like in the photos, wears a striped suit, and has a serious expression. I don't know his exact age, but he appears so much older than Lu Lu.

When my cousin finally lets me go, I dig into my purse and hand her the red envelope containing money.

"Thank you," she says and places it on a pile in the middle of the main table. Of course, she won't open it until later.

"Please join us," Lu Lu adds.

"No room for me."

Instead I sit with Mother and my immediate family. It was an honor to be invited to sit at Lu Lu's middle table, but accepting would have been impolite.

Meanwhile, many other relatives arrive, the pile of red envelopes mounts and I wave to various aunts, uncles and cousins. They bring children, aged from babies in carriages to sour-faced teenagers, and the great, distant elders who smile with unclear expressions. I can imagine the old folks being reminded time and again who all these people are. I need to be reminded too. Actually I recognize only about half the group. Some of the attendees are friends and some the groom's business associates. I think it's a shame that there are so many here whose names I don't even know.

I hear my grandmother yell because my niece, Mimi, is playing a handheld computer game. She speaks in the Hakka language, and I don't understand the exact words.

"Mimi, don't worry," I tell the child. "Grandma just talks in the grownup fashion. There's no reason to feel upset." Appearing consoled, Mimi goes back to her game. I eat.

While many of the elderly here are content and quiet-minded, my grandmother on my mother's side always shows a very strong personality. She's never afraid to speak her mind and order the members of younger generations to do as she counsels.

I eat more. Dumplings, fish, and a terrific pork soup all arrive in front of me. I'm glad that I skipped lunch and kept my appetite.

Looking around, I see a television on and a crowd of middle-aged men smoking and watching a sports match. The aunts indulge in gossip. The awkward teenagers in their school uniforms talk about tests. The small children play with their toy cars, robots, and games.

My attention switches back to my grandmother, who has enveloped one of my aunts, Lu Lu's mother, in discussion. I can pick up some of the spoken Hakka that resembles Cantonese, and I realize that they are no longer talking about the disrespect of young children playing computer games, when I will get married, or complaints about the food. In snippets, I hear, I believe, a different sort of judgmental attitude.

"My granddaughter. Should be proud. Not proud. Expect better."

The words hit me hard. If my very traditional, strong-willed grandmother disapproves of my little cousin marrying a rich man, then what does she think of me? Even with all of my attempts at being a modern and progressive woman, what would it take to earn her respect?

Later as my belly bulges from the big meal, Lu Lu approaches me. By then, I suspect that she's a bit drunk from all the *baijiu* that the men have passed around. "You're my favorite big sister," she declares.

"Ha, ha, you smell like a distillery."

"No, don't say that." Then she whispers, "Big Sister, I peeked at your gift. You're crazy."

"It's okay," I say. "I work so much overtime these days that I have lots of money saved."

"You gave more than any of these cheap people. I'm humbled by your generosity, truly."

"It's nothing."

"Sheila," she suddenly says to me sarcastically, "do you really think I'm ready to get married?"

"If you think you should be married, then you're ready."

"Sometimes I feel so lonely. The sex isn't even very good."

When she says that, I cover my face and blush.

"But I can't wait to get this over with," she continues.

"Lu Lu," I say, "these days we don't need to rush to marry young. We're free to do as we wish."

"We're not always free. Besides, I don't want to become an old maid like…" She pauses.

"Like me?"

"Sorry!" She's definitely drunk, but also seems sincerely ashamed.

"This isn't like you. What're you talking about? Please drink some water, sit down and sober up before you say anything else that's rude."

"Oh, I'm so jealous of you. You're totally independent. I want my husband to buy me a home quickly, and then I can quit my job. I don't want to be a poor Chinese. I never will have a better opportunity. It's my last chance before my beauty fades."

"Lu Lu, no! You know that won't happen for a very long time yet."

"Elder Sister, it happens sooner than you think. And I have no education. For me, this is the best thing."

"How can you say things like that?"

"You know it's true."

Exasperated, I don't know how to respond.

Suddenly Lu Lu laughs and offers me a drink. No longer do I think much about what's polite, but only about drinking as much as I can until this night ends.

* * *

Of course, I feel happy for my cousin, but I also must admit that all this talk of marriage leaves me with strange feelings that I can't place. Am I anxious? Is this feeling loneliness? Perhaps not. It isn't quite a romantic thing. Yearning for love certainly isn't at the root of this ache. Horny? Yes, that's the word. I feel horny.

My mind knows that I'm doing the right thing by being independent, but my body desires something else. All day at work I feel a heat rise inside from deep within the core of my body. It starts behind my stomach and works outward along each of my limbs. I almost look at pornography, that Westerner website that my friend recommended, but I have more self-control than that.

When I arrive home and have some privacy, I don't watch any yellow movies, but I do scour the dating websites. I sit with my notebook computer on my lap as a television show sings in the distance. I drink a can of Coca-Cola and scroll through the men of Sina Match. When I find one I like, I email him just a wink and a question.

To the first man, I ask the title of his favorite novel. To the second, I ask if he can cook, and if so, which region's dishes. By the fifth man, I'm bolder and ask how many women he has had. I feel very mischievous, and this is so much fun. After eight men, I quit. Then I make some tea, watch infomercials about breast cream and, periodically, check my email.

Soon it's well after midnight, but I have a date set up for the following day. It'll be a harsh day following little sleep. I plan to take a long nap after lunch and order several cups of coffee from the building's café.

At work, I spend most of my time checking my multiple email accounts and instant messages. Nobody at work minds much because many of the other staff members do the same thing. No meetings for me today, just some reports to finish.

First, it's my Sina Match account, next my Gmail and then I chat with my date on QQ. I've convinced him to meet me tonight because I'm an impatient, busy girl. He understands my meaning, I believe.

By the time I arrive home, we've exchanged numbers and graduated to communication by WeWa. I take a shower, wash my hair with two kinds of shampoo, and blow-dry it for 30 minutes. In preparation, I brush my teeth very thoroughly and carry two packs of gum in my purse. I wear my sexy underwear, the shortest black skirt, and a bit of eyeliner.

At eight o'clock, I rush out to find a taxi, and I'm already late. I call to tell him I'm on the way. The only thing left is finally to meet.

He waits at a restaurant in the mall, and my heart beats from the rush. I wipe at my forehead with a tissue and hope that I look elegant and uncaring.

Although handsome, he looks shorter than in his picture. They often do. Still, he's confident and has money. He orders a spicy Sichuan dish, his favorite. I force myself to eat daintily so as not to look too desperate. After he pays for dinner, we go for a walk inside the mall to help us to digest the food and also to look at the cinema posters. But we don't stay there.

He has a car and offers to drive me, but doesn't say where.

I almost wish that he didn't have a car because it's always possible to cuddle inside a taxi. At least, that's what I often do, I admit. But if he's the driver, I barely even can squeeze his hand. Instead we talk. I ask him how the GPS system works. He shows me the touch-screen, of which I'm familiar, but I play dumb. When he scrolls up his saved address, I act very impressed. I squeeze his hand when I get a chance. I say nothing about my address, neither does he, and we drive to his home.

Finally, in the elevator, we kiss. He's a forceful kisser. I feel the heat within me spread to my lips, chin and the end of my nose, where it tickles, and I almost sneeze. But I don't sneeze. I'm composed and sexy.

Happily, I want to sleep with this man. We arrive at his home, where soon the lights are dimmed and soft classical music plays on an expensive sound system. He opens a bottle of wine and pours me a smooth drink. For an Internet date, this certainly is going well. I picked very carefully, but still I'm grateful for my luck with this man.

As his kisses indicated, he's a strong and powerful lover. His penis is just the right size, and I think that I may orgasm just from the penetration. The thrusts are very deep and vigorous, but not too fast. He's firm and meaningful with just the right amount of tenderness. Often I orgasm the best of all from fingers, and he does touch the spot right above my opening for an exhilarating affect. At the same time, he kisses my breasts and tickles the skin on my neck just below my ears. It's an overwhelming experience.

I climax and climax again. Then he breathes deeply in a rhythm, rushing quicker and quicker, until I know he has cum too. He slumps to my side and holds me in his arms. We relax and lie into each other for a while. I think that maybe he nods off to sleep.

"What are you thinking?" I ask.

He doesn't answer, but his eyes are open. He peels off the condom and flings it into a rubbish bin beside the bed. With an arm, he rubs my left hip, and his head maneuvers the pillow into a more comfortable position.

A blanket rises over me. Eyes close, and sleep approaches, but it's not welcome. This is too unsettling. I have to work tomorrow and don't want to be here. I need to go. I need to go now.

虎

Betrayed!

For a Monday morning, I'm in a pretty good mood. The weekend was a riot, partying on Friday and Saturday and then recuperating from the double-hangover on Sunday. Today I'm well-rested, full of caffeine, and ready to go.

First things first, I think, waving to my secretary and asking her to make me more coffee. I check my email, smoke a morning cigarette, and wonder how I can kill time until lunch. On Friday, there's a meeting, and I'll need to write quarterly reviews and call some customers to confirm orders. But there's little on my schedule for the mid-week. I decide to download a movie.

Something seems to be amiss, but I can't pinpoint quite what. Is everyone here? I walk several rounds about the office and realize that my protégé, Jackie, hasn't shown up yet. He's a very hard worker and means well, despite being incompetent at times, but in true Middle Kingdom fashion, he always shows up, completely dependable as a warm body, if nothing else. It seems very off that he's missing today.

"May," I say to the secretary, "did Jackie call in sick?"

"What?" she says.

Her English takes time. It can be a struggle. "Um, Jackie. Not here today. Did he ask for leave?" I ask again, very slowly to enunciate each syllable.

"Oh." Then she says his Chinese name, which I never even remember. "He *resign.*"

"Holy hell! What?" I mutter to myself and walk away for a moment.

This makes no sense. He can't do that. There was no resignation letter and no one-month notice, not even two weeks. What the hell? Was he malcontent or planning a coup? Just last Friday, we drank beers together. I recall that last week had ended with a payday, which might be a factor.

All these thoughts stampede through my head. Suddenly, I need to get my partners on the phone, plus my supervisor, various factory managers, the building landlord, and a team of translators to sort through this.

I send several emails around, but none of the partners appears interested in this subject. After two phone calls to senior Chinese staff members are ignored, I give up.

Alright. I decide to email Jackie, off the record. He surprises me by immediately calling back. He always was punctual.

"What's going on here, man?" I ask frantically. "They tell me you're gone."

"That's right, Marco." He doesn't sound embarrassed, regretful or anything.

"What's the goddamn problem? This is highly irregular. I thought that I was here to teach you Western business practices, and we've made a lot of progress these last months. You really took me by surprise, Jackie-boy."

"Well," he says, not ashamed at all. "I thought that the company no longer suited me. I found a higher salary."

"Where?" I immediately ask.

"It's my own company. This is my dream. Thank you, Marco, for teaching me the trading business."

What the fuck! He's thanking me for *that*? Is there no loyalty in this world?

"Do you want to get together, and I can buy you a gift..."

Offended, I hang up on him in mid-sentence.

The situation bothers me all day. I try to banish it from my mind, but it keeps returning. Luckily, there's not too much to do. I download more videos and try to ease my mind by watching those for the rest of the day. MTV reality shows mostly, the first ones that come up on the site. Just what I need.

Tomorrow I really must start on the quarterly reviews for the Friday meeting. On Tuesday, I notice something else. My desk looks much too clean. No updated orders have arrived for the past two days.

"May, be a doll and print up the order sheets for our Dongguan and Panyu factories."

Those look the same as they have for the past 10 days. "This can't be right."

In China, orders always fluctuate, shipments are late, early or re-itemized, and business happens in a state of panic. Risk is simply where the big money goes.

"Now," I mumble, "it's entirely possible that things at the factories are *so bad* that they don't want to update the order sheets until the last possible minute."

Maybe I should make more calls. I didn't dig up anything yet, but a person can't be too careful. Does the budget cover another factory visit? But it hasn't been too long since the last personal inspection and dinner thing.

"Mister Jones," says May at closing time, as she peeks inside my office. "Do you need me to bring you anything?"

"No. But don't leave the office just yet. I need you on a call."

She pauses. "Okay…"

Stupid secretary! No help at all.

* * *

On Thursday night I'm still at the office crunching the numbers when I realize exactly what happened. It's obvious, really. The problem isn't that the orders simply went lax. The clients didn't just abandon us arbitrarily. They specifically abandoned us for *Jackie's startup*.

Busy on the computer and with paperwork spread out on my desk, I realize that it's 1 a.m., and I don't even feel like stepping outdoors. I'm burnt out on nicotine and caffeine. Cigarette butts overflow from the ash tray, and the stink is rising. I wander to a sofa in the waiting room and lie down, staring at the ceiling. What kind of work ethic is this? Am I in Tokyo, or what?

At 7 a.m., the sun isn't even up, but I awaken when the cleaning lady opens the door. I need to shave, brush my teeth, and wash my face, but instead I return straight to the computer. No new emails.

As the employees stride in one by one, I realize that it's 9 a.m., and I can start making calls. Everyone gives me a second look, but says nothing. I know that I should brush my teeth at least. Later I'll ask May to fetch me an airport-style travel bag.

The workday begins, and the first factory takes about 40 minutes to connect me to an English-speaking person. I ask directly if they cancelled the order.

"Well, uh, um, that is…"

Shuffling through my paperwork, I look up Jackie's Chinese moniker.

"Is your representative by the name of *Feng Quanshi*?"

Then I'm put on hold as a supervisor gets consulted. I listen in on the conversation. It sounds like they're yelling, but that's normal here. Maybe it sounds that way because I don't understand the language, or maybe they really do yell at each other.

A voice comes back on the phone. "Yes, that is right. Goodbye."

Confirmation! I hang up the phone. "FUCK, FUCK, FUCK!" While yelling, I grab the phone and slam it down several times for effect.

My secretary peeks in, and I treat her to my coldest look. This time she gets the picture and leaves me alone.

A pattern appears as four other phone calls ensue just like the first one. There isn't that much I can do. Not like there's a Better Business Bureau of Guangdong. I could lodge a complaint within the official capacity of some business regulatory commission, but I'd need to know the business-license numbers of every factory and management company, plus engage a full team of native speakers to do the proper research. And as far as I know, our firm here isn't even properly registered yet. We're less than a year old, and this is China. In the end, it would amount to a hell of a lot of work with a high probability of no return at all.

I feel helpless. This job was supposed to be easy. Why did I come to this fucking country to deal with shit like this?

If this happened back home, I'd just sue him. I truly would. Should I even bother trying to figure out how to get a Chinese lawyer?

I do a lot of soul-searching and research (English-only, keeping the information to myself for now), and in the end I conclude that there isn't much to do except to eat our losses and not invest in any more money pits. Start anew in the next quarter.

The late-Friday meeting turns into a disaster, full of unbearable silences that last for minutes and minutes. I wrote a haphazard report, working sleep-deprived on copious amounts of coffee and amphetamines, detailing how much money and projected funds we've lost and why the only prudent option means not fighting the competition.

Repeatedly, I swear to everyone seated around the big table that I'll come up with a business model by next week. I really do.

Most likely, I fail to properly get my point across. As I say, I likely should have shaved and brushed my teeth first.

The partners stare at me with eyes of daggers, or maybe *katana*s, and I almost want to commit hara-kiri right now. Wait, that's a wrong-country metaphor.

"So, Mister Jones, you're saying that all the invested capital has been wasted because...," and the speaker scrutinizes my notes, adjusting his eyeglasses, "you made a decision to mentor networking strategies to the young assistant, Mister Feng?"

"Yes, that's effectively correct, but..."

"And you lost *four* accounts within just this week?"

"Well, there's still the hi-tech factory in Nanshan, and my American contacts remain as customers."

"For now..."

"Well, that is, I still have lots of plans, if you'd just give me the time to formulate a business model, sir. In one week's time, I'd be confident... That is, um, just let me rework this thing, please, sir..."

"I see. It's under review."

God damn it! I don't feel well about this.

* * *

Needing decisive action, I go to Jackie Feng's place at exactly 9 p.m. when I'm fairly sure he'll be home. I don't call him first. The doorman lets me in because I'm a foreigner and pretty much can go where I want.

I knock on a door decorated with Chinese New Year red-lantern decorations still up from last February. Jackie opens it and reacts with an exclamation of surprise. He should have looked first to see who it was.

"Marco, it's always nice to see you," he says. I'm not convinced that he means it.

"Jackie, what the hell's going on?

"It's just business. Why are you so upset?"

"You screwed me over big time!"

"Please keep be quiet." He steps out into the hallway and shuts the door behind him. I wonder if anyone else is home. It's a Friday night. If anything, he should be preparing to go out and bring someone back here later. He wears work clothes with the necktie undone and a half-unbuttoned dress shirt. His hair looks disheveled. I don't know what to make of it.

Jackie smiles awkwardly. He's always smiling. That's what these people do when they know they're in the wrong.

"I wasn't suited to work at that company," he says. "I decided to leave and pursue my dream. Okay?"

"You can't steal every single client. That's a below-the-belt practice. I didn't teach you that. Don't you understand *company loyalty*?"

"You told me only to make as much money as possible as easy as possible."

That much is true. I remember specifically saying that, but not in precisely the same words.

Emotion gets the better of me, and I can't even blame it on drinking like I usually do. I start yelling, calling Jackie "an asshole" and "a cunt".

His smile turns bigger and faker. Asking me to lower my voice, he backs away, opening the door behind him, but I try to follow.

He takes out his cell phone and says something into it. Before I know it, his door's closing, and I hear footsteps coming behind me.

"You'll be fucking sorry!" That's the last thing I say before he slams the door in my face. I don't know if my prediction ever will come true, but then I yell again, "Remember that much if you're so damn good at learning every goddamn, fucking thing I've ever said."

The steps behind me thud louder, and I turn around to see the doorman who had let me into the building. Or is he supposed to be a guard or something?

He, too, smiles awkwardly and spouts Chinese to me. I don't understand the words, but do get the message. He leads me to the elevator.

"Alright, alright, buddy. HANDS OFF!"

Then his arms cross, and he stares at me like I'm some schoolboy being taken to the principal's office. His glare lasts until we exit the elevator and I'm escorted all of the way out the front gate through which I'd entered just a few minutes ago.

My unscheduled business meeting with Jackie had gone about as well as expected.

* * *

I make it home, but don't want to do anything much. Usually I'd go out seeking sex at times like this. That's what I need to do. But somehow I feel like it wouldn't be productive.

Leaning back in my folding chair and focusing on a PC screen, I watch some porn, but my heart isn't in it. I help myself to a beer from the refrigerator and play music from the classic-rock playlist. Then I take a piss and have a smoke. With the beer still in hand, I look at myself in a mirror for an inordinate amount of time.

Returning to the computer, I take a look at the local classified ad site. Many girls post their services there. Right now, this route seems like the least work for a distraction that I can handle. Grimly, I call the number for a "cute" one advertising massage and more. Her message appears under *Women Seeking Men*, but obviously refers to a professional service, not a date. It says that she knows English, yet when we talk on the phone, I barely can understand her. I don't know what she says, except for "500", which she pronounces very well. Just going ahead, I forward my address to the number.

Forty minutes later, I'm 50 minutes drunker, and my doorbell rings. I buzz her in, wait and hear a knock on the apartment door. I open it to the ugliest call girl I've ever seen.

Damn! I broke my own rule and didn't look through the peephole first. Then I could have backed out, but it's too late now. It's not that she's truly ugly, just so *average* for someone costing five fucking hundred. She's short, has a plain face with jagged teeth and doesn't even wear makeup or perfume.

She starts yapping at me in Mandarin, and I guess that she wants the money first, plus cab fare. When I give her 550, she shuts up.

I'd offer her a drink, but hell, we don't need pretenses, and I'm reluctant to waste my booze. She just up and takes off her shirt. I see that she has a distinct gut and small breasts. She strips to her panties, and I go to my bedroom, get naked and lie down.

She gives me a not entirely unpleasant massage. But I'm too drunk to fully enjoy it. As she works on my back muscles and spine, I just take her hands and move them to my ass. I'm rubbing her thighs the whole time, and she plays with my balls from behind. I'm getting hard, and I turn over, putting a hand under her panties.

Putting forth the show of massage, she rubs my belly for a minute, saying something about foreigners. "*Waiguoren,*" I caught that word. Then she's onto my cock.

She gets up, goes to her purse, takes out a rubber and puts it on me. It feels uncomfortably tight at the base of my cock and on my pubes, but I'm not paying enough to insist on doing it bareback.

Panties slide off, I go for a while and have a weak cum. Then she's dressed and out the door before I know it. I'm standing with the front door open, looking outside into the hallway. All the lights remain on in the living room, and I'm still naked.

I shut the door, lock it, take another beer from the refrigerator and collapse onto the couch. Maybe I'll just sleep right here.

What do I want to do with my future? I should get a loan, quit my job and make my own business. Maybe I could manage an expat bar or something. I've never thought about staying here for another gig, but now's the time to brainstorm. *Fuck this*! That much I know. Depending on other people always lets you down. I never did anything to earn this kind of stress.

I need a true happy ending and soon. I mean, I deserve it, don't I?

牛
Travel, Breakup

We watch geeky sitcoms while in bed. Kyla's high and in the midst of passing out. I know we have our Mandarin class tomorrow, but I suspect that she won't make it. She's missed the last two classes on the basis of nights quite like this.

"Danny, why don't you smoke some?" she asks me in a half-daze.

"No, thanks," I say.

I carefully slip out of bed and put away her bowl and gear (fire hazard) and then I step into my living room, hoping that Kyla doesn't sleep for 12 hours straight like she did last week.

My apartment's a nice size for being in the city. At least it isn't a studio flat and has a separate space for the bedroom. The living room couch is good for a couple to watch movies together, but not so much for lying down to read a book. It's too short, the kind of couch that cramps a sleeping person's back. I try to find a comfy position to read my novel. (A British friend loaned it to me. It's about addicts in Scotland and seems oddly nostalgic.)

Tomorrow's Saturday. Along with a Mandarin lesson, we both have tutoring. We're busy, irritable and have too much money.

On Saturdays, I go to two students' homes and tutor English for an hour at each place. They each pay me 250 *yuan*, the equivalent of about US$40. On Sundays, I teach TOEFL to an aspiring college-transfer student trying to go abroad in his sophomore year. For this, his mom pays me 300, almost US$50, per hour.

Kyla exclusively teaches TOEFL, and I think that she earns more money than I do. She has a system of stealing students from her training-center job. They spend six months paying the company, and then, when no one's looking, she talks to them off the record and starts charging without the management in the middle. She goes directly to their homes, resulting in more money for her and cheaper rates for the customers, a win-win. For the past year, she's built her client base like this, riding taxis all over the city at every spare moment, and has worked seven days a week for the past eight months. I've only been extra busy for the past few weeks, and already it's the most exhausting time I've ever experienced.

I don't know how she does it. She even still gets high every day, being an irresponsible foreigner and showing up to work hung-over. But I'm still trying to focus on Mandarin, while she is just fading away. She skips more and more classes, a real waste of money.

Not that we don't both have more money than we know what to do with. There are, of course, a few priorities, like paying back student loans, occasional travel and living the highlife in the developing world. Most of the time, I'm unsure what to do with my swelling bank account. We talk about traveling together to Guilin or somewhere in Guangdong. If only we could find the time. It's funny how that works. The more money that you earn, the less time you have to spend it.

But we've been putting off discussion about travel together these days, and truthfully, I'm not even sure that I want to travel with her. We might finally be getting on each other's nerves enough to break up.

I hate breaking up. It's inevitable in most relationships, but I'll put it off for as long as I can. Mostly I hate all of the emotion and uncertainty. I think about it constantly, but in the end I prefer the anxiety of a day-to-day routine to the unpredictable final explosion of a relationship. All of those tears, heartaches, suspicions and jealousies emerge after the fact. The worst thing happens later when you bump into her around town. You need to make your friends pick sides and everything.

Often I may think about other women, like my Mandarin teacher, but I can't imagine my life any differently. Not right now. Maybe someday, in another country, I can sift through women whenever I want without thoughts of the consequences, but not here, not now.

No, I think that I'd rather wait until one of us moves out of China to break up. That way's much easier.

True to routine, I toss aside the paperback and go to brush my teeth. The sight of Kyla's electric toothbrush, adorned with cartoon fish and resting on my sink, comforts me. I'm so used to seeing her stuff here.

After taking off my shirt, I squeeze into bed beside her under my blankets. I sleep, dreaming of America and its fast-food restaurants.

Sure enough, the next day starts as a lonely one. I wake up by myself, but that's okay.

While on a bus, forcing my way to Mandarin class, I get a text from Kyla. "*SORRY, I know I'm a terrible student! Zero points!*"

I think that she expects me to say it's no big deal and humor her as usual. Choosing a different tactic, I reply, "*WHATEVER.*"

For 30 minutes, she doesn't reply. Then during the class she only sends me an emoji of a frowny face. I don't think much of it.

The lesson goes well. I'm progressing smoothly. There are only eight of us in class, and most are middle-aged businessmen from Europe or various Asian countries. Their aging brains tend to progress very slowly.

Now that I think about it, I realize that I may even be at the top of my class.

We review our memorized speeches. Our assigned homework is to fill out 20 more characters 100 times each by next week, and after class I decide to talk to Miss Tang.

We're like old friends, and I'm no longer nervous around her. She wears a short skirt, and I don't even want to look at her long legs. I notice that her hair recently had a perm, but I don't want to comment on that.

"Hello," I say. "Sorry, I mean, *Nihao.*"

I tell her a story in my broken, struggling Chinese about the last time I watched a movie with Kyla. It was an action movie about spies, and the beginning had Greek language with only Chinese subtitles. The rest of the movie was in English. It's a Hollywood movie, of course, but it's problematic because, when it comes to fluency in reading characters, I can only say *kan bu dong.*

Somehow I feel like I talk about movies all the time. That's the central crux of my life. Well, it beats discussing work.

So I continue, telling Miss Tang how I prefer Hong Kong movies with both English and Chinese subtitles. She tells me that this is a Mandarin class, not Cantonese, and that's no way to study.

Then the tide turns. Suddenly she jokes that she should be my translator. Desperate to take advantage of this, I play along and ask her how I should pay her. Before I even know what I'm doing, I instinctively give her my all-important name-card. For networking, you know.

"Heh, heh! *Danny hen hao*," she says. Some of the other students still are leaving, and she takes a quick glance around before tugging out the cell phone from her purse and saving my number.

Smiling and perhaps oblivious, I now struggle to suppress nervousness. My heart beats like it did the first time I taught a group of sweaty middle-school students. I had thought that she didn't make me feel this way anymore, but I was wrong. My legs wobble, but I stiffen my knees and pretend it's no big deal.

The phone in my pocket vibrates with her message. These days that's the usual routine when exchanging numbers.

"Cool," I say.

"Homework," she says. "We go see a movie, but for study. *Hao bu hao?*"

"Yeah, sure," I say.

She says more to me in Mandarin, and I don't really hear, but I nod my head.

I hope that I come across as cool, not brain-dead. When she later sends me a happy-face WeWa add, I conclude that I did well.

At home, Kyla, happily taking advantage of the emergency key that I had given her, has returned and waits for me. She's in my bed, wearing my T-shirt and her panties.

She taps away on my computer. "Guess what," she says.

"What?"

She doesn't even ask me about the class. I'm angry and relieved at the same time.

"I finally booked us a trip to Zhuhai, like we've been talking about," Kyla says. "We go next Thursday."

* * *

When I next feel the vibration of a text message arriving on the phone in my pocket, I'm bickering with Kyla about the trip. My first reaction to her news was a visible reluctant enthusiasm, and she calls me on it. Then I start asking her for more details, and it worsens.

"What do you mean?" I ask, no longer pretending to view her plans as good news. "I work on Thursdays."

"Come on! You can call off for once in your life. I will. Don't be so responsible all the time."

"But I'm not talking about some part-time tutoring job. How can I take leave on a weekday from a real middle school? It's unprofessional."

"Come on, Danny. Live a little."

I take a deep breath. Despite dreading this kind of conflict, I can't let it go. "I don't understand why you didn't book the trip for a weekend."

"Oh, my God! I specifically told you that I booked it like this to avoid huge crowds. We'll have way more fun."

Silently, I pace around, and my living room gives me little space to pace. I go to the fridge and take out a cold beer. After sipping, I speak again, very calmly. "It's just that you always decide things like this for me. You could have asked me, and we'd have worked something out together."

"I wanted it to be a surprise. Why can't you be happy? I'll pay and everything."

"I never asked you for a surprise."

"Well, duh, that's kind of the point of surprises."

I take one more deep breath. "Okay, whatever! You're right. Thanks a lot. I appreciate the gesture."

"Well, don't get so damn excited and sincere about it."

Turning away from Kyla and checking my phone, I see the text message from Miss Tang. It's a chuckling little face. The dichotomy of my exterior world and the world inside my cell phone contrasts like lightening and water.

As the days pass, we calm down. I call in sick to work, although the school will deduct the days from my pay and the vice-principal sounds very unhappy. I know that, when I return, Amber and Aidan will express jealousy that I took time off during the week.

Early on Thursday morning, I meet Kyla at the Luohu Shop City bus station by the Hong Kong border. I've been here often to take trains or to shop, but this is my first time to use any of the long-distance coach buses. I've heard they're more comfortable than the trains.

One thing for which I'm grateful is that Kyla made this vacation only to Zhuhai. It's just two hours away. Right now, I don't want to leave Guangdong Province. This is the province for me, the one I've chosen, and any other sightseeing or backpacking would seem like a distraction from the life I'm trying to build here. For a few days in Zhuhai, we can enjoy the beach and soak in a hot spring, ready to return home soon. That should work.

"Hey."

"Hey. Good morning."

"Good morning to you too. Let's go." And off we go.

Soon Kyla snores, slumped right beside me. I don't know how she can sleep on a moving bus like this. She must be partly Chinese.

The dawning sun shines right into my face, and I'm too tired to read my latest paperback novel, but I find solace in occupying a window seat and watching the skyscrapers of Luohu. The King Building and Saint Paul Hotel shrink into the horizon, and the scenery fills with factory buildings and countryside. Then it reverts to city as we pass through Dongguan. Or is that Foshan? Or somewhere? I'm not even sure.

Suburbs and cityscapes rise and fall every 20 minutes. Then the bus rolls along a road in a denser urbanized area, and I see a beach to my left. First, it's in the distance. Then the road connects, and it's right there next to us, the sea and its brown water. There's a statue of an angel too. I think we're almost there.

It's no Lake Erie, but it's nice.

The traffic rumbles at its thickest around the downtown, and I know that we're close. This could be any city in China. After a while, they all look the same.

I poke Kyla until she awakens. She looks annoyed.

"Why did you wake me up?"

"We're here," I say.

She looks out the window, suddenly awake and bright-eyed. "Oh, I missed seeing the beach. Did you see the goddess-statue thing? I bet it was nice. You should have roused me before."

I just can't win.

The bus enters an underground passageway and stops, parking there. Suddenly 10,000 people surround us. The Chinese passengers get off first. Kyla and I exit last.

We take a good look around to remember this place so that we can return tomorrow to the same location. It looks less like a bus station than a shopping mall crossed with a shantytown. But a sign in English across an underground passageway reads: Bus Station Zhuhai.

"Well, we made it."

Carrying backpacks, we lurk around like a couple of obvious tourists. It feels still early, but lunchtime approaches. Through a doorway, we enter a maze of electronics and clothing shops. Signs on a wall point out north and south, how to reach Macau and where to find travel agencies. This is the rather wordy Gongbei Zhuhai Commercial District Plaza City Center Park Place.

We gulp down noodles for lunch, and the eatery even sells coffee.

"So…" I say, trying to stir conversation. "What did you dream about on the bus?"

"Huh?" Kyla ponders for a moment. "Um, something about Taco Bell, I think."

"That figures."

"What do you mean?"

"I mean…" I say, thinking fast, "maybe you had the munchies or something. Ha, ha! I dream about stuff back home all the time. The subconscious really misses things like eating at Taco Bell."

"Yeah."

Kyla slurps on the noodles and spins a chopstick around in the soup.

Watching her, I think of something more to say. "Do you ever dream about China?"

"Not really." She doesn't even stop to think about it.

"The same goes for me. Isn't that weird? In my dreams, I'm always in Michigan. My heart doesn't know where I really am."

"It's interesting the way you say that."

"I don't know. Sometimes I think like that."

She smiles at me.

After I pay for the noodles, we look at some cheap cameras and decorated cell-phone cases in shops. Then Kyla leads the way back in the direction of the border where the travel agencies hub together. Without thinking much, I follow her and find that my mind goes numb. Instead of looking at the products and advertisements, my eyes start to people-watch.

All these black-haired Chinese souls, sparse Europeans, and some Africans too rush alongside each other in the consumerist jungle. Women outnumber the men where clothes are sold, and I see many couples. In the electronics section, women still outnumber the men. This place has so many women. How could I meet some of them?

Our surroundings get more familiar. Taking Kyla's hand, I say, "We're back where we started."

"Yeah, I think we can get a hotel here. Aren't you tired of walking?"

"Here?"

"I guess so."

"Well, it's been a nice walk and everything, but I thought you were in charge of the plan. Why didn't you book a hotel before?"

"I don't know how to do that on Chinese websites."

"They must have English services too. You bought the bus tickets."

"Yeah, but the hotels online are super-expensive. Booking them is for like business travelers and rich tourists from Paris or somewhere. We're backpackers. We don't need them."

"I'm not a backpacker," I say.

"Come on," Kyla urges. "I always find hotels on the spot when I travel. Just ask around. This is China. A room will pop up."

We go into a hotel facing the bar street, and I do all the translating. It's simple enough. I ask the man at the front desk if there is, or isn't, an open room. Then I formulate some easy vocabulary words, like "one bed" and "one night". Two hundred a night, not bad, and in the early afternoon it's easy to find a vacancy. Kyla's right. This poses no problem.

Kyla practises no Chinese on the trip. It's always like this when we shop or order food in restaurants. We've taken the same language class for the same amount of time, yet she totally depends on me as her personal translator. I thought that girls are supposed to be better at languages. I've noticed that among my students.

"What's up?" Kyla asks me from across the hotel lobby.

"The man at the front desk needs to copy my passport. Then I pay a deposit, and that's it."

"Cool." She approaches me and puts our arms together. "Where would I be without you? You're my hero!"

Intent on dropping off our bags, we look inside the room. Then we jump on the bed, check the offerings on TV for anything good, and even make out for a while. It's fun to stay in an unfamiliar hotel room.

Next we meander outside. On the way, we notice hundreds of tourism pamphlets in the lobby. Kyla takes one. Although she can't read it, the pictures say enough.

"A hot-spring resort sounds nice," she says.

At one of the travel agencies, a lady explains to us that for 100 each we can take a shuttle bus and enjoy the resort for as long as we like. Every 30 minutes, a return shuttle carries people back downtown. But we must bring our own swimsuits. No problem. After getting our suits and buying tickets, we again sit together, staring out the windows on a bus.

It's a quick ride. The hot-spring resort looks like it's half a giant Chinese-style spa and half a theme park. We go separately into ornately decorated male and female locker rooms. Attendants line the walls, and one of them helps me to change out of my clothes. He hands me a plastic bracelet with an electronic key-guard attached. These come in many colors, and mine's green. I take a steaming hot shower, surrounded by dozens of naked Chinese men. Then I put on my swimsuit, and another attendant hands me slippers, a towel, and a robe.

Outside, a rush of cool air hits me, and I tie up my robe. I wait until Kyla comes out (girls always take longer), and then we walk around to see the empty swimming pool and some small water-slides.

Although various people are walking around and talking, the place seems strangely quiet. I would have expected to find plenty of children running around, but this is a school day, and we've just missed the warm season.

"Let's come back here for next year's summer break," I say.

"Alright."

We follow a path and discover the various hot-spring pools with labels like *Jasmine Flower Flavor* and *Hot Buddha Stone*. The water temperatures are displayed: 38 to 40 degrees. That's Celsius, of course. I do the math in my head. Wow, that's rather hot.

"Let's go," says Kyla, and steps into an empty pool. As she tosses aside her robe, I finally see her in a swimsuit. It's a Chinese-style one-piece with a skirt ensemble that does well for her figure.

I look closely at the spring pool. There are brown benches at the side, a pagoda above us and four pillars surrounding to give the façade of privacy. The pool itself is Jacuzzi-sized, but not bubbling.

My left foot goes into the water, getting used to the heat, and then my right one follows. I toss my robe over onto a bench and edge in deeper. Warmth envelopes me, and Kyla wears an expression of contentment not unlike the look when she has sex while high. She moves next to me and puts an arm around my torso.

"Feels great," I say.

"Yeah. Is this place natural?"

"I don't know." I look around, back and forth. "It doesn't seem like volcano country."

After a few minutes, we step out and try a few other pools. We go progressively hotter. Each pool feels better than the previous one.

Before I know it, quite a long time has passed, and I want to sleep. I jump back into a fully awake state when I feel Kyla's lips brush against my face. Smiling, I kiss her back. Soon we're making out, and I peek with one eye open to see that no one's nearby.

I'm holding her waist under the water and getting a little hard. Eagerly, I take her nearest hand and put it against my shorts. At first, she's into it and squeezes me. My other hand touches her breasts, and a finger slides under the swimsuit material. Then I hastily push my shorts to my ankles. I place her fingers right up against my...

"Danny!" She jumps away from me. "You're crazy."

Shrugging, I just laugh it off. Moments after I pull my shorts back up, a family with two small children walks past, and nobody notices me. A few minutes later, I'm soft, although anxious, and decide that we should return to the hotel soon.

It's past dinner time when we get there. Kyla says that she's tired and just wants to order food for delivery to our room. I say that we should go out again and explore more, but she says that her ankles are sore, and so she doesn't want to walk any more.

"Do you like to travel and just stay inside a hotel room the whole time?" I ask her.

"What are you talking about? We were out all day. Let's rest."

Resting is all we did today, I think, but don't say anything more. We eat local seafood and watch videos on MTV China.

Later, I decide to give Kyla a foot rub to treat her sore ankles. Soon I'm massaging her. She gets down to her bra and panties and lies down on her stomach on the bed. I remove her bra and rub her back. I'm very hard at this point. I kiss the back of her neck, and she responds with a pleasant moan.

"That's so nice," she whispers.

I touch her panties, and suddenly she slaps me away. "Don't do that." "What?"

"I don't want you to do that now, Danny."

Feeling so frustrated, I really want to just whip it out and jerk off right there in front of her. Instead, I force myself to be patient.

When I turn off the lights, a nice dim light glows from the television. I turn it to a station playing music, something to give background atmosphere without distracting. Quietly, I take off my clothes and go under the blanket with her. We kiss, but still she refuses to surrender her panties.

"Kyla, come on."

"No, I mean it."

Hopefully, I put her hand on my hard cock. For just a second, it feels so good, and then she jumps away.

"I'm not into this now," she says.

"Kyla, please."

She turns away from me in bed. Unable to see her face then, I hear her say, "I'm on my period. Duh!"

"Um, okay. But you went to the hot spring like that? I had no idea."

"You should pay more attention."

How am I supposed to do that? I wonder.

Kyla starts talking about the difficulties of finding her brand of tampons here, how they're fine for swimming, and anyway she bought the tickets a week before. Rather than listen to this explicitly less-than-erotic chat, I ignore her. Instead, I focus on the Chinese pop music, catching words in the air like "I", "love" and "you".

My hard-on persists, and I can't stop feeling playful. I rub up against her hip. There's no response. She's like dead. I try one last time, grabbing for her hand. Before I even can move it, she slaps my hand and shrugs away from me.

"Sorry," I say, and instantly regret saying it. I realize that apologizing just makes everything worse. I'm confused. Should I apologize? Am I bad person for forcing this? Is it such a big deal? She's supposed to be my girlfriend, right? But I don't want to be a bad boyfriend either.

Not for the first time, I wish that I had more confidence in situations like this. My mind swims with personal judgments, assumptions about menstruation and fantasies of hand jobs. I consider taking a shower and masturbating alone.

"If you're so insistent," Kyla suddenly says, coldly, "get out of here and go for a happy-ending massage down the street."

"What?"

"Fucking men! Go pay to get jerked off if it's so important to you."

"What the hell!"

"I want to sleep." With that, she buries her head under the covers and stops talking.

Sitting up, I pull on my boxers and walk into the bathroom. The mood here's shot, but I'm still erect, pointing at a 90-degree angle and wondering what to do next. For a minute, I kind of jerk off while standing in front of the toilet, but no results emerge.

So I brush my teeth, step back into the hotel room and put on my clothes. I'm not even sleepy. After clicking off the TV and making sure that the keycard nestles in my coat pocket, I go out for a stroll.

The elevator ride down takes a long time. Outside, I recognize the simple characters for "foot massage" at three different locations within eyeing distance of the hotel. One place shines blazing neon lights, spelling out "MASSAGEE" in English with the extra E and everything. Nah, I think. I don't want to do this, not now.

Girls in seductive dresses who stand in front of a nearby podium smile and say "hello" to me. They advertise prices of 88 or 188, and I'm unsure of what the difference entails. My heart beats rapidly, but I doubt if I can go through with it so I keep walking.

I continue walking until I'm back where I started. Feelings of sleepiness finally overtake me, and I plan to succumb to them. Blue balls or not, I return to the hotel room and go to sleep.

* * *

The next day, Kyla and I have checked out of the hotel. Carrying our backpacks, we stand in front of the downtown shopping maze.

"What are we going to do next?" I ask.

"Can you ask someone how to get to the bus station?"

"Don't you want to explore more of the city? Or how about going to Macau? It's right there."

"I've heard that Macau's boring unless you're into gambling."

"Ever been to Vegas?" I ask.

"Once when I was a kid. I couldn't even do anything except wait around in the hotel with my sister while our parents went out. It kind of turned me off on gambling."

"I see," I say. "So that's it."

"Hey, we saw a lot, and Zhuhai isn't that far away for us. We can come back anytime."

So I walk to the nearest newsstand kiosk, buy some gum, and ask the cashier how to get to the bus station. She gives me concise directions. My role as our translator is completed.

As we sit together on the bus, Kyla makes a motion that her stomach hurts and rubs her belly. She closes her eyes and leans her head against my forearm.

"You actually had a good time?" I ask.

"It was really nice. I loved the hot spring. We talked about our dreams."

"You really remember it that way," I say very quietly.

"Yeah…" she says even quieter. She takes a deep breath and leans even more comfortably into me.

"You know," she adds as the bus glides along beside the beach, "I'm going to miss this place. It reminds me of home, of California. The air smells better than in Shenzhen, don't you think?"

"I concur."

"There's something so cool, so magical, about being next to the water."

* * *

A week after the trip, Kyla takes me out to lunch and insists on paying. We go to a Chinese Muslim restaurant and get the typical inexpensive dish with eggplant, thin beef strips, and thick noodles.

Kyla raises the subject of her apartment. "You know, I'm having some issues with my, uh, living situation. The landlord wants to raise my rent."

"Everywhere is going up these days."

"Yeah, my students tell me that the real-estate market's crazy now."

"Isn't it a bubble or something?"

"That's what they say. Hell of a lot that I know about the property business though!"

"Sure, sure," I say, slurping down noodles while she drinks tea.

"So…" she slowly continues. "Do you want to move in together? I'm at your place a lot. Or, if your school doesn't like it, we could get a new place together. Splitting rent on a one-bedroom apartment would be cheap. What do you think?"

The idea takes me by surprise. My mind races and churns up infinite numbers of reasons why I can't agree.

"Well?" Kyla repeats. "What do you think?"

"It's just that… Um, I don't know."

"It's a big step. I know, right? You can take your time thinking about it."

"Seriously, Kyla, you want to move in with me?"

"We've been getting along so great lately, and I thought that it's time."

"We have?"

"You know we have. Come on! We should do this. It's major, but I really think we're ready!"

I pause, trying to think of something suitably indecisive. "Maybe…" That's all I can muster.

"For real? That's great!"

Feeling bad that she shows so much enthusiasm, I try to think of how best to smoothly lower her expectations. "What I mean by that is, maybe, and also, uh, maybe not. I mean maybe either way. I don't know. This is coming out all wrong."

"Oh!" She looks disappointed.

"Let's think about it."

For my part, definitely, I'm thinking about it. I've never lived together with a girlfriend in my whole life. Perhaps I should have known this would arise, and it is a part of growing up. As I ponder this, I realize that I've avoided growing up during this entire relationship. I don't want our intimacy to grow. I want it to stagnate, always stay like this and then when someone moves, we can break up. Meanwhile, I want everything to stay the same with none of the emotional introspection. It would be very therapeutic of me to admit all of this, if only I didn't refuse to say it out loud.

"You must have known that we were going to talk about this one day," says Kyla. "We've been together a year. I mean, it's really serious to me. I have strong feelings for you, Danny. Don't you care about me as well?"

"Of course," I say, and that's all.

"I'm going to give you some space, and we'll talk later. I understand. Sorry to shove all of this onto your plate! So, uh, I'll do some paperwork tonight, and at seven, I have a student. So I'll let you go now. Okay? Just talk to me tomorrow. Whenever. It's cool. Okay?"

"Yeah."

"Fine. That's great. Bye."

"Bye."

Right away, Kyla beckons to the waiter and asks for the bill all by herself. She can be nice at times, and I don't appreciate her properly. She quickly kisses me goodbye, hails a taxi, and rushes away.

Next, I decide to go for a walk by myself. I decide to stop at my bank to send money to my parents for paying back my student loans, an errand that I always handle at this particular corner, but then I realize that I don't have my passport on me, so I can't even do that.

After walking into an electronics shop, I look at the phones. I consider my outdated Chinese-brand phone, and it occurs to me that I've used the same one for the entirety of my years in China. It's small, cheap, and good for sending text messages in short bursts. Meanwhile, all of my friends have the latest Apple or Samsung smartphones. They have touch screens, operating systems, Androids, and Siris. They take crystal-clear photos and save thousands of MP3s. I look cheap in comparison. But it isn't about the money. It's about the commitment.

Where will I be in six months or next year? Will I stay here or move to another country with different cell-phone tower frequencies?

I know that I can be patient. It's not like I'm thinking of leaving. I'm not. For sure, I can commit to study, seek job security, and even fall in love. But I can't do what Kyla wants, not with her.

Just then, as I hold my outdated phone in my hands, I feel the vibration foreshadowing a three-beat ring. It's just a text message, but it's from my Mandarin teacher again. She's inviting me to go salsa dancing. Tonight! I know exactly the place, a Spanish outdoor pub across from the central shopping mall. I want her to teach me to dance, as well as to speak Mandarin, and I will teach her to kiss. I want so much to join her, and an involuntary grin spreads across my face.

I'm absolutely positive that I'll break up with Kyla as soon as I find the nerve.

* * *

"So how did it go?"

These days I hang out more often with Sandy, a black-American teacher whom I see at various bar scenes from time to time. I need more male friends like him and, more than anything right now, I need some *adult guy talk.* No Amber, no Aidan either, no Chinese girls and, definitely, nobody from Kyla's workplace. So I called up Sandy and invited him for a drink at Blank Slate to talk shop. Inevitably, we discuss relationships.

"Nice," I say, being in a braggart mood. "We totally made out. I played it fucking cool, dude. I'm not sure how the teacher-student relationship will survive though. I probably can't go to that class anymore. But I'm hopeful. I did learn a few salsa dances along the way too."

"That's all well and good, you idiot," he says. "But that's not what I was asking. What happened with your actual girlfriend? Did you break up with her or what?"

This considerably dampens the guy-talk feeling, but he's right. That's what I need to discuss. "I did," I reply. "Honestly, man, it was bad. She cried, called me an asshole and said that I broke her heart. I may have said a few things to her that now I regret, and so I have a few broken dishes to help me to remember her. The whole thing turned into such drama. It's probably best that I nipped it in the bud. I guess that things could have been worse if I'd continued to put it off into the future, but I can't imagine much worse."

"Well," he says, "we've all had our good and bad times."

"Didn't I do the right thing? I broke up with her as soon as the new relationship started."

"It sounds like you broke up over the moving-in thing. That is, if I heard your story correctly."

"You may be right about that, but I've always felt that it's traveling together that gives the kiss of death to relationships."

Then I think about all the tasks left to do after a breakup. "Fuck!" She still needs to come over to get her clothes, toothbrush and shit like that. It never ends.

"It happens. You needn't complain. You had a good run. Now let's get more drinks."

By then, I'm ready to ask Sandy about his own exploits in love and war. For example, he needs to update me about his Fujian chick. But for the moment, I concede and ask what he's drinking. Then I get up, make my way to the bar, and pay for two doubles.

Overall, I shouldn't feel bad. Anything I've endured is something that men worldwide get over every day. I didn't do anything that any other twenty-something guy wouldn't have done. In terms of the big picture, I'm having fun, enjoying the prime of my life and all that. The terrible involuntary feelings that I've experienced over love, or its absence, are just part of the process. All in all, I'm glad to be in this place and this city at this time. It's been an era.

兔
Good Life

I feel so strange seeing Duli and Lu Lu hang out together. They come from two separate worlds, and it's unnatural for them to appear in the same place. But since Lu Lu became a housewife, she insists on going out with me nearly every night. She wears more expensive clothes, drinks heavily, pays for us all, and seems far less happy.

This is my little cousin, the one who ran away and hid in my university dormitory just a few years ago. I've known her since she was very small. When her aunt, my mother, used to scold her for making a mess at dinner, I always tried to protect her.

On the other hand, Duli, my work colleague, represents a world of high finance and international real-estate clients. In my mind, she has no hometown or rural beginnings. She was born fully formed, wearing a dress suit and ready to talk business with Western European diplomats. This may not be true in a factual sense, but in the truth of my mind she hails from a vastly different place that should not overlap with my family.

That's why it's disconcerting when I arrive late and realize that these two have chatted with each other all evening. Out of breath from trotting upstairs in my platform sandals, I see them in the lobby drinking champagne and snacking on popcorn.

"Sorry that I'm late," I say.

"No problem," says Duli. "We're having fun. Your cousin is so funny!"

Hearing that remark stings. Later when a few other friends arrive, we enter a KTV box. Duli and Lu Lu sit beside each other and talk about jokes that they learned on the Internet.

The music selection is an obvious sort, the classics. A few Guangdong locals sing Cantopop. I do an old '90s Faye Wong number that has been sweet to me since childhood. Some of the others choose old songs originally done by Beyond, Jacky Cheung, and Aaron Kwok. The rest sing Mandopop, mostly from Taiwan, made popular by the likes of J.J. Lin, Chou Chuan-huing, Elva Hsiao, and the rock band Mayday.

Duli lets loose with some Jay Chou, Tiger Huang, and newer Zhang Jie. I dare her to sing an English song and find plenty of Madonna tracks for her to choose from, but she's too shy. Instead she sings a Cui Jian song.

I won't sing in English either, so I pick some classics and sing three in a row, coming from Andy Lau, Leslie Cheung, and Leon Lai. That means that we've covered all four of the Heavenly Kings of Cantopop.

Lu Lu, who insists on being new, contemporary, and cool, sings a few Mandarin numbers (from S.H.E., Jolin Tsai, Tan Yongling, Hu Xia and the latest by Wang Feng).

It's all great fun. We order beer and several plates of fruit and vegetables. The servers replace our drinks three times. By midnight, we're all a bit drunk. My throat's sore, but I'm laughing.

When we finally go outside, it's very dark. Since Lu Lu paid, I say thanks and hug her enthusiastically. It was fun, this single-girls' night out, the kind that keeps me happy.

Oh, wait. No, I almost forgot. One member of our group isn't single.

* * *

Lu Lu telephones me. She's crying. Sometimes she does this, and I try to be supportive and helpful. This time it's late, and I should be asleep. On weekdays, I need to wake up early.

"I'm so lonely, Elder Sister. Don't you know of any parties tonight?"

"Little Sister, I told you to check online. Many websites post events like that."

"But I can't go alone."

"I'm sorry, but you know that I work tomorrow. I can't go out now. You just need to find another way to stay busy. Take a class. Study something. How about a driving class? Or maybe join a club and make some new friends. Find an activity that fits you. Yoga's very popular these days."

"My life's so terrible," Lu Lu says, ignoring all my suggestions and just wanting someone to listen. "My husband always goes away on business, leaving me bored. Even when he's here, he acts so coldly."

"I know, dear. I know."

These phone calls hardly leave me in a good mood.

Work raises my spirits. Although I'm a bit tired the next morning, I recover after several cups of coffee. Then good news arrives. Thanks to my hard work and seniority, I've earned yet another promotion and salary increase.

The company thrives, and its profits rise. Even with the economic downturn overseas, Shenzhen property prices still climb, and we're doing well. More foreign customers, joining their Chinese business partners, hope to invest in the construction and advertising departments. We're expanding into Guangzhou, Zhuhai, Meizhou, and Zhongshan.

Now I'm an assistant manager, and my supervisor tells me that I'm required to travel more often to site locations. I'm introduced to a new driver who stays on call every day of the week. By the end of my promotion day, I feel like I'm in a whirlwind. Plus I realize that I must print new business cards.

I can't discuss any of this with Lu Lu, but my promotion excites Duli, who, when I see her, wants to go out later to celebrate. But I explain that I'm so tired.

"It's true," I insist. "My sleep has been very disturbed lately."

"You don't seem tired today."

"Believe me, I work very hard and need to rest. We'll meet on Saturday, okay?"

"Oh, *Sheila*," she says, pronouncing my English name very sarcastically. "You're no fun anymore."

Eager to avoid debating that point, I wave goodbye. After work, I rush out for some quick shopping to buy presents for my niece and nephew. At a children's stationery shop, I spy some small plastic robots and a cute notebook. I browse more before buying pens and matching erasers, all adorned with cartoon rabbits.

Realizing that I'm just one metro stop away from where my elder sister and grandmother live, I decide that maybe I should go to visit them. So I descend to the subway entrance and scan my metro card at the kiosk. Within a few minutes, I'm in the right neighborhood. But before I reach the complex where my grandmother and my sister's family live, I see something that greatly surprises me.

There's plenty to do in and near the garden-complex where my relatives live. Located in central Futian District, it's not only near the subway station, but many shops and restaurants operate along a road leading to the gated community.

For some reason, my eyes wander, merely gazing about and people-watching. Noticing some police officers, I casually glance to where they're going. I spot a small satellite precinct station squeezed between two fruit shops, the kind of place that's easy to miss.

Inside there, very strangely, I think that I see Lu Lu sitting on a waiting-room bench by a window.

Jolted by worry, I wonder if I should rush inside and ask her what's gone wrong. Why would she be sitting at a police station tonight?

But she also might feel embarrassed about whatever has happened to send her there. I want to be courteous. By nature, I'm discreet. Perhaps I don't need to expose our whole family to whatever personal issues she has.

Strategically, I veer into a Hong Kong-style diner (one of those *cha chaan teng* places that I like) across the road. There, I find a seat near a large window that gives me a good angle to spy.

The diner's relatively empty because the dinner rush has ended, and so I can sit wherever I want. A young waitress in an ugly orange uniform hands me a menu, plus a cup of tea, and asks what I would like.

Hastily, I glance at the menu and just say, "Mango juice smoothie".

Seen from my vantage point, the sky outside has darkened. Looking out, I see Lu Lu stand up and shake hands with an attractive young police officer. From the bench beside her, she picks up a thin brown box and hands it to him. What could that be? I wonder.

As if to satisfy my curiosity, the officer opens the box and takes out some cloth. He unfolds it, revealing a shirt. I can't see the details, but I would assume that if Lu Lu bought the garment, then it must be expensive and stylish.

The officer waves the shirt in front of himself, as if evaluating it in front of a mirror at a clothing store in one of the shopping malls. He appears to approve, judging by his giddy body language, although I can't see clearly enough to tell if he's smiling. I certainly don't know what the two of them are saying.

My smoothie comes, and I take a sip while still looking out the window. My lips find the plastic straw, and then my tongue experiences the taste of delicious juice and sweet milk, all while my eyes taste something very unfamiliar.

Soaking in the visual taste, I decide that it doesn't look likely to become any sweeter or increasingly bitter. It only melts into more confusion.

My cousin and the police officer just talk. Then he goes behind the front desk, and she follows. They sit together at a computer monitor. She leans on his shoulder. Are they examining some official document related to a legal manner? Or are they watching a comedy program on PPTV?

It's all very suspicious, and I don't know what to do. When Lu Lu finally leaves, I decide not to visit my elder sister's family on that day after all.

After paying my bill at the diner, I take the first taxi that I can find and rush home. I shower before cooking myself a dinner of rice, chopped vegetables, and shelled shrimp. Next, I watch television alone and soon put on my pajamas. But I can't sleep, partly because I'm used to staying up late and taking Lu Lu's phone calls. On this particular night, she doesn't call.

* * *

Abruptly, Lu Lu has stopped telephoning me, and it turns out that I miss her. We still hang out as friends at times, but less often as the days pass. She's less flamboyant than before. Duli and my co-workers no longer laugh at her jokes. Yet I sense that my cousin feels happier, content in ways that mean she no longer needs me or my group as distracting entertainment.

The weather simmers and steams us. Springtime has come and passed, giving way to a southern China summer. It's muggy and wet. At home, the air conditioners blast from every angle. Anyone who steps outside walks straight into a wall of sweat.

When socializing with Lu Lu, I routinely feel liquid form on my brow and blame it on the sultry heat. I try to forget what I saw and not think about her personal life. After all, it's none of my business, and I have nothing to say about it.

But I can't help myself. One evening after a family dinner, as my relatives complain that Lu Lu's husband never joins us, I listen to what she says and then make a decision.

"I don't mind," Lu Lu insists. "I live a happy life."

She wants to leave early, fleeing from the family's constant judgment. My grandmother says some disparaging words in Hakka, and the children hide in a corner, like they always do during family quarrels.

"Let Lu Lu be," I say, but then I stop my cousin before she rushes away.

"I'll join you, Lu Lu," I tell her. "Let's have some pleasant company for once."

"You two girls enjoy yourselves," says my aunt. "One of you is a single old maid, and the other has a missing husband. Don't the two of you care at all for family, for respecting your elders? Your generation has no concept of filial piety. What a disgrace…"

Hand in hand, we run out through the doorway and giggle as I push the elevator button repeatedly, hoping that somehow it'll arrive faster to hasten our escape.

"Little Sister," I say. "You must be careful."

"Careful?" she repeats, incredulously. "I'm an adult too, and a wife. I can take care of myself."

"You must be careful when you always leave dinners early. Don't let them suspect."

"Suspect what?"

"Just don't let them suspect anything. Make them think that your life's perfect, and they'll be happy."

"You're so cryptic right now, Elder Sister. It's very strange. My life is my life."

I take a deep breath as we step into the elevator. That's when I say what I've been dying to say for weeks. "You must be careful because if I saw you, then perhaps Mother, Grandmother or someone else has seen you too."

"You saw me?"

"I saw you," I say.

"Who was I with?"

At that moment, my suspicions are completely affirmed. I knew there was a "*who*".

Reading my facial expression, Lu Lu understands that her secret has been revealed. Then she changes her disposition from annoyance to calm. Perhaps she even feels relief at knowing that we can talk about this. "Where did you see us?" she asks.

"It was in the small police station, the one down the street, about a month ago. Since then, you've seemed happier. So I made a guess."

"He said that we never should meet in the local station. He thought that it was too close, but I didn't care."

"Don't meet there anymore. Anyone can see you. And please make sure that your husband never finds out," I tell her in a condescending tone.

Suddenly I feel like I'm a middle-school student again, that she's in primary school and that I must lecture her on how to avoid trouble with teachers. "You must be more careful."

"Oh, what do you care? You don't understand what it's like. Let me be happy."

"I do want you to be happy."

"Then leave it alone. Keep my secret, and that's all I ask."

"So… Little Lu… Is there anything that you want to tell me?"

The elevator bell rings, its door opens and we step outside into the enveloping heat. As we just walk, she tells me the story of how they met. It's a long tale and a long walk. She calls her husband "an old man" and explains about how soon after they married, a bag was stolen and she reported it, meeting many police officers. She liked one of them. They exchanged numbers and became friends. She never found the bag, but continued to see the young officer. Their friendship turned into an affair.

Lu Lu tells me that she had felt intensely lonely with her husband away so often and acting distant even when he came home. She found the police officer more attractive, both in looks and in spirit, and she made the first move. Bluntly, she asked him on a date and made her situation very clear. They go to love hotels and small bars. She even pays, and he knows that she's married, but never asks questions. My cousin says the situation is the best that she ever could do for her life. She insists that the policeman makes her so happy, so much more than her terrible husband does. She insists that she stands in the right.

"At first, I felt guilty," she concedes at last, "but then I thought about the *old man* and how many whores he must see on his travels."

"Come on, how do you know that?"

"I know men. I know them well."

On this, she sounds very confident, and I have nothing more to say.

* * *

Many holidays, such as the Qingming Festival and Labor Day, fall during this season, creating lots of opportunities to meet with family members. Being a Shenzhen local, part of a small minority, I never need to travel out of town for family reasons. So I see my family often, being sucked into the bottomless ocean of family obligations. I'll never truly escape while living in this city.

Last year at this time, my friend Duli and I traveled to the lovely beaches of Hainan. This time my mother insists that I must stay in town. The children don't have to go to school, and so Mimi and Little Fo regale us with tales about their recent adventures at the Happy Land Adventure Park. I hear about roller coasters, pirate ships, and delicious sweets. My elder sister sits beside me on her sofa and shows me pictures from the day-at-the-park using her touchpad screen. Her finger waves and offers another picture. Her finger waves again, and the show continues.

The whole family's here, and with full bellies from a big dinner. My mother also sits next to me to bask in the delightful moments of childhood. "So cute!" she raves to the screen.

Fearful of a coming speech, I mentally prepare to explain that I'm very busy with work and that I'm a modern, career-oriented woman so far content without a marriage and children.

But before Mother seizes the chance to guilt me into breeding children of my own, Lu Lu interrupts with an announcement. "Hello, everyone," she says. "I want to announce some good news. Please be quiet."

The scene grows still. Everyone puts down their phones, games or other electronics. Mother makes Father turn off the television. Still-silence descends. Once the tension builds, Lu Lu, always knowing how to put on a show, tells us all, "Thank you. I want to let you know that we'll gain a new addition to the family next year. I'm pregnant!"

"Congratulations!" declares her mother, my aunt, whose eyes turn tearful. All the old ladies rush to hug Lu Lu and rub her belly. The men begin to pour wine and liqueur.

After waiting in line, I take Lu Lu's hand and wish her the best. "Life is so happy," she says to me with a quick wink.

The celebratory activities of drinking and eating desserts commence, and so I find no chance to talk to Lu Lu privately. All we shared was that wink. The night turns into a late one, as they often do, until finally I'm allowed to leave.

These days, I lack much time to myself. My job gets busier every week, and still I have no boyfriend. So immediately after leaving the joyous glow of my family, I stand alone on the street. Not caring for such a lonely feeling, I decide to seek out some other companionship.

I ride in a taxi to the nearest pub and order two whisky sours in a row. Removing my dress jacket, I bare my shoulders to all the patrons. Then I smile at several men, but it's a slow night. No one approaches me.

As I sit at the bar, a tired-looking businessman sits three chairs away. So I get up and sit beside him. He ignores me and watches a football match on a television screen high up near the ceiling.

"Pardon," I say. "I'm low on money. Please buy me a drink."

He looks over at me with a surprised expression on his face. His glasses droop, and he's much less attractive up close. I regret speaking to him.

"I'm sorry," he says. "I can't."

What's this? I feel so ashamed. Can't I even find someone to love me on this lonesome night?

Really, my life has no time for this kind of thing so please let me just get it over and done. I have so much else to do. For example, I need to visit my dentist and call my landlord to fix the stove. I need to buy laundry soap and recharge my SIM card, and I want to look into taking Spanish lessons too. I must wake up and arrive at work in just six hours to manage my own suburban development team. But first I need this simple thing and can't even achieve it. I feel, very strongly somehow, that no one wants me.

No one wants *me*. *Me*!

Exactly who am *I*? Well, several answers apply. My name is Chen. My mother calls me Dau-Dau. My cousins and brother call me Big Sister, while my elder sister calls me Little Sister. In Cantonese, my friends call me Siu Chan. In Mandarin, I'm Xiao Chen or Xiao Dou. When I go to Hong Kong, my name is spelled C-H-A-N. It can be written in traditional characters or in simplified ones. My ID card fully states Chen Dou, spelled C-H-E-N. My business card has two sides, and when I turn it over, I see what my English-speaking friends call me, and then I know that I'm Sheila too. Somehow, right now, at this time, thinking about all these different people within myself only makes me feel all the lonelier.

虎
Times Change

This year, everything would be different. That was my promise. I made a vow to myself, and somehow, I took myself up on the offer. I'm a changed man. It's goddamn true.

I've invested. In myself. Being my own boss. Settling down. And I'm married too. Can you believe it?

The thing of it is that to own property in China, you must be a Chinese citizen. To successfully conduct your own domestic business, unlike trading, for which you can register an overseas address, it's best to have the most trustworthy partner possible. So the logical thing for me was to get married.

On paper, the bank accounts and licenses, little May owns my business and heads up its management. I'm a silent partner, but also the face of the company. It's funny how that works.

Together we run the Stone Bar in Shekou. It's this little dive behind a big club. You may know it. We've been a staple location on the foreigners' nightlife scene for the whole season.

Last year when I retreated back to New York with my tail between my legs, I decided to live off my financial portfolio temporarily and to focus on doing some research about thriving small businesses. Restaurants weren't for me, being too high risk. Nightclubs required massive capital and high-profile connections. As for running a bar, I learned that getting a liquor license is the most complex issue. But keep in mind that doesn't matter in China. So my choice looked easy. I'd offer alcohol plus a humble venue.

For starters, I interviewed bartenders and tavern proprietors in Brooklyn, asking about the histories of how they started up, what loans it took, and their rent per square foot. Then I began factoring in housing prices in square meters, current conversion rates to *yuan*, and the much cheaper real estate.

I learned how to handle both domestic and international issues, focusing specifically on Asia. Then I studied how to set up an interior and what decorations would fit the mood. I advanced to lighting, audio, wiring, and how to screw an all-important television onto a room's corner ceiling just before a big-game night.

After borrowing money, I came back to Shenzhen and set myself up to live in a long-term hotel. I started dating my old secretary. She's the one for me, I decided. I captured her heart, and within a matter of a few months, she was ready to marry.

We held two separate wedding parties, one in Shenzhen and one in her hometown. My mom and brothers couldn't make it, but they emailed messages of their love. In the process, I met more in-laws than I'll ever be able to keep track of, and we made a hell of a profit on all those red envelopes handed along as wedding gifts.

Then I took May on a honeymoon to Thailand. That was her first time abroad. One day, the two of us will travel to America. I know it! Every day, she falls for me harder and harder.

Together we moved into a nice place in the Nanshan District. It's not too far from the new bar. May wanted me to buy her a home, but

I patiently explained that I need to invest all of my available funds into the new establishment. We're still renting an apartment.

At dirt-cheap prices, we bought the bar location and hired workers to renovate it. After just a month, I felt ready to show off the place, and so I hired promoters and graphic designers to start spreading the word. That part became a tad more expensive. Flyers got around, ads appeared online, and on opening night we drew quite a turnout. We booked a DJ from Hong Kong. We hired cute waitresses too. My little lady became the boss of them all.

That very first week, I started to recognize my regular customers. After the excitement of the big opening, the business took hold. In the ensuing weeks, the place got a little busier night by night. Profits rose. I started to pay back my lenders. Ever since, my bank account has risen exponentially.

Sometimes I even tend bar myself, mixing drinks and chatting. It's not my area of greatest expertise, but we have flowcharts to explain how to do proper cocktails. I get better at it all the time. We also have some on-site cooking, just simple things like fries or nachos, and I help out with that too. It's easy enough, nothing compared to the stress of business meetings and sales deadlines.

I like to hang around near the bar's front counter and make sure that everyone sees me. I figure that's a big part of the business model. Soon, I'll become a pillar of the community, a local character loved by everyone.

Maybe I'm getting a bit ahead of myself. But I'm fairly certain that this will work out for us. The key to economic success, I realize, isn't climbing up the ranks within an established company. In that scenario, the company always screws you over eventually, unless you get all the way to the very top and then screw over everyone else first. Damn, but I'm totally over that rat race!

Nor does economic certainty lie in *creating value*, whatever that means. Subjective philosophical concepts of the free market or not, value remains subject to the limits imposed by an unstable society and local regulations. I'm so over Friedman, Smith and Rand too.

The key thing is to market to those who already have capital. They can hoard it, corrupt the government, rise or fall with the world economy and do whatever they want. They can be bailed out or escape to the Caribbean, and you can protest, or Occupy them, to your heart's content, but it makes not a damn bit of difference.

No, the best way to make it in this world is to have something to sell to that elite class and then let good things trickle down directly to *you*.

Yes, my business educational background serves me well.

Hey, I'm telling you this profound story, and you're barely listening. No wonder! You're the only one left in here this late tonight, drunk beyond all comprehension, and I'm a little buzzed too. Well, I just happen to like sharing my knowledge. I see that your eyes are closing and your body slumps, but please hold on a bit longer. I'm almost done.

* * *

My new hangout, Shekou, forms a part of the western Nanshan District, to the deep southwest of Shenzhen and at the end of a peninsula, geographically so desperately trying to grab onto Hong Kong. Literally, the name Shekou means "snake's mouth".

Within easy reach of Hong Kong by ferry, this place is where most of the Westerners with capital have decided to set up shop. I'm talking *major capital*. There's no other way to describe it. This is a modern colonial village where many of the high rollers in Shenzhen choose to live. As I've concluded in my savvy business model, if they continue to come here and buy overpriced drinks for the sake of *atmosphere*, then I'll do well.

For the moment, I still need to build a reputation. That involves the people, the real masses of Shekou, who make up the crowds. How about bottles of champagne on reserved tables for the one class, and Tiger or Tsingtao beers for the rest? That's perfect for everyone. With every demographic covered, I can't go wrong.

One day, I notice a certain English teacher. I've seen him around the scene at Blank Slate and Santa Maria, and when he comes into my place, he gives me that cold look. So another American thinks that he's special. Well, he has no capital, and he's just here for the show. He's easily replaced. When he starts rattling on about the watered-down drinks, I happily give him a free drink and hope that next time he'll bring friends in here with him.

Another time I see an attractive Chinese girl whom I recognize. I'm pretty sure that we had sex together a few times, although I don't remember her name. Those were my younger days, almost another life. The girl arrives during happy hour with a group of females and acts like she doesn't know me. I hope that they'll stay for the evening, lure in men, and repeat the cycle next weekend. I keep watching her, but she doesn't respond to me, and I don't want to make a performance out of it, so I back away and let my employees take care of her group.

Looking down at my stomach, I'm reminded about how much weight I've gained since moving back to China. As if I could go back to picking up the likes of that girl! Well, this happens, thanks to my age, no gym membership, restaurant food, and settling down. Maybe that's why the girl doesn't recognize me. Who knows?

A journalist, scribbling in his notepad, sits across from her at the next table. I think that the restaurant and bar reviews are supposed to be anonymous, but it's such a small town for us foreigners that anonymity's nearly impossible. I know that journalist. He's young, doesn't dress well, and writes for the *Pearl Delta Expat*, the expatriate 'zine of choice for the whole province, and his drink isn't watered down.

Late into the night, my regulars come in, balding middle-aged men, full of capital and conversation, and they ask me where little May is. I tell them a story that she's gone to her hometown attending to my in-laws. Then I joke about how lucky that I am to stay here and hang out with "you guys". That earns me a good laugh, and the group lingers for another two hours. Mission accomplished!

"Ding Ding," I say to the head waitress, who has become sort of my assistant lately.

"Yes, boss," she answers in the charming way that she always calls me "boss".

"I'm going outside for a while. Keep the place lively."

"You got it!"

She's great. I should think about promoting her to an official management position. After all, a position's open.

It's late, and we're busy. Really, I shouldn't leave the premises, but I must. I feel compelled to call the Shekou Hospital. They have an English line, and the night nurses know me well by now. Ritually, I call from time to time. The nurse, or whoever answers, never minds that it's so late. I say "hello" and mention a report number that I've long since memorized. Then I'm told that there's no change in May's condition.

The nurse thanks me for my concern, and I hear a rustling of papers. She adds that I must wait until after the surgery for any real updates. Next she reminds me about my appointment on Friday and asks me to make sure that I bring along my insurance papers. She thanks me for my time and hangs up.

When my wife had the car accident, I didn't know how I should react. To me, it felt unreal. Honestly, I didn't know what to do. I received a phone call, saw my wrecked Acura and, suddenly, my wife had turned into a hospital bed.

Since then, I've survived on my own. I do utilize my employees for translation services in various day-to-day affairs, but that isn't what I mean by not knowing what to do. Now I have no idea what'll happen to my life. We had everything all planned out, and then this happened. I didn't realize it until May was gone, but she's become my whole world. Without her, I can't imagine a future.

I really had thought that things were going well. Why now? May lies in a drug-induced coma and needs surgery. She has a spinal injury with slips of plastic dashboard right between her vertebrae. Life hardly resembles TV dramas with medical miracles occurring as if delivered from on high. Even if miracles did happen, I don't deserve one. May does, but not me.

And the worst part is that I know where the fault lies, and it's not with her. Why couldn't the accident have happened to me instead?

Really, I have little reason to step out and call the hospital every night. May's not in unstable condition. The night nurse is right. There's nothing more to report until after the surgery. All that I can do is to go along as scheduled on Friday, sign some documents and make sure that the payment's in order.

If she dies… If she dies… Well, I can't think about that. Stepping into an empty alley, I cry for a minute or two. Hopefully, nobody sees me. It's lame, but that's what I do now. Constantly, I talk myself up, take a deep breath, and somehow muster the strength to continue.

Damn! I promised May that I'd take her to America someday, that she would see everything there, my family, the cities, the sights, the places of my childhood. I want her to see the places that shaped me. If I don't get to do that…

You'd think that life in rising China would make you hard. It doesn't. China makes you soft.

With a tissue, I wipe at my eyes one more time. Stiffening my heart, I go back to work, back to my life, back to the Stone Bar. That's the name of the place, and that's the point. I need to be like a stone.

羊

Epilogue I: Tears, A Few

It's time for the Mandarin class, and I stand outside a clear-glass door overlooking the lobby. For, like, three whole minutes, I've been peeking into the classroom. I notice the receptionist looking at me oddly, but I don't care.

I've already traveled all the way here. I took the elevator to the 17th floor and cautiously edged closer and closer, looking suspiciously like a cat burglar or something. Luckily, the security people leave me alone.

So far, I don't dare go inside yet. My eyes are still red from crying last night.

"What are you doing here?" I ask myself. I do that at times when I'm stressed and upset. I know. It's crazy, right? We all get crazy sometimes.

I'm here like this because I want to see if Danny has arrived yet. At the same time, I'm refocusing my eyes, trying to decipher reflections on the glass to see behind me. I don't want Danny to sneak up on me either. Will he really show his face here? Would he do that?

My heart beats super-fast, and I feel a thousand conflicting emotions. I'm depressed. I want to go home, get high, and go to sleep. I'm embarrassed and hope that the receptionist doesn't say anything. I'm angry and want to scream at Danny, making a scene in front of everyone. I'm so afraid, and if he comes here, I'll want to just disappear forever.

"Hello, how are you?" I say to the Indian fellow who always sits in front of me. He answers in Chinese and squeezes past me to get inside. I move my body, but not my head or eyes, and I watch him enter and sit down.

"Here goes nothing," I quietly tell myself. Then I follow his steps one by one through the doorway, around the lobby desk, and into the classroom.

Anxiously, I sit down. To my left, a seat remains empty. Danny's not here. I don't know whether to feel relief or disappointment. Come on! It's mostly relief. As I watch the clock, 10 minutes pass, and I'm pretty sure that Danny won't be here.

There's nothing worse than bumping into an ex, especially so soon after the breakup.

With all this on my mind, I pay little attention to the teacher. Like, really, none at all! I embarrass myself, I suppose. Miss Tang calls on me once, twice, and I feel like a teenager failing in Spanish class again, which I'm almost used to by now. After the first two times, she doesn't call on me anymore. On some level, I sense that she's slightly annoyed at me, but why would that be the case? I doodle in my book, creating some pictures of cutesy pocket-monsters and magical girls. Before I know it, the class is over.

"I can't come here anymore," I whisper to myself. "Who needs the heartache?"

The teacher glares at me, and I feel angry and ashamed at the same time.

"Bye, bye," I say.

She waves, makes a gesture with her eyes that I can't interpret, and says something that I can't translate. Then I'm gone.

I share an awkward elevator ride down with the Indian fellow. Once we're downstairs, I say "goodbye" and stuff, and he smiles his polite smile.

Momentarily, I walk by myself. Next to the building, there's a little park. I decide to sit there beside a tree and watch the couples pass.

"India," I say, alone and at full volume, disregarding that I'm outdoors. "I should go on a trip and get out of China. Why not go backpacking in India? How cool would that be?

"Yeah," I'm saying, agreeing with myself as I wait at a bus stop.

"India! Girl, that's the best idea you've had in ages. Ah, here's my bus."

As I clamber onto the crowded vehicle and search for a seat, I decide to go to an Indian restaurant tomorrow.

The next day at work, I talk about upcoming holidays with my Chinese manager, asking him about vacation pay, which leads to discussing travel. "Did you ever go to Tibet?" I ask him.

"Yes, it's so beautiful."

"I'd love to go there," I say, "and to a lot of those surrounding countries too."

"Like Nepal," he says.

"Yes, and Pakistan," I say, although I don't really mean that one. Then I pause, before adding, "And India too."

"So exotic," he says.

"Yes. It's just that, say, if I wanted to go there, then I'd need a lot of time to see everything because it's such a big country."

"Two weeks in the summer should be no problem," he says.

Yes, he approves! "It'll be so hot."

"Well, I never mind that," he laughs. "Living in southern China makes me used to it."

Then I make my move. "But the only thing is… it's hard for me to book a ticket. I kind of need help from a Chinese friend. To, like, get a cheap online ticket from a Chinese website. You know?"

"I see."

On our free time between shifts, my manager shows me some good local websites for booking flights. During my spare moments in the next week, I check in, playing the game, gambling at finding the cheapest ticket on which day and trying to snatch it quickly.

Then late one night after instant messaging my girlfriends back home, I browse one of the sites, refresh the page, and see "Hong Kong to Delhi" available for only 1,800. I make a mental note of that.

The next day I go to an ATM so that I have the necessary cash in hand. Then, on my lunch break, I check that the ticket's still listed at the same price. As I coax him, my manager orders it for me.

Way to go! India! I don't need Danny or any man at all.

This turn of events gets me thinking about how my contract will be up soon and how maybe I'm about done with this China thing. Having had some travels, I could say goodbye to a few friends and go back home. Everyone here moves on eventually. Nothing really ties me down. I have no real relationships in this country, not anymore. Now that I think about it, all of my friends are only shallow acquaintances. I could just as well never see them again. Here, I'm truly close to no one. Not like back home.

But I have money and a backpack. Imagine no more Chinese smelly street food, no more creepy businessmen hitting on me, and no more gross hot weather. I should go home. Totally!

To me, this place isn't the real world. And Danny was no good for me. Now I see how selfish, negative, and no-fun he was. I may miss him, and tears may well up inside of me, even right now, but I know that I'm better off alone. It's ridiculous how this emotion swells and spreads to my arms and legs. I know that it's stupid, yet it's like I watch myself have this reaction and I can't stop it.

So, sure, I cry a little, but that doesn't mean anything. I know better. I'm so happy now. At least, I'm pretty certain that I am. The future looks wide open.

Gosh! I'm so totally happy right now. Aren't I?

雞

Epilogue II: A Blessed Thing

I feel so fabulous. No sickness at all today. I'm playing pop music on my top-of-the-line smartphone as our private driver, Ah Yan, takes me to the driving school. All the tuition's paid, and this will be my first lesson. I'm fantasizing about which kind of car I soon will own: possibly a BMW.

Diligently, I practice in the driving-school version of a Korean car. It's difficult. My driving instructor, a middle-aged migrant from Dalian, speaks perfect Mandarin, but I wish he was fluent in Cantonese. In fact, we don't go anywhere. We just use the simulator indoors. But overall, it's a fun experience, and I can't wait to get behind the wheel of a moving vehicle.

After the one-hour lesson, Ah Yan takes me to Starbucks. There, I chat with my older cousin on my lightweight notebook computer, the one that fits so neatly into my purse. Then I go shopping in the adjacent mall, buying shoes, sunglasses, and another handbag. When I call the driver, he picks me up and takes me home.

By then, I'm thirsty. The housemaid comes in only twice a week, and she hasn't appeared for the past few days, so my dirty dishes have piled up, but I don't want to wash them if a servant will do it tomorrow anyway. So I pour myself a drink of fruit punch in a plastic cup. Next I watch a film, a Ge You comedy, on the movie channel. Feeling sleepy, I take an early nap. So far, I'm having a good day.

My stomach starts to hurt, and I wake up to use the toilet. I always awaken alone in my king-sized bed, something that takes a long time to get used to, at least for me. During this season, my husband comes home only one weekend per month. Now he has another three weeks to go, and I feel lonely.

Although we expect an addition to our family, that isn't due to happen for many months. I'm hardly even showing yet. Meanwhile, I want to get a cat, but my husband says that he doesn't like cats.

After a light lunch, I go to an afternoon yoga lesson. Prenatal style. My doctor says that's okay as long as I take it easy. The gym's only a few blocks away, still inside our complex, and I can walk there. Once the class begins, I enjoy 40 minutes worth of good stretching. Then I chat with other housewives about some nearby restaurants.

Returning home, I take a shower. I send a text to my girlfriends to make sure that we still plan to meet this evening. One of them has a birthday next week, and I must think about buying her a gift.

After dinner, I have a late appointment with my gynecologist. She examines me in the stirrup chair, says that everything's in order, and describes me as remarkably healthy. Morning sickness has not affected me like it did in the first month. But I always feel a need to go to the toilet. The gynecologist says that's normal, and she prescribes no medicine.

Once back outside, I decide to buy some Chinese-medicine tea at a traditional pharmacy, a kind of tea that my grandmother always recommends. It tastes so bitter, but I think that it helps. Indeed, my health has been rather remarkable.

We remain far from knowing the gender of our child. Of course, my husband wants a son, but I believe that either sex should be okay. These days it doesn't matter so much to have a son. My husband can be too traditional sometimes. Besides, even if this child growing inside of me isn't a son, we can always have another.

I just hope that in the end our family isn't too big. If we have a boy, then I hope that he doesn't grow up with his father always away on business. I hope that any daughter will grow up to respect and think highly of her mother. Most of all, I hope that my family will be happy forever.

Sometimes these hopes make me feel lonely, and sometimes overwhelmed. Sometimes life seems slow, and sometimes so fast. I suppose what really bothers me is a feeling that I'm not in control.

And on some evenings, I feel hormonal and horny. Then I can't stay alone. As a secret among women, my grandmother once told me about the need to address such cravings. It keeps the body healthy.

So I telephone my good friend. He has known me for a while now, and we've grown so close. I book a room in a hotel and charge it to my husband's credit card.

My friend meets me. His uniform's so sexy, and he takes me into his arms. He makes love to me with passion and the strength of his entire body. I don't let him kiss me though. He tries, but I turn away. He bites my neck. I feel incredible.

After we both climax, I'm layered in perspiration. I go to the toilet and then take another shower. Returning to bed, I lie in the space near my lover's armpit and his shoulder.

We watch television together. He asks me when we'll see each other again. Not wanting to say that I don't know, I just make up an arbitrary date. Later he'll remind me, and I'll cancel if it's inconvenient.

Truly, I don't know what'll happen. For now, I feel comfortable, although tomorrow, or the tomorrow after that, probably I won't.

At this moment, my life's good. As for what tomorrow may bring, I can't say with certainty. I only can hope.

鼠
Epilogue III: Gloriously Rich

Happily, I invite my parents and extended family to see my new apartment. I've just purchased it. My new property-development business goes well, and so I organized a small party for my relatives. My uncle and auntie accompany my parents, and we all eat catered food while watching variety shows and sports.

"What's your English name?" my mother asks me after looking at my business card.

"Jackie," I tell her. She often forgets and asks me again.

This time she tries to pronounce it. I feign that I'm deeply impressed and recommend some English lessons to her.

Auntie commends me on buying a property and asks me if I have a girlfriend. "No," I say.

"Why don't you get a girlfriend? You should be married when living in a beautiful apartment like this."

Reluctant to tell her about the many girls I'm dating now, I succumb to her advice somewhat, and suddenly it appears that I've agreed to meet her friend's daughter on Friday. Having enjoyed so many dates lately, I laugh to myself at the luck. I profusely thank my aunt for the setup.

After my uncle and aunt leave, I decide that my parents are ready for the surprise that I've prepared for them.

"Please follow me," I say.

We go to a nearby apartment in the west building. My parents don't question why I escort them there, not even when I take out keys and we enter an empty apartment.

"Surprise, this is the new home I've bought for you!" I shout.

Instantly, Mother cries, and my father shakes his head disapprovingly. "Son," he says, "this is too much."

"No!" screams my mother in passionate disagreement. She lectures to him, he gives in, and then they already start discussing plans to move in within the month. Mother always excels at telling him what to do.

I think this home looks perfect for them. It's much better than where they live now across town. I pay their rent already. This mortgage will cost about the same and, since I own it, give me an investment to resell in the future. It's a full-win deal, and I'm happy to do it.

However, I'm not so traditional that I want them to move in with me. Certainly, I'm not ready for that. Their new place and my own are in the same complex, but far enough away from each other that I can bring home girls, have parties, and maintain my private life. They don't need to be around me at all times, but just near enough that they feel appreciated.

I'm very pleased with myself because I've done well and am the perfect filial son. All this, and yet my bank account remains so loaded that I don't know what to do with all the money. I could buy more properties, maybe invest in my own office space, or travel abroad. I will definitely take my parents to Hong Kong for shopping on my father's birthday in the autumn.

Soon I experience another typical week as my commissions and clients pile up. My new business does even better than expected. At first, it was hard work and long hours, but in recent months, I've hired plenty of fresh college graduates to handle the work that I used to do. Gradually, my own workload eased. I train the newcomers for a day or two and then let them scramble to outdo each other at hard work. That way, I can sit peacefully in my cold, spacious office, waiting for my usual "meeting" at the end of each day. Meanwhile, my employees scatter, stay busy on phones, rush in or out, and write reports that my assistant reads.

With so much leisure time today, I decide to leave early and go on the date that my auntie helped to arrange.

"Hello," the girl greets me. We meet at a northern-style restaurant. I still wear my suit, and I think that she's impressed by my money. She's a cute girl, short, with a modern attitude, and she's not Cantonese.

While eating, we talk about my auntie, about mutual friends, and about her family. Her relatives live far away, and she misses them. I talk about my "complex". She already knows that I've bought my parents a new home.

"I think that you're a very good person," she says.

"Please, come with me, and we'll take a look at my property."

Reaching my home, we stroll through the central park behind the gates and guards. "After a meal, it's good to go for a walk," I say.

Families walk their dogs, and she comments "how cute". Old men sit on benches and play Chinese chess. In the main square, 100 elderly ladies dance in unison. Looking at flowers too, we walk along the path until we finish a complete circle. The sun is setting, and although the weather remains hot, I feel a comfortable light breeze rise from the mountains.

"This is a beautiful garden," the girl says.

"You must see the view from the rooftop," I tell her. "That's a magnificent scene."

"Really?"

"Yes. From up there, you can see all the way into the New Territories in Hong Kong, beyond the river."

"Wow!"

With ease, I convince her to ride with me to the 34th floor, the very top. Moments later, we step out onto the flat rooftop and take mobile-phone pictures of the wonderful view. So much land spreads out below us.

Sensing a great moment, I curve an arm around her hip. Gently, I lean in, but she backs away and won't let me kiss her.

"Let's go," she says, and so we do. But I press a button to stop the elevator at my floor.

"Why did you do that?" she asks.

"Of course, I'd like to invite you for a drink at my place."

"No, thank you. I need to go home soon. Tomorrow morning, I must work, and it'll be very busy."

Although disappointed, I just smile. "No problem," I say. Somehow I like this girl and want my chances to improve for the next time.

Courteously, I escort her to the front gate and hail a car for her. I quietly peck her on the cheek before wishing her a pleasant evening. She promises that we'll see each other again very soon, perhaps on the weekend, and then I make her solemnly pledge to meet me then. She climbs into the car, tells the driver where to go and they speed away.

Life's grand. Maybe I've never felt more content than I do today. Along all avenues, I'm satisfied. I know that I'm a good person. It looks like a happy ending for everyone.

Then near the front gate, a disgusting old beggar approaches me holding out a pan partly filled with one-*kuai* coins. She touches my shoulder, and I jump away. She looks like a witch and must be hundreds of years old. Her skin resembles crumpled paper, her clothes are ripped and gray, and when she opens her wide mouth, empty spaces reveal the grim reality of missing teeth. No one possibly could look more out of place here at this luxurious villa.

She asks me for money, speaking in heavily accented Mandarin from a region that I can't identify. Ignoring her, I walk briskly to the other side of the gate.

There, I glare at the front security guard in a very disapproving manner. He lowers his head slightly, and I hope he understands that as a tenant I dislike such people wandering into my view. The guards need to control that problem, or I'll lodge stern complaints with the management.

Soon the disgusting woman walks away, and I ascend to my comfortable new home to rest and enjoy a little solitude. Except for meeting that beggar, it wasn't a bad day.

I don't want even the unpleasant memories of seeing beggars to spoil my community. Well, I suppose that no place is perfect.

BOOK II
廣州
Guangzhou

Prologue: 1, 2, 3

New Town
Art, Inspired
Monkey
Adventures in Estates

Interlude I: Guangzhou

Ting Ting Two Two

Interlude II: Guangzhou

Cantonland

Interlude III: Macau

Casting Call
He Never Mentioned My Hair
Officialdom

Prologue: Guangzhou

1
豬

I don't like to judge people based on appearances. I'm more attracted to personalities. It's what's inside a person that counts, as I always say.

Eric has a strong personality. Older and very confident, he's sincere, really. Certainly, he doesn't have much fashion sense. That's for sure, especially with that thick beard. But he's really funny, and everyone laughs around him all the time.

At the moment, he's dressed in a silly Hawaiian shirt like a stereotypical American on vacation.

"Mexican brown," he says.

We're at a party, and he's showing off a small plastic baggie of brownish powder. A small crowd forms around the dining-room table, and he asks for a metal surface.

"A mirror maybe?"

We're at Rina's place, and she replies that she has no mirror. "Just use a magazine."

"This isn't like rolling a common spliff, but whatever."

Six thin lines appear, each about an inch long. "Nor is it similar to coke," Eric says, "for if you take too much, do not assume that the buzz simply will go away after twenty minutes. This will go on for *hours*. Hence, you must start small."

He rolls up a pink 100-yuan bill and sniffs a line. "Yes, I love the feeling down the esophagus!"

Then he passes the bill to me. "I'm next?"

"And why not? Welcome to the neighborhood, Amber."

I suck it up my left nostril and feel congested, but nothing else. I know these things take a while to kick in.

One by one, the others take their lines. Then Rina brings her laptop and screws open a bottle of Sauvignon blanc, although Eric warns us not to be too heavy on the alcohol. We listen to the music shuffle from her computer.

"Do you feel anything of the potency yet?" Eric asks me.

"I think so."

"Just chill. Be lovely."

Casually, I touch my cheek. Then my finger goes to my forehead, and I realize that I'm covered in a film of liquid. My breathing feels a little weird. It's hard to describe this feeling. Basically, I know that I'm highly intoxicated.

"Look at my pupils," says Eric and leans right into my face. His eyes appear nearly empty with just the tiniest dot in each of their centers. "Like pins, am I right? I'm positively loaded."

"So what happens now?" I ask. "I'm not going to embarrass myself, am I?"

"Of course not," he says. "The most that would occur is that you'll get tired and pass out. But you're certainly, ahem, still in control of your faculties."

He scratches at his forehead and neck, and his face turns red. "Are you okay?" I ask.

"Yes, I'm well," he says. "It's a pleasurable sort of itchy." He scratches away.

I do feel tired, but no skin irritation. My mind remains soberly attentive, and I could continue chatting. "It's not like in the movies," I say.

"What's that?"

"I don't know."

We're kind of talking slower. My mind wanders, and now it's getting more difficult to maintain conversation.

That's when Eric starts asking me the obvious questions. "So, Amber, what brings you to Guangzhou?"

"I worked in Shenzhen before."

"You had to get away from all that business nonsense and come here where there's true culture. Am I right?"

"Actually, I like Shenzhen," I say.

"I'll never understand it," he says. "Shenzhen people hate Guangzhou. And we in Guangzhou hate Shenzhen. Why is that?"

"Well, I don't hate it here. I'm giving this city a chance."

"And how long have you been in the Middle Kingdom as a whole?" he asks.

"Forever and ever," is all that I say.

"Me as well," he says. "Are you fluent at Mandarin?"

"I'm alright."

"How about speaking Cantonese?"

"*Lei hou ma*," I say.

"*Ngo hou hou*," he replies.

"That's about it," I confess. "Maybe I should study it while I'm here. I don't know."

"I'll teach you more," he says, and continues. "*Kung hei fat choi*. That's for the Chinese New Year celebrations coming soon."

"Is that like *gong xi fa cai*?"

"Hey, the lady learns fast."

I repeat it, "*Kung hei fat choi*."

"Come with us on the New Year," Eric says, opening his arms. "We'll watch fireworks, go to the flower market and, if we're truly desperate, watch the gala on TV."

"That sounds great."

"I love the New Year holidays, with all of those black-market combustibles, the red ash on floors and the sounds of grenades and car alarms, like a war zone. Smells like a war zone too, I should guess."

I'm just giggling while he goes on talking.

"I've always thought, if there ever was going to be a war, that the Chinese New Year would be a good time for it. No one would notice. People here wouldn't even be able to blame the Japanese."

I laugh.

"Or at least it'd be a good time to steal a car."

I laugh again.

"Fireworks, literally meaning 'smoking flower'."

"I know that. Why're we talking about fireworks?"

We sit silently. All conversations in the distance have evaporated too. We need only enjoy the buzzing feelings in our bodies.

Some of our fellow partiers are nodding off on the couch. Some close their eyes and tap their fingers. Some just stare. I just stare.

I think that Eric dislikes silence, even when he's high. He needs to keep on talking. It's his way.

"Well, dear," he says. "Where were we? Tell me more about your travels."

"Um," I begin, struggling to form words. "I wanted to see more of China, and Guangzhou was so close. It only cost me five hundred to move all my shit. I've accumulated a lot of stuff, especially clothes. If I'd moved to Beijing or Shanghai, it would have been so much more trouble to do."

"As for me, I just live out of my suitcase," Eric says. "I move like the wind."

"I can understand that," I say, slurring my speech, but sensing my mind is still sharp. "A lot of us foreigner teachers do that. But I just can't. I'm too old already."

"How can you be so sure that I'm a teacher?" he asks me.

"Um, I just assumed."

"Perhaps I'm a trader or an architect." He smirks.

"Come on. You?"

Eric stands up, takes a chopstick from the table, taps it against his wineglass and makes an announcement. "Attention everyone, please raise a hand if you're an ESL teacher."

A few hands struggle to rise, but most of the crowd has descended into a living sleep.

"Well, take my word," Eric says. "It's a good guess."

I laugh, which drains a lot of energy out of me. The high is catching up to me, and I'm so tired. My body feels heavy. I want to collapse. "May I lie down on the couch?" I ask.

"Of course, you may." Eric takes my hand and walks me carefully to a couch. Right now I see three set up side by side. Two other girls, focused on their own quiet conversational mutterings, politely inch away to make room for me to rest my weary head.

Thankfully, I lie down. From my horizontal position, I watch two boys set up an Xbox next to the TV to play some shooting games or something.

I didn't tell Eric, and the subject keeps changing, so I don't think that I'm appearing overly obtuse or anything, but the main reason that I moved here was because of my ex-boyfriend. It's a story told all too often. I needed to retreat an adequate distance away from Hong Kong.

Since I'm sensing some chemistry with this Eric guy, I decide to keep a few details to myself. I mostly told the truth about how I didn't want all the trouble of moving to Beijing or Shanghai.

An air of exhaustion rushes over me, but I can't close my eyes, and I see so many lights. Despite the noise of several conversations swimming around me, everything seems quiet. Even the sound of video-game warfare makes a pleasant, distant music.

My mouth feels terribly dry, and so I look toward the water cooler back in the kitchen. I get up and take my water bottle from my purse. Then I drink the contents and go to refill it at the water cooler. Next I lie down once more. Soon I drink the whole thing again and repeat the cycle one more time. By then, I need to pee very badly.

Time has passed. It's quiet. Others are asleep. I go into the bathroom. Although there's no squatter toilet or anything; it's one of those Chinese bathrooms with no shower curtain.

I sit down, and as I pee, Eric comes in and starts to brush his teeth. He jokes that it's time for bed, acting so casually that I don't feel any embarrassment. None at all, despite my panties at my ankles. So I finish, dab myself with paper, flush and pull myself back up.

Eric smiles, looking in the mirror, and spits out toothpaste.

I ask if I can use the mouthwash. They have purple Listerine.

Eric's so nice. He gives me a blanket and pillow for the couch, and he doesn't pressure me or anything. Once the lights are out, I fall into a comfortable sleep, thinking that we'll all have sober conversations tomorrow.

It's just my second night out in Guangzhou. And I'd thought that Shenzhen was special. What have I gotten myself into?

* * *

Later I learn that Rina and Eric share this apartment as roommates. Not only that, but they've handed out flyers to everyone as invitations to another party, a show for her band.

When morning arrives, most of the previous night's party has gone. Just four of us remain, drinking coffee and rubbing at our eyes.

"Thanks for everything. You guys are so nice," I say.

I look at the flyer that Rina gave me. It shows Snoopy with a word bubble spelling out the party information. The band's called Puppy-rama. There's Chinese text for the address too. The show will be on for Saturday night at a bar that I don't know, but I'm open to exploring in this new-to-me city.

"I'll be there," I say.

"So how did you like it?" Rina asks me.

"Well, I haven't heard your music, but the graphic design on this flyer looks good, I guess."

"No, silly. How did you like *it*?"

"Oh. I've never really gotten into opiates and stuff. I mean, I've tried things, but this was the first for me in that particular category. How would I describe it? Cool. Super chill! Not as extreme as I expected. It beats weird pills and the usual getting stoned. I'd give it three-and-a-half stars."

"What I hate," the other guy says, "is that you can't get mushrooms in Asia. What the fuck?"

"The way I look at it is that it's like going to a film," Eric says. "I pay money, and then I'm entertained for several hours. Very economical."

"Hey," it occurs to me, "how much do I owe you?"

"First one's free, and then I get you hooked," Eric says in an evil voice, and we all laugh. "It's cool, baby. Don't worry about it."

"You guys are so cool."

"Just be careful," Eric says, suddenly very serious. The tone changes, and he lectures to me like he's an adult and I'm a teenager at my first party with drinking. "Don't let yourself make a habit of it. We're all responsible here. I'm sure you understand."

That's the beauty of Guangzhou, of moving every two years. I'm new here and have no good source. So I couldn't do this sort of thing every day even if I wanted, not now. I'm grateful for the experience, but I know how to keep it at arm's length and not let myself fall in too deeply.

I walk outside with Rina, Eric and the other guy, who happens to be Rina's boyfriend. He also has a hipster beard and dresses in a skater style. He's quiet, saying little. As we walk, I overhear conversational blips between bouts of chain-smoking and realize that he's in the band too.

"What's your music like?" I ask.

"We mostly do covers."

* * *

Maybe I was wrong about Guangzhou. I came here to see the mythical *real China*. Get out of the fakeness of Shenzhen's rapid development and experience the true country. Visit temples on weekends, meet the elderly relatives of my Chinese friends, live life at a slower pace and maybe learn some Cantonese.

Hell, I was totally wrong.

Really, and I thought the chemicals flowed freely in Shenzhen. I thought too many rich people flaunted there. I thought that city formed the pinnacle full of spoiled students, hung-over foreign teachers and easy money. I had no idea.

My new job is teaching at the Garfield Kindergarten, part of Garfield Estates. That's not just a usual gated apartment complex with guards and high-rises. This one has a hospital, night markets, a whole street full of restaurants, and its own school district. You could spend your whole life hiding behind the gates and never miss the outside world.

All of my workmates look like functional alcoholics. Functional may be pushing it too. They're all in their 30s. They have Master's degrees, snobby attitudes, and tendencies to sneak whisky into their desks to sip during lunch breaks.

The Garfield school system, including its kindergarten, offers an international curriculum. It's accredited in Canada. That means that my students theoretically can come from all over the world, and we do nearly everything in English. When the students grow up, they're expected to attend universities overseas.

Here, I'm an official teacher. Not just an ESL specialist, but a real fulltime teacher. My students are much younger than at my last job, but the work's more serious than what I did at Qian Shi Tou, and I'm paid twice as much.

In Guangzhou, everything's bigger, including the highs and lows. It's easier to score and easier to fail. Sex is easier too. I can shut myself up inside my gated estate or explore the biggest city where I've ever been. Either way, I'm surrounded by strangers, and the more strangers to surround you, the more you can disappear into the crowds. Let's see how well I can disappear.

2
龍

At the hair salon, I tell my stylist to cut my hair real short. I want to reinvent myself.

The gay guy working there gives me an old-fashioned sort of bob style. "A sport haircut," he calls it. But I don't like it. I don't want to be some innocent middle-school girl.

So he cuts my hair even shorter and says that I look very professional. But I don't want to be a middle-aged office lady either! I want to be punk rock.

I spin around the chair, give the haircut one more look and say, "Not short enough!"

So he cuts and cuts as I repeatedly ask him to snip it shorter. This guy complains through the whole thing, but I keep insisting. Finally, I decide that it's good, almost shaved on the sides and with cool bangs that I can style with gel. "Awesome," I say.

"You look like a boy, a crazy boy," says the stylist.

"No way." What I look like, I tell myself, is a crazy lesbian.

As it happens, I'm not a lesbian, but I think it's a cool look. Lesbians have a lot of style. If I want to reinvent myself, then this works. I've just arrived in this town and don't want anyone to recognize the shy girl I used to be back in art school.

"Where are you from?" the stylist asks me. He knows that I'm not Cantonese.

"I just got back from Beijing," I say, but don't reveal my hometown. Everyone here speaks such bad Mandarin. I'll have to get used to that.

"Beijing's so beautiful," he says. "I love the Great Wall."

"Oh? Have you ever been there?"

"No, I haven't. But I hope to go one day."

I shrug. And he calls himself Chinese. These Southerners, they've never been anywhere.

What I don't tell him is that I've dropped out of art school in Beijing, but my accommodating father has loaned me enough money to live off for six months. So I followed my old college roommate to Guangzhou, her hometown, and here I'm going to seek out my destiny.

I'm excited. I'm thinking about how well I could do here. Maybe I should do some postgraduate work. I'd just have to decide on which university. There are lots of good ones in Guangdong or even in Hong Kong. I could possibly study online. It's easy these days.

But first, I want to make plenty of cool friends. I want to attend parties, network and make *guanxi*, so that when I do find a job, I'll find the best one. I also want to get the best boyfriend and see all the interesting places in this city.

For that matter, I need to get a new camera and try my hand at photography again. And painting too! And interpretive dance! Then after school, I should become a famous art-magazine editor, and I won't have to work so hard. Everyone will like me! I can't wait!

After the haircut, I go to a beauty shop and buy a dark-red-mixed-with-auburn dye. The place happens to be near my new apartment, where I go next.

"So short!" says my roommate after a shocked glance at my head.

Her name's Siu Choi. In college, I used to call her Xiao Cai, but wanting to adapt to a Cantonese environment, I try to remember to call her Siu Choi now.

"Siu Choi, you haven't even seen what's gonna happen next," I say.

Then I lock myself inside the bathroom, open the box, and pull the plastic gloves onto my hands. I mix the ammonia and cream. The air starts to fill with a heavy stink.

"Oh, gosh, that smell's so strong," Siu Choi says from beyond the locked door.

"I know. I'm sorry. Just open a window. And wait."

Continuing, I take off my shirt and just wear my bra. It's okay. No boys are here. I place the coloring on my hair and rub it into my scalp, although the directions warn not to do that. I rub it in like shampoo.

Soon my black hair roots will grow in, but I want to postpone that as long as possible. Little beads of red drip down my ears, like blood. It's a sacrifice.

I place a bag on my head and walk back into the living room in my topless ensemble.

"Ha, ha," Siu Choi laughs. "You look so crazy."

"Shut up! You'll feel jealous soon."

I boil water for tea, and we watch TV together. For now, I still wear no shirt. The instructions say to wait twenty to thirty minutes, but I wait one hour because I really want this color to come in strong. My scalp starts to itch and then burn. I ignore it.

During every commercial break, I go into the bathroom, look in the mirror and wipe at the cream draining down my ears and along the back of my neck. Each time I sit back on the couch, I'm very careful to avoid letting my head rest on a cushion.

I've invested my whole soul into my hair. Don't disappoint me, I urge.

"Are you okay?" Siu Choi asks me.

"I'm fine."

Finally, I take a shower and shampoo my hair twice, using lots of conditioner. It feels so good. Circles of red liquid rotate into the floor drain, and I feel almost like the lead actress in a violent movie. When I dry my hair, flecks of bright red stain the towel. Oh dear, I think. It's my friend's towel. Now I'll have to steal it and buy her a new one.

Stepping again into the living room, I ask, "What do you think, girlfriend?" I say "girlfriend" in English, playing it really cool.

"Wow, you look so great!" Siu Choi's reply pleases me.

My skull's on fire, but I feel amazing.

* * *

I feel confident, cool, and ready to take on the world. Although the weather's too hot, I buy a leather jacket. Mainly I'll wear it when shooting pictures of myself. I've been exploring the city and plan to take pictures at all the famous sites.

Carrying a small tripod, I go to Canton Tower, Baiyun Mountain, Yuexiu Park, Chen Clan Academy, Tianhe Sports Stadium, and the Sun Yat-sen statue. For effect, I flick off the camera with my middle finger and show an evil grin while wearing enormous sunglasses and the jacket. My blog is called *TING TING, FUCK OFF, GUANGZHOU!*

It's been a long day, and I'm so tired from traveling everywhere. At rush hour, the metro line's crowded, but not as bad as in Beijing. At each subway stop, a recorded announcement speaks three languages: Mandarin, English and Cantonese.

Back home, I upload the pictures to my blog. Then I crave a nap, but Siu Choi arrives and bombards me with screeches of joy.

"Hey, did you get my text message? You didn't reply."

"What?" I go check and see the invitation.

"Let's get ready to go."

Before I even catch my breath, we change clothes, pick out accessories, and depart. Already I'm back on the subway. Tonight I'll get no rest. At any moment, I could pass out from exhaustion. We disembark at the central Tianhe station and take a taxi from there.

"Where are you taking me?" I ask.

"You'll see. It's cool. You'll love it, totally the Ting Ting style."

Siu Choi tells the taxi driver to go to the music conservatory. Soon the bright lights of downtown dissipate into a broken-down college-town. Suddenly, we're in almost the middle of nowhere. When my friend instructs our driver to do a U-turn and drive to the side of the highway up a hill, it doesn't look right at all. We stop behind the conservatory. This time Siu Choi pays the taxi driver, and I'll pay on the way back.

We're in some secret neighborhood, but I'm comforted to see bright graffiti. A big map on display shows design studios and art galleries. Peeking inside some of the buildings, I see elegant studios.

Light rain starts to fall. We react by running to a bar. At a big, lone house, a sign reads, GOLF BALL CLUB. Looks like the right way.

"Let's go inside."

Striding past the smokers clustered outside, we pay a couple of fifty notes to get in, and that comes with drinks. The band, with a foreign-girl singer, a Chinese guitarist, and a foreign-guy drummer, has started.

"I've heard that everyone in this band comes from a different country," Siu Choi tells me.

"Wow, so international!"

She was right. This scene perfectly suits my style. And suddenly, I feel so overwhelmed and anxious. How will I make friends with all these cool people? Looking around, I see faces from all around the world, even a few scary black guys, and I even hear the bartenders speaking good English. So many people! So many interesting faces! I want to meet everyone, but I'll never keep track and remember their names. Each and every person must be an artist, writer, or musician. I'll bet that their blogs get a lot more hits than mine does. I bet their incomes far exceed the tiny sums I used to make selling paintings on the street corner. They're so very successful, I know it. How will I catch up?

My one friend and I order drinks.

3
猴

Here at the bar, I see nobody fucking important. But there's room enough for me to take the corner sofa alone and sit comfortably, jotting scattered thoughts in my notebook. Later, I'll need to email my editor and try to convince him to pay for a review of a rundown hipster bar that's rumored to be closing down any day now.

The band does some cover songs from Pink Floyd, David Bowie, the B-52s and the Smiths. I liked the last one, although they did kind of butcher it.

As usual, just a couple of fans dance in front, Chinese men at tables play dice games, a few white guys prowl for Chinese girls, and the waitresses display that tired look. One of them bobs her head to the music. She's cute, and I consider talking to her.

"Hello," I say, waving to her.

The waitress comes over, immediately talking fast to me in a language that I can't understand.

"Bourbon?" I ask.

She shakes her head and talks more. I seek a menu nearby, find it, and point to the Chinese translation. She nods, smiles, and goes.

I should really brush up on my Mandarin.

Drinking alone, I look around, observing and thinking about how everyone here represents an archetype. There are teachers, the real ones with degrees who know what they're doing. There are ESL teachers, often dropouts who come here because they have nothing else. The obnoxious Americans and the drunk Europeans. There are international traders and their Chinese managers following suit. The business majors, the backpackers, and the housewives. This place accommodates the good crazy and the bad crazy. There are migrant workers from the North and teenage girls who just want to get married. Plus the artists with dreams, the trust-fund stoners draining away their inheritances, the lucky and the unlucky.

But I find it hard to fit into any of these roles because I'm right in the middle of two of them. I'm from both the Chinese and foreigner worlds, but I don't fully match the labels of either one.

ABC, people call it. American-born Chinese. Mom and Dad moved far away for a better life, and I went and moved right back.

By virtue of ethnicity, I'm Chinese, but I was born American. I get yelled at for not speaking the language of my facial features. When I shut my mouth, I can get lost among the crowds. Nobody stares at me. Yet when I speak up, it turns confusing.

Well, I came here to make the most of myself, and I'm glad that I did. Hell, we all have our unique experiences and complaints.

When people ask me where I'm from, I use the old cliché: I'm a citizen of the world.

One day, I'll finish writing an epic memoir of my life story. But first, I need to pay the bills.

I scribble away at my notes for the review, and I already have a pretty good draft in mind. Five hundred words about the atmosphere and the house wine. Then the music stops, and Rina sits down beside me.

"I'm so pissed off," she says.

"What's wrong now?"

"Nobody's here!"

Whether or not she's right, I encourage her to cheer up a little. "Order your free drink. You've earned it, and at least you got fucking paid."

"Trust me. The pay isn't enough to cheer up about that."

"How much?" I ask. "At least a hundred *kuai*?"

"I'm not quite that cheap of a whore," she jokes. "It's two hundred."

"Ha! Don't worry about it. I'm doing my part to get this place on the map," and I wave my notepad.

The waitress from before notices me do this, and Rina displays her handful of drink tickets.

"Want one?" she asks me.

"I thought you'd never ask."

As a chaser to my whiskey, I suck down the beautifully free beer while watching Rina's bandmates take apart the drum set, roll out amps and carefully rest guitars into their cases. Rina and I sit together discussing books. She's a reader. The last time I went to Hong Kong, she asked me to buy a few banned nonfiction tomes for her. Tonight I left those books at home, and so I promise to bring them the next time. She insists on paying me back first, but I won't accept it, not after free drinks.

"Fucking no," I say.

Rina later helps to load the musical gear into a van owned by Vinnie, the bass guitarist. He's Chinese, a Guangzhou local, and the only one in the band who can legally drive in this country.

I'm a bit tipsy and feeling very literary. Trying to act like Hunter Thompson or Christopher Hitchens or some shit, I carry my drink over to a couple of ladies. I strut like a college professor, the sort who's screwing the female student body.

"Pardon me, do you have a light?"

They giggle, talk to themselves in Mandarin or Cantonese or some shit, and then start babbling nonsensically to me.

"Please ladies," I say. "This is an expat bar. English only."

Taking out a cigarette, I perform the international gesture to request a light. They continue to giggle, but the cute one with short hair pulls out a lighter for me.

"Wowee!" she says. "Your English so good."

I get that comment all the time. One advantage I do have.

Waving goodbye, I go and talk to the band for a while. Then I return to the girls and sit down. Having seen me with the band, they ask about the musicians and I reveal that I'm a writer interviewing them for an article. That allows me to jot down the cute one's email address in order to send her some of my writings. We promise to meet again soon.

Inevitably, she asks me where I'm from.

"I'm a citizen of the world, girl."

When I finally arrive home, it's very late, and I think that maybe I've lost that email address. I'm half-asleep with heavy eyelids weighing down on me. But the first thing that I do, after hopping out of the cab and walking up to my second-floor apartment, is check my email. Then, with the computer already on, I quickly outline my article, the review about the bar, while it's still fresh in my mind.

I completed my Master's thesis in Asian-American literature for this?

Then I enter another folder. It's right there on my desktop computer, reminding me. So I open the Word file titled "*Memoirs*". Some twenty sparse words of scattered brainstorming and notes appear. I feel like I should write something now. Something witty and interesting must have happened tonight.

But it's not in me, and nothing comes. I can write countless restaurant reviews, blog comments, and shorthand of interviews with aspiring entrepreneurs. All of that I can handle with my eyes closed. I wonder why it's so hard to write about things that matter.

豬

New Town

"This district is called *Zhujiang Xin Cheng?*" I say. "Really? As in Pearl River New Town?"

"Amber, it isn't a district," Eric tells me. "We're in Tianhe, but that's simply the name of a neighborhood near the metro stop. Or wait, are we technically in Haizhu? I forget. I think this is Tianhe."

"This city has a lot of districts to remember."

Eric explains more about just how big Guangzhou really is, but I'm not listening, just looking around. We step out of a subway train, and everything's so crowded that I can hardly stand it. I'm cramped in among grandmothers, babies, and office workers. After passing through an exit, we're herded like sheep up an escalator toward fresher air. Finally, the fresh air signals that we're free as the swarms of people disperse.

"At last, I can breathe," I say.

Although full of skyscrapers and shopping malls, Guangzhou remains more spread out and airy than Shenzhen or Hong Kong's crowded markets. Apart from the congested subway system, it feels slightly more like home, and I like it.

Eric takes me for a walk in a park, and we look at the sports stadiums and opera houses. One strip has some bars and pizza restaurants. The roads here are squared off like a grid, some of the better city planning I've seen in Chinese cities.

"This is the up-and-coming place," Eric tells me, pointing at different locales faster than I can keep count. "It's very happening."

"I see."

"Excuse me for a second," he says. He goes into a public toilet, and I wait. When he comes out, he's sniffling.

"Let's sit here," I say, nodding toward an eating establishment.

"Cool."

We enter a pizza restaurant, and I'm happy to sit after so much walking. I wore the wrong kind of shoes for a date on foot. I wore the kind for being picked up and driven.

"Tell me about your new work situation, Amber."

"Oh boy," I start. "It's different from what I did last year, and I work so much harder now. I have to grade papers. They're full of easy ABCDE-kindergarten stuff, but that's still paperwork. I have my own in-class desk and office hours. The money's ridiculously good though. Overall, I can't complain."

"Amber has finally become a professional grownup," Eric says. That's funny to hear from him, because with his beard and silly cartoon character T-shirt, he looks nothing like one himself.

"It's true," I say. "I have a real job now, but maybe I could do better."

"How so?"

"I don't know. Somehow I still feel like I have a lot to figure out in life. Like, is this my career? This year I'll turn thirty."

As I speak, I regret disclosing my age, but fuck it. Eric's a lot older than me so he won't judge.

"I just wonder where I'll be ten years from now," I add. "It's not like I want to rush back to Canada."

"Yes, the usual anxiety. Hey, shall we order?"

The poor waitress has stood over us patiently, waiting during our whole chat.

We order. The food comes. We continue talking.

"Tell me about your job," I say, shifting the focus away from me.

"You want to know about just one job? I have many. There's tutoring and ESL, of course, plus sporadic bouts of acting and modeling."

"Really?"

"There's much money to be made by standing around looking like me. But as the literary type that I am, these days I primarily do proofreading. It's one of those learning periodicals that you see on newsstands.

Officially, I'm an editor, but, well, you can't really call it editing *per se*. More like, ahem, *helpful typing*."

"Wow," I say. "I feel like everyone has a cooler job than me."

"Don't be jealous. I fell into it, that's all. The publication's but a humble English 'zine, a way to market for college students learning the language. Mostly it's about lifting articles from *Reader's Digest*. I don't do any original writing or have much of any connection to the editorial staff. Basically I rewrite the headlines so that the grammatical mistakes aren't too glaring."

"Ha! You gotta love China."

"Exactly," Eric agrees. "Do you know how the copyright law and residuals work here?"

"I don't know." So I think about it. "China just doesn't have those things, right?"

"In theory, on paper, copyrights are just as valid here as anywhere else. But, of course, companies here never pay residuals to publishing houses, to Hollywood, or anything like that until *after someone overseas catches it*."

"I think I follow you."

"Basically, people here have a right to steal anything that they want and publish it. The government keeps a fund set aside to pay fees for original copyright holders abroad. But it isn't until after, say, a company like Disney, finds out that it's been bootlegged that anyone can go to the government and file for due payment. The responsibility rests with the foreign companies and intellectual-property holders, all after the fact."

"Um, fascinating," I simply say.

"At least the situation keeps me busy. The legal side isn't my expertise, but I fear that the ride won't last too much longer like this, not if Beijing wants to look good to the World Trade Organization…"

I dislike talking about economics. It's even worse than politics. But men like this, with their beards, bookshelves and blogs, always like to blab on about such topics.

"Hey," I interrupt. "Let's finish eating and go to my place."

* * *

This time we take a cab. I don't want to ride on that horrible subway again.

"Damn, you live far," Eric says.

"Yeah, I'm out in the 'burbs."

Garfield Estates, the particularly enormous gated community in a nation full of enormous gated communities. I moved there just two weeks ago and still often get lost.

Inside the estates, I explain to him, the residents have their own private security force, a rent-a-cop on every corner. We also have six supermarkets, four bars, a string of restaurants and outdoor markets, a long-distance-coach bus station, a complete K-12 school district, five-star hotels, and a hospital. Only a university and an airport are missing.

"This is where my employers set me up, where the rich go to get away from it all," I say.

"Nice," Eric says, sounding sincere. "I've heard a lot about Garfield, but never had an excuse to stop by and take a look."

"Here, we shun the city," I say.

"The city's not so bad."

"My place has distinct advantages. It's not the city, but it's not bad. It's almost like parts of Canada, except hot."

"We need to get you into a proper downtown setting, get you civilized."

"Never gonna happen," I say.

Then I talk to the cab driver, directing him through the maze of internal roadways to my neighborhood. Once I show my ID key-card, the north-gate guards let us pass. During eight more minutes of driving, the taxi racks up a massive bill as we tell the driver to turn left and then right, turning constantly until I find my block, and we pull up to the building.

Eric hands me a fifty to split the fare, but I insist. "No, no, let me get it."

"You're serious?"

"Chinese style, okay? I'll pay."

"If you truly insist, then I cannot refuse a lady."

Truthfully, I'm kind of annoyed that he didn't argue more, but I pay. Trying not to hold it against him, I take him upstairs.

"Thanks for coming,' I say. "It's time for the big tour."

"Lead the way, my dear."

Here we go. "See my empty living room. Notice the furniture and lack of bookcases. There's a high-pressure shower in the bathroom, very modern. Here's the kitchen, an empty refrigerator, and the dining-room table. The place came fully furnished, of course. It's a hundred and twenty square meters with two bedrooms, king-sized beds and way too damn big for me. And there's a walk-in closet. That's a rarity this country, right?"

I notice Eric doing the math in his head, meters to feet, as Americans always do. "You surely do live the highlife here. No roommates, all alone?"

"Just me, all set up by the Estates. I'm a valued employee."

"Lucky you indeed," he says.

"And you haven't even seen the balcony yet!"

We laugh, and I open a bottle of wine – the cheap stuff – and pour some glasses. Then we return to the bedroom part of the tour. When I sit on the bed, he practically jumps on top of me, and I shriek, warning him to be careful not to spill the wine. As a precaution, we place our glasses on the floor.

Then Eric starts to talk about biting the insides of my elbows.

"What?" I blink, surprised.

"The skin behind joints usually stays hidden from the air, and ergo, 'tis the most sensitive part of anyone's body. Behind the knees too, you see," and he touches me there.

"Back to the elbow-joint area," he says, touching the inside on one of my arms. Then he bites the same spot, and it tickles so I shriek again.

Eric backs away. Bending his neck, he points to a place under his ear. "Bite me there."

"What the hell are you talking about, Eric?"

"Just try it."

I edge close to his neck, and he looks so full of himself.

"Shut up," I say. Grabbing his head, I turn it to face me. "You don't need to go through this routine with me."

I close my eyes and kiss him. Hairs around his lips stab my tongue. I like that.

"So very forward," Eric says as we gasp for air.

Where does he get these lines? Shushing him, I stand up and turn off the lights.

We begin taking off our clothes. It's my first time in a while, my first with a white guy for absolute ages. Eric's chest and arms are so hairy, but that's okay because men are supposed to be hairy. It all goes slower than I remember. His size appears average, I guess, although I don't get a good look in the dark, but I feel with my hands, and he's definitely circumcised. The biggest difference between Eric and my ex-boyfriend turns out to be how gentle this is.

Maybe I'll regret it, but I just had my period last week, and I'm so horny. Since I've been taking birth-control pills, I had might as well put them to use.

"Is this, ahem, pleasant?" Eric asks.

"Harder," I say.

He goes faster, squeezing me tighter, but it's not enough for me. Soon he cums, but I don't.

After about twenty minutes, we're resting under the blankets, and he cuddles next to me. It's not that late, but he looks like he wants to sleep.

"What's your plan for tonight, honey?" I ask.

"Getting hungry," Eric says. "Do you have any take-out menus here?"

We order in food. He stays all night. We watch TV, play on the computer, and watch the stars. Damn, can't he take a hint at all?

* * *

The next day, Eric's still in my home. I wake up in my underwear and go to pee. Passing the kitchen, I see a shirtless man digging through my refrigerator.

"You have nothing to eat, nary at all," he says.

"*Hmph*," I mutter.

"Pardon?"

"Can you make some coffee? I have that instant crap. Just turn on the boiler."

Honestly, I'm not a morning person.

Despite my refrigerator's meager contents, Eric somehow makes a couple of egg-and-cheese sandwiches that actually taste rather good.

"So what's up for today?" I ask, hinting that he needs to go.

"No plans."

"Oh."

"That is," he continues, "I need to get some shopping done. As for the office, I'm not due there until Tuesday. Even then, I just need to pick up a hard copy of a document. Most of my work happens at home via computer. We must love this modern age, yes? As for my to-do list, let me see…"

Eric wanders into my bedroom to retrieve his smartphone. While walking back to me, he begins pressing buttons and resumes talking. "…I need to go to Tianhe and pick up some ingredients for spaghetti sauce."

"You like to cook, huh?"

"Most definitely. Got to have standards."

"Then what?"

"Late tonight I'll return to Taojin and meet someone there, anonymous-like."

"Your fuckin' drug dealer?"

"No comment."

For a while Eric sits next to me and taps at his phone.

"I need to work tomorrow," I say. "It sucks."

"I thought that you liked your job," he says, still not looking at me, peering instead at the phone.

"My job is okay."

"What's the problem?" He still taps on the phone.

"GO MAKE ME COFFEE!" I snap.

This jerks his attention back to me. "Whoa! Sorry. Yeah, I'm on it."

He gets up and soon pours hot water, mixing in the coffee powder from packets.

"I'm just not good with mornings," I say as sort of an apology.

Eric comes back and sits beside me. As I sip the coffee, he looks right at me.

"I guess that my work's okay," I say. "But look at my life. I live in this giant apartment. My job's full of money and no future. None of it seems real. Do you know what I mean?"

"You could invite people to stay with you," he says. "Why not join an online travel service that I'd recommend?"

"Is that safe?"

"Sure."

"Whatever. Not my point."

"You're lonely?"

"Maybe I am."

"You want a family?"

"Eww," I sputter, "and you called *me* forward!"

"Not at all what I meant by that," he hastily reacts.

Suddenly Eric looks visibly distraught. He gets dressed while I crouch like an old shrew and sip my coffee until feeling more awake. By the time I stumble back into my bedroom and pull on pants, he's fully dressed.

Standing together on the balcony, we look out, and I point to indicate which way he should walk to catch a cab. Below us, families walk their dogs, and couples stroll along arm-in-arm. I don't want to go down there with him.

So I say goodbye, and Eric rushes away. Maybe he'll avoid me now. Did I do something wrong? I'm so confused by this morning. Too awkward for my tastes.

I sense that this thing won't work out between us.

Then I spend a lovely day at my computer. I read all the classified ads on every local expatriate website. When emailing my resume, I present myself as an English expert, adept at writing and editing.

Sternly, I make a promise to myself. "Amber," I tell the mirror, "by this time next year, you'll be an awesome career woman. You'll have a cool job and ooze with self-respect, but no anxiety. No depending on men."

Usually, I keep promises to myself. The hunt begins.

龍

Art, Inspired

Xiao Cai, I mean Siu Choi, takes me to the Green Square Factory district. The name's a riff on Red Square, and the place is an old factory area redesigned into spaces for galleries and exhibitions with restaurants and coffee shops too.

"This place totally copies 6789," I say.

As it happens, 6789 in Beijing also is an old factory space turned over to artists. Here, it's the same thing, but on a much lower level. In Beijing, the original fills a space the size of several shopping malls and attracts just as many people. There you find energy, color, and hundreds of people on any given day. Here, everything looks half-empty and lacks the charm. I see brick roads and crumbling buildings. Everything looks like it opened too early and remains unfinished.

"In Guangzhou, we take what we can get," Siu Choi says.

As students, the two of us spent so much time at 6789, seeking inspiration among the towers, musicians and expensive paintings. In our first job together, we worked at a teahouse that doubled as a gallery. Up north, we used to hang out with artists all the time. This version just isn't as cool. The south disappoints me again.

For a while, we walk around without entering any buildings, making sure to circle the whole place. We look at some outdoor graffiti and peek into restaurants. Then we sit down to drink black tea at an outdoor shop.

"Do you know Dafen Village in Shenzhen?" Siu Choi asks me.

"No, but everyone says that Shenzhen has no culture."

"True. People call Dafen an art village, but everything there resembles a factory. A thousand students painting the likes of Van Gogh or Monet reprints. Some capitalist entrepreneurs go there to bargain, maybe buying in bulk to decorate restaurants or hotels. Really, it's wholesale business."

"That sounds terrible."

"It is. So be thankful that you ended up here and not there. Many of our Cantonese classmates moved to Shenzhen. I almost did."

"But you turned out great. You're a real artist."

"Ting Ting, I'm no artist, only a graphic designer. We make packaging for plastic toys and underwear. I play around on Photoshop. That's all."

"You're still cooler than me. I want to be an artist like you and get a real job."

"Good luck. I'll let you know if my company's hiring."

"Well, I kind of want to be another kind of artist too."

"I understand," she says compassionately. "Do you know what kind?"

Her question requires some thought. I studied painting, realism, video-editing, and a semester of dance. I like to make collages and play around with my camera. Mostly, I just want the whole world to pay attention to me.

"That's what I'm trying to figure out," I tell Siu Choi. "Come on! I want to take some pictures for my blog. Let's go and get inspired!"

While we walk around, I ask her about Hong Kong. I've never been there, but I watch a lot of movies and always wondered what it's really like.

"The art scene in Hong Kong?" she says. "I don't know. Everyone there only wants to make money."

"But Hong Kong must have lots of cool Europeans, perhaps French painters, like that."

"Maybe, but honestly, I don't know the scene. I've only been there a few times. I heard that Beijing's so much better."

I want to go to Hong Kong, but for me to get a visa means doing paperwork first back in my hometown. I don't know when I'll get the opportunity. For now, Guangzhou looks like the next best thing.

As I ponder this, we enter a gallery and view a black-and-white-photography show that focuses on impoverished children in small farming villages. Some of the pictures convey a lot of emotion. It isn't an opening party or anything, but I see from a pamphlet at the front door that the photographer comes from Germany. I wish this was the opening so he'd be here and I could meet him, but he'd never come out on a dull day like this. The artist biography shows a picture of an older white guy with a beard. He looks so smart and wise. I wish that he could be my mentor and teach me everything.

I fantasize too much.

"Ting Ting!" yells Siu Choi, breaking me out of my spell. She knows that I daydream sometimes. "I want to introduce you to someone…"

So it's time for me to practice my English. I'm introduced to Maria, a businesswoman from Russia whom Siu Choi has met before. Maria enjoys visiting the Green Square too. As a career, she trades in jewelry products.

Since Maria looks so beautiful, I feel shy. She's tall, taller than most Chinese men, almost two meters. Okay, maybe not quite that tall, but to me, she's like a statue or a billboard on the side of a building. She has long blonde hair and a high straight nose. The ridge between her big blue eyes is just perfect. She wears an expensive vest, tight jeans and laced yellow boots. When we shake hands, I feel the firmness of her palm. By comparison, I feel underdressed. Wow, I'd love to take pictures of her.

We talk about the photography show, and Maria says that it's nice, but she keeps checking messages on her phone and soon tells us she has to go.

"It was a pleasure to meet you," I say.

"Wait," says Siu Choi. "Do you have a business card?"

"Of course," says Maria. She takes one from her handbag and gives it to me.

"Thank you," I say. "I'm sorry, but I forgot to bring my cards today."

"No problem. See you around." Maria waves and turns away as I stare in awe.

Once she's gone, Siu Choi whispers to me excitedly, "Oh, my gosh! We need to get you a job interview."

"What are you talking about? You're crazy."

"No, think about it. It's perfect."

Staring at a photo on the wall in front of me, I think about it. The photo, measuring one meter by one meter, framed in glass and with simple silver borders, shows a poor child in ripped clothes looking up at the cameraman. It's wide angle, and the foreground is curved. The child looks thoroughly confused by this big ugly world, and I completely understand.

I met so many people this past week and I'm getting dizzy trying to keep track. When we get home, I upload a few pictures to my blog and reflect on the day. I should check the classified ads for design or freelance jobs. But I also want to produce art of my own, not for money, but for myself. It's so very hard to decide what to do.

I hope to return soon to the Green Square, preferably for an opening-night party, and begin to meet the owners, managers, artists and dealers, gathering the *guanxi* so that I can set up my own show.

But even if I do that, I still must produce some art worth showing!

* * *

Maria has invited us to a nightclub in Haizhu, a beautiful place alongside the Pearl River. Siu Choi says that Russian girls love to go clubbing. Well, she has more experience on that subject than I do.

The place isn't my usual style. In Beijing, we'd go to the island and visit small bars to watch friends play in rock bands or DJ to small audiences of students. In Guangzhou, people like bigger clubs full of businessmen, dancing girls, and champagne. The lights and sounds clash in my brain, creating an overwhelming experience. The good music makes me want to dance.

"This place is quite small," says Maria, screaming over the drum and bass beats.

"WHAT?"

"SHANGHAI CLUBS ARE MUCH BIGGER."

Wow, I can't imagine.

Maria later walks out with some people in her group, Russian businessmen, and they smoke near the front door. Moments later I follow, taking a break after dancing and curious about what Russian businessmen like to discuss. They offer me a cigarette.

"I think that the art here in Guangzhou is, how to say, passé," says a tall man.

"No, avant-garde," says a fatter, older guy in glasses.

"I disagree," says Maria. "Did you see the recent show at Green Square Factory?"

"The photography?" I ask. "I think it was nice, but one couldn't describe it as very avant."

"No, no, the other show, the cartoons," she says. "Did you see it?"

We all shake our heads.

"It was a kind of political cartoons, but on rice paper. Like classical Chinese art, but with modern themes. Very interesting! But, alas, I can't say the artist's name in Chinese."

How did I miss that? I make a mental note to visit the Green Square website and see what I can learn about that artist.

"But that's very rare," says one of the men. "Most Chinese art is too much the copy."

"Yes," Maria says, "copies of Japanese and Korean art."

"I don't think so," I say.

"I mean no disrespect," she answers warmly. "Is like in Europe. We all follow the French style in fashion. The whole world follows the Hollywood style in film. The Eastern style, I believe, soon will be led by Beijing. Just wait."

"On that," I say, "I can agree with you."

"I think not," says the tall man.

"Maria, you're unrealistic with your predictions," says the older, chubby man in glasses. "You always put too much of your faith in this country. I am business-investment expert. You trust me, yes? Soon all collapses."

"No, no," answers Maria. "We don't have time for one of *those* conversations right now. I merely want to express my opinion about art."

"Fair enough, and what's your opinion?"

"I think," Maria begins, "that Asians who grew up on the character writing system are better at visual design. It's different than for us who learned from alphabets. They can draw, paint and Photoshop with ease. Perhaps Russians better at poetry, theatre, and novels. I think Chinese better with the graphics."

They all nod and pause to think about it. "Makes sense," says the taller man.

"What do you think?" asks the fat man in glasses.

Me?

He gestures in my direction, waiting for me to speak. It seems that unsmiling Russians like to communicate with their hands.

Everyone looks at me, awaiting my expert opinion, so I clear my throat and say something. "I never thought of it that way. My own art teacher always told me that most people have no art in them and that you only learn it from hard work. I don't know which country has which skills because only a few people anywhere are truly skillful."

"Yes, yes," they say, nodding.

"But maybe Maria has a point," I add, "because we value good handwriting and hard work here. A lot of brilliant kids of this generation do the most amazing work, maybe more on average than in other countries. Basically, now that I think about it, yeah, I think that the Chinese are pretty great with art."

"What did you study?" I'm asked.

I narrow it down to a simple answer. "I studied classical realism." Feeling them wait for me to say more, I add, "In Beijing."

"No, no, no, little girl, that's precisely not what we're talking about," the oldest man says.

"For fine art and classical realism," I explain, "the best universities in the world are in Beijing."

"No," the same old man says. "You not know what you say, little girl."

"It's true!"

"Even if so, let me ask you this. Have you been to New York and the esteemed art galleries there?"

"No, I haven't," I meekly answer.

"Paris?"

"No."

"Then you can't possibly understand of what we mean."

This old man's arrogance is starting to annoy me. My hands make fists, and I squeeze them. Energy surges up from my belly and comes out my mouth. Not in a gross throwing-up way, but similar to the feeling when energy flows from my center into my fingers when painting. Only this time it emerges in speech.

"First of all," I begin, "you can't have a solid understanding of expressionism, or cubism, or postmodern abstract, or pop, or any of that, unless you learn realism first. Everybody knows that Picasso was a childhood prodigy in painting realistically before he joined the cubism movement and became so famous. Matisse and the Fauves are like the same thing. Pollack was thirty three years old and studied art profusely before the whole dripping technique. Andy Warhol was a professional graphic designer fully educated before the silkscreen prints and pop art. In contemporary work..."

I pause and do translations in my head. It's hard to remember the English names for Japanese characters. "...Murakami Takashi and the superflat movement came out of a historical context, like all the others. Definitely it's because of the artists taking the time to learn realism first.

"Many of the young modern and postmodern westerner artists want to be avant-garde, but they skip the middle process. They're poseurs, and their work sucks! With no foundation, they're just shallow, lazy, wannabe artists. Weird for the sake of weird isn't avant-garde. It's lazy!

"I don't know about your Russian galleries, but I do know why Paris and New York aren't growing in the art world. They reached their peaks so long ago. According to magazines and the major art critics, everything new comes out of Asia. There's a real connection there, why you can't study classical realism on a high academic level anywhere except in Beijing, and that makes it the most forward-thinking art city in the whole world."

Stopping, I catch my breath, but before knowing it, I have more to say. It spills out in brief spurts, and I continue.

"It should take decades to learn the rules before making up new rules. You can't fake it.

"That's how art really works. You can't skip the middle part.

"So don't tell me about Ai Weiwei. There's much more to it.

"In the 1920s, France had it. In the 1960s, America had it, and you'd better watch out in this new century for China."

By the end, I just mutter about how I dislike foreigners acting in condescending ways toward China and how much I love the brilliant Beijing art scene. When a sense of closure comes, I slowly lower my voice and my speech ends. I almost feel like I should wait for applause.

The Russians in my audience don't clap, but they don't talk back to me either. The men only nod, and Maria laughs. Not in a condescending way, but very approvingly. She knows that I've won, decisively, and our eyes silently exchange messages of female solidarity.

"Let's go to get drinks," Maria says. "It's time to change the subject."

We go. Maria and one man form a couple and move on ahead while the oldest man shuffles along beside me. "I'm impressed by you, little girl," he says.

"Um, thank you."

"We must do business together. Please email to me your portfolio, images and such. I know that in your generation, you always must have website. Am I right? And I shall see paintings in person one day soon, yes?"

"Okay, I guess."

"Give me your phone."

We're still walking, but, fumbling a bit, I take out my phone from my purse, and he snatches it away. Quickly he calls himself, and I hear his ring-tone. It plays classical music. He smiles, tugs his own phone from his pocket and presses buttons, saving my number and texting me his email address on WeWa.

"Soon we'll meet again, little girl," he says, handing me back my phone.

I do wish that he wouldn't call me a "little girl".

猴
Monkey

I wake up wearing just my boxers and see that it's 3 p.m. I'm home alone. Was someone here yesterday? I have no memory, but my brain feels like it has remnants of shotgun shells stuck in the gaps between wrinkles, and it smells like that too. I wouldn't trust a brain like that.

Stumbling to the toilet, I piss and don't flush. Then I just let gravity drag me back down onto the bed, and I drift back to sleep.

My home has one bedroom and no living room. Elsewhere, we'd call it an efficiency unit or a studio. So that means that the bathroom's really close to the bed, and there's little other space.

The sun glares onto my face, but I ignore it. Squinting with partly open eyes at my cell phone on the floor, I see that I have four WeWa messages. Well, I can't be bothered with them now.

When I awaken again at 5 p.m., the sun has set much lower. My stomach feels like it's been emptied out from the inside with a rusty spoon.

Opening the refrigerator, I drink straight from the water-boiler kettle. I don't like hot water (not very Chinese of me), and you can't drink what comes right out of a tap here, so I like to stash the boiler in my fridge and drink from it when I'm thirsty. That's a habit you'd form only in China.

Empty *baijiu* bottles fill my kitchen counter right to its edge. Just one of them falling would trigger a chain reaction, turning my floor into a death trap of jagged glass, like a barbed-wire rug. But all I care about is that they're empty.

After putting on a bathrobe and slippers, I take the elevator downstairs. The building's doorman just ignores me. Not quite outside, a convenience store called Fam Fam Mart connects to the lobby. It pays to live downtown.

In the store, I snatch up a cup of instant noodles and then hear the clink of bottles as I grab three tall ones of the cheapest domestic beers they got. The cashier, an old lady, starts yelling at me in some shit Chinese dialect, and I almost can't take it when setting the bottles as carefully as I can in front of her.

It's too bright in here. I should have brought sunglasses. While squinting again, I also cover my ears.

The cashier scans the items. I pay.

"Yeah, yeah, yeah," I say.

At home again, I resume drinking. Removing the water-boiler from the fridge, I turn it on, impatient for it to heat up. While I'm waiting for water, I usually kill time on my laptop. For a moment, I nearly panic when I don't see it on my desk, but then I find it on the floor half unfolded under a blanket and several layers of dirty pants.

I take it out of the mini-fridge and plug everything in, but still must wait for the damn thing to turn on.

Checking on the water-boiler, it seems hot enough. I pour water into the cup of noodles, cover it with a dirty plate and wait.

The computer powers up and goes online. I click on my web-browser, of which the home page stays set to my email, logged on as always. Just then, I remember my phone and find it buried beneath several undershirts and powerful-smelling socks. The screen informs me that the number of unopened messages has graduated to ten.

At almost the very same instant, I look at who sent the texts and my twelve unread emails. I couldn't even tell you which list that I read first. Most of the messages, except for spam, came from my editor. Fuck! Apparently I'm several hours late for an important deadline.

"Fuckin' damn it!"

Quickly I type with my left hand and text with my right. "*Didn't you get my email?*" The texting works fast, and I hit Send on that. Tossing aside the phone, I start to type at a record 200 WPM. "*Sorry for the technical difficulties. Electrical emergency here. I have the final draft and thought I sent it. I don't know what happened. Must be that annoying Great Firewall."*

Opening Word, I frantically write some partly plagiarized drivel about the serene atmosphere at a new Turkish restaurant, about the sights and scents that please the eyes and nose as you enter the establishment. Mind you, I've never set foot in the place.

I find the restaurant's website, and it displays a menu so I randomly choose two dishes: mixed kebab and something called *Kuzu Pirzola*, which I assume has a succulent taste.

One more problem troubles me. I don't know how to end this review. It needs to be 800 words long, and that's so much harder than 500 words. That's not just due to the 300-word difference, but it's the whole tone and organization. Having already done a decent intro, how do I handle the outro? I think of another sentence. The onscreen arrow hovers over Word Count to inform me: presently tallies at 672. I think of two more sentences, and now it's 719.

Urgently I need some witty and cultural Turkish-related phrase to end on a high note, but I know next to nothing about the region. Suddenly my vast knowledge of culture saves me, and I write a sappy regurgitation of the lyrics to an old swing song, "Istanbul (Not Constantinople)". Humming the tune, I hit *Send*.

That's 804 words.

I hope that the editor, his colleagues and their readers will all appreciate the good review.

Well, that covers rent.

* * *

With the crisis now resolved, I need to relax. I jerk off and finish quickly. Out of breath, I collapse onto the bed again where I look at my semen-stained boxers and don't even do anything about them. I close my eyes, refusing to think. My preference is to wait it out and wake up with dry shorts. Maybe I could find this place cleaned up too. I want to awaken from this bad dream, open my eyes, and enter the life that I was supposed to live.

The lamp shines right into my face, but I'm too overwhelmed to turn it off. Squinting yet again, I look at the haphazard bookcase in front of me, full of paperback novels and nonfiction about East Asian economics. My books are stacked precariously, almost ready to tumble. I read some of the authors' names. Chandler, Shelby, Welsh, Bukowski, Thompson, Cheever, Ellis, Hemingway, and Stephen bloody King. Obviously, I'm a pale empty shadow, undeserving of the literary satire that's my life.

"My God," I mutter. "I'm such a fucking cliché."

*   *   *

The great thing about having friends who are DJs is that you always know where the next party is at.

I've attended parties like this one tonight for years, and the faces change, but it's always the same thing, especially the rehearsed lines. Whether at an Irish pub, Taiwanese nightclub or elsewhere, it's all the same.

I wonder if I should settle down, forget all this and write the Great Chinese-American Novel. I could get married and spit out a few kids. Would a family help or hinder my writing goals? Any and all experiences theoretically should help with whatever kind of memoir, if only I had it in me to write one.

At tonight's venue, I wave, order a Scotch, listen to the music, and nod to various acquaintances. I want to meet a girl. I always think that way, instantly falling in love with every other girl I see. Yet when did I last have a serious girlfriend? I barely even remember.

Even if I were in a player mood, I can't take anyone back to my place, considering the dirt and disarray of that hole. Won't stop me from trying to score, but generally having an apartment that smells like fermented socks isn't a good strategy.

Why don't I just hire a maid already?

Or at least buy some air-freshener.

"Hey, Monkey, what up, you common bastard?" someone yells from across the room.

"What up, bitch?" I retort. That guy, Eric, has all the good bud, and I'm trying to get in on his group.

Yes, my nickname's Monkey, but that's not as racist as it sounds. It sounds pretty funny in English, but in Chinese it sounds even better. At least, so I'm told. *Hou-hou.*

On my way toward Eric's scene, I'm snatched and pulled to a table occupied by my editor Jonas and his trader friends. They all wear jet-black suits and smell of cologne.

"Aren't you going to buy me a drink first?" I half-joke to Jonas.

On cue, he motions to a waitress, and I expect a free drink to arrive.

Jonas supplies my main source of revenue and seldom calls me Monkey. He's the editor-in-chief at *Pearl Delta Expat*, the leading province-wide, English-language magazine that's free to pick up at coffee shops. I've eaten literarily dozens of free meals for the sake of its restaurant reviews. Occasionally he even subsidizes my travel expenses for longer pieces.

Jonas is middle-aged, balding, and, I suspect, Jewish, but I've never asked. He likes me, and apparently my alma mater happens to be the same university where his son from New Jersey now studies. Blessed with an amazing ability to blend in with the suits crowd, Jonas probably could earn much more money if he really tried. But he works in publishing for the long haul, no matter how much money he gains or loses. His heart, like mine, remains in literature.

Usually, Jonas and I like to drink beers and talk about James Joyce or Lu Xun, sprinkled with discussions about articles for submission and baseball statistics. Every once in a while, he invites me in on a new investment opportunity.

"Check this out," he says now, as everyone at his table huddles over the latest shiny smartphone.

"What am I looking at?" I ask, like a true investigative reporter.

"Wait for it."

"You grabbed me for this? I could be fuckin' picking up girls."

"Like you're going to get laid in that shirt," he scoffs.

"What's wrong with my fuckin' shirt?"

"I'm trying to make you money here," he says. "Boy, take heed."

My free drink comes, and it's a Long Island Iced.

Soon Jonas punches in his new app for some kind of tour-guide system. "A company out of Shanghai does work like this," he says. "Take a look. This is about Xi'an."

I see pictures of the famous terracotta warriors, and with each touch-screen movement, historical trivia pops up like a cartoon word balloon. It's impressive and looks nice, user-friendly and informative. "I want to market this in Guangzhou," Jonas says.

"Here?"

"Think about it. We're just beyond Hong Kong in by far the most major and historical city of Guangdong Province. Tourism profits should soar with all the general development. The company already has apps like this in Chinese, Japanese, Korean, and French."

"French?"

"Believe it."

As it turns out, the suits at the table are investors, and I'm designated as the project's head-writer. All that I need to do is to conduct research about Guangzhou's scenic sites and format the information into pithy prose to fit comfortably onto two-by-four-inch screens. They want a young tech-savvy journalist who fits undetected into the crowds. Somehow they think that I'm their man.

"What's the pay?" I ask.

Jonas types a number on the screen.

"You flatter me, Jonas. How about an advance? What percentage up front?"

He types another number.

"Alright, I'm in!"

That covers rent for an entire year.

* * *

With camera on hand, I get off at the Peasant Movement Institute metro station and look around. There's a big library, a park, and a shopping mall under construction. I walk to the library, go upstairs, and ask a lady at the desk where to find the English section. She shows me, and I browse through some graying, dusty books, but soon get bored and leave.

Nearby at the Peasant Movement Training Institute, I wait in line amid some tourists. With the usual mix of Chinese-student girls and European backpackers, it could be a party in Taojin. I see the original classroom where the revered revolutionaries once studied. It's a hot day, and so I wonder how people could have studied in this place ninety years ago, long before air conditioners. Maybe back then people were used to the searing weather. Even now, fans are blowing here, but I'd prefer AC.

I shoot some pictures of the front gate, chairs, desks, dormitory bunk beds, blackboards, old wooden tables and peeling red-paint walls. My camera, a Canon EOS Rebel T3i, cost me a sweet penny, and no one will reimburse me, but with it I feel somewhat more like a legitimate journalist. Unfortunately, I'm not really here as a photographer. The investors most likely already have a stock library of professional photos. No, this is for fucking *inspiration*.

As for my value as a professional travel writer, I'm confident about that. I'm good at headlines, pithy summaries, and taglines under blurry photos too, but I prefer having something to work with, something to summarize. A menu or an interview to paraphrase always helps me, something more than just my own experiences walking around and absorbing the atmosphere.

On a wall, I see an English section beneath old black-and-white film photos of Mao Tse-tung and Sun Yat-sen (none of this digital-photography shit back then). My camera fits nicely onto the strap tied around my neck so I let it dangle, take out my notepad from a back pocket, and scribble some notes.

It's too damn hot, I'm tired, and, after about twenty minutes of this, I abandon my mission. I take a taxi home, asking for a receipt because maybe they'll pay me back.

Once at home, I dig out my copy of the travel book, *Lonely Planet China*, and toss it onto my bed. But if I'm honest with myself, I probably won't even open the book.

Instead I open my computer, Google the place, and start writing.

The Institute was founded on July 3, 1924, not by the Communist Party, but by the Kuomintang (KMT) back when it was led by Sun Yat-sen. At that time in history, the KMT had an alliance with the Communist Party. I hope that part won't be censored.

Chairman Mao, the Institute's sixth director, had its largest class or something. Maybe that's just propaganda, you never know.

From studying literature and writing, I've learned two things. For starters, you never really know anything. Historian-scholars refer to this as revisionism. In literature, you'd call it the unreliable narrator. The second thing, which I've learned from journalism specifically, is that almost nobody ever checks up on these things.

So I write in short hundred-word bursts, like sprint running, inserting a quip about Mao's success here and an observation about the architecture there. It amounts to just taglines, like on the backs of cereal boxes.

Maybe Jonas has me pegged. This all comes kind of naturally to me. It's easy too. After an hour's work, I have twelve word-balloon-sized factoids, each of which would read nicely on a handheld screen.

Going to the fridge, I reward myself with a cold one.

Next I log on to Wikipedia and learn what I can about the Canton Tower, Baiyun Mountain, Chen Clan Academy, Yuexiu Park, Martyr's Park, Ching Long Amusement Park, and that big Catholic church cathedral building thing in Haizhu. I bookmark each page and prepare myself a schedule on Excel to keep my writing at a good pace for the next three weeks.

When the chance arises, I'll visit all these places, I tell myself. I'll absorb the air, get a feel for them, and then really write. For now, I read what others have written and merely summarize. That's what I'm good at.

* * *

All week I've looked forward to this.

"Baby doll," I softly say into the phone. "Go to sleep early tonight. I'll meet you at the metro station tomorrow morning."

Gigi is a local girl with whom I've had an on-again-off relationship for the past year. I met her, guess how, through the fuckin' WeWa app.

"Goodnight, Monkey," she coos.

We met online, and although it wasn't serious, she proved rather good in bed. When it did start getting serious, I up and went to Washington for the summer. After I returned to Guangzhou, I heard rumors that she had forged another relationship, and so I didn't pursue her. Occasionally I'd call her for help with translations, like for my bills and when I need to communicate with my landlord. She's nice about that sort of thing, and anyway, she likes an excuse to hang out with me and practice her English.

For the last few months, she occasionally contacts me for late-night booty calls. Three times so far. When we do this, I tend to stay at her place, which is much nicer than mine.

Sometimes I feel rather lonely, and we went out together two weekends in a row. Almost like real dates with dinner and everything.

When I got the travel-writing job, I stuck to myself at first. Then, as the job continued, I figured out that I could better utilize the free, reimbursed cab rides. I even studied the fine print and realized that for ticketed-fee locations, I could claim reimbursement not just for one ticket, but for two, on any assignment.

So, with savings at hand, I figured that I should make a date out of my day at the Ching Long Amusement Park.

"Bye-bye," I say, disconnecting. Tomorrow will be a long day, and I need to wake up early. This time I mean it.

I figure that a glass of white wine can't hurt to help me nod off. While I'm at it, I can go online and check my email to pass the time while drinking. That's a bad habit, I know. Many-a-night this sort of logic leads to hours of drunken masturbation and sleep deprivation.

When I open my laptop like a flower's petals blooming, it fails to turn on automatically like it usually does.

"Huh?"

I check the battery. It's plugged in so I unplug it and plug it in again, but still nothing.

"Oh, what the sweet fuck is this?"

I bought this Toshiba model about a year ago. It should be good quality. It's definitely no knockoff. Sure, my Windows Seven is most certainly a bootleg, but luckily the hardware has given me no problems. I've downloaded, uploaded, typed, printed, shifted, and deleted with nary a worry.

After spending some time with a machine, you develop a certain emotional attachment, and it hurts your feelings by abruptly refusing to respond to you. It's like a lover suddenly angry at you and she won't say why. If not similar to the feelings of a broken heart in all the subtle ways, at least it's just as fucking frustrating.

When thinking these poetic thoughts with no format to record them, I smell something burning. Just a little, like the moment before ramen noodles burn and the smoke alarm goes off.

A tiny puff of smoke rises from the keyboard's left side. I levitate my nose just above that location, and no question, detect the smell of melting microchips.

"FUCK!"

I raise the laptop toward my nose and sense something worryingly familiar. Sticky, wet, and I'd taste its sweetness on my tongue if I was a centimeter closer. White wine seeps into each and every crack between the keyboard's letters.

"FUCK, FUCK, TRIPLE FUCK!"

Rushing to the wardrobe, I dig underneath my winter blankets for a small luggage case in which I keep a plastic bag filled with receipts. For the next twenty minutes, I rummage through the receipts, examining each and every one. Not only are they all written in a complex, character-based language that I can't understand, but they're crinkled and faded too.

Finally I find it, my warranty for the computer. It's good for one year. I remember that much, but can't recall on what date I bought it. There! I see the date in tiny print.

The Chinese receipts use numbers instead of names for the months. So I can make out the date: *5-4*.

Distrusting my judgment, I need to look up today's date. I want to see it in front of me. Unable to use the computer, I go to my pants on the floor and dig out my cell phone from a pocket. What's today's date?

May 8.

"FUCK, FUCK, FUCK, FUCK AND MORE FUCK!"

I pace around the room and then try to sleep, but too much roils my mind. Realizing that it's after 2 a.m., I can't call Gigi now, not yet, and tell her that tomorrow's plans have changed. So I make a new plan, set my alarm for 9 a.m. and try again to sleep.

* * *

This is epically unjust. I feel like shit, and I'm not even hung-over.

I dreamed of roses and missed deadlines. Once awake, I send a text to Gigi saying that my plans have changed. Then I pass the fuck out and wake up again at noon. I stumble to the water-boiler, fill it and wait so that I can make instant coffee.

When I check my messages, not even bothering to read the nine unopened ones (this can turn into a habit), I call her.

"I'm so very, very sorry. There's an emergency. I promise, promise, and promise to make it up to you. Let me buy you flowers."

She's a sucker for that romantic stuff. Yet this truly is a sincere apology.

Spitting forth my smoothest game, I beg and plead for forgiveness. I tug at her heartstrings and play them like that traditional musical instrument that you see blind people playing on the sidewalks as you toss coins to them.

I almost have her won over when I add, "One more thing. Baby, will you be a dear and meet me at Gangding? I have to fix my computer and kind of, uh, need a translator."

Gangding is the kind of place that gives nightmares to copyright lawyers. It's the electronics district in the third-biggest city of the world's first-biggest copyright-infringing nation. A hundred-building theme park of unhinged electronics and bootlegged software, a shanty town straight out of cyberpunk literature, and it's not even remotely where a girl wants to go on a date.

We meet at the metro station. More precisely, we meet in the station's attached underground shopping malls that sell video games and novelty mouse pads. I lug my dead laptop inside a bag and can't wait to make this 6,000-*kuai* paperweight useful again.

"Hey, girl," I say, waving.

Gigi, of course, is delighted.

"Hello," she says in monotone.

Yeah, delighted, is that the word?

She does look cute. Gigi is short. I'm one head taller. When frowning, she looks irresistibly lovely. With her arms crossed over her big round breasts right now, she looks like she may want to hit me.

"Where you want to go?" she asks with little-girl venom.

"First," I say, "I need to visit an Internet café."

My phone won't work without Wi-Fi, and I'm desperate to check my email, not having done so for over twelve hours. We find a nearby *wang ba* within seconds. This is grand central for such things.

Chinese Internet cafés are like the bars were in mid-America until New York took over the world. That is, a haze of tobacco smoke hangs over everyone's heads. You hear occasional coughs, but mostly notice the teenagers playing online games and yelling to each other.

Gigi goes to the front desk, hands over her ID card, and explains that I'm a foreigner. It costs only four *kuai* to use a computer for an hour. Fucking glorious, indeed!

Luckily, nobody has emailed me about any lapsed deadlines that I'd forgotten. Then I surf some news sites, listen to music, read reviews and soon it's time to go. Meanwhile, Gigi sits beside me on QQ.

I'm enough of a gentleman that I generously pay for the hour for both of us.

"Thanks so much," I tell Gigi. "I couldn't do this without you."

"Okay, okay," she says. Maybe she doubts my sincerity.

I put an arm around her shoulders. She backs away.

"Next week I'll take you to Ching Long," I say. "I promise. We'll have a great time. Go on roller coasters and shit. Do they have a teapot ride? It'll all be paid for. But for work, you know, I need to do this now."

We just walk, and I follow behind Gigi, my head lowered in shame. Several blocks later, she leads me into a small repair shop behind the fourth shopping mall. She talks to a guy there, and I twiddle my thumbs. He looks at my computer, takes it to the back of his shop, and I wait and wait. Gigi and I don't talk. The guy comes back and quotes a price.

"He says it cost five hundred, fix the power."

"Can we bargain it down?"

"No," she simply answers. Perhaps I haven't given her much incentive to fight for me.

"That's fine then," I say, desperately appreciative of her translator acumen.

Accepting a receipt, I'm instructed to return here tomorrow after 2 p.m., but before 6 p.m. I take a name-card with the shop address, and I'm pretty sure that I can find this place again.

"Let's go," says Gigi.

So I treat her to dinner. We go to a kind of modern Chinese restaurant with little phone-like devices so you can punch in your food-and-drinks orders electronically. The waitresses look like they're texting on cell phones, and I can't help feeling offended. I'd prefer the old-fashioned way, a server with a notepad.

"Isn't that funny," I say. "It's like the waitress receives and sends text messages. I'm like, no tip for you."

"It's very good technology," Gigi says. "The cook in the back can see too and make the food very fast."

"I know. Just joking. No tip, ha, ha!" I say unenthusiastically.

"No tip in China? I don't understand."

Chalk it up to cultural differences. We eat in silence. I don't try any more jokes or attempt to lighten the mood.

Being hopeful, I'd brought a condom in my wallet. I wasn't sure where I'd end up tonight, at my place or hers. Now I'm not even going to try. I fucked up this date well and proper. My literary idols would be proud.

"Goodnight, Monkey," Gigi says, since the sky has darkened when we return to the metro station. I'm going west, and she's going east (so symbolic).

"Please don't call me that," I say. "Call me by my name. Call me Terry."

"Bye-bye," she says, turning and walking away.

It's an anticlimactic story. I wonder why I even tell it. It's self-destructive, solipsistic, and beneath my education and ambition. Maybe I'm doing alright, but I should do better, right?

Well, I haven't quite hit rock-bottom yet. I think I'll keep going.

豬
Adventures in Estates

"Guangzhou's like Los Angeles and New York put together," Eric says. "But maybe more like L.A."

"I wouldn't know," I say. "I haven't been to either one."

"It's like this," he explains. "Guangzhou simply isn't an easy city to figure out."

"I agree."

"Indeed. Amber, you'll never get used to it. I've been here for years, and I'm still constantly lost."

"I see. But how is that like New York or L.A.?"

"For one thing, it's big. It has big culture and tall buildings."

"Doesn't seem that tall," I say.

"Canton Tower is the tallest building in China."

"Really, is it?"

"Certainly, and recently it was the tallest in Asia. That's saying something."

Eric gets up, goes to the sink and rinses a cup. He pours himself a drink from the water cooler and sips slowly, as if trying to impress me with his worldly knowledge. My anticipation builds. I've got to admit that he's good at this.

Crawling back into bed with me, he continues. "If you ever do have a chance to go one day, you must. New York is stupendous. You walk around Manhattan and Brooklyn. You bar-hop, and people just give you flyers. Immediately you find the cool scene.

"You know," he continues, "Guangzhou is China's third or fourth-biggest city, depending on how we measure these things, and yet it's far larger than America's biggest city. Population-wise, it's more than comparable."

"I wouldn't know," I say. "We don't have such big cities in Canada."

"Another thing about New York is that it's not, in fact, *that* big. In a geographical sense, I mean. You can walk across the island in an hour. Of course, there are the other boroughs too, but you get my point."

"I guess so."

"Let me continue. On the other hand, Los Angeles is smaller in population, but there you need a car."

"That sounds more like Canada."

"And likened to most of Middle America too," Eric says. "When you live in a city where one needs a car, everything tends to be spread out, far away. Guangzhou's massively spread out. It's a fucking *sprawl* in the sprawliest sense of the word, in-fucking-deed."

"Yeah."

"This is what I mean by L.A. and New York put together. Guangzhou's like downtown Manhattan's Times Square spread out in every direction from Pasadena to Orange County."

"Okay, I guess."

"We're in a place far bigger than the biggest city in the world's richest nation, yet only third-biggest in this country. I mean it when I say that Guangzhou is geographically a combination of New York and Los Angeles, but even bigger by all measurements. My intention is to impart upon you the *massiveness* of it."

"I get what you mean, Eric."

"I'm just fascinated by cities."

"You're fascinated by a lot of things."

"Yeah, baby. That's why I'm such a good teacher."

We're naked. He spent the night here again. So I guess we're fuck-buddies. It's better this way. Nowadays my track record on relationships looks pretty bad.

Next we discuss how it's hard to maneuver in Guangzhou, but what I really want to say is that it's hard to find a job here.

I'm hesitant to ask for Eric's help. After all, it's not like he's my boyfriend. He comes over every few weeks and avoids me in the intermittent times. I get confused, but when he's here, he acts like it's no big deal, like everything's normal. Perhaps I just get caught up in his attitude. Guys can have that effect on me. I just give in to them, and I hate that!

Really, I wish that I was more independent, but since moving into this apartment, I've hardly left Garfield Estates. For a while, I felt so excited to meet people and planned to find a new job. Then what happened? I fell into a deep rut.

Since I rarely go out exploring in Guangzhou, I don't even know where to start. I thought that I'd make more friends in this city, especially after the crazy first few weeks, but it turns out to have been easier to make friends in Shenzhen. For some reason, in the two months that I've lived here, I've only gone out with Eric's group a few times, just at the Chinese New Year and for several shows and after-parties. I've met very few other people. I did go to a work party once and to the Canadian consulate in downtown Tianhe for passport services one afternoon. That's about it.

I'm never in the heart of the city because I'm stuck in the Estates Bubble. That's what my co-workers call it. My whole world exists within the gated community's walls. I go shopping, to the gym, and to work inside the zone. I even hear that the Estates will build a movie theater this year.

Well, girl, I think. Do you want to depend on guys like Eric to bring you news of the outside world? No way! Stand up for yourself.

After a few more hours, Eric leaves. He knows his way from the shuttle bus to the subway and back to his place downtown. In fact, he knows how to get around from here better than I do, and I live here.

Don't get me wrong. I have plenty of energy. I'm not in one of those depressed funks. My complaint is that I'm stuck in a pattern of staying within my little neighborhood. Other than that, I'm working hard and enjoying life.

The main problem is that something always interrupts my time on the computer, time best spent job-hunting online.

Getting out of bed, I notice that now I'm wearing Eric's T-shirt. It's not from last night, but from another night three weeks ago. I slip off the shirt, throw it on the floor and catch myself in the bathroom mirror. I'm wearing pink cotton panties, and my tits are out. They could be bigger, but that's alright.

I put on my slippers, cute bunny ones left over from away back in the Chinese Year of the Rabbit. Reaching my wardrobe, I put on my sports bra too. Before stepping into my shorts, I run back to the mirror and gawk at myself again. My nose looks too big and my hair too curly, but below the neck, I see improvement. For confirmation, I suck in my stomach a bit and push my girls together.

"Yeah, you look hot!"

Smirking to myself, I finish getting dressed, adding shorts and socks with Adidas logos. I find the cute purple headband in my socks drawer and push my hair back.

Next I unroll my yoga mat and play music from my computer, some old poppy punk from the '90s, what used to inspire me as a kid. I stretch my arms and thighs, do a splits position and hold it for 30 seconds. I used to be much more flexible back when I did gymnastics in high school. Hopping up, I perform jumping jacks for a full minute.

I groan, moan, and work up a short sweat before I feel limber enough to put on shoes and go out into the world. Glancing toward my computer, I tell it, "I'll be back for *you*."

Grabbing my keys, I depart. As for the lights, music, and air conditioner, I'm pretty sure they're all turned off. After trotting down three flights, I turn left and two blocks later arrive at the gym.

The Garfield Estates Clubhouse, a big structure in the middle of the garden, has a five-star restaurant where I've never gone. There's an Olympic-sized swimming pool, a beauty salon and endless amenities for ping pong, tennis, pool or snooker, and sometimes I notice little girls in ballet classes. See what I mean about how a person can get stuck with an active life and never leave the gated world?

I flash my card up front and enter the special room. The gym isn't that nice compared to what I'm used to back in Canada, but it's suitable. To come here, I didn't need to sign any insurance paperwork. No problem as long as I'm never horribly injured.

In fact, the gym's just a big room upstairs that could have been an emptied-out apartment. The carpeting looks out of place. It has four treadmills, wall mirrors, a bench press, a cluster of Nautilus machines in the middle, and some free weights on a rack to the side.

Nobody's here. That's perfect. I want no shirtless meatheads distracting me. This works the best when done alone.

I turn on the ceiling-hanging television to MTV and do some stretches again, just for a minute to get my laterals and thighs in order.

MTV China's so weird, actually having music, I notice, and chuckle to no one in particular. Too bad that no one's ever around to hear my best jokes.

Snatching up a plastic jump rope from a corner, I adjust its length to my height. I'm taller than most women in China and about the same height as the average man. So how much adjusting that I need on the rope depends on who used it last. I do 200 rotations to work up my heartbeat. Out of breath, but feeling good, I follow with 30 sit-ups. After resting on a leg-pulling machine for a few minutes, I feel ready to get onto a treadmill.

First, I take the TV remote and elevate the volume to its highest. Then I go to the water cooler and drink, emptying a plastic cup three times.

"Let's do this, bitchez!"

So I set one of the treadmills to six kilometers per hour and a level-two incline. After one minute, I raise it by half-a-kilometer. Each minute thereafter, I do the same thing, reaching 7, 7.5, 8, 8.5 and 9. That's my routine.

Seven minutes and one kilometer after starting, I'm really sweating. I look at my reflection in a mirror to my left. For 30 seconds, I hold onto the side handlebars, lean on them, and rest.

Then I raise the incline by one level and go to 10 kilometers per hour. A minute later I lower the incline two levels and raise my speed another kilometer. Then another kilometer, and soon I'm sprinting at 12 kilometers per hour.

I can last only one more minute like that, after which I lower the speed back to 10 and hold the sides, trying to catch my breath. My heart beats fast. Sweat soaks into my headband, but I still need to wipe at my eyes.

A peek at the display screen tells me that I've run two kilometers. I ease the pace by half-a-kilometer every minute. At nine kilometers per hour, I take my legs to the side and rest for 30 seconds.

Finally I put the incline back to level two and run for 90 seconds before gradually reducing the difficulty for six more minutes until I'm trotting again at just six kilometers per hour. Then I look at the timer, speedometer, and distance spent. Not bad: three kilometers in 21 minutes.

I know that's a lot of details, but when jogging, I constantly think about these numbers. It calms me, helps to pass the time. When I'm lost in this world of math, breathing hard and furiously pumping blood, nothing bothers me. Nothing out there, no stress, no love, no darkness, can penetrate my heart. For about 22 minutes, I'm all alone. Sometimes that's just what I need.

Now with the run finished, at least I don't need to think about numbers. I lean on a wall and breathe deeply, quickly. At the water cooler, I gulp down four more cups worth of liquid. A glance at the TV shows pop singers, but I hardly even hear them.

"That's cardio," I say, marking the box on an invisible checklist in my head.

Sitting on a bench, I rest to regain my strength. Then I decide to do some weight training. That's not my main thing, and I'm always a little scared to look all buffed out. I don't focus on my biceps very much, but do many repetitions using small two-kilo dumbbells for triceps. Next I do some squats while holding the dumbbells to my shoulders, although my thighs and calves still twitch from the jogging.

I believe that my whole body has toned well. I touch my chest. "That's my heart," I say.

Then I touch the sides of my thighs. "Those are my legs."

And I put my hands to my belly. "That's the abs."

Only one thing's missing, my ass, and I'll check that when I get home.

Stumbling outside, I travel home at a very slow trot. I'm drenched in sweat and wearing a murky odor. Fortunately, I live alone.

Once back inside my apartment, each item of cloth peels off me as sticky as if I was dipped in lukewarm ketchup and not smelling nearly as nice. I throw the clothing into a corner.

Naked, I return to the mirror, look at my backside and shake it a little bit. "That's my ass."

I flex my arms, but can't really flex my ass the same way. It doesn't look as nice. Putting on a towel, I take my clothes to the washing machine.

My place has the washing machine outside on the balcony. So I can't just wash my clothes when naked. But I always wear a towel and enjoy the summer breeze on my bare shoulders.

I pour detergent and press the Chinese-labeled buttons. Although I can't read them, they always do the trick. *Beep.* I hear water flow and know the machine's working.

If anyone's watching me, I hope that I give a nice show.

Going inside, I drop the towel and take a shower. Full of energy, I sing to myself and soak my hair, lather, rinse, and repeat.

"UNDERNEATH MY UMBRELLA, BRELLA, BRELLA!"

I dry my hair. Tangles collect in the drain. Picking up a blob of bleached brunette, I throw it into the toilet. "Yuck!"

Planning just to relax at home, *alone*, I change into clean pajamas. I feel so fresh. With my teeth brushed and my skin moist, I'm finally ready to get on the computer.

Fully pumped, I vow to land a new job, maybe even tonight. All the necessary sites are bookmarked. I'm revving my engines like a race may start. Let's see. There's acting, trading, modeling, proofreading, voice-recording, editing, and international restaurant management, the possibilities beckoning like every white girl's dream for an anything-but-teaching job in China. This shapes up as a night of hunting like never before. The entire country should take notice and read my freshly polished resume.

"Watch out, everyone. Amber's coming to get you."

But first I'll check my email.

Oh, what's that? It's from my little brother. I haven't heard from him lately.

Hey, he's coming to visit me next week, flying into Hong Kong on Tuesday. That's sudden.

Maybe I'll need to change my plans somewhat.

* * *

My brother's journey may be an exhausting one. First, there's a four-hour drive across small-town Manitoba to reach Winnipeg. Of course, travelers must get to the airport two hours early and wait around. Then he flies five hours to Vancouver for a transfer and more waiting. Next it's the full 13-hour flight above the Pacific Ocean and crossing many time zones before landing in Hong Kong.

Even after that, he still needs to reach Guangzhou.

I think about these numbers, instead of my usual ones, while on the treadmill. They help me forget the sensation of my heart and lungs ready to explode out of my sweaty chest. But pondering the numbers doesn't work right because I'm still stressed out about everything.

Damn! Before I know it, I've covered three kilometers in an even 20 minutes. That's a new personal record.

Tip-toeing away from the treadmill, I go to drink water and then sit for a rest. Although barely able to breathe, I can think clearly, remembering my first journey to China all those years ago.

Right now, my little brother and his fellow passengers glide through the sky. He's watching bad movies or trying to sleep under one of those thin airline blankets. He must be wondering what he'll find in this strange country, but he holds two advantages that I never had: me to take care of him and a return ticket.

Tomorrow I'll skip work and take an express shuttle bus all the way to the Hong Kong International Airport. My ride will cost a couple of hundred and will take several hours, passing through the Shenzhen Special Economic Zone and entering the Hong Kong Special Administrative

Region. I'm going to meet Michael, my brother, whom I haven't seen for two years. The last time I saw him, not including Skype, he was only *17 years old*.

Chinese people often ask me if I miss my family. Sometimes I do, but I also like being far away. I feel more independent and free. The filial Chinese always want to know how often I visit my hometown, and I just say it's so far away and expensive to get there that I go only every two or three years. I tell them that I can't make it for every Christmas (or Spring Festival), and they say that's so sad. They really don't get it.

Now two years have passed since my last trip home. Instead a member of my family, my 19-year-old little brother, my only sibling, comes here. We haven't been that close, and I must dig deep into my memories, back to before my parents divorced, before I went to college, to recall much. He attended middle school and really enjoyed action figures and video games. I think he's still into video games.

Mom wants me to take care of him for a week. He hasn't even gone to university yet. I don't know what his life is like now. He works at a restaurant and probably hangs out with his friends. I suppose that Mom thinks I can inspire him to see the world and make something of his life. Maybe I can, but I'm not sure.

After all, I can't even inspire myself properly. No one back home knows how I'm stuck in a rut. They think that I'm living the highlife backpacking through Asia, that I have some classy job, and that I'm going back to nature in the Tibetan mountains or some such shit. In reality, I'm just another white girl in a sea of white sub-par English teachers, and I can't even improve my lot as a *professional white-skinned person*.

I guess that Guangzhou's more interesting than Manitoba. But that's hardly saying much.

Michael should have visited me when I lived in Shenzhen. I felt more confident then, when China was new to me. Now I'm just living out a stereotype.

Looking at the clock high on a wall, I realize that I've rested, deep in thought, on the abdominals machine for 20 minutes. I'm too stressed out to continue with this workout. Well, at least, I got in my cardio.

I go home, take a shower, and plan for next week.

* * *

I'm on a bus bound for Hong Kong's airport. Thirty minutes more should take us to the Shenzhen Bay customs border. Already we're in Nanshan. It's strange! Looking out the windows, I recognize everything, but I'm not even going to hang out in Shenzhen. There's Shen Uni, and there's Seaworld Mall. I wish that we could have passed Window of the World, the fake international photo-op theme park. Maybe I'll take Michael to see the miniature Eiffel Tower and mini-Big Ben. After all, it's his first time overseas. That park's kind of a stupid place though.

In my purse, I carry two books. One's a mystery paperback that I bought on Khao San Road in Bangkok ages ago and never got around to reading. I'm on page ten and probably won't finish it today either. (Not finishing what I start is becoming a running theme with me.) Whatever! No trip to an airport would be complete without a book I don't finish.

The other book, a travel guide to Hong Kong, also came from Khao San, and it's very handy. I've flipped through it on the whole bus ride and gained lots of ideas. I look at the Mass Transit Railway (MTR) map and think about it. To begin with, we'll both need some colorful Hong Kong money. Michael will want an adequate number of mainland RMBs too, and we'll joke about how Chairman Mao appears on every banknote.

From the airport, we can take an express train to the Central Business District and go up to Victoria Peak for a view of the skyline. Then we should descend and take a Star Ferry to the Kowloon side of the harbor for a look at the Hollywood-like star-adorned walkway that celebrates Hong Kong cinema. We'll go shopping along Nathan Road. I want to buy blush and conditioner there. We'll eat Indian food and go into Kowloon Park.

I just hope that Michael didn't bring too much luggage. We'll restrict ourselves to a quick tour because I need to get home tonight and work tomorrow. Just riding on this bus eats up so many hours from our day in Hong Kong.

Too bad we'll have no time for Michael to check out Shenzhen. Then what for the rest of the week? He'll have to stay inside the Estates for the next few days unless he wants to explore on his own. On the weekend, we'll go into the city.

Amazingly, my Hong Kong guidebook offers four whole pages devoted to Guangzhou. All this time I didn't even know I had a local travel guide at all.

At least I finally have an excuse to begin exploring the city properly. I'll ask Eric and some other friends to show us around. No doubt, it'll be an awesome weekend. And by Saturday night, I'm sure there'll be some party somewhere to attend. There always is.

The bus makes steady progress. Hong Kong border, here I come.

* * *

"It's so weird," I say.

"Don't say that," Eric tells me. "He's your brother."

"I'm right here," says Michael.

We do tend to talk about him as if he's not in the room. Michael has been around for the past four days. He's tall and stands out, but he's shy and just *so young*.

About a dozen of us are at Rina's place again for an after-party, and we're talking about family. We discuss whose parents have visited, what it's like to go back home, and even getting married to someone with a different passport. I'm just telling them how weird it is that Michael's here.

"It's like different worlds are colliding," I say.

"Good *Seinfeld* reference," says Eric. Everyone laughs, except for Michael.

"I feel like there used to be a big barrier between my lives in China and in Canada," I say, "and that I'm almost a different person when I'm here. This unsettles and confuses me. I don't know."

"But don't you cherish the time with your family?" Rina asks. "It's so great that your brother has come to visit."

I pause before saying, "Yes, definitely."

"Well," says Eric, "I can understand a little anxiety. A cousin of mine visited last year. He was roughing it in Laos and Singapore so my aunt suggested that he come here so that I could show him around. We hadn't been close up to that point, but it turned into a great opportunity to get to know each other better. He was the first family member who came to visit me. Prior to that, I'd hidden in my own little alternate reality. Then he thrust me into an overlap of my previous life with my contemporary one. So, yes, I know what you mean. It's an odd feeling at first. My cousin and I went out drinking, and I learned a lot about him. He's studying sociology. We had plenty to talk about, you see. Now maybe my life is more, shall we say, *real*? And my relationship with my cousin strengthened. Ultimately, there's nothing like family."

"Yeah, family's great."

"So what do you think of China?" Rina asks my brother.

"Um," he says after having been quiet all evening. "It's so different."

"How so?" Rina says. She wants to prod him to open up and keeps trying.

"It's difficult to get around because I don't speak Chinese."

"Well, obviously, but tell us more. What's your deeper impression?"

"It's so big too! First, Amber met me at the airport, and I couldn't believe what I saw in Hong Kong, especially the flashing lights and big crowds. Now I've learned that Guangzhou's even bigger. I truly can't believe it. I've never even been to such a big city like this, not really, except maybe for when we went to Chicago. Remember that, Amber?"

I nod, hoping that he doesn't say much more because there's an embarrassing story that he could tell about long hours on the road and nature's calling...

Michael spares me. "I took some good photos here," is all that he adds.

I feel a sense of relief and also annoyance. It's good for me that he didn't tell the need-to-pee story, but it would have been much more entertaining if he did. Everyone would laugh and be impressed, making my brother the life of the party. I'd feel stupid and then laugh too. But he missed the chance and just sits there being *boring*.

"It's annoying that you can't put the pictures on Facebook from here. Am I right?" says Rina.

"Yeah."

"Tell us more, Michael. It's always great for us to be reminded of the feelings when first getting here. Being 'fresh off the boat' again…"

Somehow, Michael relates a few mildly interesting anecdotes about street food and the currency exchange rate, and we make it through the night without revealing too much of how small-town we folks truly are. He offers nothing personal. After a bit more superficial conversation, he steps back and stays in a corner, occasionally taking pictures and flipping through them on his phone or using other handheld gadgets. I guess that he's playing video games. I never know for sure.

Culture-shock's one thing, what with being so far away from home for the first time, suddenly being a minority, noticing that everyone looks at you, standing out and struggling with the language barrier. It always feels weird, but we can get over it.

It's really the generational gap that sets Michael and me so far apart. Most of the people at this house party are around 30. I usually feel like I'm the youngest one, and now here's this big awkward teenager trying hard not to be noticed, but just standing out all the more because of it.

On that first day, the one in Hong Kong when we dragged Michael's luggage through shopping malls and up the mountain, things felt weird, but not so bad. I forgave a lot of the distance between us, recognizing his jet lag and my own exhaustion from a bus ride across Guangdong Province. We were completely "out of it", just going through the motions. Under the circumstances, that was understandable.

I'd waited at Hong Kong's airport that morning, browsing through expat magazines and *South China Morning Post* newspapers, sitting in the arrivals hall full of loving families and sign-holding limo drivers. As soon as Michael appeared among the travelers, I felt a rush of disappointment. From then on, we indulged in fake enthusiasm, which gave me the blues. I could have renamed the newspaper right there. *South China Morning Blues* felt more like it.

When we took a quiet train ride headed onto the Chinese mainland, I instructed Michael on how to fill out the necessary border-crossing card, write the tourist-visa number and get his passport stamped without drawing too much attention to himself. Once the border vanished far behind us, when we reached Guangzhou and he stepped out into the real China, I could just *feel* his six-foot frame and lone white face jump out from among the masses. In Hong Kong, nobody cares if you're a foreigner, but when you're suddenly on the mainland and all of those strange eyes hit you, no one fails to feel it. To me, it felt like they were hitting my whole damn family.

From the Guangzhou East Station, we waited in line. Gosh, I hate taking taxis in Guangzhou, but after about forever, we made it to my suburban apartment.

On the second day, Michael wouldn't even leave. He stayed indoors playing games on his phone, Game Boy or whatever that gadget is. I encouraged him to take a walk through the Estates complex or boldly catch a random bus into the city. He barely made it across the street to buy junk food. On the way, he took pictures of the street signs like they were the biggest deal ever.

Those four extra pages in the Hong Kong travel book came in handy. All weekend, I chaperoned. Michael and I went to Yuexiu Park, to the zoo at Ching Long, up the Canton Tower, and to every old temple along the way. At least, Guangzhou has a lot more places of interest like this than Shenzhen does. We went to eat at the Tianhe Mall, and I showed off that I could order food in Mandarin. Finally we took a taxi to the bar where Rina's band played.

Everything that we saw and did was worlds away from the tiny town where we grew up, the long drives through empty land or days spent watching TV together with the grade-school friends we'd known for our entire lives. Back home, life stays so comfortable and dull while Guangzhou brings an endless array of strange new experiences.

As we sped along the Chinese roadways in taxis, I texted my friends while glancing to see my little brother, with his mouth agape, staring at the bright lights flashing by the car windows. Then I thought back to my own first days in China and how it felt when everything was new to me.

In truth, Michael embarrasses me. I'm not quite sure that I know who this kid is. Apparently, I lack motherly instincts and the feeling of family debts to repay. What fate of destiny and genetics has set me up to take care of this guy?

Now we're stuck together for however many days longer, and I realize that I can't wait for my little brother to go home and leave me alone. Does that make me a bad person?

If I am a bad person, then I don't know what I can do about it. Other than live really far away from my family.

Interlude I: Guangzhou

狗
John

I'm on the street-corner, like every day. This a common day here in this land, hot and wet. I'm used to hot, but this a different thing from the sun of my continent. There's the humidity, a dirty feeling. But I don't sweat it – been here long enough that it's okay. I wear Nike, very stylish, and a necklace with its gold cross dangling. Relaxed and chill, I want these white boys to trust me, like a normal hip hop boy from their own countries.

"Hey, man, what you need?"

That guy make eye-contact with me, then walk past and don't even say "hello". He rude, but I don't care. I still do my business.

Here it's the international district, you might say, people from all over cruising along. My Muslim brothers have a restaurant down the street. European big rollers stay in the Garden Hotel. All the Chinese hotties are dressed to pick up the white boys and black boys, everyone headed to clubs on both sides of the *Huanshi Lu*.

Another white boy walk past me. He smile at me, and I smile back.

"Yo, dude, help me out," he say. "I hear that you got a cash-flow problem, and I got a *hash*-flow problem, ha, ha!"

"I help you, friend." We walk into the alleyway where I hide my stash. He give me two notes a hundred each, and I hand him five grams.

When I pocket the money, I keep half in a separate envelope in my coat pocket. That's for the boss. He always tell me not to write down numbers, but to immediately separate the loot. At the end of the week, he add up what I put in the envelope and how much weight I got left over. I'm one of his good boys and almost never fail to add it up right at the end of a night.

For a while I talk to my honey on a mobile. Then I eat some kebab. After that, I'm back to my corner.

Almost at the end of my shift, this one white boy come over. He act like he's my good friend. We meet here every week. He even have my number and usually call first, but I guess I missed his call because I was chattin' to my honey.

He a regular, the white boy in the beard playin' the holy man. These American white boys, they always think they the black man's best friend.

"Did you read about the recent developments in Uganda?" he ask me.

"I'm not from Uganda," I say.

"No, no. I didn't imply that. Just, ahem, speculating about your unique perspective."

"It's a tragic situation, sure."

Man, I don't like talkin' politics. Chinese-boys ain't always so good to me, but at least they never talk politics. These American collegiate boys won't shut up. They think just because I ain't Chinese, they can talk Mao and shit with me. Don't they know I here to do a job?

"Look man, what do you want?"

He buys the usual and gives me a hug. I put three in the envelope. Nice pocket change for me.

And I got one more customer for the night, a Chinese white boy who also come down here every so often.

When I say Chinese white boy, I say that because he don't speak no Chinese, and he just as American as the last one. Basically he a yellow-skinned white boy. No disrespect meant by that. I know black-skinned white boys too, if anybody wanna call them that. Just using my own terms, my own way of distinguishin' my fellow man from country to country.

So we do the business, and now I got a burnin' hole in my pocket. I gotta go to the bank. I know peoples see me in my outfit, lookin' all hip because that's what I like to buy. Nice shoes, bright hat. They always respect me at the bank, they know it, and I go to the window, deposit a few thou.

Lastly, I put a few more notes in my underwear and make sure that envelope tucked deep in my coat because that's my only inventory for the night. With that envelope inside, my nice coat be even nicer.

It's a knockoff, but I know coats. Hell, I know clothes. I came to this country to sell clothes.

Sure, when I came here, I wanted to do right, but as soon as I'm off the plane, my cousin here tell me the way it really is. He tell me we go to the factory, ship boxes, and back home people wear our product, but that ain't all it really about. What he tell me, it's really about shipping the herb, the pills, and the powders.

Now I just stand here on the corner. I don't know it all, but I know what I know. My cousin, he the one deals with the boys at the bay, the shipment, the politics, the boss, and the *big money.*

Some nice Chinese boys don't like us black boys. They blame us for the whole world, but they don't even know where the real thing come from. The white boys, they don't trust the Chinese, so they come to us. They think that better? It's all a joke because ain't nothin' like economic incentives, and the real money and product ain't comin' through no black boys or no white boys.

But that ain't mine to know. No sir!

Sometimes my momma, she email me letters and ask what life like here. She want I should make money and send it over, buy a plane ticket to visit right away, or get married and give her some grandsons and quick. I tell her be patient on all fronts. About this city, I tell her it's like Lasgidi. Construction all the time, dirty and always people out to make money any ways they can. She say can't believe it, but I tell her the biggest difference from here to back home is that it even bigger here.

I decide to write my momma an email. Let her know life's alright. First thing tomorrow. Now I gotta strut my stuff and take the metro out west just one-ways.

So I go home to my honey, quiet night in and no clubbin' tonight. I'm happy and content cuz all over the world I got family out there waitin' for me.

龍
Ting Ting Two Two

At two o'clock, I come in and change into the robe. My handbag's big so I can stuff my clothes into it. The class begins at half past two.

The teacher is Mrs. Tai. She's middle-aged and very nice. We chat for a while about the week, and she repeatedly asks me if the room temperature's okay.

"It's fine. It's fine, thank you."

No students have arrived yet. I walk around the room, looking for any new sketches that I haven't seen yet. Mostly I see small 8-by-12s. This is a fashion-design institute so a bunch of the pictures show tall and beautiful women wearing extravagant, impossible dresses. There are gowns, black and white with touches of colored pencil at the edges, flowing frills, bare shoulders and twisting high heels.

Only a few of the pictures show nudes. I look at them, thinking, *I could do better.* Way better. I used to love my life-drawing classes.

Now I'm on the other side of the lens. Well, it's not a photography class, but that's still a good way to put it.

The students come in one by one. They bring their own art supplies in purses, but the institute supplies the large 20-by-26 Bristol boards.

Wooden drawing horses, those tall desks, are set up. Looking at the stage in the middle, cluttered with props, blankets, and a rocking chair, I wait for the butterflies in my stomach to digest. Every time I come here, I feel nervous, a little less each time, but it's still there.

Since it's a Tuesday afternoon and not a real university setting, only eight students attend. This daytime class consists of seven housewives and one gay guy. The women, I think, all have rich husbands and lots of free time so they come here for fun. I don't know what the gay guy does for a living or why he's able to participate at this hour. Ha! Maybe he has a rich supportive husband too. I do like him; he seems like the most serious art student.

I don't mind that these women are trophy housewives. It's a good thing and means that this job pays me 400 per hour, more than even English teachers earn, and so I can support myself and my own art projects. I don't need a real job, can buy all the supplies I want, pay rent, buy my own cocktails, and still have time to find artistic inspiration and paint.

"Let's begin. Everyone's here," says Mrs. Tai, directing me to start.

"Hello," I say, waving to everyone. I hop onto the stage and pass my robe to Mrs. Tai. Now I'm standing nude in front of these people. My heart beats fast, and it's not too cold, but I'm worried that my nipples will turn hard like the last time.

Everyone looks at me! And that's fine. That's the job. I can only wait to see how the pictures turn out.

"Ting Ting, please begin with a standing position."

I place my hands on my hips and stretch my shoulders back. There really is an art to this. I need to stay still for 20 minutes at a time. Of course, I want to look dynamic and cool. I also don't want to look fat. I hope my butt looks good.

Mrs. Tai applies white tape in front of my toes so that I can return to exactly the same spot after my break later. She lectures to the class, and I listen. It's all good advice.

With this job, I've learned a lot about patience. It's amazing how in the beginning each time, I feel nervous, and then after just a few minutes, I mostly feel bored. I think about what I want to eat later today, and what I'll buy with the money I earn.

"Take a break, everyone."

Finally! I stretch my arms and legs, put on the robe, and sit down. I don't want to look at the pictures until after an entire hour. I let my body rest for five minutes.

"Please begin again."

I place my toes in precisely the right place, get naked, and it's the same thing all over again. My muscles soon get sore, my back hurts, and I'm straining not to let my legs shake. It's certainly a workout.

On the next break, I put on slippers and the robe and go outside the room to drink some water. The students are on break too. The gay guy, as always, goes out to the hall to smoke. All of the ladies start chatting and texting on their phones. I walk around to look at the pictures.

Charcoal, deep blacks, greys smudged with little thumbprints going lighter and lighter. Each one depicts me from a different angle, through different eyes and hands. They're all *true*, kind of, but there's no such thing as just one truth. A certain corner of the room shows one truth, and another spot shows a separate truth, and that truth looks a little different from another truth. Different hands, different experiences, different angles and different talents, all bringing different memories.

The pictures represent different worlds. In one, I have bigger breasts, and I like that world. In another, my head looks a little pointed, and my eyes are closed. Eight different images appear during each hour spent here. I guess maybe that's the point of art, to think of stuff like this.

Then the class resumes. "Let's do a sitting position please, Ting Ting."

That's great to hear. I'll feel much more comfortable now. For the second hour, I'm in the chair. Having my arms crossed makes my shoulders get tense, but for the most part, it's much easier than the first hour. Mrs. Tai knows this. She's a veteran art teacher and works easily with models. Things go much better here than my Fridays do at the university with young Mister Hu. I can't stand it there.

In fact, I prefer Mrs. Tai to Mister Hu for a bunch of reasons. Besides the usual poses, Mister Hu makes me kneel, lie on my side, or stick my butt out in all kinds of awkward positions. Not only that, but the university class has 20-plus students, and half of them are *boys*.

But I'm a professional. I can handle anything as long as I'm paid.

Hour three comes, and I'm lying on my back. Despite the fluorescent lights shining into my eyes, I think that I really do fall sleep for a brief moment. Nobody ever remembers *going* to sleep, but always recalls the instant of awakening. I have that feeling. True, I'm a little embarrassed to nod off while nude in a room full of people, but I guess that it just shows how tired and bored I am.

Mrs. Tai calls my name, and I open my eyes, immediately pretending that I was awake the whole time. I don't know how long I was out. I must have kept still. Nothing could have happened. It was probably for only a minute. But during that minute, or however long, I was so *exposed*.

And that's my job. At the end, I put on the robe and say goodbye to the students. I'll return here in two weeks. Next week, this class will have a male model, and I can only imagine what that's like for the students, especially the gay guy.

I circle the room one last time to look before the students put away the work into their oversized black folders. As usual, most of the pictures are so-so, but a few hold my interest. The gay guy's still the best.

Mrs. Tai gives me an envelope. Inside I'll find 1,200 in cash.

"Thank you," I say and bow a little.

Well, that's my work for today. There's something oddly nostalgic about it all…

My bag's stashed in the backroom, and I look around to make sure no one's there before I change into my clothes. That's funny, right? I'm nude all afternoon, but when getting dressed again, I really need privacy.

Going outside, I find a taxi fairly fast. Unlike the university campus, the institute's situated in the middle of Tianhe, and from here, it's easier to get around town.

Arriving back home, I hand the driver money, wait for change, and then hop out. I'm in a good mood and give my three *kuai* change to a beggar.

Before entering our building, I walk to a bank across the street and deposit five hundreds. I check my balance, which now shows over ten thousand.

I'm so happy. In a sense, that isn't much, but I earned it myself, and I feel independent. I'd never tell my parents where my money comes from, but still, I think they'd be proud if they had a general idea. At least I'm working in the art industry.

Now that I've reached my goal of one *wan*, I should move out soon. I have enough money to pay a deposit on an apartment of my own. I fantasize a little about looking online, paying a moving company and then I'll be there. It won't be easy, but I'll be able to focus better on my art, maybe even turning my private place into my own little studio.

All that's left is telling Siu Choi, my roommate. That will be the hardest part.

* * *

The gallery party is going very well!

"Hello, darling," says Rina.

"Darling?" I ask.

"It just feels more glamorous to call you 'darling'."

She says it like this, "*Dahling*".

All of her *laowai* friends laugh, and so do I. Honestly, I don't always understand the *laowai*, but I think that they're cool so I follow along. Everyone's more than a little drunk.

My paintings hang beside us. I call them "reverse-lifes". They're inspired by my time as a model. It's no mixed medium, simply oil paintings of human figures. I take humongous vertical canvasses, pretend that I have a camera lens bent at extremely wide-angles (I have no time for photography anymore, but don't waste my training), and paint art students staring directly at you, the viewers. I think it was a clever idea, the way I did it. Big, exaggerated heads and eyes look at you, sneer, and judge. I almost want to make people uncomfortable with this message. *You all see what it's like.*

"I'm making a statement about the artist and the audience," I say. I want to explain the whole feeling, but it's hard to express, especially in English. "It's about, like, the art staring back at you, and that's the last thing you expect."

"Yes, yes," they always say.

Every few minutes a group of French, northern Europeans or Hong Kongers pass through, and I nervously introduce myself as the artist. The people look for a few minutes. In front of each painting, they nod, scratch their chins, and read the pamphlet. Then they move on to the next one. Sometimes they say, "Bold, original." Sometimes they say, "Dove-tailing, derivative. It's been done."

I smile, thank them, and that's all there is.

Here at Green Square Factory, we have all sorts of people passing through with an even mix of locals and foreigners, all colors. Many come just for the free wine. And no, I'm not the star. Many artists have work on display here tonight, including people older and more talented than me who've lived in Guangzhou longer and have more devoted followings. I only have Rina, her friends, and a few colleagues. My roommate didn't even come! I'm just a small player, but maybe I'm the one who will turn into the next big thing…

I look around. Then I enjoy a quiet moment, realizing that I've already talked to everyone. I go to the toilet, come back into the gallery, and pour myself some chilled white wine into a fine curved glass. Some familiar faces pass, but mostly strangers, and I feel kind of lonely in this crowd.

"Ting Ting," says the gallery's director-manager.

I turn around. He's a tall, handsome Cantonese man who wears expensive suits, flies to Germany to deal paintings every season, and sets up art parties like this once a month. Since taking me under his wing, he has given me confidence by letting me in here for my first real show in Guangzhou.

"Yes," I say.

"Congratulations. You've sold a painting. I'll prepare the check and statement later this evening."

Four of my pieces are displayed for sale. Three are priced at 6,000 and one at 8,000.

"Wow," I say quietly. "Thank you."

"And it's only the opening night. Maybe you'll sell another. We have five weeks left."

Oh my! I must have made an impression on someone. Going back to the corner where my work hangs, I see my name and little summary. Next to the smallest 6,000 painting I see a green sticker. Enjoying the moment, I drink my wine slowly and say nothing.

Curious, I carefully scan the room. Somehow it's totally noisy, but quiet. I'm a new person here, a professional artist, and I wonder how

I'm supposed to act. This is no longer hustling tourists on Tiananmen Square in Beijing. It's the real thing. So many thoughts flood my head. Should I act confident? Or should I play it cool and humble? Should I put this on my resume, immediately sell out, and get a design job? Maybe I could use my cash to take a month off and travel? Move to Paris? Or Tokyo? What should I do?

Sometimes I overwhelm myself by thinking too much about such things. I try to remember that there's nothing I can do for now, except to put one foot in front of the other and keep doing what I'm doing.

I put my wineglass on the floor, shut my eyes tightly, and let the sounds become clearer. I take a deep breath, open my eyes slowly, and my vision returns to normalcy. "Okay, good."

So I pick up my glass and enjoy another slow drink, deciding just to take in the situation. Looking more closely, I notice that even more people are here than I'd realized. There's Rina's crowd near the bar.

I did invite Mrs. Tai and Mister Hu too. Suddenly seeing them together now, I watch, almost spying. My work associates from separate schools appear to know each other, and I hear snippets of their conversation at the nearby life-sized plastic sculptures. They're a little antagonistic, snapping at each other with differing interpretations. Mrs. Tai shakes her head. Mister Hu points his finger and calls her a name.

Although I don't know exactly what they say, I suspect that they're slightly jealous. For poor art teachers, coming to galleries can't be much fun. It was cruel of me to invite them. That's probably why they haven't looked at my work or said "hello" yet. Mentally, I vow that, whatever happens to me, I never want to become a teacher.

Then I see a tall, western-looking woman. Hey, it's Maria from the nightclub scene! I wave to her, and she notices me.

"Hey, darling," I say, using some newly learned glamorous lingo.

Maria approaches me, and I see a group of Russians behind her. I notice one aged man in particular. Oh no! It's *him*!

"I'm very impressed," Maria says.

"Thank you."

"I knew you were serious about this. You have a very brilliant talent. We must catch up over coffee sometime."

"Of course."

"And where's your good friend?"

"I don't know. Busy elsewhere, I guess."

"Oh! Well, keep in touch, dear."

"Yeah, it's nice to see you, Maria."

She moves on when seeing another friend, and they talk.

I look out toward a video display, the exhibition's real star attraction, in the middle of the gallery. There, the group of Russian men, including *him,* still hasn't noticed me. With a sigh of relief, I look away, but then I hear it.

"Little girl!"

I don't want to respond, but I turn, look, and smile politely.

"You remember me, yes? It is I, Dmitri."

"Oh, yes. Hello."

For a long time, this bald, fat, old man had bombarded me with text messages, constantly inviting me to his flat. At first, I made excuses as to why I couldn't go. Then I just stopped replying and totally ignored him. Even so, he needed weeks to take the hint.

Although Guangzhou's a big city, it can feel small. Being busy, I haven't gone to many parties, but I should have known that one day I'd bump heads with this guy again.

"You have a kind of idiot-savant, you know?" he says.

"I don't know," I reply.

"You are very young and display great aptitude." He looks at my pieces with a condescending attitude. "Yet you are too new and will need many years to become a real artist."

I can take criticism, but I wonder where he's going with this. "Thank you for attending," I say.

He pauses, takes out a pack of Chung Hwa cigarettes, and offers me one. I shake my head. "You have to smoke outside," I remind him.

"Come on, little girl, is China." He finds a lighter.

"No, really, you can't smoke in here."

"Join me outside."

"Um, I need to stay in the gallery."

He slides his lighter back into a pocket and shoves the cigarette onto his ear like a pen. Is that supposed to look cool or what? The fat old man raises an arm, rests it against the wall and leans in, touching my shoulder. His face looms, just up against mine. "You are not very friendly to me. What can I do to get you alone, little artist?"

I don't even know what to say.

Just then a Chinese man approaches. We make eye contact and suddenly he taps the old man on a shoulder and starts speaking fast in perfect English. "Pardon me, but I'm writing for *Pearl Delta Expat*, and I need to talk to the artist. Absolutely, I must interrupt. We'll be four minutes, tops. I mean no disrespect, but a profession is a profession, ya dig?"

"What?"

He extends an arm, and the Russian can't help but shake hands. "I'm going to borrow her for a few minutes. I don't mean to block like this, but it's vital for my article. You wouldn't want me to get into trouble with my editor, would you? Not a fine man like yourself, a lover of the arts, right? Stay nearby, and I'll get a quote from you too. A vital member of the audience, as I'm sure you are, could give me perfect street-side interview material. But first, I need a short time alone with the lady."

"Well, that is, I suppose, if only for a moment," Dmitri says.

I stay silent.

"Thank you for your cooperation," the Chinese man says. "You're a scholar and a gentleman."

"Yes, well, of course."

"Cheers."

The Chinese guy grabs me by a forearm and drags me outside. He carries a notebook and a pen held up in his armpit, and as we pass through the doorway, he winks at me.

"Let's get out of here."

When I don't reply, he takes me to a café down the block. Alright, maybe the gallery can wait.

"Americans gotta fight Russians, ya know," he says.

I do laugh at that one.

He pulls out a chair for me, and we sit in the café. A waitress in a black apron hands me a menu. Without looking, my companion just asks for an Americano.

"Um, I'll have an espresso".

"You know," he says, "people always misspell that word."

"Okay."

"Just something I've learned, working as a writer. So…" he begins.

Taking his notebook, he begins scribbling. "Shall we?"

He asks me where I came from, how long I've been in Guangzhou and who my favorite artists are. After peering into my eyes, he looks away and jots more notes. I peek at his page, but it's in a messy cursive that I can't decipher.

Opening up, I tell him much of my life story. The coffee comes, and he drinks his fast. I sip mine slowly. He only asks a few questions, but my answers grow longer with each one. I talk and talk as he puts pen to paper. I don't know how much time passes. Finally, he asks me what I hope to accomplish with my art.

"That's hard to say. I want to be famous, for everyone to like me and to earn lots of money by expressing myself."

"No," he says and doesn't write anything, for the first time refusing to accept one of my answers. "Give me something deeper. I know you can do it."

"It's something like that, truthfully. We all want to be heard, don't we? You're a writer, so same thing. I want fame and everybody to like me, or at least notice me. I want my voice to be heard because I think that I'm very special. Thinking that doesn't make me a bad person."

"That's a bit more like it."

"I suppose it can be rather annoying, right? I get a little attention, and then bad people start to show up too."

"I know," he says warmly. "As we've just seen."

"But it's worthwhile. Good things outnumber the bad. The world has beautiful art, and I really want to participate in it, for myself and for the world too."

"I understand that," he says, scribbling. "More than you know."

"Then I hope to see you at the next show."

"Fuckin' right on!"

At the end, he pays for the coffee, and we exchange cards at nobody's suggestion. We just naturally offer cards at the same moment. I give him my personal cell-phone number and everything.

He's slightly familiar to me, I think. It's a funny thing. I'm sure that we go to the same bars and the same shows all the time, yet we've never really noticed each other until tonight.

It's like, if I fell in love with this man and someone asked me how we met, I wouldn't know what to say. What happened today would make a good story to tell, but isn't the true start. I'm sure that I've seen him around before. But there's no specific starting point. It's like a fuzzy blend of how he's always around, and I'm around too, until one day we meet again. There's no precise second of our first encounter that you could identify on a clock. It's like two paints mixing, and you can't cut a line saying this side's blue and that side's red. Some things just fade into existence with no exact point of entry. Our meeting today resembles the color purple, a light purple. Tomorrow it may be dark purple, and before we know it, life will change to red.

I look at his name-card. It has one side in English and the other in Chinese. I laugh at his nickname.

"Ha, ha, do you know what this means?" He doesn't laugh.

* * *

What a night! It's very late when I arrive home. After opening the apartment door, I shove my keys deep into my purse, burying them beside a stack of cash.

"Why didn't you come to my showing?" I ask my roommate.

"Wha…?" Siu Choi sits up on the couch. A laptop lies beside her on the floor, its white light shining. "Oh, hi, you're back. I fell asleep."

"You should have seen the party," I say. "So many people! I know it's not like I was the only artist, but it felt really cool to see so much activity. Plenty of people you know were there. They asked about you. Lots of cute boys!"

Siu Choi yawns. I know how it goes with artists. We need to be careful when telling each other about our successes.

"I'm just so busy these days," she says. "So tired."

"Yes, of course, very tired."

"What?"

"*Nothing.*"

At first, I didn't mean to sound rude or sarcastic. But when I said the word "nothing", real scorn dripped from my voice, and anyone could see it.

True, I wouldn't be here in Guangzhou right now doing what I am if not for Siu Choi and her connections. She was the most ambitious one right out of college, not me, nor any of our other friends. I'm proud that she works hard as a designer, and I'm sorry that she never got into a gallery.

But she should be nice. She should congratulate me. I come home, and she says nothing. How can that be right?

My old friend rises from the couch, folds her thin notebook computer, and carefully places it on the coffee table. She goes into the bathroom.

I think about how I've come into my own scene recently. Now I hang out with Rina and Maria and other cool friends. I dress up, go to bars, and meet artists. Everything went by so very quickly. I don't need Siu Choi anymore. These days I see her less and less. Sometimes we say nothing to each other for days. We even chat online with happy faces, a wink, an expression, but no words to type. No words to say.

She thinks that I'm using her, but so what? She can use me too if she wants.

When she emerges from the bathroom, I'm standing in the same place. She sits back down and smiles up to me.

I want to tell her that I made a sale! A journalist interviewed me! Soon I'll be famous and take her with me. I owe her everything. If she but asked, I would help make her dreams come true, whatever they may be…

"I'm sorry," I tell her, "but I'm going to move out."

"What's that, Ting Ting?"

"I'm moving!"

She sighs loudly to express annoyance. "You want to talk about this now? It's so late."

"I just think it's important. At the end of the month, I'll move. That's coming up."

"Did you find a new place?"

"I almost found one."

"Almost? What's that mean?"

"It means," I slowly put it, "that I'm not comfortable here, and so I'm ready to go. Do you understand, Siu Choi?"

"I've told you that you don't have to call me that. What do you mean by 'not comfortable'? You're acting very strangely, *little* sister."

Siu Choi stands and stretches. "I certainly can't go back to sleep now," she says. "Okay, we'll talk about it. First of all, you owe me money. It's already been a week, and I'm still waiting for your part of the rent. I was nice and didn't say anything, but if you want to talk about it, now I'll speak."

"Okay, how much?"

"You know it's one thousand."

From my purse, I grab a large handful of fresh pink notes, each one with Chairman Mao's face glaring out at me.

Siu Choi opens her mouth, leaving it agape, as I slowly count. "One. Two. Three. Four. Five. Six. Seven. Eight. Nine. Ten. Want me to count it again?"

"No, that's *fine*."

The way that she speaks infuriates me, and I throw the money to the floor. Immediately Siu Choi crawls around, scrambling and picking up the notes one by one.

"Money's all that you care about!" I shout.

"How can you say that? Do you know what life's really like without rich parents to take care of you?"

"AHHH!" She makes me even crazier, and I look around, searching for something to throw. My insides boil, and the whole situation suddenly erupts into something that I can't handle. I just want to break something!

A potted plant occupies one corner on top of a short wardrobe. I snatch up the plant, hurl it onto the floor, and the impact makes a loud *crash*. The poor plant sprawls as crumbs of dark brown dirt spread everywhere, almost like residue from an explosion in a war movie. Or splattered watercolors!

Siu Choi drops the money. "What's wrong with you?"

When she pauses, I see her confusion transform into fury. Then she jumps at me, scratching my neck and pulling my hair.

The ensuing moments turn into a blur of emotions and jolts. It's like smeared paint all mixing together until it's too dark for me to make out anything. I don't know if the blur lasts for seconds or minutes.

We roll around on the floor. My vision turns red. I feel a snap to my nose. One of my shoulders hits a corner. Mindlessly, I flail my arms. Sometimes they hit hard dirty floor, and sometimes they hit soft flesh and cloth.

Despite the late hour, we scream and cry, thinking nothing about the time or our neighbors. Then for me, everything goes black and silent.

Finally, I open my eyes. It's hard to breathe, and I feel bruises starting to form all over my body. I'm crouched next to the couch while Siu Choi lies against a wall near the broken pot. She sobs loudly.

Slowly I get up. Above all, I really want to say that I'm sorry, but I absolutely can't form any words. Feeling confused, I struggle even to understand exactly what has happened.

I check to make sure that I'm wearing my shoes. Without even taking my purse, I just go. The door doesn't shut behind me. Lights glow at all of our neighbors' places. My body hurts a little, but I run to leave the building as quickly as possible.

Now it's even later, and I feel empty in every sense. No money, no keys. Vaguely, I remember a small pub nearby. If I walk there, maybe I can find someone to buy me drinks and take care of me just for tonight so that I won't need to go back home.

I place one foot in front of the other and move down the dimly lit street. I have nothing to do except to continue.

You know, we weren't even fighting over a man. Yet suddenly I've turned into one of *those girls*.

The night had started so well, and I'd wanted to remember it. But now I want to forget everything.

My future can't arrive fast enough. I can't wait until the present turns into a distant memory. It'll be worth it, even if I end up forgetting some of the good times.

Interlude II: Guangzhou

蛇
Eric

I'm bored. It seems that all my friends are busy, and I am left alone.

The sun is descending, and I haven't even left the apartment all day. Indoors for twenty-four hours, not a healthy situation. My roommate's at work. Nothing social is planned. I think about working out, watching a movie, masturbating, smoking herb, or perhaps trying my hand at something stronger. But whatever I'm going to do, I don't want to stay alone. I'm going stir-crazy in here.

This is but Tuesday. No plans whatsoever exist on a weekday such as this. I get online, check my emails, and observe naught but coupons and news updates. Perhaps I shall read later. I check my personal social-network page. No invites, no new friends, and no events worth noting, except for lady's night at a bar in Panyu two hours away by metro.

I know that I should be productive and engage in personal growth. A pile of books waits on a shelf for me to read. I have a grant letter to write, articles to edit, and a lesson plan to draw up for tomorrow's tutoring, not to mention my ever-procrastinated thesis. All in due time, I think.

Next I look at my phone. No text messages. Nothing on WeWa. So I go through my contacts and select five interesting women to simultaneously text.

"*Today is so beautiful, and it makes me think of u. It's been too long…*"

Then I wait. Within a minute, I receive three replies.

One comes from Amber. "*Busy with skool. U know I'm not free weekdays.*"

That ditzy white girl. It's always so damn overwhelming with her. No fun at all. I'm starting to really get frustrated with that woman.

So I send an obligatory appreciation for the reply. After that initial SMS, she doesn't respond again, and I can only think that's good riddance.

The other replies come from Jessica and Cherry, both to be summed up as "*Happy to hear from you*". Nice Chinese girls. I met them on the subway months back and haven't seen them in absolute ages. I did sleep with Jessica. Cherry strikes me as a nicer girl.

Busily, I simultaneously carry on two conversations, back and forth, until…

"*I want to meet,*" Jessica texts.

"*Let's have dinner.*" That's Cherry.

Uh-oh! Double-booked here. It's time to choose.

On one hand, sex with Jessica would look a bit more certain. At a platonic level, I sincerely enjoy her company as well. Truly, I do, but I readily admit to having that certain male impulse that can affect judgment.

On the other hand, and I insist on being honest about those base male feelings of mine, sometimes a challenge proves good for the spirit. I recall all those eons ago how when I tried to kiss Cherry goodnight at a car window, she turned away. She's such a good girl. Yet by now she must recognize my motivations. Perhaps if I try harder with the charm and let her erotic-self open to me, I could experience a wild and delightful night. A new notch on the belt never hurts one's ego.

So I go for the latter.

"*Let me check my schedule,*" I send to Jessica. After all, I may change my mind later. It's never in poor taste to have a backup plan.

Then to Cherry, "*Let's eat!*"

Hastily, I take a shower and freshen up. I trim a bit around my beard and carefully place a condom in my wallet, hoping that it won't get flattened. I do this just in case. After all, we must put safety first. Most of the time, I try to be a gentleman. Most of the time!

I send Cherry a message recommending the Turkish restaurant on Jianshe that I've heard so much about. With satisfaction, I smirk to myself, thinking that my drug dealer often works near that same corner. Shall I greet him too?

Cherry and I agree on a time. Jessica hasn't texted me back, but probably holds no hard feelings. At least, nothing negative is indicated, so I conclude that all goes well. I'm happy to have alleviated the day's boredom so positively.

Soon I'm riding in a taxi to the agreed location. When I arrive ten minutes early, I'm patiently alone and so the lovely hostess offers me a seat.

"No, thank you," I say in Mandarin. "I'm still waiting for another person."

I smoke a cigarette outside. I lean against the front door. I check my phone intermittently. Now Cherry lags five minutes late. That's not necessarily a problem. Girls often show up late for this sort of thing, and it wouldn't be prudent for me to make a big deal out of it. No, I must play it cool.

"Alright then," I tell the hostess. "For now it's just me, and I'll wait."

Not holding it against me at all, the hostess smiles and escorts me to a two-seater table with a conspicuously empty chair across from me. I fantasize about dating the hostess. She is certainly cute, but it's usually a mistake trying to game on waitresses and the like. And I'm not exactly showing my best attributes by being stood up.

Perhaps I need some appetizers. I order hummus, and it arrives quickly. Next I add Tabasco sauce, which I've been told isn't the authentic palate. What can I say? Even I can be a Philistine.

I eat slowly and delicately so as to let the time pass without being too bored. Yet again, I check the time.

Well, it's been forty minutes. I have officially given up, and the hostess looks at me with what I assume to be sympathy. I'd have no chance with her now.

The point of no return has passed, and I have no reason even to contact Cherry. That would just place me in the weak position. Although I'm frustrated, there's nothing I can do about it except try for damage control.

I text to Jessica. "*My evening has opened up! Guess what! You've got to check out the new bar on Huanshi. Mmm, absinthe...*"

She promptly replies with an economical choice indeed: a lone angry-face.

Ah, well! It was a noble effort. Hell, what else would I do with my time? These women! The experienced, surefire sexual ones have an uncanny sense for knowing when they're the second choice. And the cute, innocent ones are flakes who don't know how cruel they are with this sort of thing...

Later when I'm already back home and lazing in front of the television, Cherry calls and profusely apologizes. She went shopping, and the bus got stuck in a traffic jam, and her phone ran out of power. It's a rather ridiculous story, but I'm nice and say that it's no big deal, that we'll catch up another time. Well, I shan't try that one again anytime soon. If so, I'd have to be quite desperate. Then again, anything's possible.

Well played, Ericson! Or not! Damn, it's all that I can do just to laugh.

猴
Cantonland

One of those conversations ensues, the sort that foreigners have when we're only a little buzzed and it's still early, but the moon's high. You know the kind. It's epic, all-encompassing, a great Unified Theory of Chineseness. We have our strong opinions, our bellies are full, and no girls share our table.

There are four of us – my editor Jonas, his friend who happens to be an older businessman associate, a random old American who joined us because he saw no one else here with whom he wants to hang out, and me. We're at Indian Towers, a bar right across from the city's most expensive hotel, but here the drinks are reasonably priced. We're adjacent to class, and that's good enough.

The place has a whole Bengalese vibe with statues of Shiva, Krishna, and other blue god dudes chiseled into the walls. It's an elevated balcony type of venue. To get here, you need to walk uphill two floors. We sit in the outside-patio area on sharp metal chairs. The weather has just started to cool. Each of us holds a Tsingtao beer. In the distance, we hear the soft sounds of a DJ's beats from a dance floor beyond the horizon.

"Guangzhou has no identity," Jonas says, "because it's developing too fast. First-tier it may be, but it's a city of economic nonsense with a hodgepodge of Lego buildings randomly and maniacally stacked everywhere. From the avant-garde Germans to the Vietnamese plagiarists, anyone hired as an architect for new luxury high-rises here rushes to build, and there's no consistent style. No city planning. Shopping malls and ethnic bars like this one appear, built over ghetto-like village settings on the cusp of being labeled shanty-towns. With nine-per-cent growth every year and massive internal migration to lift the demand for space in Guangzhou, and the rising wealth gap in turn, well, there's no time for culture in all of this."

"Although," says Jonas's companion, "Chinese people may differ with you on that conclusion. They see culture differently. Look at a Northerners' stereotypes of the Cantonese. We don't necessarily see the subtle cultural differences because of our outsider perspective. From our vantage point, it's all construction and pubs, but if we had the eyes of a local, we'd spot the elusive identity thing of which you speak, that flavor of the city."

"I completely disagree," says Jonas.

"Why so?"

Before Jonas answers, the graying American, new to our group, interjects. "I think Guangzhou has a ton of identity."

We all wait for him to continue with examples, details or something. "It's so different from back home," he adds.

"Oh?" answers Jonas. "Have you been to Beijing? Shanghai? Osaka? Mumbai?"

"No," the old American says. "Only here. I'm from the great state of Georgia."

"I see. Just checking."

"This year I left the United States for my first time, and I'm getting married too."

The rest of us look at each other and silently agree to pretend we didn't hear that.

"Well," begins Jonas. "Thanks for that segue. Now here's the thing. Although Beijing and Shanghai have their charms, I'd still say that the vast majority of Chinese cities lack much in the way of real culture.

There's a big contrast between the top two and everywhere else. Think about it. For the bulk of China, there's nothing beyond those two places. Everywhere you go, it's either villages at one end of the spectrum, or the same damn bars, offices, factories, and karaoke places at the other end. Just a smidge of nightlife entertainment exists for us international investors and the newly mushroomed rich. Everything else is plain *bland*."

"You can't just discount the cultural identities of Shanghai and Beijing," says the business associate.

"I know what you'll say. Yeah, yeah, there's the Bund, modern art, the 1920s Republic era, and the Forbidden City. Still, bear with me."

"Go on."

"Maybe back in olden times, things were different. Maybe back when this city was called Canton, the place had more flavor. But it's been more or less a blank slate for the past, what, fifty years?"

"I think that I follow you there," I say.

"Compare the situation in Guangzhou to other Asian cultures of note," says Jonas, now on a roll. "In Thailand, you have that cultural rule about not touching kids' heads. In Japan, people bow. Almost everywhere else in Asia, you constantly need to take off your shoes."

We all raise our hands to make a point, but Jonas beats us to it and resumes. "That last one about shoes kind of applies in China too, but it's very inconsistently enforced compared to other countries. Meanwhile, look at the jay-walking and the driving here. No rules! My point is that if you look at the unique history, post-Revolution…"

"Which revolution specifically?" I ask him.

"Terry, that's just it. Allow me to get into more detail on that. The point is, *all of them.* You've got 1911, a tumultuous time, followed by civil war, Japanese invasion, and civil war again. After that, along comes 1949, the Great Leap Forward, the Cultural Revolution, Deng Xiaoping, and the Tiananmen Square protests."

Jonas says the last few words quietly. The American quickly looks back and forth. Usually you can say whatever that you fucking want in China, and newer expats tend not to understand that. Only a few truly taboo subjects exist here, and the government's brutal crackdown on student protesters in 1989 happens to be one of them. Not to mention, no one at our table says anything about the Dalai Lama or Falun Gong either.

Back at normal volume, Jonas continues with some choice comments about Chairman Mao, and nobody bats an eye. "In Mao's bloody Cultural Revolution purge, people spent years with no school, no education. No culture was produced, just propaganda and violence. What does that do to a nation's soul?"

"Some say that food is the only Chinese character trait that survived the 20th century unscathed," I add.

"Exactly, but don't get me wrong. I'm not complaining. From a business perspective, this lack-of-culture thing has its advantages. You could say that with the post-1980s and '90s reforms, with starting from scratch on culture, it brings out a certain adaptability and open-mindedness that many more stubborn Asian cultures lack."

"From a marketing perspective," says Jonas's companion, who with those words identifies himself as definitely a businessman, probably in trading, "some might disagree with that assessment. How can we generalize about 1.4 billion people? Yet we try."

Conversations involving Jonas tend to burgeon with every drink and each passing hour. Elaborate theories sum up the destinies of billions. Only editorial-staff types can comprehend his grand scope. We talk like this at every opportunity, yet each new theory fades from memories by the next morning. Seeds for more theories grow at the back of Jonas's brain, nurtured by wine and cigarettes, ready to bloom on the next Friday night.

As I consider what to say in response, suddenly the old American asks me, "Aren't you Chinese?"

"Yes and no. I don't feel like telling the whole story."

"I bet that you're from California. Am I right? We don't have much Chinese-Americans down South, I watched that TV show *Glee* and..."

"Let's stay on topic," I interrupt. It bugs me that he guessed correctly.

"Well, what do you think your parents would say? Are ya Cantonese?"

"That's a good question. They're from Taiwan. By way of Fujian as for the hometown village anyhow, but I know what you mean. I can't be sure how old Dad would chime in on this discussion, but maybe he'd prefer Taipei to Guangzhou for cultural flair and identity. Maybe he'd agree that it's developing too fast here. You know, my parents never once even travelled south of Xiamen."

"So I wanna know, what do you think?" the old American asks me. Okay, now I'm starting to like him a little more.

"Well," I say, "probably we all can agree that there's a lack of, what can we call it? *Flavor*. Especially compared to other famous Asian cities."

"Sure."

"But I think we also can say that Shanghai and Beijing do have that indefinable charm that we're discussing. Maybe less so than Bangkok or wherever, but they have a lot more than here. There's a reason for that. Up North, things are a bit more well-defined, like the borders, cuisine, and even dialects. The thing about the South isn't just that it has developed too fast. Surely if you look at Shenzhen or Dongguan, those are the places really hit by the brunt of economic growth. Obviously, everything did develop very quickly. But I think the key issue is that it develops *too spread out*."

"Certainly it's a crowded province down here."

"This is the South China conundrum, the angst and blues of it all. We have Hong Kong, with as specific a style as anywhere, and those border towns that I mentioned. There's a similarly weird relationship with Zhuhai and Macau too, and Foshan, Zhongshan, Huizhou and just everywhere. One day it all even might turn into the biggest city in the world."

"That future megacity plan, right? All these places will link together someday?"

"We'll see if that ever happens. But yes, this is it. 'Megacity'," I repeat.

"I don't know if that's a good term for the fuckin' place," says one of my listeners.

"Does it include Shantou?" asks another. "You know, that's also in Guangdong Province and the fourth-biggest city, but not within the megacity territory."

"Shantou's boring. Let's at least limit our being overwhelmed to the immediate area. Just around here. Do you know the megalopolis of the Northeast American Seaboard? I think it has forty or fifty million people from Boston to New York to Philly to Washington, D.C. That used to be the peak of the civilized world. But now, do you know how many people live on the Pearl River Delta?"

"Not off the top of my head, but I assume you are about to enlighten us."

"Somewhere in the region of one hundred and twenty million," I say. "With so many people living in endless sprawl in every direction, it's akin to cyberpunk dystopianism, if you want to get literary about it. The Gibson-esque Sprawl exists, and it's here. We're sitting in a postmodern *Cantonland*. Culture and identity can't keep up, and everything gets spread thinner and thinner. Tens of millions of migrant workers enter the area every day, and hundreds of thousands of us aliens from overseas mix in too. Maybe this is what the future of globalism looks like. It's prosperous to be sure, but not very romantic."

I pause and take a big swallow of my drink. "Anyways, I don't even know where I'm going with this fucking thing. The whole damn place is just too damn much to even sketch some mental picture of what it all means."

And that's it. That's my theory for the night. It's not exactly clearly defined, but I like to think that at least some of my theories are a touch more poetic and subtle than most.

Then Jonas and I look trade glances, each reading the other's mind. Writers both, we know that with beers in our hands, we can come up with almost anything. But if only we could express as much in long-form at a computer keyboard, deep and well-organized, yet in ditties longer than a mere 800 words.

"What I hate," says our American Southerner, who grapples with other big issues, "is how when girls be on the rag, they can't drink anything cold at night. I'm like, 'Have a cold one with me, dear'. But she's like, 'No'. What the shit is with that? Or at other times, it's no spicy food, that yin-yang claptrap. Why do they believe all that? I mean, *Jesus.*"

"There is no 'why'. *Mei banfa.*"

"Listen to me," he says. "All complaining about the missus. You can guess what brought me out here tonight, am I right?"

We say nothing.

* * *

By recent events, I drink, I talk, and I don't work much.

As it happens, I decided to take a vacation, a sabbatical if you will. In the end, I was paid well for minimal work on the travel-writing app gig. No magazine articles interested me, and Jonas has decided to put me up on a pedestal above the usual restaurant reviewers. He says that I came through, showed tact and professionalism, and that I'm truly the most functional alcoholic of any writer he knows. So, I'm on a retainer until the company does an app for another city.

Jonas explains that if the number of subscribers grows and creates a big revenue stream from downloads, then my next app-writing project will likely be for Hong Kong. He says to wait a few weeks and see.

Although Hong Kong's a bit obvious, and plenty already has been written, it's required for the region. After that, the more untapped tourism markets could take me as far as to Inner Mongolia, in which case the company will pay for my flights and all expenses.

It gets even better. On a few occasions, Jonas has dropped hints that if he finds any other writing jobs even more prestigious and higher paying, then I'll be first in line. It seems to me that he's become more than just my mentor and editor. He almost could be my literary agent. It feels positively like New York.

So I've taken the last seven weeks off to "find myself" while embracing my own drunken stupor.

I could have used the money that I'd earned to move into a new apartment or hire a cleaning lady. Instead I've spent it all on booze and pot.

It's been phenomenal. I've never had so much fun.

Just last week, I bought two bottles of *Maotai* and got a hotel room out in University Town in a wretched attempt to pick up coeds. After several rejections at a small pub, I decided to try my luck via a fierce alcoholic stupor. I don't know exactly what happened next, but I blacked out and woke up later to the sound of a policeman yelling at me in an indecipherable language.

By then, I was at the edge of some park next to the dirtiest roadside tributary of the Pearl River ever seen by man. What a mess. Drenched in slime on the muddy street, my face bruised, and no coeds whatsoever.

"Holy shit!" I muttered. Did that policeman just ask for my fuckin' ID?

What to do? In certain situations, no matter how bad things may look, you only can play the foreigner card. Find a way and power through, like the undying cockroach that I am.

So I insisted that I was Taiwanese-American in a long memorized phrase that I've learned, and I demanded a translator. I keep a folded photocopy of my passport picture in my wallet, and it was still there (although I discovered the wallet to be totally devoid of funds). The actual passport remained back at the hotel. Fuck the law that says I'm supposed to carry it with me at all times! Can you imagine how much worse the situation would have been if I'd lost my passport to boot?

Other cops arrived and made a minor scene. A crowd formed. When the police finally gave up because of the language barrier, I somehow scrounged enough *jiao* coins to pay for a random bus that hopefully led back to the hotel. That's the kind of situation when I tightly shut my mouth and blend into the Chinese crowd. It's my special magic trick.

Jonas and all my white friends know that I have this ability, and they don't. Perhaps that's another reason why he has such faith in me, not for my writing flair or professionalism, but for my undercover skills.

In the end, things worked out alright that time in University Town. Just barely, but they always do.

These weeks have taken me on an exhausting journey, but I haven't hit rock bottom quite yet. Even Alcoholics Anonymous says that I won't change my ways until then.

Maybe I could get used to this sort of a writer's lifestyle. It's a bit of a cliché, but what the hell? Every six months get a job and then have as much fun as I want. It's almost like being a celebrity, some kind of an actor or rock star. Work on a film-shoot one month out of the year or produce an album and tour once every three years. In the meantime, party as much as you want. Get it together on time for the next money-making scheme. What could go wrong?

Of course, even if I really want to do this, the next level remains unchanged. I need to write that damn book.

I'm back at Indian Towers. The night's no longer young, and good conversation has descended into drunken nausea, as often happens. By the time that I vomit all over Jonas's brand-new loafers, we've long finished with our Sino-sociology brainstorming.

"Terry Chang," my editor addresses me. "I might have been wrong about letting you relax for all this time. You may be getting lazy. A writer needs to get his dick wet every so often, or else he forgets how to get it up. Already it's been too long so I want you to write about a little art gallery event next week. You know the place. It'll be good for you."

I'm agreeing to the art gallery thing and saving the date on my calendar app so that I won't forget this conversation tomorrow morning. Meanwhile, there's something else that I'm typing onto the handheld touchscreen. In the old days, we used to carry notepads, and I still do when I need to write fast, but for simple note-taking, I use this. It's my digital pad, and there's something I really need to not forget.

No matter how bad the world spins in my brain, I still have enough in me to record this. It's the curse and boon of the digital age. When I want to take my epiphanies with me to keep them for after a hangover and when sobriety kicks in, I can record them. I don't want them to vanish like that sense of a dream that seems so profound upon awakening, but fades within minutes. When the waking life takes over, let me remember this.

Back home, my file titled "Memoirs" may amount to little more than an empty screen, but finally I've decided to give it a proper name, and that's a big first step. There it is, in print, CANTONLAND.

Interlude III: Macau

馬
Steven Lee

It's Tomb-Sweeping Festival, and I'm on holiday. Without work to do, I agree to cross the border into Hong Kong and visit my family. They live in the New Territories, and so we all enjoy a nice meal together with the grandparents. Then I insist that I'm a very busy man and so can't stay the night, although I'm not really busy at all.

That evening, I take a long taxi ride to Central on Hong Kong Island and consider my options for the night. I don't have a change of clothes with me, I broke up with my girlfriend months ago, and I'd just sleep alone if I went home tonight.

Then I see an advertisement for the ferry services to Macau and going there seems like a good idea. I haven't been there for a few years, and it should make a nice novelty for a few hours.

The boat ride takes an hour, and I read a newspaper's entire business section. When we arrive, I leave the newspaper on my ferry seat. If other passengers want to pick it up to read, they're welcome to it. Or a janitor can throw it away. Not my concern.

A short walk takes me right into the casino district. Macau isn't very large, and not much happens beyond the gambling houses. I recall once coming here on a school trip as a boy and walking along the path of old European stones from the Portuguese church to the market. That was during the old colonial days, and a lot has changed. Tonight I have no desire to relive the past.

The streets are lit up by grand hotel-casinos with endless entertainment and extravagant restaurants inside. But outdoors, the city looks strangely empty. The native Macanese live on the outskirts, leaving the downtown surprisingly quiet, almost peaceful. It's difficult to believe that chaotic Guangdong Province lies within walking distance from here. This place resembles another world.

When I enter a luxurious resort building, the bright lights and the sounds of gaming hit me with the same force as the air conditioning. The resort's signs appear in multilingual excess: Japanese, English, Portuguese, Korean, Traditional Chinese and Simplified Chinese, in that order. The place takes four different kinds of currency, and Hong Kong dollars are totally acceptable.

Sitting at a slot machine, I lose a few ten dollar coins. When I win a ten pataca Macau piece, I decide to call it a night on gambling. My shoulders feel stiff. I'm a bit dirty too and could use a shower.

Once I'm back outside, just beyond the doors of the resort, a man in a suit calls out to me in Mandarin from across the street. "Sir!"

When I approach him and say "hello" in Cantonese, he quickly responds in a perfect Chinatown *Taishanese*. "You look so tired from business travel. Would you like a sauna and a massage?"

I nod and follow him down an alleyway between two major hotels to a side door. The sign there welcomes and glows.

The slickly-dressed man hands me a menu, and I read it carefully. A simple massage costs only 500, more than on the mainland to be sure, but this is a high-quality place, I'm already here and I do want to take a shower.

I'm embarrassed about the sexually explicit parts. It's something unique about Macau culture: the open advertising of hand jobs and blow jobs. I make a weak promise to myself to limit any services for me to a massage.

"Very good, sir. Very comfortable," the man says.

Quickly, I look to the left and then to the right to make sure that no one will see me. I do this out of instinct, I suppose. It's not as if I'd know anyone here. Plus the entrances to places like this are along alleyways for a good reason.

"Let's go, mate." From habit, I say the word "mate" in English.

The man leads me inside. We ride up in a lift, reaching a front desk where two girls wait. The doorman passes me off to them, and one girl leads me to a locker room.

Unlike at saunas in other cities, she doesn't pass me off to a male worker. She walks right in, and we stand in front of a locker where she directs me to take off my clothes. I peel off one layer at a time, setting aside my dress shirt, T-shirt, trousers and socks.

My heart races as I remove my underpants. I haven't done this sort of thing for a long time. The girl smiles slightly, but mostly looks quite bored. She folds my clothes, puts them inside a locker, hands me the wrist key, and goes to get me a towel.

Covering myself with the towel, I rush to the facilities where I shower, wash my hair, brush my teeth, and examine myself in a mirror. I'm not a bad-looking guy. My stomach's toned, I have a stylish haircut and my cock's okay. So what am I doing in a place like this? I work in sales, have charisma, and don't need to be here. I can take a girl home any time I want. I do it all the time with girls from all around the world. For me, today just isn't a good day. That's all. I feel slightly lost.

The other customers within sight are overweight, balding men. Asian managers or CEOs who seldom see their families and relieve sexual stress with money. Because money's all that they know. For sure, I'm not that kind of a person. I've lived in Europe, have an artistic side, and know that there's more to life than just earning money and shooting your load.

So I dry off and wrap the towel around my waist. I walk to the swimming area and find a Jacuzzi with two men inside. They're watching a football match on the ceiling flat-screen. Girls in bikinis walk around, offering their services and massaging shoulders. They're tall and beautiful, but their faces betray looks of profound boredom.

Not too many people are here, and the girls outnumber the men. Everything seems so quiet that I hear only the game commentary from sportscasters speaking in a familiar London accent. Traditional Chinese subtitles roll across the bottom of the TV screen.

A very beautiful and very tall girl in a tiny two-piece walks up to me. I look at her long thin arms, smooth belly, and small breasts. When she notices that I'm staring at her, she takes my hand, saying nothing. I think that she's silently waiting to hear what language that I speak. I'm naked under my towel and feel damn horny.

"Oil massage," I say in Cantonese.

"*Hou, hou.*"

She takes me down a hall to a dimly lit private room. It has red-flower wallpaper. The massage table looks more like a bed. There's a flat-screen HD television with the latest cable box. When she asks, I say that I don't care what's on so the girl channel-surfs, finding a suitable Mandarin drama. I listen to it in the background.

Slowly, the girl removes my towel and hangs it on the door. She tells me to stretch out face-down on the table, takes oils from a shelf, and begins rubbing me.

She's good. The kinks in my neck flatten. My collarbone feels pushed back into place. She does a bit with her elbow on my back and then squeezes my arms and thighs, right and left, until they feel like melted ice cream. Soon I'm almost putty, softly easing into the earth.

Then she goes for the space between my legs. She does this deliberately and raises my hips. I don't feel soft anymore. She circles the area and…

A seasoned professional, the girl knows exactly how to touch me just delicately enough. She seduces me in this way, slowly. I feel her fingernails and a light brush against my scrotum. She raises my waist higher and higher, until there's more room to touch, and sensitively nudges the base of penis. She raises me even higher and then asks me turn over.

I'm on my back. With no more pretenses, she unties the string behind her neck, and the bikini-top falls. It's tossed aside. In the dim light, her budding chest looks like it could have been painted. She's not big, but her skin looks so smooth, and her breasts form perfect half-circles with pointed nipples precisely in the middles.

As she uses her hands, it's no longer any massage. She simply squeezes my cock with her left hand and cups my balls with her right. She speaks quietly in Mandarin: "*Xiao didi*," meaning "little brother".

Under the circumstances, I'm unsure exactly what to do. Should I grab her ass? Her breasts? Jump up and fully have my way with her? What would that cost?

I'm about to explode. She's topless, I rest a hand on her nearest thigh and she slows to a still. The pulsations from her hand get briefer until she stops. I suppose that she wants me to make the next move.

"*Yao bu yao? Yiu m yiu?*"

"What?"

Suddenly she lets go, takes my hand and puts it to her crotch. I feel pubic hairs below the fabric of her bikini bottom. It's all that I can do to decline. I pull my hand away and shake my head. "No sex. I don't do that."

She nods, and I assume that she interprets my rejection to mean a preference for just hand service. She resumes the previous position and starts pumping me, her small breasts jiggling and her slender fingers tight. Not objecting, I close my eyes and let it come. "*Ahhh.*" It comes fast.

In the immediate aftermath, I feel fucking terrible. This is pathetic. This isn't me. I feel like shit, lowly, not a proper man.

She cleans me up, and I'm ticklish. I close my eyes. She brings a blanket. I feel tired. The light goes off. We're finished here. She waves goodbye, and I decide to take a nap.

When I wake up, I wonder about the time. Did I sleep the whole night here? They let you do that in these places.

I wrap the towel around myself and walk back to the lockers. Absolutely no one's here. Quickly, I shower away the oil, using copious amounts of shampoo on my body. Then I use the wristband key to retrieve my clothes.

My cell phone reveals that it's 8 a.m. I dress, go out and pay money to a lone hostess at the front desk. She looks tired and sad. With the gratuity and other fees, my total well exceeds a thousand. Not even arguing, I use my credit card.

Outside, the morning sunlight momentarily blinds me. Staring at the casino-resort across the street, I mull over how much money that I might win if I stayed longer. I could eat breakfast at a buffet and then, at this time of day, have a whole casino floor to myself. Or I could take the next ferry away and quickly forget about this holiday.

I should decide soon. I lean towards going. It may be about time to abandon all thoughts of this cold and empty place. But I'm not quite sure where to go…

豬
Casting Call

Already I've spent three hours in this waiting room. I had to call in sick just to be here today. I'm surrounded by Russian models, all of them a head taller than me and with clearer skin, thin arms and legs, plus nose jobs. But they have accents, bad attitudes and frowns on their faces while I struggle to maintain a smile.

"Next," says the casting director.

The girl lined up in front of me enters the studio. I don't know exactly what she does in there.

We all carry folders with our photo albums. Some of the photos form portfolios organized by professional photographers for a fee, and some are just pages ripped from magazines. I've heard that pages ripped from magazines may be better. They show real experience.

So far, I've appeared in no magazines. My face graces no Guangzhou billboards. When I started chasing this kind of work, I took a photo of myself and emailed it to an agent whom I found online. The agent got back to me, saying that higher-paying jobs require a portfolio.

Therefore, I made an appointment and posed in front of fake painted backgrounds. It was fun. The place had a makeup artist, a hair stylist and lots of outfits, like wedding dresses, Shakespearean-period pieces, and even those sexy Shanghai 1920s *qipao*-style dresses. I felt like a movie star.

I paid for it myself. Gotta spend money to make money!

This month I've gone to an audition every week. All the modeling agents choose the Russian girls over me. I hope that this time it's a speaking role and my English helps.

I thought this was supposed to be easy. People told me that Guangzhou advertisers like foreigners to make the companies look more international and that they need women most of all. Supposedly, I could show up and just make money. I don't know why it's been so hard.

Maybe it's easier in small towns with less competition. This city's too big. Maybe the industry's drying up in the bad economy and so there's less work. Or maybe it's just me. I haven't figured it out yet.

Eric does work like this sometimes. I'll bet that it's easier for him, for men. They aren't judged in the same way I am. It's not fair.

Wanting to be independent, I refuse to ask Eric for help.

The auditions average forty minutes per girl, and I'm so fucking bored. I didn't realize that being an aspiring model/actress was so *dull*.

And depressing as well! It seems I'm thinking too much, and I revert to playing a game on my phone.

"Next."

Finally! I hop up, paste a big smile on my face, and enter.

The photo studio is large with a desk in one corner, a green screen, big lights, tripods, and crew members smoking cigarettes. As carefully as possible, I walk toward the guy at the desk. I sway my hips, stick out my ass, and balance on my high heels.

"Hello," I say and hand him my folder.

He's young. A camera dangles around his neck. He glances at my photos and throws them onto a pile.

"Okay, let's take picture," he says.

"I want to share that I'm from Canada and speak English with a perfect North American accent. I can bring a level of professionalism to acting and speaking roles that I consider unique."

"Okay, okay! I know you speak fine."

"Um, do you have makeup and costumes? Should I prepare anything? What's the motivation for this shoot?"

"No, nothing, we just take picture."

Doing my best, I accept direction and hold up plain brown cardboard boxes, doing it as sexily as possible, stretching my body in every conceivable way. I have no idea what the product supposedly is. It's all still-photography. There's no video and no speaking. And it's so slow. The guy takes pictures for about five minute. Then the lighting crew adjusts equipment for about ten minutes. We repeat the process a few times. I feel sorry for the girl waiting to go after me.

Finally, I hear this. "I get back to you next week."

"Thank you so very much for this opportunity."

Then I rush home, eat ice cream, and watch old episodes of *Sex and the City*. I can't believe today. I'm working so hard and without results. Sure, I want a shoulder to cry on, but I can't let anyone know how hard this is for me. Not Eric, not my brother or mom, and not my friends or co-workers. I'd thought that I could put myself out there and burst onto the scene fully formed. I didn't realize how hard it would be.

Look at all the actors on TV. Was it as hard for them? I'd always thought that anyone could do it. Now I kind of respect the celebrities more. It's unbelievable, right? I don't know. Maybe it's all just luck. But that thought makes me feel even worse.

Today was only one kind of job. I still have a voice-recording interview next week, and what I really want to do is English editing and proofreading.

God, tomorrow I return to the kindergarten. I dread that. If only any other job in the world would come to me pronto.

* * *

It's a normal day at my real job. We begin with breakfast: porridge and apple slices. My classroom contains twenty little munchkins, the world's cutest rich kids. After eating, they sing Chinese songs, and I get to take a break. Then it's 10 a.m. That's one of the English times and my turn for songs.

"ALLIGATOR JOE, everyone!"

That's a new one that the school assigned to me based on a textbook. Sometimes I do my own research, download something from The Wiggles or *Sesame Street*, and the school lets me design a curriculum. We have a pretty relaxed atmosphere at the Garfield Estates Kindergarten. I can do what I'm told or make up something more interesting.

We play musical chairs, duck-duck-goose, and a racing game with Team A versus Team B, all of which I learned from my online TEFL course so many years ago.

Then it's time for lunch. The school would give me a free meal, but it's not very good so I always prefer to go home. I live just a few blocks away. After ordering in some fried rice, I check my email and take a short nap.

After awakening, I gulp down coffee and rush out again. It's always like that at 2 p.m. I'm almost late constantly.

Back in the classroom, my students are finishing on basic math. That's in Chinese. Only when we're on an English-numbers lesson do the subjects overlap. As it happens, this week I'm teaching about animals.

Our arts-and-crafts session begins. I'm always nervous about this because we don't use safety scissors here. On our current theme, the children cut out rabbit and cat shapes.

My assistant's still angry that I cancelled yesterday. She's on one side of the room with half of the students. I'm in my own corner with the other half, sitting on the floor and arranging different-colored construction papers.

"Who can try to make a blue dog?" I ask.

"Lemme try!" the little ones cheer. It's really the cutest thing.

"Teacher Amber, look me, look me! Yellow giraffe!"

I want to leave this job desperately, yet I know that I'll miss it. These kids, they're so familiar to me. Nothing could be cuter than Chinese kindergartners.

It can be hard to keep track of them. This kid runs here, and that one runs there. I keep counting heads to make sure that all ten stay in my group. They all have English names, and I even named many of them. But they're too small to go by their English names, and I never can remember Chinese. So I've given them little nicknames, for my use only, to organize them in my mind.

Big Ears is a naughty one who always hits girls and steals crayons. Sparkly Dress is the cutest, very well-behaved and her parents dress her so nicely. Tall One's awkward and shy. Short One is best friends with Crybaby, and Pigtails excels at drawing. Fatty always sneaks candy and dislikes sharing. Daydream stares out the windows and keeps to himself. Lead Guy acts like a natural leader and the other kids follow him. But my favorite is Nosepick. Although sometimes a little gross with the nose-picking, she's very smart, and I hold high hopes for her.

Little by little, I've watched these children grow and improve in language. They learn so fast, and regardless of the stress, teaching still can be a rewarding job. I'm glad for the experience, and if I ever decide to have children of my own, I'll have the necessary skills to do a good job. Yet this work just isn't for me anymore. I need to go. For a while, I'll miss the students. Then I'll be okay. It's just time to move on with my life. I'm selfish and want something else.

After all the cutting, we paste the pictures onto a wall, clean up and it's time to sign out for the day. I go home, take another nap, and then make a salad. Too tired for the gym, I stay in and binge-watch some TV.

Before going to bed, I take a shower and shave my legs. And that's it, that's my day.

* * *

For the first time in years, I'm working somewhere that isn't a school.

An agency finally called me back. It's a Saturday morning and way too early.

After a dozen of us meet in downtown Haizhu District, we ride on a bus out to the middle of nowhere. We arrive at a former airplane factory or something converted into a studio. Inside a hangar, we find an enormous airplane cut out in the middle. It's torn apart and surrounded by lights, but inside it's the roomiest plane I've ever seen.

We're all supposed to be passengers. Tall Chinese girls in red uniforms play stewardesses. That's what the commercial involves. The Chinese girls know how to act, and we foreigners are the extras. We sit down, toy with our phones for a few hours, and get paid for it.

The director speaks Chinese, the primary cast is Chinese, and this turns into the most incredibly boring day of my life. The tall girls walk along the aisle, giving us napkins and speaking. Then they restart and do it again. We shoot from a dozen different angles, each time with the lighting equipment set up differently.

At noon, there's a free lunch. Taking a break then, we get to know each other. Some of the other extras are English teachers too, and some have done this kind of thing for years. A few even rely on it as their main jobs.

We chat, relax, and complain. Then we sit down again in the airplane seats and chat some more.

The guy next to me claims to be a full-time actor, but he's not that good-looking and earns the same pay as a novice like me. "I used to live in L.A.," he says.

"I'm from Canada."

"Cool, I love British Columbia."

"I'm not from there."

"So," he continues, "I used to do non-union background work in L.A. too."

"Sorry?" I ask.

"As in being an extra, you know. The business there's all about being in SAG, in the union. So if you're not, they call in nonunion."

"Oh, I see."

"I'm just saying. Although I used to be in the acting business there, I didn't exactly make it in the big time. But I did work as an extra on lots of big-budget sets and meet plenty of celebs. I know what you're thinking. Amazing, right?"

I just smile and nod.

"But let me tell you what," he continues. "It's not really much different from here in GZ."

"Really? I find that hard to believe."

"Ha! The biggest difference between L.A. and GZ is the food." He chuckles, and I don't say anything. Guys of a certain variety always love to compare cities.

"The catering services in L.A., truly things of beauty. They're like the best part of the business in Hollywood. You have to go there someday."

Belatedly, he introduces himself, and we shake hands. Talking's the only way for us to pass much of the time. Despite having little to say, I still listen.

"For me, L.A. provided perfect preparation to live in GZ." He keeps saying the letters "GZ".

"For years, I struggled as a starving artist in L.A.," he adds. "Nothing that you do there's based on merit. It's all networking, like *guanxi* here, but even worse. It's like training on a handicap. You push yourself, finally come to a place like China, and really get rewarded. After a minimal payoff in Cali, I bring the same skill-set to GZ, and already I'm shooting commercials."

"How long have you been here?" I ask.

He continues without answering. "I constantly go to business dinners with executives. I know all the agents. My phone's full of numbers I can't even recognize. It's too easy. Am I right, or am I right?"

"It's okay here."

"I'm not gonna lie. The advantage in GZ over L.A. is that we're white. So now I get more money and maybe less serious roles, but man o' man, this white face sure gets me through the doorways."

He pauses, waiting for me to say something. But I don't know how to respond. I'm barely qualified to listen on this subject, let alone to talk. "Sure, I guess. It's okay."

"Of course, everybody totally agrees," he says after my modest reply. "It's awesome."

He doesn't listen to me much. Instead he just waits for a response and then says whatever he planned to say. Like a TV actor pausing for applause and canned laughter. (Hey, I've done my research.) Maybe he really has acted for years.

"Well," I say, "it's alright."

"White, white, white," he repeats, stressing the benefits of his skin color. By now, I'm no longer even responding. At least he's not one of the chronic complainers, but when he diverts to discuss Chinese girls, I decide that we've reached a point when I need to tune him out.

This fellow really starts to make me uncomfortable. Not just with his obnoxiousness (he's quite a normal expat with that), but it's the white thing.

Part of me feels guilty for even being on this TV-commercial set, like I'm cheating. I feel the same thing about earning 10 times what my teaching assistants do. It's the same when I see street-cleaners or beggars. And I feel it the most of all when I meet losers like this guy who have so much fun in China. Why do we get to enjoy these middle-class lives just for being born in English-speaking countries?

I almost wish that I was more like some of the white guys, the ones who come here with no skills, become actors, fuck Chinese girls and don't think much about it.

I don't know. These days I have a lot on my mind, and I'm too stressed out, so maybe I shouldn't think too much.

My seating partner talks more about Hollywood. Now he critiques American girls.

I'm just smiling, listening and thinking about how I'll spend the 1,000 that I earn today. I want to get a facial at the Garfield Estates spa and buy new shoes, plus I can't forget to go to the pharmacy to take care of that thing.

After ten hours (a *fast day*, I'm assured), we wait in line as the agency manager hands out envelopes of cash, one for everyone, each holding ten pink banknotes.

"Hey, Amber," says the ex-Hollywood guy, standing behind me, tapping me on a shoulder. "We're going to keep in touch. Westerners gotta help each other out. Hey, I know a great restaurant in Haizhu. We can celebrate breaking into the business, you know?"

Although his line's smooth and confident, I see it coming from miles away. I can't blame the guy, and it's always flattering, but… "I'm sorry. That's probably not a good idea."

He takes out his cell phone. "Let's swap digits."

"I'm not going to do that."

"Huh?"

"It was nice meeting you."

That's that, and our ride back downtown passes quietly. We're all worn out. After waving goodbye to everyone, I take the metro back to the suburbs and transfer to a cab to reach my place.

Wearily, I just want to rush inside and collapse onto my bed. I'll go to the spa tomorrow. But now I have one more thing left to do, and I've avoided thinking much about it all day.

Detouring to a pharmacy, I buy a pregnancy test. For the last few days, I've meant to buy it. My period's more than a week late.

Last month I slept with a British guy, and I don't even know why I did it. He was so full of himself, a big, drunk asshole watching football at a bar. But I really needed it, and from the way he talked, I thought that he'd be a good lay at least. Not at all! Even my ex-boyfriend was better than that.

The Brit talked a good game and showed me off to his friends. When we arrived at his apartment and were alone together, he got nervous. He rushed, fumbled, immediately came inside of me, and then passed out abruptly. I can't believe that I didn't make him use a condom.

At school, I logged on to Google Translate and very secretively printed out the Chinese for "pregnancy test". I folded the paper and kept it in my pocket.

Now at the pharmacy, I show that paper to a girl working there. Her eyes light up and she claps, congratulating me. Fucking Chinese pharmacists!

I buy the piss test. In preparation, I also buy a bottle of water. Then I rush home and make sure to drink the bottle's entire contents.

Everything printed on the pregnancy-test package appears in Chinese characters that I don't read, but I've done this before and know all about it. It's a matter of plus-signs or minus-signs. What's that hormone called? I just read about it recently. Oh yeah, human chorionic gonadotropin.

My best friend back in college used to joke about this with me. She used to say that these tests were so much fun, like video games for girls. I giggle to myself at the memory.

Squatting over the toilet, I take aim. Then I put the test into the sink and just wait for results.

I should go online and check my email to see if I got that editing job. And I should email my friends to tell them about my new acting job. I should read the news. Check my phone. WeWa updates. See what's up in the world. I should wash my hands, get out of the bathroom and do something productive.

But I can't move. I just wait. That's the worst thing at times like this, and it's all I can do.

What timing! Just as my so-called "new career" looked ready to begin. What'll happen to me now? Maybe I could get it "taken care of" or move back to Manitoba and work at Walmart. I could find that British guy again. Perhaps I could give it away. I could raise a family. In fact, I guess that I could even tie it up in a plastic bag to drop into the Pearl River.

Meanwhile, I just wait.

龍
He Never Mentioned My Hair

My new apartment is nothing but a big, empty living room filled with brown cardboard boxes. They're *everywhere*. All my stuff's scattered across the floor. Some boxes are taped shut, still unopened. Some have turned into makeshift cupboards, full of dishes and art supplies. Some lie on their sides with clothes and shoes spilling out onto the floor.

One box, next to the door, holds extra importance. I ordered the contents online, and it arrived today. It's full of hair dye, a special color.

When starting a new chapter in life, it helps to change hairstyles. I always do this. Life's a cycle. Besides, my roots have grown in since the last time.

I open the box, remove the dye, and toss the empty box into a corner with others. Going into the bathroom, I sort out the tubes and start to prepare. I've done this so many times. I love it.

Living by myself now, I can walk around topless whenever I want. I'm totally used to that from work anyway, so I take off my shirt and bra to make sure that I won't stain anything.

The new apartment's too big. I walk all the way across the living room, zigzagging past boxes, to throw my surplus clothes into a hamper by the washing machine. Returning to the middle of the room, I play some music from my computer on the floor. Only then do I walk back to the bathroom to begin.

When I take out my contacts, the world turns a little fuzzy. I squint to read the directions, mixing peroxide, ammonia, other chemicals, and finally the bright purple dye. The smell's strong, but I'm used to it. So I pull on the plastic gloves and stand in front of the mirror. I can make out which hair strands I want to dye. Very carefully, I rub in the dye, up and down, and then wrap the line of hair in plastic to protect the rest. I do this four more times. I don't want my whole head to be purple, just certain kinda highlights, like a plum-colored zebra.

With twenty minutes to wait, I post a microblog about my new hairstyle. Time goes fast when I'm surfing online. I check my QQ, and someone video-calls me. I almost answer before remembering that I'm topless! That could have been hilariously embarrassing.

Ignoring the call, I take off my underwear, step into the shower, and wash my hair using special conditioner that came with the dye. I blow dry. While I'm at it, I carefully shave away my scratchy pubic hair. Then I apply some facial cleanser to moisturize and keep the skin looking smooth. Put some on my ass as well. An old model's trick!

With my hair dry, I peer into the bathroom mirror and see how it looks.

"You're so sexy," I whisper.

I'd never, ever pay hairdressers for this. Truly, it's like another kind of painting, part of what I do. Looking at myself, I'm like a work of art.

* * *

Today I have a date. I can't wait to learn what he thinks of my new hairstyle.

After sleeping late, I finally roll out of bed at about noon. I spend most of the afternoon slowly unloading boxes and putting together my bookcases for various art volumes. I also need to turn the bedroom into a studio, but I haven't gotten around to building the desk yet.

Earlier I drank coffee. After dinner, I make more because I want to stay up late tonight.

Sweaty from wrestling with the boxes, I take a shower and again apply the special conditioner to my hair, and between my legs. The purple streaks are bright, like grapes in the sunshine, and the color drips down my body onto the white floor. It's like dark grape-wine spilling everywhere.

As evening arrives, I lay out my best outfits on the sofa. I want to wear something that matches my hair. It should be casual, but I don't want to wear jeans. I put on a skirt over black tights, plus a shirt and my boots with the fuzzy accessories.

That's about it. I put in my contacts, apply deodorant, floss and brush my teeth, gargle, and spray perfume onto my wrists. Finally, I pop a stick of gum into my mouth and rush out the door.

The shopping mall's big. We planned to meet at a coffee shop on the first floor. I'm a little late and looking around. While hoping I'm not too late, I really hope that he's not even later, putting me here first. Then I see him, sitting in the corner with an empty cup and reading a magazine. He looks bored, lost, and alone in his world.

I jump up alongside to surprise him. "Hi, Terry!"

Glancing up, he smiles. Then he stands and takes my hand. At first he appears unsure what to do with it, but then gently shakes my hand while I stand there.

"Ting Ting," he says. "It's so nice to see you."

"For me too," I say and sit across from him. He looks nervous, not like at the gallery when he came to my rescue.

"I have a surprise for you." He hands me the magazine.

"Oh? Thank you."

"Wait. Let me turn it to the right page." He leans over and flips through it to a page that immediately looks familiar. "Look."

"Wow!" I say, truly surprised and gripping the magazine. "This comes from my exhibition."

I see a two-page spread in a popular design style with lots of little boxes showing art pieces, all from the Green Square Gallery. I see the sculptures, the video piece, and my own reverse-life paintings. Three pictures of my works appear right in the middle of the page. I browse through the text, but it's not in my native language so it's hard to find my name quickly.

"It's a good review," Terry says.

"I can't believe it. Thank you."

"You're the famous artist. Thanks for giving me an interview."

"How did you publish it so fast? The exhibition opened only a week ago."

"Oh, we always work at the last-minute. I finished writing the story on Monday, and it's hot off the press."

"Wow! I can keep this?"

"It's free, and sure. That's yours."

Now I can't wait to frame this article and hang it on a wall in my new studio-bedroom. I want to tell my parents about it. All my old friends should know too. It'll be a source of inspiration to me, a new muse!

"Hey, did you take the pictures?" I ask.

"No, we had a proper photographer there too. That part isn't my job."

"Oh," I say, slightly disappointed. I'd wanted to ask about getting a job as a photographer, but I'm hungry so instead I say, "Let's eat!"

Carefully I place the expatriate magazine in my purse. Then Terry leads me upstairs to the top floor and a nice Thai restaurant where the mood's soft and romantic. We're surrounded by statues of Buddha and elephants. We talk about traveling. Terry has been to Thailand, but I haven't. He says it's the world's best country for street food. I like the Thai noodles.

We talk more about travel and about Beijing, agreeing that it's a better city than here. When I ask Terry why he came to the south, he says that he was raised in California and so hates the cold. I laugh.

Later we ascend in an elevator to the cinema. Terry already has two tickets to a movie. I sit beside him, and although it's old-fashioned behavior, I squeeze his hand and lean my head on his shoulder. I barely even remember what happens in the movie. I don't watch many movies, but Terry can talk about them all day.

After the show we go to Golf Ball Club nearby. It's quiet, and we have the whole place almost to ourselves. Terry drinks many beers and talks on and on about the movie's director, its under-appreciated screenwriter, and the novel it was based on, covering all the differences, the similarities, and the process of adaptation. I just listen.

Terry asks for my artistic opinion about the cinematography. I tell him that I love photography, but consider most films dull and predictable when it comes to that. He mentions some independent directors that I must see, including Wong Kar-wai, whom I know, of course, but I play along like I don't.

"You should take me to your home, and we can watch together," I say. "That should be more comfortable than the cinema."

He turns quiet, and his eyes shift.

"What's your home like?" I ask. "Any roommates?"

"No," he says.

"I also have no roommates. I did have one, and that sucked. No privacy. I moved out recently, and it's nice to live alone."

"That's cool," he says.

"And for artists like us, we need our solitude to work."

"I know."

"And..." I continue, flirtatiously drawing circles on his arm, "you can invite anyone over. Nobody knows."

I wait for him to invite me, but he says nothing. "So where shall we go next?" I ask.

"Well, I'm not sure, but if you have any ideas, please just say."

"My place," I say, and his eyes light up, "is kind of messy because I just moved."

"I'm sure it's fine," he declares right away. "I'm totally a bachelor, and there's no way that I could regard your home as a mess." Then he nervously laughs.

I wonder what could be so bad at his place, but I try not to dwell on it because the night's going so fabulously. "Well," I say. "I know it's late, but I guess that you can come to my new apartment and help me to unpack."

Then his eyes really light up!

During the taxi ride, I sit close to him, put my head on his shoulder again, and he kisses me. He's so much more confident after a few drinks.

Foreign guys always like making out in taxis. I'm kind of embarrassed because the driver keeps looking back in his rearview mirror. Terry doesn't even consider that. He grabs my thigh, and I feel I could melt. He's definitely more American than Chinese.

I'm aroused and in my own world. Then the taxi driver announces that we've arrived, and I must snap back to reality. "Oh," I say.

Terry pays for the taxi, and we quickly go upstairs. It's a dark journey until I open the door and turn on a light.

"This is the place," I say.

"It's not that bad at all."

"Here, come look at my sketches."

We travel through a maze of boxes to a coffee table in the middle of the room, and I hand him a sketchbook. I usually leave it nearby on the sofa, conveniently placed for any random bursts of inspiration.

Terry flips through. "Quite good," he says.

"You saw just one style of my paintings. I want to show you some of my other pictures."

"Wow," he says, his eyes widening. "You do a lot of nudes."

"That's a part of art."

"Where do you get the models?"

I don't tell him about my part-time job or my colleagues there. "Why do you ask? Do you want to apply for the job?"

"Ting Ting," he says playfully. "Are you asking me to take off my clothes and model for you?"

"Ha! Why not?"

"Like the opposite of what happened in the movie, *Titanic*. Okay, one day…"

He flips through to see more of my sketches. We stop teasing each other, and he's too quiet.

"Come see some paintings," I say. "I have images on my computer."

We sit on the sofa, and I show him some of the pictures. From my early art-school years, they're simple, but I feel proud. It can be fun to share and talk about my past, but the night has cooled us off, and I need something to fire us up again.

"I have a bottle of wine in a box here somewhere," I say. "Want to open it?"

"Do I?" he says excitedly.

I find the bottle, and we drink from plastic cups. Terry quickly empties his cup three times. When I get up to tidy the table a bit, he stands as well and winds an arm around me.

"When will you paint me?" he asks with his face near mine, the smell of wine heavy on his breath.

"Um, for now I'll just use my imagination."

"You're so talented," he says and kisses me again. He's taller than me and leans down to kiss.

I step back, and we hit a wall. Distracted, I drop the plastic cups, and they fall to the floor.

Then I grip him tightly, pulling his waist into me. I feel his crotch throbbing and stiffening against my stomach.

Pausing for breath, I suggest, "Let's go to the bedroom."

He squeezes my wrists and drags me into the hall. "Wait, which way to your bedroom?" he asks. "I'm a little drunk."

"You're so silly. My place must be too big. Let me lead the way."

We go into the bedroom. I undo his belt buckle. He takes off my shirt and struggles to unclip my bra. Soon we're lying on our sides, making out in our underwear. His chest is smooth and wet. He slides a hand up and down my back. That feels so good, and I want more. He takes my hand and places it against his underwear, on the crotch, and I play with the tip, squeeze, and go lower until I feel balls. I creep with my hand under the cloth, touch flesh and hear him shudder. Then I slide the underwear down to his ankles, and he tosses it aside. He plays with my ass, and I take off my panties. We're both breathing very heavily. I feel sweat and can taste salt from the edge of his lips.

"Do you have the, um, you know?"

"Yeah," he says. The mood's broken, but he gets up, goes to his pants on the floor and takes a condom out of his wallet. He rips open the packaging with his teeth. As he stands, his cock sticks straight out.

"Come here," I say. He lies back down, and his head almost hits me in the stomach so I laugh. "Let me help you. I love to do that."

Carefully I look at each side of the condom to see which way it unrolls. I squeeze his cock with my bare palm and rub it up and down to make sure that it stays hard. Then I slowly place the condom down. He moans loudly. For a second or two, I scratch at his balls.

Then while he's still sprawled on his back, I climb on top. I maneuver and ease down so that he enters me.

Now I hop up and down with the momentum of bedsprings. I shriek, and the feeling's great. Taking his hands, I put them on my breasts, and it feels even better. I scream loudly and don't care who hears.

Terry's very good at this. It's interesting to have sex with an ABC guy. He's aggressive like an American, but doesn't look the part. He's not very big, but his hands are so strong and they pinch me tightly. Although I'm the one on top, I feel so much power surge from his hips.

He turns me around and jumps on top while biting at my neck and squeezing my ass. I lose it, and the orgasm comes.

"AHHHHHHH!" I tend to scream.

Terry's orgasm soon follows. "*Ahh*," he moans softly.

We toss aside the wet condom. Tomorrow I'll clean up the place a little, I think. If we become a couple, I should probably go on birth-control pills.

The blanket covers us. We turn off the light. Wrapping my arms around a warm body, I close my eyes. We fall asleep, exhausted. As I drift into happy dreams, I think about how much I want to paint this feeling, to record it and share it with the world. This wasn't a bad night.

Suddenly I realize something. We spent the whole evening together, and he never once mentioned my hair.

猴
Officialdom

"Dude, the girls there are so hot."

"But how much that gonna set ya back?"

"Check it out. If you go there, like, in the middle of the night, you can bargain it down to only two hundred. Full service, dude."

"They do oral?"

"Hell, yeah, they do!"

"That's awesome."

I'm on a bus, crowded and lurching like a genocidal train ride. Plastic bags tightened around my fingertips cut off my blood flow almost to the point of numbness and may induce amputation. I needed to go to a supermarket across town to buy cheese and cleaning supplies. Usually I like to listen to music on these long bus rides, but this time I noticed the two overweight Western men. Curiosity got the better of me, and I just had to listen in.

"Here's what you do, bro. Go to the club late at night, at closing time. They have one of those pink-light joints behind the building. Go in and bring just a hundred or two. You can totally get away with oral and full service. They got the hottest bitches."

"Oh, I'm on it. Love the monger scene here."

I'm intrigued and disgusted at the same time, not only by how openly that they discuss prostitutes and brothels, but also by their attitudes. What pride they take in underpaying, what miserly degenerates they are and how fucking *fascinating*.

The guys keep it up, laughing and trading high-fives. They sneer like juvenile caricatures of '90s MTV cartoon characters. As far as I can tell, the surrounding Chinese people on this bus ride have no idea what the two Westerners are saying.

"The bitches love it too, dude. They love a big white dick. All day long, they deal with little Asian-chink dicks, and as soon as you walk in, they're totally into it. The hookers act like they're bored and shit, always looking at the clock. But you know that deep down they love it."

"You said 'deep down.'"

The talk about penis size especially disturbs me. I've certainly met many obnoxious folks from all around the world in my years, yet this reaches a new level. No offense to my home country, but I would absolutely guarantee that these guys are Americans. I don't know if they're tourists passing through or workers settling down and taking root as they partake of the local businesses, but either way I feel a sense of shame about the country that issued my passport.

It's not just how undeniably crass their conversation is. I've been around and heard about worse things done by many nationalities, including Chinese. What turns me off so much is how they talk so obnoxiously within a crowd and yet act like they're having a private conversation. I may not know how many others might be listening in like me, but there very well may be a few English students on this bus. These Westerners don't consider that at all. How can they speak in such a way with impunity and arrogant confidence? Perhaps they visit foreign countries all the time, like global sex tourists, and constantly insult the natives while living in a bubble of superiority and obliviousness... And soon I can't fucking stand it anymore.

Here's my stop. Before I step down from the bus, I must say something.

"Hey, fuckers, you should know that I'm getting laid tonight and not even paying for it. Just sharing! I hope that you'll get your money's worth and catch something really contagious."

Sudden flashes of comprehension glimmer in their eyes. They look around, surprised to realize that they're surrounded by real human beings, some of them even able to talk.

The two men say nothing back to me, but only tilt their heads, looking at the floor like naughty children caught stealing sweets.

I step off the bus, and it drives away. Watching the vehicle depart, I feel great. This may be the most fantastic feeling that I've ever experienced while sober.

After entering my apartment, I hop over the strewn newspapers, magazine back-issues and empty bottles, put my cheese in the refrigerator and then plop down on the bed while still wearing my shoes. I open my laptop, just where I left it, and immediately start writing about the bus-ride incident in the file titled CANTONLAND. Already I have 20,000 words there. By the end of the year, my memoirs should be finished.

Before I know it, I've written 900 words about the bus incident. I still need to brainstorm about some chapter titles. FAT AMERICAN PIGS comes to mind. I'll decide on that later.

While I'm at it, I go through some drafts of my features for *Pearl Delta Expat*. I have a puff-piece interview with an acquaintance, a guy who runs a trading company, because the magazine needs something business-related, and one of the usual short reviews of coffee shops and dim sum. I reread them, tidy up a few sentences, and correct two typos which eluded me the first time. I'll rewrite the stories one more time tomorrow and then email the drafts to Jonas. I'm still a week early on the deadline.

What has triggered all this productivity? I can't be sure, but it just might be that feeling of having a girl to impress. In the past, getting laid tended to leave me lazy, and long-term relationships caused irritability. But at this time in my life, I can't think of anyone I respect more than her, a productive artist in her own right, and I just want to match her pace.

I've had a good day. But something's missing.

Standing, I maneuver toward the fridge, anxious to bite into some cool cheddar. Clumsily I step on a bottle cap that lodges right into my heel. "Ow!" That makes me angry, and it's not just from the pain. I feel foolish and can't even blame it on being drunk.

So far, I've slept with Ting Ting three times, always at her place. If I want her as a steady girlfriend, then I should bring her here. Soon the time will come. But first, there's something really important that I must do.

* * *

Feeling manly. My shirt's off. I'm sweating. In my boxers. Speed metal playing in the background, at maximum volume. Testosterone flows through my veins. (Does it really flow through veins? I should look that up.) Catching glimpses of myself in a mirror. Biceps and pectorals glistening.

It's a hot day, and I'm spending it cleaning my apartment. It is something of a workout.

Clink, clink, clink.

That's the sound of me hauling out the dozenth-or-so garbage bag full of glass bottles. First, I pile them outside my door, and then, one by one, I drag them down the hall to a rubbish bin near the staircase.

"Oh, fuck!"

As I return for the last round of glassy garbage bags, I casually try to open the front door as I did thirteen times before. The doorknob doesn't turn. Instinctively, I pat my right thigh looking for the keys in my pocket and realize that I'm still wearing just my boxers.

I've locked myself out of the apartment while in my underwear. Is this really happening?

"Goddamn it! Embarrassed, I run downstairs and try explaining my dilemma to the doorman.

"Um… *diu le… wo de yaoshi…*"

The building-management people here know me. At least, they realize that I'm a foreigner (kind of) and hence inclined to act a little erratically. So they call a locksmith. While waiting, I rest, sitting on the stairs, and I'm thirsty, but without pockets in my boxers, I lack the money to buy a bottle of water or a Tsingtao beer.

When the locksmith comes, he unscrews the door handle and shoves various instruments inside. Once I get through the doorway, I grab my wallet and pay him a few hundred. I have to laugh at the situation and make a mental note to write about the episode in my memoirs, which are turning increasingly comedic.

Well, where was I?

Having already rested, I drink some water. On the subject of water, I then dump some onto the kitchen floor. Next I spatter on dishwashing soap, toilet cleaner, and bleach. I take an old towel, wrap it around a shoe and rub at the floor, especially in corners and near the edges of cupboards.

When I start opening the cupboards, I see the quick movements of cockroaches. Gross indeed! Recalling a long-ago suggestion from a friend about dealing with insects, I pour some bleach into a spray bottle and get busy with it. Roaches scurry around, but I keep spraying. Then I add Raid and continue. The heavy stink starts to sting my eyes. I'm in a cloud of smoke, and my tongue feels a tingling sensation. Maybe it's time for me to retreat from the kitchen. I shut the door behind me.

My last load of laundry finishes, and I hear the telltale beeping nose. It took hours and hours to wash my clothes, one load at a time at 90 minutes each. I hang up the latest laundry on the small balcony, where the wet garments press together like moist pieces of meat. At this rate, they'll take forever to dry, and I only hope that tomorrow's sunny.

With the clothes and trash handled, I look down and notice my floor for the first time in recent memory. Walking here suddenly feels like a totally different process.

Grabbing up a few scattered leftovers, some books and periodicals, I toss them on my bed to organize later. I find the broom and sweep. Giant clops of dust form. I collect them in a dustbin and take it out to the hallway, this time remembering my keys.

Next, I mop with that towel from the kitchen. The hardwood floor's beautiful, worth seeing more often.

The whole apartment looks completely unrecognizable. Totally unfamiliar, it's spacious, seemingly twice as big. I just may be inclined to invite someone here…

One more task relates to the bed and its blanketing layer of books. When the floor looks dry enough, I dump all the books back onto its hardwood and start organizing.

This is the fun part. I could do this all night. Hours pass. It's long past midnight, and I hardly notice.

First, I try to arrange my books in alphabetical order by the authors, but that doesn't work at all. Some oversized volumes don't fit vertically on the bookcase shelves, and the results don't look right. They're too messy and zigzagged. There's that, plus the travel books don't exactly have credited authors.

I arrange all the books again, this time initially by size with hardcovers, trade paperbacks and pocketbooks. Next it's by genre. The novels work well alphabetically. Other sections cover Chinese- and Asian-themed nonfiction, various popular nonfiction and the travel guides.

Several more times I rearrange until finding a nice intuitive order that compromises between genres, book sizes, and authors. Each shelf has its own theme with the most important ones at the top and then in descending order.

As for the magazines (plenty of *Pearl Delta Expat* back-issues) and a few newspapers worth saving, I just stack them straight up under my desk.

Now, I can't wait for someone to come to visit, get drunk, and discuss books with me.

The only thing left is to wash my sheets and pillowcases. But for the moment, I have nowhere to dry them. So I decide to postpone that part for a few more days. I hope she won't notice.

* * *

"Wow, your home's so small," she says.

"Yeah, we know that your place is bigger," I snap back. "You want to brag some more?"

"But I thought you're rich," she says, playing along.

"I used to be, but then I spent all my money."

"So now I'm richer than you."

"Will you hold it against me?"

She answers by jumping on me and making out. We fall onto the bed (which isn't far from the front door) still in our street clothes, and I'm almost glad that I didn't wash the sheets.

"I'm so horny," she says. "I like a poor boy."

We begin to shed our clothes. I lick at her ear the way that she loves, and she shudders. We undress haphazardly, starting with belt buckles and going waist-down from there. In our socks and T-shirts, with only the legs and crotch areas open to the air, she rubs me till I'm hard and quickly starts maneuvering me to enter.

"No condom?" I bluntly ask.

"Hey, it's okay."

"Are you...?" I ask.

"I take the pill," she says.

"Oh, well then, girl, let's go."

I'm not ashamed to say that, over the years, I've had sex with quite a few horny Chinese girls. It's often rough, harsh like the taste of undercooked meat, something that tastes great when you're starving, but less appetizing with each repetitive lunch special.

I suppose it could be like that with any ethnicity. That's part of being a man. After a while in a relationship, sex becomes only about that final push to orgasm. What thrills the first time quickly dulls. Scratches feel fiercer and the squeezing of flesh more painful until it takes all you got not to imagine blondes and get it over with.

I don't know why I'm thinking like this as Ting Ting's ass sticks up from my bed and I'm rock hard, slamming into her. It's as "in the moment" as this writer can get.

Mind you, I think, not wearing a condom makes this considerably more enjoyable. I don't need to imagine blondes. I'm reaching around and pinching her clit. She's screaming, and her ass looks so smooth. Quickly I feel like I'm going to explode, then I do, and it feels great as my ejaculate drips back out of her onto my naked skin.

It should be a long time before I ever grow weary of sex with Ting Ting.

We collapse onto the bed, and the sheet feels sticky. I don't mind. Slowly, belatedly, she takes off her shirt, bra, and socks. In the soft light, I see her dark nipples. She takes off my remaining clothes too and takes me under the blanket to cuddle. I'm so relaxed that I could fall asleep at any moment.

She laughs loudly, waking me. "Ha! That was wonderful. I thought you might never bring me here."

"What?" I say, my eyes slowly opening.

"I thought you'd never take me to your home."

"I took you, didn't I?"

"It's funny now," she says. "I thought that maybe it was because you have a wife."

"Why the hell would you think that?" Suddenly I'm wide awake.

"You never wanted me to come to your home."

"Oh! No, mostly I was just busy. There was never a good time. We always hang out nearer to your place, right? And I worried that it's too small. I'm only a writer, you know, and not a famous one. We're all poor until we become famous."

Ting Ting pauses to absorb all this. I don't think that she's angry at me, just relieved that I finally brought her here.

"It's true," she finally says, calmly. "You are poor. Your apartment's small and dirty. But that's okay. I understand because it's the same with artists. We're either rich and famous or very poor. There's no middle. You should have seen where I lived before."

"But come on, Ting, your place is nice. You're no starving artist."

"Maybe I'm not so starving now."

"Then does that mean you've already skipped from poor directly to fame?"

"Fame?"

"You know what I mean."

Quietly, she thinks about it. "Maybe."

* * *

Proud of having such a fabulous girlfriend, I'm ready to show her off to my friends. For me, this represents a very rare occasion. Usually I prefer to keep those worlds separate, but there comes a time to grow up.

Hanging out with friends and hitting on girls in a bar atmosphere is one thing. More often than not, those less-than-ideal pursuits are more about having a laugh than really succeeding with women. But as for being in a meaningful relationship, and letting my editor and his drinking buddies in on this, and that whole process of going out to socialize as an official couple? That's a big step.

Regardless, I take Ting Ting to Indian Towers. I wanted to impress her with the luxuriousness of the location, but when we get there, she only says, "*Oh*, you mean this place. I've been here before."

By now, Jonas is already here, quite drunk and spending money with his people. "And who is this?" he slyly asks, stepping forward to kiss Ting Ting's hand.

I introduce them to each other. "You're the artist," Jonas says.

"So I guess you really are famous," I say to Ting Ting, essentially answering for her.

This makes it real. Here I sit at a table with my girlfriend. There's my editor and his whole circle. Briefly, we talk about culture and art, and Ting Ting keeps up with the best of them. I could get used to this.

But we barely have time to order our own drinks before Jonas changes the subject and starts talking business. "I liked your last three pieces," he says to me and winks at Ting Ting. The exhibition review was one of those pieces.

"After your sabbatical thing, I'd almost worry that you're getting lazy," Jonas adds. "But you still have it in you. I want to give you a big assignment. I've hinted lately that something might be in the works, and here it is."

"Lay it on me," I say.

"You know the Chen clan?"

"Do you mean the Clan Academy Museum over on Line One?"

"No, a different Chen clan."

"Like Jackie Chan?"

"Is that the same surname? I never can tell with Cantonese and *Putonghua*."

"I think so," I answer, although we both know that I'm not fluent in either language. "It's a very common name, Chen or Chan. Or Cheng. Same difference."

"Well, be that as it may, one of these Chen clans recently uncovered an ancestor's diary."

"Whoa! I can't do translation," I say.

"Let me finish. It's already translated, but it sounds terrible. Too much Chinglish. The clan needs a proofreader. This is almost more of a ghostwriter gig with rewrites and edits, ideal for someone who can work fast, meet a deadline, and has a way with prose. This is a professional gig with a heavy workload. Think literature. There's guaranteed high pay, but minimal exposure. If a non-disclosure agreement appears in the works, don't put the job on your resume."

"So you think that I'm only in this game for the money?"

"And the experience," Jonas says. "You can tell yourself that."

"Where have I heard this before?"

It does sound interesting. We continue on the subject of Chinese biographies and diaries and famous translations in literature. My girlfriend contributes with some questions of her own. Jonas's businessmen friends offer us all second and third rounds of *Maotai*s. I keep refusing, and they keep insisting. Jonas repeatedly calls me Monkey, and I reveal how I just learned that the nickname means "gay tweaker" in the local slang. We all laugh like we're buzzed indeed, although I'm not.

This shows all the makings of a good night. I bask in my surroundings, having work, a girl, and respect. The only thing missing is money, and it sounds like a nice slice of that will come my way soon enough. Like the rising moon, full and reflecting light above us, I'm doing alright. About now, I consider officially declaring all this as a happy ending.

Just then, I notice Gigi at the bar. And behind her stands Dmitri, the creepy Russian. They appear in my field of vision both at once, as if I'm being tested by the fates. This seems almost too ridiculous.

Both of them see me and scowl. They approach. The bickering begins. Within moments, my girl starts to yell at the other girl and then at me, the business associates flee in wretched embarrassment, as the old man sneers and I'm expected to defend. And defend I do, and then the situation escalates, flaming up like the fires of an arsonist's barbecue. In the end, I can only be amused.

The drama, it never ends. I am overcome with a powerful feeling: I need a drink. This is going to be harder than I thought.

BOOK III
香港
Hong Kong

1
鼠

Yes, I'm first. I always arrive first at these kinds of meetings.

I'm seated at an expensive restaurant near the new client's office in Kowloon, in the city of my namesake *Cheng Long*. We scheduled the meeting for the client's lunch break, but people say that in Hong Kong offices, the bosses don't even give enough time for anyone to nap on lunch breaks.

Looking to a window while waiting, I observe all the people outside. Nathan Road stays so very busy. Many of the pedestrians are tourists from other countries. It's a very diverse crowd out there, and I think maybe with almost more *laowai* than Chinese. I see Europeans of all shapes and sizes, black people from South Asia or Africa, and many Muslims wearing strange clothes. The long skirts on the men remind me of the fashions in ancient China, like during the Qing Dynasty. The Muslims must be here because of that famous mosque across the street.

From the ethnic businessmen in all types of suits to the tall blond families traveling in light clothes, everyone on the sidewalks appears to be in such a hurry. They're cordial in their own ways, whether standing and talking business or rushing to take pictures of everything they can see. Whatever they're doing, they do it politely and fast.

Momentarily, I watch a Germanic family of four across the street. The mother pushes a baby carriage. The overweight father wears a colorful shirt. The child's in flip-flops. They walk in circles. A Pakistani man approaches them. Although I can't hear him, I know he's urging the European man to buy a tailored suit. I know that because such men accosted me many times when I have walked on this street. For a moment, the father looks interested, but then the child starts tugging at the mother, the mother tugs at the father, and soon they vanish from my sight.

Weary of people-watching through a window, I switch my attention to inside this densely packed restaurant. I tune into the overlapping sounds around me and hear more English than anything else. But surprisingly, I also hear Mandarin. Someday the border between Hong Kong and the rest of China will disappear. Then everyone here will speak Mandarin.

To amuse myself, I examine the money that I'm carrying. It's odd to see money without the Chairman's face on it, and so many coins too. They feel heavy in my hands.

Next, I read the menu full of outrageous prices. Luckily, I'll charge the cost of this meeting as a business expense. Perks are nice.

My client finally arrives, just in time. The waiter was getting annoyed with me because I wouldn't order, and yet I'm hungry so it's a big relief that I can eat soon.

I stand up and shake hands with my client. "Hello, Mister Ota," I say in English. "Good to see you again."

"Thank you for coming the very far way to here, Mister... Feng-san." He pronounces my name very badly.

"You're welcome," I say and bow.

He shrugs off my bow and pats me on a shoulder so I raise my head.

"How was your journey on this excellent day?" he asks.

"Very efficient on the public transportation," I say.

Mister Ota sits across the table from me. We make small talk about recent additions to the Hung Hom train station, but we lack much else to chat about so very quickly our real discussion begins.

Diligently, Mister Ota persists with his broken English. Having worked in an investment firm in Hong Kong for the past decade, perhaps he also speaks some dialect of Chinese, but when working with international clients in places like Kowloon, it's always best to use the world's most international language. His English pronunciation is poor, and our conversation goes slowly because I must pause to understand him.

I order noodles and continue to listen while eating. In fact, Mister Ota says nothing interesting or new. It's all a summary of what our employees already discussed. Nevertheless, this all forms part of the process of meeting in person.

The investment firm that Mister Ota represents wishes to expand its business onto the Chinese mainland, and it's very late to act. In the technology trade business, many Hong Kong companies already hold high controlling shares in Shenzhen. However, I lead a fresh young company seeking new clients. Through mutual networking acquaintances, I contacted his office, and our employees set up this meeting.

As Mister Ota and I know, Shenzhen still grows all the time, and just by looking around in this crowded city, anyone can see that Hong Kong has no more room to grow. The wisest place to put one's money is right across the border.

For companies and countries worldwide, the best place to invest happens to be precisely where I live. The whole world knows it, even the high-rollers in Mister Ota's disgraceful country. I feel such a fierce national pride when thinking about the prevailing trends in economics and development.

Mister Ota is Japanese, but I don't hate him. I try to stay as open-minded as possible. I know that his ancestors were dogs preying on the people of China, but we're in the 21st century now and must be civil.

At the end of our conversation, I make sure to bow again. I want to say "*sayonara*" and almost do, but decide that'd be overreaching. We've had a pleasant and formal discussion, very successful, agreeing that when we meet again, it'll be to sign contracts.

After lunch I feel pleased with myself. Having some free time, I walk casually around parts of the tourism district, passing many congested shops. Then, hidden across the street from the restaurant, I discover Kowloon Park, and that's nice for a stroll.

Here in Hong Kong, I notice the use of many languages. It's interesting how different the traffic signs look too. Where I come from, such signs show Simplified Chinese script with English at the bottom. Yet here,

English appears foremost with Traditional characters as the subtitles. How unbelievable that this place belongs to China! Equally astonishing to me, in all of the brochures, shops and restaurants, Japanese seems like an unofficial fourth language.

Leaving the park, I find my way back onto Nathan Road. I consider going next to the Mong Kok District to browse for electronics products, and so I stroll north.

Noticing a bookstore, I decide to look inside. Its air conditioning feels good after my walk. I take my time and slowly examine some books. There's a selection of biographies about the Chairman. Maybe this shop isn't so different from the bookstores anywhere else. I see a few unfamiliar books about Tiananmen Square, but they don't look very interesting, so I pay them little attention.

The main difference here is that the prices are much higher, like everything else in this city. Yet Hong Kong's buildings are older and dustier, the cars drive on the wrong side of the roads, and nothing feels optimistic. I do love that I see no beggars. I don't know where local officials have put the beggars, but for all that I care, they could have shoved them into the sea. Overall, I mostly sense that the best days for this city are long gone. Although the native Hong Kong people might smack me if I said this too loudly, I much prefer my city, my own side of the border.

Pondering the past as well as the future, I go to the bookstore's history section. There I find many fascinating books about the Pacific War, most with gruesome photos of the devilish Japanese soldiers. Glancing around the store, I wonder how many of these customers come from that island nation.

It's intriguing to think about that small country with no natural resources and a culture derived from China, full of violent samurais and sexual deviance. The Japanese came to this city in the last century trying to control all of Asia, but they failed. I always attributed that failure to heroic efforts by the People's Liberation Army, but all the books here mention American soldiers, and I hardly believe my eyes.

In any case, the cruel Japanese soldiers failed. Fifty years later, people from the same country returned as businessmen. As *sararimen*! And I don't care! They're welcome to invest and contribute to the economy all that they want. So long as I'm a part of it.

Like all the rest of this world, the Japanese have no choice except to yearn to participate in the blossoming economy of my beloved homeland. World peace through globalism sounds like a good idea. Peace indeed, but we're the big winners.

Perhaps our economic miracle is just that, a true miracle.

* * *

My girlfriend phones me. She's on Hong Kong Island, inside an enormous shopping mall in the Central Business District. I walk to the Star Ferry Pier, crossing the streets carefully because I can't keep track of which direction to watch for the oncoming cars and buses. A green-and-white ferry takes me almost directly to the shopping mall.

Boat rides are often pleasant, and I carry my digital camera to shoot some lovely photos of the sea. But after doing that briefly, I feel a slight nausea from the up-and-down motions. Thankfully, the entire ride lasts less than ten minutes, and then I arrive.

When stepping out from the boat, I phone my girlfriend. "Honey, where are you?"

Immediately she begins a detailed report of her shopping day, which slightly annoys me due to the roaming charges. Whatever. Technically, I'm not supposed to charge the company for personal calls, but I often do.

"Just tell me in which shop to find you," I say. "Look for a sign."

Finally we meet after both getting lost and several more phone calls. She looks much as she did this morning when we took the train together, except that now she wears a bigger smile and carries so many bags.

"Help me carry," she says, and I take four of them.

"All name-brand," she declares. "The prices are wonderful! Don't you just love it here? I never want to leave."

"Okay," I joke. "You stay here. I'll go home."

"Fine."

"But first you must give me back my credit card," I tell her.

"Never mind," she says. "I'll go back with you tonight."

We sit on a bench and joke some more. "So," she asks me, mildly interested, "how was your meeting with the little Japanese man?"

"It went very well."

"Did you eat raw fish?"

"Yes, so delicious. I brought some for you!"

I pretend to stuff sashimi into her mouth, and she laughs loudly. Suddenly, I feel very happy in this place. My girlfriend hugs me, and although it's rude in a public place, she quickly kisses me on the mouth.

"Let's go," she says.

"Go where?"

"Shopping, of course."

"You aren't finished yet?"

"Shopping for you, dear."

She leads me into a men's clothing store. I do want to look nice, but don't enjoy lingering at shopping malls like she does. Hastily, I choose designer dress shirts in a few colors, and my girlfriend recommends the light-blue ones. She says it's my style. I purchase two of them and a matching necktie.

"What would you like to do now?" I ask.

"I'm not tired," she says. "I drank so much coffee today that I know I'll be up all night."

"I didn't book a hotel."

"Yes, I know that too. I'm finished with the mall, but I wonder what else to do…"

"Then I suppose it's time to go home," I say, and she doesn't disagree. "And yet earlier you mentioned wanting to stay forever."

She thinks for a moment before responding. "This is such a great holiday. The cross-border bus service from Wan Chai operates twenty four hours a day. We can cross the border anytime. I promise to carry all the bags. Let's go for drinks in Lan Kwai Fong."

That's a good idea. The famous bar-street should be within walking distance, but we don't anticipate the steep hills, and the staircase-roads leave us hot and tired, even as the sun sets and an ocean breeze blows. My first cool beer will be welcome indeed.

To begin our night out, we choose a small pub. By mainland standards, it's a tiny place, but with twice as many people stuffed inside. Next door there's another pub, and then another. All looking similar, they're tightly crowded places so different from the more airy venues I've known. The designs are simpler, and the drinks more expensive.

After drinks at the first stop, we hop to the next bar. Again we order drinks, look around, and go to the next place. On the sidewalks we zigzag among women (many in tiny dresses) of all ethnicities and fashionable men. No poor people come here at all. That's grand!

We do a hard turn beneath the escalator. There, I can't help but stare at all the foreigner girls with big breasts and the beautiful Chinese in heavy makeup. I try not to leer.

At the fifth place, my girlfriend suddenly shrieks. It's noisy, and only I notice as she screams right into my ear. "OH, MY HEAVENS! LOOK WHO THAT IS!"

Sitting at a VIP table in a far corner of the bar are several Cantonese pop stars! I recognize a man who has starred in many action movies and a young girl regarded as a new idol-singer who also appeared in a romance film. A big group surrounds them. About ten people are crushed together at the table. They're playing dice games.

"Do you think I should walk over there and take a picture?"

"No," I say. "That would be rude."

"This is so great. Nobody back home will believe it."

We stay at this place the longest. The celebrities don't move, but we must. Feeling bored, I suggest a change of scenery. "Have you seen enough?" I ask.

"Not at all."

"We can't just watch celebrity-stars from afar the whole night. That's too strange. We should go. Do you want to try a dance club? But maybe we have too many shopping bags."

"I don't know," she says. "I'm still not tired."

By now, I believe it's time to go home. "We've had a really good time and seen amazing sights."

We walk to the door, and my girlfriend says, "Tonight I feel so high and full of energy. Everything's just too cool. What else can we do?"

"Nothing's left to do."

"AHHH!" she shrieks again. "I have a great idea. Look!"

My girlfriend points to a bulletin board covered by small paper flyers taped over each other. I don't know which one excites her so much.

"What?"

"That one." It's an orange flyer stapled up in the middle among greens and pinks.

"Big music-festival party on Lamma," she reads. "It's tonight. They call it a rave."

"Lamma?" The information appears mostly in English. I look closely and read some small print at the bottom that includes translated directions in Traditional Chinese characters.

"Oh," I say. "*Lamma*, the island."

"*Nanya dao*," says my girlfriend in Mandarin.

"Yes."

From the bar, we walk for a while and reach a row of ferry piers. This area's much quieter than the bar-street. We'd hold hands if not for all the shopping bags. All the same, it's nice and romantic. We notice couples, joggers, backpackers, and even a few drunks. There are many shops, but they're closing for the night, leaving only the smells of pizza and noodles.

Hungry, we snack from some vending machines. At a kiosk, we ask for directions and finally find the boat that goes to Lamma Island.

"The next ferry leaves at 10:30," I say, studying a large poster-type schedule pasted to a wall. "To Yung Shue Wan, wherever that is."

"Let's go there," she says.

"But look," I point on the schedule. "Soon the ferries stop for the night. We probably couldn't catch one back until after 6 a.m. tomorrow."

"That's okay. I want to party all night," she says. "It'll be fun, much better than Lan Kwai Fong. Rave parties always last until morning, and we'll meet so many interesting people. Please!"

Honestly, I can't say no to her. It's my one flaw.

2
牛

I'm in communication with the new teacher, directing him through his mission step-by-step. Cell phone to my ear, I speak very slowly, enunciating clearly, with quite a few deep breaths. It's his first visa run.

"You're at the border now," I say. "Get the departure card. Fill out the whole thing."

"What's my travel-document number?" he nervously asks.

"That's your passport number, buddy."

"I see."

"Just get to the other side and look for a bus to Tsim Sha Tsui. Call me when you get off that bus. Oh, and you might need to buy a SIM card at a 7-Eleven shop or wherever."

"Okay. Thanks."

"And don't convert too much money at those exchange stands. They'll rip you off on the rate. Did you go to the bank yesterday like I suggested?"

"Yes," he says, but only after a pause. He may be lying. Well, it's his dime. Or rather, it's his *jiao*.

"Talk to you later," I say. "Bye."

Poor kid, I think. It's too early for this.

* * *

I agreed to help. The mission began when our school administrators figured out that the kid's tourist visa had been expired for more than a week and that they needed to pay his fine (500 a day) and get him to Hong Kong quickly. And after that, get him "legal" again and back to work as soon as possible.

The kid is a colleague of mine, part of a new batch of teachers this semester. Our bosses don't know what they're doing, and the kid's so inexperienced that responsibility fell onto me to facilitate the process.

It's like this. I have an official work visa because I came to China years ago, and every year I can transfer the Zed-status visa to a new employer. I never had the problem that so many new kids have, but I've been around and heard from other foreigners so I sure do understand it. For me, the school would simply take my passport to the local provincial Public Security Bureau (PSB), and then I would sign paperwork. For almost everyone else who comes from overseas to teach, it works a little differently...

Most people in my profession don't care much about proper legal visas. They just show up as tourists, start working, and nobody checks up on them. When the school got desperate for new teachers, it started hiring, using a shifty agency to find foreigners, and flying them into China. Then the agency takes a fee equivalent to 50 per cent of the first month's salary for each new teacher. That's how it often works in the ESL community.

New teachers arriving this way aren't legitimate to work in China, but who cares? This country isn't exactly known for its stellar rule of law. From time to time, I hear about crackdowns on illegal English teachers, but that's rare in the grand scheme of things and doesn't appear to be happening this semester. My school hasn't been raided by the police for years. Even if that happened, we can eat up some of the cost of arrest, a calculable risk. Still, if even one teacher does get deported, that's not exactly good for business.

As the school's senior *waijiao*, it's up to me to clean up the mess. The company will pay the bills, but the research and direction are all on me. This situation, as all the expats around here well know, calls for a Hong Kong visa run.

So I prepared a list of directions and addresses and sent the kid on his way. He printed a two-inch-square passport-sized photo, packed his own clothes (it's an overnight stay), and walks on his own two feet. But apart from the kid's actual physical presence, pretty much every aspect of this project lies under my control. Not the least of which is stringing him along like a puppet via cellular communication.

Step One. It's Friday, and he needs to cross the border. Begin at the crack of dawn, and we all still should be asleep right now. From Lo Wu customs, he reaches the tip of Kowloon.

Now he's texting me every five minutes to find the travel agency in Tsim Sha Tsui. I tell him just to ask people for directions. By that, I mean people other than me, those actually there sharing the sidewalk with him. Everyone speaks English.

He keeps replying about how he's scared that the government won't let him back into Guangdong Province, and I tell him not to worry. He asks me to pack up his things and meet him tomorrow, if it comes to that, and then he'll need to borrow money to fly back home. I promise him that won't be necessary. We go back and forth like this all morning.

A very important part of my job, I realize, is morale boosting.

Step Two. My phone buzzes. New Hong Kong number.

"Hello?"

"I'm eating lunch," he reports.

"Alright," I say, unsure how he wants me to respond to such big news. "Good job."

"I found the travel agency."

"That's good. How did it go?"

"They told me to come back tomorrow afternoon after 4 p.m. I didn't realize it'd be so late."

"Don't worry about that," I say. "Think of the whole thing as a mini-vacation."

"What should I do stuck in Hong Kong? It's going to be so boring."

"I don't know." Hmm, now I'm a tourism agent too.

"Maybe see a movie," I advise. "There must be something good playing. Eat dim sum. Take a walk in the park. Grab a map, buy a day pass to ride on the MTR trains and go sightseeing. It's easy. I like the movie-star-walkway at the edge of the harbor. That's very Hollywood. The view from that mountaintop, the Peak, looks beautiful too."

"I just don't want to spend too much money."

"Then stay inside at the guesthouse and watch TV."

"Where's that again?"

Oh my! This tries my patience, but I'm a professional, and these are my job responsibilities. So figuratively speaking, I continue to hold his hand.

"I wrote down directions to the Peking Guesthouse for you. Did you find the note? The guesthouse is near the travel agency on Nathan Road. Just call the place, ask if there's a vacancy, and then look for the building. There should be lots of Africans and South Asians there, but you'll be alright. You can do it. Try to bargain, and don't pay more than two hundred for a night. You'll have a small room, but that's the way to save money."

"I just want a cheap place."

"Relax, man. Enjoy your first trip into the Hong Kong Special Administrative Region. When you're back at the travel agency for your appointment tomorrow, just text me to let me know that everything works out. I'm really sure it will. Got it?"

"Oh, yeah. Okay, I'm headed to that guesthouse now. Thanks."

What a very rewarding job I have!

Step Three. It's the next day. After several texts during the night to complain about his room's smell, I chose to ignore him. By now,

I'm numb with each message's narration duller and duller. But this afternoon, he finally tells me that he's checking out, and I simply reply: "*Don't be late.*"

Then a bit later, I receive the most important text of all: "*Got my passport back from the agency. Visa says Category G.*"

So he got a business visa. It's not a Zed-class work visa, but perfectly acceptable under the circumstances. I feel a genuine sense of relief and happiness. I'm almost proud. This time I call back and ask him to read me the details.

"What does it say under 'duration of stay'?" I ask.

"Um. It says thirty. What does that mean? I have to leave after thirty days? Oh God, I can't do this again."

"Not like that!" I yell, trying to impart the urgency while still sounding encouraging. "As I explained before, alright, it means that you have to leave China and come back every month. That is, you need to cross a border every thirty days. But in reality, it only means that you go to Hong Kong. You quite literally can turn around after getting your passport stamped. It's so simple."

"Okay, if you say so."

"Just don't overstay again. Now listen closely," I say, again trying to sound urgent, yet hopeful. "What does it say under 'entries'?"

"It just has an M. What does that mean?"

"So far, so good. M means 'multiple' so you can cross the border and re-enter the mainland as many times as you want. This is how it works. This is the process."

"Okay. I'm glad."

"Last question, what's the expiration?"

"Um, six months from now."

"Cool. You can even stretch that to seven months. All goes according to plan."

"Really?"

"Really. We're all done. Congratulations! Just take the train up from Hung Hom, and be careful about the Lok Ma Chau or Lo Wu route. Either way, you're back so no big deal. Just get to the other side already."

"Thanks so much. Is that really it?"

"That's it. See, it wasn't so hard. As a next step here, we'll get your address registered under the new visa with the Public Security Bureau during the next few days, but no hurry on that. Just remember – if anybody asks you questions, you're a consultant. Not a teacher."

"I'll see you tomorrow. Thanks again for your help."

"See you. Oh, and you have the receipt, right? Give us the receipt, and the school can reimburse you."

"I didn't know that I was supposed to keep the receipt."

Now he's going back for the receipt, and it'll be a while yet before he crosses into the mainland. He may get lost along the way, but he'll be alright once on this side again. It's not like he's African or Southeast Asian or anything. The police won't ask too many questions to an innocent-looking white kid. The hard part's over, and I no longer need to worry.

This whole thing might get to a lesser man, but today I proved my ability to handle it.

Step Four of my personal plan calls for talking to the school principal first thing tomorrow to demand a promotion. I want to become the new manager in charge of recruitment and maintenance of foreign talent. The people running the school have no idea what they're doing. They need me and badly. At least, that's what I hope to convince them.

Without this promotion, there's no more future for me in ESL. I can't just teach here until I'm too old to do it anymore. Instead, I need to invest my time into a real long-term career. My wife keeps pushing me to make more money, buy her a home and all that. I've spent too many years in this dead-end job. It's been a terrific time in China, and I wouldn't change it for anything, but now I'm pushing thirty. After a certain point, I should focus on what I'm doing with my life.

Back home, my old college classmates are surpassing me. The world economy's starting to turn around, and I'm stuck teaching while studying Mandarin and with no discernible international business experience.

I've wasted all these years living in the moment and not planning for the future. But no, I won't teach forever, nor help these new teachers for free.

My best option is to become a foreign-teacher manager and pitch that to the school, or else move on to start my own recruitment agency. Either way, I know that I intend to stay here and move up as best I can. I mean, what else could I do with a resume like mine?

3
虎

This takes me back to my old ways. I've been on my own for two hours now, and already I'm on a boat sailing to a party and half-drunk from the beer in my gut mixing with minor seasickness as the waves slosh my fluids up and down.

I came here for purely noble reasons. I really did! What? You don't believe me?

You see, the old lady has done well with her physical therapy at the Shekou Hospital. So I decided to take her to the nearest First World locale. You'd be surprised. Hong Kong's way more handicapped-friendly than Shenzhen.

I wheeled her all the way. No line at the border. A free train ticket for her. We met some very friendly Hong Kongers along the way. After a late lunch, I dropped her off for an overnight stay at the King George Hospital.

That's a private hospital over on the west end of Hong Kong Island, one recommended for expats and upwardly mobile mainlanders. Its spinal-cord department is considered top-notch. I know that Hong Kongers get upset these days when mainlanders arrive to take advantage of the healthcare system, but it's not like that. We simply need the best. It won't be cheap, but hell, that's what money's for, and at least my business is finally making a profit.

After the hospital's visiting hours ended, the nurses kicked me out. "This ain't no hotel," they said. So it was time to kiss goodbye, time for silent prayers. I'll check back early tomorrow, but in the meantime, I need to occupy myself.

I came prepared for the encroaching free time. You know, I even heard about a party on "the other island". Lamma! I remember that place well. It used to be a great vacation spot to take girls. You could walk on the beach, eat vegan health food, shoot scenic pictures, and smoke dope with the local hippies. I have good memories of Lamma, but never did take my old lady there. That's sad. One day!

Right now, I don't want to think about that. I take another swig of beer. A slight nausea ripples from my intestines to my throat as the boat thrashes. I'm on an empty stomach, and I keep drinking.

I'm doing the right thing here. Of course I am. I deserve some fun.

I look across the ferry seats. I hope to find some young scenesters to let me in on their little cliques. Among the people sitting nearby, I see clusters of lower-class Chinese whom I assume to be migrant workers, a few healthy-looking Hong Kongers in suits and ties, and some thinner mainland tourists taking pictures of everything. Almost half the passenger list is composed of whites, ranging from fashionably hip kids to aging hippies.

The couple sitting across from me looks familiar. "I saw you guys back at the Central Ferry Pier, right?" I say, holding up my beer. "You stocked up on supplies, huh?"

"Hello, my man. What's up?" says the dude. He has a full-on beard and heavy necklaces visible through the facial hair that jingle as he leans to shake my hand and introduce himself. The guy's dressed like a mystic holy man, or at least a Western parody of one. The girl introduces herself too.

"Do you two live in Hong Kong?" I ask. They tote camping gear so I assume that they're not from Lamma. Although resembling backpackers, they carry themselves confidently enough that they don't look like visitors. I hesitate to ask where they're from, saving that question for later, so I throw a shot in the dark to see if they're Hong Kong expats.

"No," says the girl, who shows some skin, but gives me an impression of being more modest than all the crazy hippies on the boat. Her accent's a bit ditsy. "We live in Guangzhou."

"Ah, I see. I've been to the Canton Fair a few times for business. Can't say it's my favorite city. I'm based in Shenzhen myself."

"Really?" she reacts, sincerely interested. "I totally used to live there. What do you do?"

"Enough about business," I say. "After the party, we'll do the exchanging-cards thing. Right now, it should be all about partying."

"I do hear you on that, compatriot," says the guy. "Who wants to talk about the usual workload when we're all here to get away from it?"

Observing their tents and sleeping bags, I ask a party-related question. "So you plan to stay for the whole weekend?"

"As long as they'll have us," says the man.

"It's going to be so cool," adds the girl.

"Looking forward to it myself," I say.

For a moment, we don't say anything. Without work as a subject of conversation, it isn't easy to make small talk.

The bearded guy breaks the ice and brings up another topic. "Without inquiring about anything too personal, allow me to ask, do you smoke?"

"Sure. What, are we hinting? Want a cigarette?" I pull out my pack.

"No, no, I'm fully stocked." He takes out a box of menthols from a compartment in his backpack gear and then picks up the whole thing. "Shall we step outside and have a smoke?"

I follow them. The ferry's big with two levels. Upstairs you can go outside. A few people are seated out there smoking and chatting.

Walking behind my new acquaintances, I try to read the situation. Are they a romantic couple, just platonic friends, or what? They aren't holding hands or anything, but then again, they don't seem like the types for that. What are their types? The guy's an intellectual stoner, someone totally fitting in with the Lamma scene, yet he lives up in Canton. The girl's ditsy and not exactly the alternative sort. So they backpacked together. They traveled a long way, and maybe they're just acquaintances both wanting to check out the beach party. Hell, even if they're fuck-buddies or whatever, they're definitely not boyfriend and girlfriend. I'm sure of it. Maybe I have a chance with this woman.

True, I shouldn't entertain such thoughts. I know it, okay? But old habits die hard.

Outside there's a nice breeze. We find a corner and light up. "And by smoke," the bearded man says, "I also mean this." He pulls out a glass pipe with a thick stench of marijuana.

"It's cool?" I ask, unsure of how to get away with this sort of thing here on a public ferry in Hong Kong. One thing I've learned on my travels is that you must be careful with local laws and customs. Get a sense of what you can get away with in certain countries, municipalities and regions. San Francisco, for example, isn't Iowa. Canada isn't Singapore. But how much of lax PRC soft-drug policy translates to Hong Kong?

"As long as it's cool with you," the man answers.

So I assume that it's lax enough here.

He lights up and takes a puff. The girl silently goes along.

When they pass the pipe to me, I take a deep puff and cough until small tears appear in my eyes. It's been a while.

"You okay?" asks the girl. She's sweet, comforting. The guy just smirks at me.

"I'm good, I'm good," I say, my throat itchy with smog. Really I'm kind of embarrassed. You'd think that smoking a pack a day of Hunan-brand *Baisha*s would have toughened me up more.

I pass the pipe back, down some beer, and look at our surroundings. Another group across the aisle ignores us, probably smoking the same thing.

Beyond the boat, it's dark, and the sea looks almost black. The waves undulate. I like it here. Time seems to stand still. Yeah, I think, this shit's starting to kick in for me. Good stuff!

We smoke silently, and I take a few more hits. We're gliding across a watery abyss with no visible evidence of mankind. Then some lights appear.

"Almost there," I hear from somewhere in the distance.

"I hope it was some enjoyable herb," someone says to me.

"Ah, well," I say. "That did make the trip go well."

"Nice." The man pats me on the back.

"I thank you heartily."

"That's nothing. In my possession, I have certain products and concoctions coming with much stronger experiences to await us…"

Watching from above on the ferry, I see the lights turn into a village of low buildings along an otherwise dark shore. The boat rides up next to the Yung Shue Wan pier and does a U-turn. We pull in backwards, and docking procedures begin. A ferry crewman lowers the platform-bridge thing. Hey, I'm not a nautical man so I don't know all the technical terms.

Following everyone else, I line up to disembark. It's time to go.

Once off the ferry, the arriving herd walks not quite in a full stampede along the pier until we get properly onto the island. Too many people surround me to keep track of them, and I'm a bit fucked up too. Hundreds of bicycles are parked to the sides. I notice concrete at the edge of the sea. Graffiti on walls welcomes us all. There are tiny hotels, seafood restaurants, and small grocery stores still open, the lights blinking.

Blurry sounds of conversation penetrate my hearing. Farther along the street we go.

I feel slightly nostalgic and a little nervous. You can do this, I think, pushing myself to go forward.

"Hey," says the bearded guy, suddenly beside me again. "You coming?"

"Sure."

"You merely need to follow us, my man. There's a bit of walking yet ahead."

"What?"

4
兔

First, I go to a shopping mall at Tai Po Market in the New Territories and browse for handbags and shoes. I don't see anything that I like, but I do buy a phone case.

After stopping for coffee, I ride on an express bus to Happy Valley on Hong Kong Island. There, I window shop, take pictures, and sightsee. For me, it's a very normal day. I often visit Hong Kong for business or pleasure.

But today I've made a firm promise and must go to one more place. If anyone asks, I'll simply say that I've come down with a sudden cold and need a doctor's opinion. That gives me a reason for visiting a hospital.

After I walk for a while, an MTR train takes me due west. Then I transfer to a bus until reaching the Pokfulam valley. There it is, the famous King George Hospital.

I never have liked hospitals. But I'm here to do a job.

This hospital looks very different from others that I've seen. It's cleaner, much bigger, many floors high, and everything's so white. The place smells like strong chemical disinfectant mixed with meat, an unpleasant odor.

Having entered through the emergency-room front gate, I don't sign any paperwork. No nurse approaches me either. They all leave me alone, and I simply walk around. I follow a hallway and read a directory on a wall, trying to find the maternity ward.

Sick people appear everywhere. I see old men in blue gowns leaning on canes to walk, young wives being pushed in wheelchairs and children in school uniforms crying from the aches of bruises. Some patients wait for surgery. Others may be here for simple checkups. People of all ages facing various levels of emergencies come here to regain health.

When I go to the opposite end of the building, I hear babies crying. I smile at the sounds, knowing that I'm headed in the right direction.

I find a lobby of sorts where several pregnant women and anxious husbands are completing paperwork, waiting and reading magazines.

"May I help you?" a nurse asks me. She looks at my belly, sees that it's flat, and then waits for my answer.

"I'm here for a friend," I simply say, and the nurse leaves me alone.

Looking around, I find some pamphlets. I circle the phone number for making appointments and save the emergency number to my phone. I also jot down the ward's suite address to help me find this section more quickly the next time I need to come here.

But there are no lists of prices, and I can't very well ask about those. I've heard of almost-free public hospitals for Hong Kong citizens, paid for by the local government, but this is a private hospital for rich people, and I'm sure that nothing's cheap here. Although we mainlanders must pay, I know that Hong Kong people still grumble about us having babies in their city. That's because the babies become citizens here and are born with certain rights. Hong Kong's size is small so it can't accommodate much of the mainland's population. Yet isn't this city a part of China too? It's a strange and complex social problem.

Of course, I'm not here to meditate on Hong Kong issues. I can't solve those. All I know is that I'm here to learn what I can, but if I ask too much then people will grow suspicious.

Going for a walk again, I search the hallways. Cute paintings of cartoon animals adorn the walls. A few nurses and doctors walk past. It's quiet now. This ward lacks the same sense of emergency as elsewhere in the building. If any baby-related emergencies happen now, they're behind closed doors.

I turn a corner and see a nursery, a row of small beds behind a large glass window. Nurses wearing clean white hats rock the babies and place bottles to the tiny lips. I see some pink and blue gifts too.

The babies look so adorable, so tiny. I wish that I could go behind the glass and pick one up to hold. They're so fresh with innocent hearts, so much potential and long futures to anticipate. I can't hide my smile.

A paunchy man stands next to me. His smile dwarfs even mine.

"Hello," he says.

"Hello."

"Which child is yours?" he asks.

"The one on the far left," I say, not wishing to explain my real mission. "Um, my elder sister's new daughter."

"Mine's in the center. My first son! Do you see him?" He points for me. "I'm so proud."

"He's beautiful," I say. "Congratulations."

"Thank you."

As we talk, I fear that my accent betrays me and maybe he knows I'm not a native Hong Kong person. His smile stays wide, but his eyes show curiosity.

I know what he thinks. What would a mainlander be doing in a nursery like this?

"Babies are wonderful," he says. "We need the population to grow, don't you think?"

"Yes."

"I hope to have many children here. And I hope that damnable Beijing keeps its One-Child Policy for many years to come."

"Oh," I quietly say.

"Where are you from, miss?"

Pretending to receive a call, I put my phone to my ear and turn partly away. "Sorry, I must go. Good luck to you and your family. I hope that you'll receive many red envelopes."

Now I think it's time for me to leave. I've had an excellent day and learned all that I can by coming here. Knowing the route means that next time I can get here very fast. Tonight I'll meet my pregnant cousin and give her the pamphlets. Tomorrow she'll cross the border…

My cousin has procured forged papers from medical professionals, indicating that she's only six months with child, and an internal visa pass with 30 days duration of stay (arranged by her husband's company). So she can make it past the border officials, and they won't suspect. In reality, she's more than eight months along and ready to have the baby as soon as possible.

Her husband must travel elsewhere on business, but he's made all the accommodations so that his wife will stay in a nearby hotel for a few weeks. She can shop and temporarily entertain herself however she wishes. He'll visit when he can.

If the child does not come within a month, my cousin and her husband will make an appointment to induce labor. A maid will stay on call, and I'll come to help as often as I can on the weekends.

We've prepared all that we can. The plan, of course, is for the baby, by being born here, to gain automatic Hong Kong citizenship. While the parents also considered flying to Taiwan and letting the baby become a Taiwan citizen, they chose Hong Kong because our family lives so close.

It will be a girl. I learned that some time ago.

When she grows up, she'll have rights beyond any of which her mother's family ever dreamed. She'll secure a quality education, a Hong Kong passport, chances to study abroad, an amazing career, and a life that I can't even imagine. This marks the start. In the future, I hope that she'll appreciate her aunt's efforts to make sure of all this.

Ha, ha! I feel like a spy. My cousin and her husband will even pay me for my trouble, although I didn't ask for that. Really all that I'm doing is taking a look around and snatching some pamphlets. My cousin herself must do the hardest part.

Finished with my mission here, I start my trek back home. I transfer at Central to catch another bus in Wan Chai. Looking out a bus window, I see darkening rainclouds and the glowing city. It feels good to help family members, but otherwise this evening seems dull to me. Today I took leave from work, and tomorrow's Saturday, but I won't even spend the weekend here.

Somewhere out there in Hong Kong, so much more must be happening. Family obligations bring me close enough to sense what I'm missing, but keep me too far away to see it. A part of me wishes that I could go out and have fun on this night. Imagine what I might have done, perhaps clubbing at cramped bars, meeting interesting men, taking boat rides, or attending beach parties. Instead I'm going home ready to wake up early tomorrow to see my cousin off as she departs.

We must keep our lives normal and make little sacrifices for the sake of the next generation. This is my culture.

5
龍

"Fucking so cool, so amazing," I say. This is the greatest. I feel *glorious*.

Everything all led up to this. I've prepared for months, ever since my last holiday when I went home to Beijing and applied for a Hong Kong/ Macau internal passport. It's unfair and annoying, but that's the only way that we Chinese people can come here. So then I got the visa and asked around until I heard about a good chance to travel.

Now here I am at the big Lamma Island rave party. All these famous DJs are here, and some of them are my friends. Even better, my art gets exhibited. I so had to be here.

"GIVE ME ANOTHER SHOT," I yell.

Hundreds of people mingle. Flickering lights come from glow sticks and fire-dancers. I'm wearing denim shorts and a spotted bikini top. I feel sexy. The men are almost all shirtless, and many of the girls wear less than I do.

There's an enormous tent with lots of people gathered on a hastily put-together plywood stage in the middle. It's so hot. Industrial-strength fans whirl at the edges of the tent, but in the center it's one big mess of hot sweaty funk.

I'm tired from dancing. So I want some drinks and to cool off.

"ANOTHER SHOT."

Standing at the open bar, I present my pass and then down another drink. Most of the partiers paid good money for their drink passes, but mine came to me free because I'm part of the crew.

Before my head spins too much and I'm too drunk to remember it all, I should play out the day's journey that led me here.

Early this morning, six of us set out on a drive. Our group had two DJs from the United Kingdom, a technical expert from America, one Chinese girlfriend (of the American guy, I guess), me (the video artist), and my boyfriend the writer. We split the fee for a minibus rental, which came with a driver, and shared the petrol costs too. That took us to the Shenzhen border. From there, we transferred to a Hong Kong driver, paid a much higher fee and reached the Central Pier, where the same driver agreed to pick us up again tomorrow.

I played it cool, telling no one except my boyfriend that this is my first time in Hong Kong. But I took pictures in every direction, capturing the mountains, the shopping malls, the streets, and the sea. Anyhow, photography's one of my many talents.

Hong Kong's just so Cantonese. And all the traditional Chinese characters here can be hard to read. Any Chinese people whom I met along the way spoke to me in Cantonese, and when I answered in Mandarin, they sneered and paused, but they understood me. I can't wait to practice my Cantonese more and explore in Hong Kong on my own one day. But today we needed to reach Lamma Island.

We loaded our boxes onto the ferry and arrived on Lamma in time to eat a delicious seafood lunch. An event organizer took us the rest of the way to the beach in a small delivery vehicle, really just a motorized cart. There was so much audio equipment that we needed to make three trips.

Then we started to set up on the beach. The tech expert helped me to connect the projector to the generator, adjust the screens, tape up the sheets, and plug it all in to the right computer outlets.

After nightfall, the beats began with slow and soft bumps. Swimmers from along the beach gradually approached, curious and excited. Bit by bit, set list by set list, more people came, paid, and watched my video. In time, I'll receive a small cut from the party proceeds, but it won't be much. I probably won't break even, but at least this makes for an affordable little vacation.

It's great to see my video up there, all the cuts and photos, distortions and edits, infinitely looping, all from my very own heart, for everyone to see.

Now it's late, the party's full on, and I want to have another shot, but I'm tired of screaming at the bartender. So instead I walk toward the portable toilets. It's time for the pee that I've been delaying.

Along the way, I see a familiar face, that of a man with a bushy beard who wears loud clothing. He acts like he can do whatever he wants and doesn't care at all what people may think of him.

But I don't know him that well and can't remember his name. He's friends with the musicians in that band back in Guangzhou, right?

I tap him on a shoulder and yell, "HEY, WHO ARE YOU AGAIN?"

"What?"

"Sorry, didn't mean to scream. Can you hear me?"

"I hear just fine," he says, teasing me. We're in a quieter spot. I don't need to yell.

"Who are you?" I bluntly ask.

"It's me, Eric."

"IT'S YOU, ERIC! I know you. You're that guy. You're late getting here. Sorry, but I'm a little drunk."

"You must pace yourself, dear. Where did you say that you were going?"

"I need to pee! Follow me to pee."

"Ahem. Well then, for sure."

He follows me, and I go to the portable toilets. They're gross and smelly, but when nature calls, there's nowhere else here to go, except maybe in the sea.

When I come out again, Eric's still there. "Here you are," he says, handing me a bottle of water.

"You have no idea how much that bottle cost me," he adds, pointing with a thumb back to a row of vendors at the edge of a beachside walkway.

I feel a little more sober after going to the toilet. We can't have that, I think, gulping some water.

"How did you get here all the way from the provincial capital?" I ask.

"We took an express bus from Garfield Estates. Brought camping equipment – tents, sleeping bags, the entire arrangement to stay for the whole weekend."

"That's cool. I'm here with DJ Estaz and DJ QQQ. I'm doing the video art. But we're going to leave when the sun comes up if I don't fucking pass out. Ha! And who came with you? Is what's-her-name here? You know, from the band?"

"No, I'm here *sans* Rina and her crew. I believe they had a show elsewhere, contractual obligations, you see, but there's no possible way it could be as good as all this," and he waves his hands around. "So it's simply Amber and me, with the addition of a weird old dude we met on the ferry."

"Cool. Um, no Russians, right?"

He shakes his head for "no".

Then I hear a song that I like, and so I edge back toward the central dance area. Eric takes out a cigarette, asks people in a nearby group for a light, and then starts a conversation with them. He waves goodbye to me as we go our separate ways, and I think that I overhear him say, "When did she become such a party girl?"

On the plywood dance floor, I'm full of energy and want to sweat the drunk out of me. Then I see Amber and give her a big hug.

"HI, AMBER!"

"HI, TING TING!"

"I JUST SAW ERIC."

"YEAH, I CAME WITH HIM. WE JUST GOT HERE."

"I KNOW."

"WHERE'S YOUR MAN?

Good question. "HE'S HIDING SOMEWHERE, WRITING. HE NEVER DANCES."

"THAT'S SO BORING."

"I KNOW."

I'd almost forgotten about my boyfriend. Now Amber has prodded my curiosity about his whereabouts. Thinking back, he really didn't want to come here. He said that he needs to cut down on drinking, and there'd be too much temptation. I told him I don't know what he's talking about. He said that he doesn't like Hong Kong and already comes here too much for work. I practically begged him to join me for my first time here. Finally, I convinced him by saying that the party would make a good story.

I see Amber dancing with an overdressed white man. He's a little fat, and maybe he's the weird old guy mentioned by Eric. My other friends are scattered all over the place. I keep wandering from one group to the next, my attention span too short to stick to one clique. Also I'm kind of wary of all these guys staring at me. I want to keep moving.

Soon I decide that it's time to locate my boyfriend. Taking a walk, I find him sitting on a reasonably quiet part of the beach. The music's still loud, but heard from here, the sound fades. With flashing lights and fire pits on each side, he seems to have found the loneliest place on the whole stretch of beach. He sits on the sand, staring at something in his hands.

"Do you even get any reception on that thing?" I ask, joking.

"What? Oh, it's you. Hi, baby. No, I'm just writing a little."

When he turns toward me, I see that the objects in his hands aren't a phone and stylus, but a normal notepad and pencil.

"What are you drinking?" I ask.

"Just a bottle of water."

He drops the notebook into a pocket and sips the water. I sit beside him. Sparks of light flicker in my peripheral vision, but straight ahead all that I see is the peaceful dark ocean. Silently, he puts an arm around me.

"How are you," I ask, "really?"

"I'm doing great."

"Okay then. Um, go for a walk?"

"Let's just sit here for now."

"Oh."

"You're getting antsy, aren't you? You want to return to the party?"

"Well, it's only that I still need to talk to some people. Eric and Amber from Guangzhou are here, and I want to ask the organizers about galleries here on the island. I need to keep in touch and network. There are lots of people to meet and stuff."

"Damn, girl. You've got it all planned, a full itinerary."

"I am busy. It's true. Sorry, I don't mean to ditch you."

"It's cool. You go and have fun. We'll have plenty of time to spend together all weekend."

"You're too nice," I say and kiss his cheek.

"See you later, girl."

Slowly I walk away and then look behind me. He's so content, just sitting, staring at the water and scribbling away. I thought that we'd party together, but he isn't really into it. Oh, well.

I take off my sandals, carry them in my hands, and step where the water touches the sand. It's a little cold, but feels refreshing. Wet sand sticks to the gaps between my toes, scratching me gently.

Down the beach I see a group of men mingling, and I recognize some of them as the guys who came here with me. From the two British DJs in our crew, I know Estaz better. He's less famous, played his set too early and has long since finished. He's conversing with one of the organizers, a guy who lives on Lamma.

I met that organizer when we arrived and set up shop. He was helpful. I guess maybe he's a professional promoter. His accent's hard to place, maybe Australian. Like most of the men here, he wears no shirt. Unlike most of the others, he has solid chest muscles and a toned stomach.

"Great job with the party," I say to him.

"Thanks, bird," he says in a way that sounds insincere as if he receives praise all the time. He shrugs me off and goes back to facing the others.

Annoyed by his attitude, I try to show off a little. "It's not as good as the parties we used to throw in Beijing or anything, but it's kind of fun."

"Is that a fact?" he says, and we all laugh.

"It'll do," says Estaz. "What I love about Lamma isn't just the raving. It's the community. Here, it's not just about money and getting high. It's truly about the music."

"Not about getting high?" I say. "Tell that to Eric. Heh, heh! Maybe he'd disagree."

Estaz and I chuckle, but the promoter doesn't get it. He's too serious, and I see that his mind goes in only one direction. "Now, now, should I be meeting this Eric fellow?" he asks.

"American bloke," says Estaz. "Also in the, what do you call it, the Canton Contingent. He often has the best shit, but I can't guarantee that he brought any from across the border. Is he really here, Ting Ting?"

"Yeah, I saw him at the toilets."

"That's fitting. Geez, is it just me, or are there more people at this little shindig from the mainland than from Hong Kong?"

"I don't know."

"Well," says the promoter with the solid chest and flat stomach. "I could meet someone new, ask about some stuff."

"It's worth a try. I'll introduce you."

Estaz leads us back to the dance floor and pulls Eric out from the crowd. I decide to follow them, curious about where this will lead. We find a corner behind a loudspeaker and perform introductions.

"I must say that I'm surprised," says Eric when the talk of business begins. "You see, I only brought a bit, for trade, because I assumed that all would be of a purer sort on this island. What's your stock?"

"Just some Mollies… What did you bring?"

"Interesting! Well, my good sir, I might be willing to part with a tad dosage of liquid GHB. Are you familiar?"

"I'm very familiar. That sounds interesting too."

"One sip, a big sip, for one pill. Fair trade?"

"That works as long as your mate vouches for the quality of your stuff."

On cue, Estaz nods.

"Let's do it," and Eric goes to his tent, vanishing inside. Everyone follows him with arms crossed, playing it cool, but with giddy, childish smiles.

I follow too, still curious about all this. I'm barefoot, and the sand on my feet is drying. As I wiggle my toes, it still feels scratchy. I don't remember what happened to my shoes. Or were they sandals? I'm definitely still drunk.

"Any art galleries here?" I ask as we wait outside Eric's tent.

"Huh?"

"Well, you're like a promoter, right? What about other events besides parties? Are there any art galleries and, like, exhibition shows? I'm, uh, an artist."

"Sure, whatever you want. I'll email you and keep in touch."

"Cool."

Essentially he's ignoring me, anxious for what Eric has to offer.

"We'll trade email addresses later," I say.

"Yeah."

We wait longer. Eric has zipped up his tent and won't let us inside. He shouts to us from within that he needs to sort out some measuring equipment.

"So," I ask, "how much does it cost to bribe the police not to interfere with a beach party like this? At the warehouse shows in Beijing, we used to..."

"What makes you think that I bribed anyone?" the promoter interrupts, hostile.

"I don't know," I say meekly.

"Organizing something like this isn't easy, and it isn't cheap, but I can bloody well assure you that we all have the proper permits."

"Oh."

Then I hear only the rustling of tarp and the zipping of bags opening and closing. Somehow, anticipation lifts those noises above the music.

"So you lived in Beijing," the promoter says, probably reluctant to leave our chat stalled on a bad note and because there's little else to say. "Do you speak Cantonese or Mandarin?"

I answer in some very poorly accented Cantonese and make a joke. But he doesn't get it. "Mandarin, and just a little Cantonese," I say in English. "What about you?"

"Not a word of any Chinese, no matter what the dialect."

"I see." Still waiting, bored, I ask more questions. "Do you ever go to mainland China? Like the Guangdong capital? That's where I live now. Or even that famous border town? Not a good place or anything, but it's so close. Hong Kong's great, but it's pretty cool that you can go to such a different kind of place very nearby. One country, two systems, right?"

"Never went to any of them," he tells me.

"Really?"

"I have no interest in going there."

"Not even for a quick visit?"

"Not once. It sounds too crazy for me, too dangerous. Come on, bird. Listen to the way you describe it."

"No way, it's not that bad. I've lived in China my whole life. It's a normal place.

"I think," he says, "that you people living there are certifiably nuts."

"We are?"

He laughs at me, and I experience strange feelings that are a mixture of confusion, embarrassment, patriotism, resentment, and a slight sense of shame that I respect this guy's opinion at all.

Silently I watch as Eric finally emerges from his tent with a measuring cup of what looks like normal water. In the moonlight, the liquid's color seems almost grey. The two men make an exchange that involves a handful of capsules that the promoter guy had in his pants pocket all along.

They both see me watching and make no effort to hide the deal. Then they gesture toward me, eyebrows knitted and shoulders raised, showing off the acquisitions, as if asking, *You want some?*

I smile and shake my head, *Thanks but no thanks.*

I hope that they'll have fun. They talk together and then fade away inside the tent, from where a light flickers on and off.

Next, I decide to find my boyfriend again. He still plays it low-key, sitting there so relaxed on the sand, and I drink some of his water. I hope he has no drugs in there. Just kidding!

Then I go for another shot of liquor. Along the way, I happen to find my sandals on the sidewalk. Although glad for the discovery, I don't want them right now so I throw them behind the DJ booth.

After yet another shot, I dance and dance, forgetting the time. When I go for another swig of water, I see that my boyfriend has disappeared and I don't know where. Detouring to my own tent, I find some of the colorful Hong Kong dollars, and I go to buy some extremely expensive water from a vendor.

Then I dance more. A short drunk guy hits on me, rubbing the side of my ribs as I dance. I ignore him, and he goes away.

When the DJs change up, there's some technical difficulty, and the music suddenly stops. The abrupt silence hits like a reverse bang, jolting everyone into paying attention. Hordes of people on the outskirts of the dance floor immediately look to us in the center. A communal groan of disappointment replaces the musical sounds.

"Sorry, folks," someone says into an echoing microphone, "we'll be right back up."

A high-pitched feedback screech erupts, and I cover my ears. At this point, people start to disperse.

When the music resumes, there's no crowd anymore. The unlucky new DJ needs to work hard to attract everyone back.

At this point, I decide that it's a good idea to catch up with Amber. I wander all the way back to the main village before I catch sight of her in the glare of a streetlight. Trying to close the distance, I follow her down an alley off the Main Street.

She's talking to a tall Chinese guy. He's handsome. From how he carries himself, I instantly think that he's a local Hong Kong person. He wears what looks like a genuine polo shirt, sports shorts, and leather sandals.

The two of them seem very familiar with each other. I stop, concealed by darkness, and try to listen. I can't hear much, but my observations of body language tell me that they're both upset.

Suddenly Amber makes a violent slapping motion, aiming for the man's face. From my vantage point, I can't tell for sure if she connected, but the guy recoils, stepping back.

"I'm leaving!" Amber abruptly yells.

I wonder why she struck at him and yelled like that. Suddenly, I don't want her to know that I saw them together. It was a very private conversation. I kind of spied.

I give Amber a minute after she walks away from the man. Then, back on the Main Street, I cautiously approach her. (I always seem to jump into these awkward situations.)

"Hey, Amber," I say.

She puts on a big happy face and hugs me. "It's nice to see you again!"

"Yeah, you too. Now we're in a quiet place. We can talk and catch up."

"Sure, sure."

"Tell me," I request, "what's up with you lately?"

"Not much," she says. Seems she doesn't want to mention the man. "I'm busy with the usual things, like working, partying and vacationing here. I've, uh, done some modeling work lately."

"Wow, that's cool," I say, still curious, but knowing better than to ask about that guy. Still, it's interesting that she's modeling. That's something we can discuss. "I used to model too."

"Then you must agree," she says, and looks over her shoulder, "that there's nothing wrong with that job at all."

"Sure thing, it's great."

We talk about work and struggling and art while taking our time to walk back to the beach. As we approach the outdoor bar, I have an idea. "Let's drink! I can get you free drinks!"

I run up to the plastic table where there's a cooler full of melted ice, souring orange-juice mixers, sodas, and warm bottles of beer. Endless empty aluminum cans litter the sand so I must step carefully.

"What do you want?" I say to empty air. Nobody answers.

Far behind me, Amber walks slowly. "Fine then," I murmur.

I smile to the bartender guy as if asking if he knows me after all my visits there. "Um, vodka with soda," I tell him. "Two of them. Yeah!"

Amber finally arrives despite my worries that another man might steal her. "Sorry, it's warm," I say, handing her a drink. "It's so late."

"Thanks honey," says Amber. "What's in it?"

"Vodka."

"Good choice." She takes a sip. "Speaking of vodka, isn't that Maria?"

Whirling, I look in the direction that she points. "Who?"

"That girl. Sometimes she goes to Indian Towers or Golf Ball. I didn't think she'd come all this way. Wow, she looks damn sexy. I have to go and say hi."

So Amber and I separate again. For my next activity, I stumble onto the dance floor and fall down a few times. After my final tumble, a boy helps me up. He asks my name, but I stick out my tongue and go to dance again. I think that maybe I get drunk too easily.

Every time I start to feel slightly sober, I go back for more drinks. The music's bumping, and I reckon that the new DJ's really starting to take off. It's very Euro-trance, I guess, very danceable. I feel like I may know everyone here. Really I do recognize a surprising number of faces. But I hold no deep conversations with anyone, merely saying "hi" and asking how they like the party.

When I see that Amber has returned, I hug her again and again. With my boyfriend missing and that crew of DJs and technicians getting higher and more distant, she's like my new best friend here.

I don't know how much time passes. Closing my eyes, I dance for as long as I can. When I open them, I see that Amber's still with me and dancing drunkenly too. A layer of sweaty moisture covers her skin. I touch my forehead and chest, realizing that the same goes for me.

"LET'S COOL OFF AND HAVE A REST." I don't know if she hears me, but she does follow.

We catch our breath. The shoreline's near, and I have a new idea. "Let's swim!" I take her by a hand and propel my bare feet along the walkway. Then we detour onto a darker part of the beach.

"Shall I change?" Amber asks. "My bikini bottom's in my tent."

I pull down my shorts.

"Or swimming in my underwear's cool too," she reacts.

"Silly, who needs underwear?" and I take off my top.

"You're really doing this. You're crazy!"

"Let's skinny-dip," I say in a loud whisper. "Nobody can see us. Come on! It's a quiet spot."

Stealthily, we move to the very end of the beach. In the distance, the party's lit up by fires, flashing stage lights, and my video. I see no one near us, except for a few couples sitting on a blanket, and I don't think they're looking this way.

I want to experience this so I shove my clothes into a pile and run fast into the water. The wind blows across my entire front as I run and run. When I hit the water, my toes feel a rush of coldness. I adjust to the temperature, squat to my knees, and splash myself with salty water.

At first, I shriek, but then slap my mouth shut when realizing how loud I am. Kicking at the sand, I push forward, deeper and deeper into the sea. Then waves start bobbing me up and down. Soon I no longer feel the little rocks and shells under me, and I'm just barely wading. Only my head stays above the water.

I can see Amber. She's hesitant to join me. "The water feels fine," I say, waving, not sure if she hears me.

After looking back and forth, she pulls off her top, quickly drops her shorts and underwear, and then runs into the water with her hands covering her chest.

She swims right up to me – she's a good swimmer – and laughs and splashes. "I'm not even that drunk," she says. "I can't believe that I'm doing this with you. Ting Ting, you're well and truly crazy."

"When I was a model, I was always like this."

"Really? I can't imagine you as that kind of a girl."

"So you should be used to modeling like this too."

"No way, I won't do nude!"

"I didn't mean anything like that," I say, wading. "It's like… I was an art model for the university. Even when I was a student, we had life-drawing classes, studied anatomy and all. It's cool. It's true art, not porn or anything."

"I see. That's really interesting. I never knew that about you."

"I'm, uh, very involved in the art world."

"Sounds completely tasteful. I mean it."

It's nice to be floating out here and conversing like this. We chat and swim until we're tired. Every so often, I go close enough to the shore to see that my clothes remain there. The third time over, I see that my clothes are fine, but several people linger there too.

I recognize one of the men. It's Eric. "I can't believe that you beat me to it," he yells to us, dropping his swimming shorts and running into the water. The others laugh, but don't dare follow him.

"WHOOO!" Eric yells.

"That guy always gets naked," says Amber.

"Now there are so many people nearby," I say. "How will we get out?"

In no time, Eric swims over and splashes us. I see that he hugs Amber. She plays along and doesn't act offended, but I don't want any naked hugs from him. I back away.

The tide brings me closer to shore, and I see men leering at me. They drink beer and lean forward, getting their feet wet, but not coming in to swim. Feeling embarrassed, I keep my torso low.

As the tide pushes and brings me higher, I crouch lower, making sure that only my shoulders and wet hair can feel the wind. That just makes the men gawk at me even harder.

"Okay, guys, the show's over," my boyfriend announces, suddenly appearing to save me.

"Hey!" I say and wave to him. But I wave carefully to make sure that my breasts stay under the water.

My boyfriend chases the men away, and they scatter. Then he carries a large towel, takes off his sandals, and walks to me. His shorts get wet, and he doesn't care. I stand, and he covers me up. I give him a kiss.

"My hero…"

"Hero?" he says. "Saving you from yourself?"

"Oh, you're no fun."

He kisses me again. Then he makes another announcement to the lingering crowd that forms a widening half-circle around us, this time louder. "I *really* mean it. Show's over!"

He wraps me tightly in the towel, and I wear it like I've just emerged from a shower, like it's a dress. I'm vigorously guarded, and the other men back away as we pass.

Without such modesty, Eric charges out of the water, his dick swinging and words raving. This distracts people, and they all look to him. He's singing a song, I think, but he's almost screaming, his voice such a noise and going so fast that I don't understand much. It's something about God, the stars and animals, I think. I can't be sure what he's on, but he's really on it hard.

We ignore him, but everyone else nearby walks over to see the spectacle. My boyfriend takes the chance to pick up my clothes and offer me a water bottle. I drink some, but as it reaches my stomach and mixes with my insides, I feel a pain welling up inside me.

Immediately, I'm overcome with dizziness and exhaustion. Before I know it, vomit comes right out of me. I cover my mouth with my hand, and the spew gets all over my chest and the towel.

My throat burns, my eyes water, and my nose's clogged. The smell resembles a mixture of sickness, rotten fruit, and seawater. I hardly can keep my eyes open. I want to go back into the ocean, fall down, and wash away this mess.

"Oh, gross! I'm so embarrassed."

"Let's get you cleaned up, girl."

Right now, I don't feel very sexy. But at least I'm sobering up some.

"I need to get dressed," I say.

"We'll get you dressed."

"Where are my sandals?"

I feel terrible. Why do my most eventful nights always end up veering from coolness to regret? Is it too much to ask that they should stay cool the whole time?

And that's just my problem. What's going on with everyone else? As I look around, wondering where I should go to get dressed and have a rest, I notice Eric. Up close. There he is. His mouth is foaming.

6
蛇

"It's all relative," I explain. "Very Einsteinian. You wouldn't understand. Relatively speaking, suffice it to say, I have a high tolerance with these things."

"Yer crazy." So says my new compatriot of the night. He's humbly named Pete.

I procure my measuring cup from one of many pouches in my heavy and durable camping sack. "Take this beaker," I say, beginning my lecture. "A reputable cookbook might quote adding so many milliliters of oil. Say, up to here," and I point my finger to a relatively low level.

"But I'm on a diet," I continue, "so I subtract that by a third. Or rather, let's speculate about another time and place, and I happen to like this brand of olive oil. So I'll add a quarter." I shift my finger up and down, intentionally portraying the measurements as ambiguous.

"What're ya makin'?" he asks, totally not following. "I can do a mean batch o' cookies."

"Please don't miss my point. Fine then, cookies. I ask you, does the recommended oil consumption truly make such a difference? There's a certain threshold, to be sure, in which needed ingredients must have a minimum dose for the desired effect. And in reverse, a maximum until the taste reaches... damn, but I do hate to word it in such loaded terminology... *overdose*."

"Wait, are we still talkin' about cookies?"

"Gamma-Hydroxybutyric acid, MDMA, and Grandma's fucking recipe for chocolate biscuits. You know what I mean? The point being that there's far more leeway in the middle than most care to admit. Whether your palate is suited for spices, sweets, or just directly connects to the serotonin-releasing glands, it takes trial and error to find the percentage of key chemicals that work for you. And it isn't such a big deal to play around with that. Cooking's an art."

"I'll drink ta' that!"

"Or take this spoon," I continue, removing the next item from my pile of personal gear. He looks at the spoon, burnt-side-up.

"Um, like for sugar?"

"Whatever. Let's say that we're baking a cake, and the recipe assures us two tablespoons of sugar. But mine is a *sweet* tooth. And I dare to go overboard, not just by half a tablespoon, or even sixty to seventy per cent. I add three extra tablespoons for a total of five, *more than twice the dosage.* If you like sweets, it's all good. Otherwise you simply learn and take into account for future recipes. We never know until we try. It matters not and all works out the same. In Mandarin, we might say, '*cha bu duo*'."

"I don't know no Mandarin."

"Fair enough. Keep this in mind too. About crossing the specific lines from minimal dosage to OD, it's fuzzy indeed. Like Mandelbrot fractals, infinitely indefinable and multi-dimensional. They don't conform to specific sets of measurable and verifiable integers. It's infinitely subtle, as we must never forget. Not to mention personal metabolism and just plain taste. Etcetera, and so forth. Fuzzy math. Personalize your order. Don't be afraid to customize. You're a paying customer! Only by being intuitive do we respect this as the art it is, and…"

"Um, what?"

I can see that I'm talking over him. It happens at times.

"My apologies," I say. "Sometimes my mind races and I can't help myself. Let me get to the point, being which, I know how much shit that I can handle."

"I guess I follow ya there, mate."

"Indeed. Let's bloody do this. Please, Peter, come into the tent."

I invite him deeper inside and do a quick turnaround to make sure that no one watches us. That girl has left us, perhaps to the detriment of my companion, but it's all the same to me. She rejected my advances ages ago, and frankly she's not my type.

After getting rid of her and, of course, having delivered the obligatory speech explaining the disparity of doses for me and for my new customer, all has been checked off, and I'm finally ready to partake.

"By the way, you organized a splendid party here."

"Thanks."

I zip up the plastic and tarp behind me. In here, it's rather dark at this time of night, despite everyone being in the midst of a Dionysian romp outside. I don't want anyone getting the wrong idea so I immediately turn on a flashlight, although I wonder if it makes a difference as far as the inappropriate mood goes.

"Ahem, keep your hands where I can see them."

He gets that joke, and the subsequent laughter eases the tension.

I reorganize my camping bag and its various pouches, standing up the flashlight as a sort of lamp and carefully placing the beaker beside it. I take my specially marked water bottle and carefully pour into the beaker. The liquid slowly rises until hitting a previously marked spot.

"Here you are," and I hand it to him. "Straight from the *Liwan* factory. Grandma's home-cooking."

He gulps it. "Tastes like water."

"Not bad, right? Not too mediciney at all. Expect a pleasant inebriated effect, a mix of drowsiness with heartbeat acceleration and a feeling of body vibration. But you surely will stay in control of your faculties. Enjoy!"

My turn! "Now I'm going to take a big chug of this GHB, the large margin within being far less than the lethal amount, but far more than I'd recommend for you. Once combined with those other entheogens swimming around in my bloodstream and nervous system, we'll soon see what the hell happens."

Not even looking at the beaker, I wing it and take a thirsty drink. This is kind of the point.

"What else are ya on?" Pete asks me.

"The standard concoction. Your THC, the skunky spliffs going around and, obviously, copious amounts of alcohol and cigarettes. The special part will be the pills, those pure Molly capsules. *Mmmm*, do you feel that? Suddenly the weather took a turn for the, um, windy, cool, breezy. Let us. Let us open. Let us open the tent. Go out. Out of here. Here."

Whaaaaaaaaaaaaaaatttttt?

"Well, that's coming on rather strong."

* * *

I experience a not-unfamiliar time jump, but it's unexpected because this trip wasn't supposed to be the psychedelic sort. (Nor ketamine, as I know of no veterinary factories in the area.) Of course not lysergic acid diethlymide either since this isn't Southeast Asia backpacker country. I'm simply at a party, high, stoned, in the moment, yet here I am with blacked-out memories and left very confused. The whole thing's a surprise.

Suddenly I find myself next to the ocean, hanging out with Pete, and we're looking at girls.

"What do you think of that bird?" he asks.

As often happens when I'm, shall we say, *loaded as fuck*, I speak in a sort of autopilot that betrays my better vocabulary. It just spews from my mouth.

"You mean for a strapping, young party-dude like yourself? Fuck! You could do better."

So far as I can tell, I have yet to completely embarrass myself. This is lucky.

"Man, that buzz sure has kicked in, huh? You too?"

"I'm cool, man. I guess."

I sense bad vibes. Around me are various couples in states of distress. I see two men, one of whom I recognize, in a verbal cuff with looks of fire emanating from both pairs of eyes. I'm overcome with a need to interject, to impart my wisdom of universal love upon these poor unwashed masses.

I walk over, stand in the middle and interrupt.

"Hey!" shouts the man whom I recognize, perturbed.

"You are M," I say to the middle-aged gentleman I'd already met.

"Give me a minute, buddy. I have something to say to this little weasel here."

"Why must you quarrel with the Chinese man?"

"It's personal. Go. Away!"

"All is love. Take it easy. None is the big deal with think it is."

"I'm in the middle of something here. It's business, something I'm sure you wouldn't understand. Respect that, and get the hell out of here."

"Simply ingest some methylenedioxy-methamphetamine, my friend, and roll as to one with the cosmos."

"Wha…?"

"And be one."

"Er, are you feeling alright?"

* * *

There are no visuals, so I still may not call this one psychedelic. But certainly a chronological distortion exists to it, and a most peculiar feeling. I next find myself wandering near the sea with wet sandals, and I'm seeking some sort of feminine companionship.

"*Ambeerrrrrrrrr,*" I droll out.

Vague dreamlike reflections cloud my mind. I feel that she was talking to some guy before, I think.

So I want to find a single girl to fancy, but here there are none. They all are paired off in couples, attached at the forearms or mouths. The beautiful half-naked ones in their short shorts and bikini tops, with cute stomachs and fluttering eyes, Chinese, white, or other nationalities, all are with males. I'm afraid that I won't get lucky tonight.

Alas, I feel very lonely. Where's my male friend anyway? And I think that I should do something drastic before my next blackout. Well, I just pondered nakedness. I think, maybe, and so it's decided that I should get naked.

"I should get naked," I tell myself.

"Streaking!" someone yells. Did I say that?

It's truly to be likened to a dream, it is, and somehow I know that two nude beauties frolic in the sea. I wish to join them. My clothing falls away and disappears from this realm. I don't move, but the rest of the world does, and the water rises to my chest, and I merely float. I see one of those beauties. I know of her, but have forgotten her name. We embrace. I feel her soft skin rubbing upon mine. She talks, and I talk. I forget the words just as they disappear into the air. The words, like my thoughts, are phantoms, clouds, dispersing smoke, all gone.

There's something I must say. Something, to say. To say. To shout. To scream. To tell. To say, to the whole world. Say

that

It's relative,

Relativity,

Nativity,

Natist,

Statist,

Stasiz,

Haziz,

Whazis,

Zis,

s

sssssssss

snake,

make,

mammal,

animal,

animalistic!

Oh, wait. Dammit! I'm out of the water, finding it hard to breathe, my stomach hurts, and something really strange is happening to my circulatory system. Perhaps I overdid it. Indubitably.

Me, of all people. Really? I should know better.

7
馬

I came to this outlying island to get away from it all, as a break from the city and a chance to relax. But it's no paradise here. It's dirty, and I'm finding the place difficult to enjoy, with the sand underfoot, creeping salt water, and more than a few beer-stained T-shirts.

Despite growing up only a few relative kilometers from this place, I never was much of a beach person. Give me indoor swimming pools any day. Not here where the sand gets everywhere, sticking in your hair, pockets, and every little crevice. I can't wait to go home and shower.

"Nice to see you."

"What's up?"

"Lookin' good."

"Been a while."

Soon I've nodded to, or shaken hands with, what must be a hundred people. I can recall a lot of the faces, but not names. Mostly they can't remember my name either so we call each other "*you*" or "*guy*", anything to avoid that awkward admission of ignorance. Fine by me! Mostly I wave from a reasonable distance, close enough that the passing acquaintance and I must acknowledge each other, but far enough away that we don't say anything. Just keep moving.

It's surprising how many people recognize me and how many I know from across the border. Am I the only proper Hong Konger here?

After only about an hour, I'm getting hungry, so I follow the pathway leading away from the beach and go all the way to a little seafood restaurant. While walking, I see another party character, an American chap who runs a bar near the port, and we're passing each other so we just do the smile-and-wave thing and keep going.

When I reach the humble restaurant, which must have stayed open extra late to feed the beach-partiers, I order a beer and a rice dish. I sit outside across from the front door's display of fish swimming in dirty tanks.

Over empty plates, two girls seated at an adjacent table casually chat. One is white and one Chinese.

"You must be from around here," I say to them.

"How can you tell?" asks the white girl. She's short, wears glasses and looks a little old, but dresses in an alternative style and has her hair dyed deep red. I'd guess that she's in her 30s, but trying to play up like she's still younger. Knowing her type quite well, I'd bet that her dress was made from hemp and that she does yoga every morning.

"Because you look so relaxed," I answer. "Just chillin' at the seafood place. You're not at the beach party and not exploring the island either. Now you're pacing yourselves, but later you'll be drunk and dancing the same as everyone else. But unlike the rest, you won't be taking the ferry or sleeping in a tent. You have no anxiety about you because this is your village. You must live right up that hill," and I point in a random direction.

"Very good," says the white girl, smiling. "Anything else?"

"Oh, I suppose that I'm doing alright then. Okay. You've lived here for a while, several years." What could the mystery girl do for work? What's the job? Let me see…

I look for clues, but it hardly matters what I say. If I guess right, then I come across well. If I guess wrong, but flatter her, then it's still good flirting, and we can strike up more conversation.

So I go with an educated guess plus a touch of flattery. "Are you a grad student researching your Master's thesis? Asian studies? Wouldn't be Mandarin or anything, not down here. Perhaps design, something creative."

This elicits laughs from both of them, and they clap.

"Come on," I plead. "Aren't you going to tell me how I'm doing? Give me a sign if I'm close."

Then before anyone can give me a reaction, a Filipina waitress comes, breaking the flow of our conversation. Once I've ordered, my food and drink arrive almost instantaneously.

The two girls decide to refill their drinks. Our multilingual waitress first asks the white girl in English what she'll have and then addresses the Chinese girl in badly accented Cantonese. It all sounds good to me because the girls have chosen to stay a bit longer.

And the waitress departs.

Still speaking in Cantonese, the Chinese girl asks me where I'm from. I try to ignore her, and she asks again. I know her type too, and it's not mine.

She's got to be one of those true Hong Kongers, working in some dull business environment. She definitely moved to Lamma just for cheaper rent. A member of the young generation, she wasn't raised to speak English proficiently, but she's too old to excel at Mandarin either.

Floating on the shifted colonial tides without real language advantages, she wouldn't dream of working on the mainland, and until a few years ago, she lived in a total Canto-world. Then after getting here, she fell into the Lamma party scene, suddenly smoking dope and hanging out with Europeans ravers.

One thing that you have to give to us Chinese, we're adaptable.

But perhaps I'm too harsh.

Anyhow, I've already picked my target, and it's not her. I simply reply by saying that we should be polite and speak English.

"Where are you from?" I'm asked in the language that everyone understands.

"Really now," I say, still taking the piss. "That's the most boring question in the world."

Just as the Chinese girl follows up, I cut her off at the precise moment. "Don't ask me where I work either. That's the second most boring question. It's true. Someone did a survey. You can look it up."

"*Sooo* what should we talk about?" asks the white girl, stretching out both the *so* and the final rising tone of a question mark.

"Let me eat first, and then I'll have some ideas."

I chew in an efficient quick way so as to finish and move on to the next social venue, but I still need to chomp slowly enough to show that I have some manners. As I do this, I mentally consider a list of conversation topics. What will be interesting and make me look good? I could talk about astrology. Girls of this type always like that stuff. I could talk about the club music scene, but that may reveal where I live, and I don't want that out there yet. Independent movies would be good. Novels, maybe, but there's little chance that we'd have anything in common.

So I just go with a story that I often tell about the last time I traveled to the UK. It involves a visit to the old alma mater, almost getting into a fight outside a London club, and accidentally interrupting a commercial video being shot outdoors. The story works well. It elicits laughter and shows off my positive qualities. Just like when meeting with clients or networking at luncheons, we all need to have a few good stories rehearsed.

After another round of drinks, for which I insist on paying, we chat up some more. When we finish, it's time for me to return to the party. I walk along the path, and in a clear indication of interest, the girls trot along to keep pace with me.

I tell them that I'm meeting my friends (they don't know I'm alone here), and so I cut them both loose. The Chinese girl soon lags behind, but the white one won't let me escape, and I feel a tap on one of my forearms.

Perfect.

"Wait," she says and then giggles. "We didn't catch your name."

"Steven Lee. With a *v*. Don't forget the *v*, and don't forget the Lee."

"Nice to meet you, Steven Lee."

"Nice to meet you too."

This brings a handshake, lingering fingers, and more touching. I'm almost surprised at how well I'm doing.

"It's so pleasant to talk to someone new on Lamma," she says.

"New? I'll bet that you get visitors here all the time."

"Well, just tourists. And this lot here tonight, coming mainly from the mainland."

"I know!" I exclaim in an emotional reaction that's a bit too obvious. What the hell? I'd might as well cut the mysterious-man act and talk about myself. "Alright, I admit it. I work on the other side in that little border town. You must have heard of it, the one everybody hates."

"Oh, I've heard of the place," she says, "but I've never been there."

"Never?"

"I've heard a lot, all of it bad."

"Sure. Well, tonight we're not allowed to talk about where I come from, remember?"

"How many banned topics do you have? I take it that China's another one in that boring-subject survey that you mentioned."

"Nope, China's not a boring topic at all. If anything, it's as interesting as interesting can get. But it's kind of a downer. That's all. I came here to stay positive, to get away from all of that for a while, you know?"

"So what will we talk about?"

"We'll find something eventually. I'm still enjoying this back-and-forth right here. Don't let it end."

"Ha! Do you realize that we're talking about talking? How meta is that?"

As we really get into the conversation, we walk at an ever-slower pace, almost standing. We take our time, joke around and tease, stopping at various landmarks to comment on the beach and nature.

When we make it all the way to the party, our surroundings get much too loud. Like the proverbial frog getting boiled, we now yell and don't even notice it.

But I do notice that the other girl has disappeared, and so I decide to make my move. "DO YOU HAVE ANYTHING GOOD TO SMOKE?"

"LIKE WHAT?"

"I THINK YOU KNOW!"

"AT MY PLACE! LET'S GO! WE'LL BE ABLE TO TALK THERE!"

At this point, I feel confident enough to slither an arm around the low curve of her back. I motion for us to turn around, leave the beach, and follow the path again. The dancers, drinks and rubbish all vanish behind us.

"LEAD THE WAY!"

At first, we walk without speaking, and I don't move my arm from her back. Just as I must be able to carry a good conversation in pickups, it's equally important to portray comfort and confidence in silent situations. It will be extremely important later.

Some tardy party-goers drag their feet, walking in the opposite direction. A few of them instigate that maybe-I-recognize-you experience.

I see a wealthy-looking mainlander yuppie, exactly the type of person I bloody hate, and his trophy girlfriend. Somehow they've carried shopping bags all the way here. She actually wears high heels on her way to a beach. Apparently they've just arrived, still looking for the party. When the man smiles toward me, I just automatically nod my head. They follow the music, and then they're gone.

We continue walking. Now the girl tells a story about her experiences when travelling across continental Europe and how she arrived on Lamma due to an ex-boyfriend's work. I interrupt with a few witty quips, but mostly I listen, letting her speak. In the process, I learn that I was right about her being a graduate student. I learn a lot about her hometown, favorite books, and main complaints about the local culture. Once women feel comfortable and start to talk, they can go on and on.

That's okay. I know what to do in such situations. With each step, I sense that we're growing closer to each other, and I know she feels it too. Soon we'll reach her apartment, and I'll reap the rewards for my good efforts. In my head, we're snogging already.

We pass the same little restaurant where we met. This island has a downtown of sorts, the Main Street in Yung Shue Wan, which is a quaint little island village. Soon we reach a cluster of restaurants, coffee shops, and grocery stores. This should be the area where everyone hangs out, at least when there's no beach party.

To the left, we hear the sounds of waves. Then to the right, a steep staircase leads uphill to a residential neighborhood. Many of the homes sit halfway up a hillside, mostly in little three-story apartment buildings hobbled together with what looks like minimal urban planning. More like make-it-up-as-you-go-along planning, something I'm all too familiar with from beyond the border, but don't expect to see in Hong Kong. The shadowy grey buildings look like half-unfolded cardboard boxes thrown together after retailers finished unpacking.

Looking up, I wonder where exactly my companion lives. When my attention returns to the street ahead, I see a familiar girl holding a one-liter bottle of water step out from a grocery store. On instinct, I wave to her with my free hand before I even recognize her.

My body had moved before my mind could properly process it. Now realizing her identity, I have no choice but to control my surprise. Having made the first move, I need to say something. I must make contact. Bloody hell!

"Hi, Amber," I say to my ex-girlfriend. "It's really you."

"What a surprise," she answers.

"I didn't expect to see you here."

When I let go of the other girl, she instantly knows that something's wrong. I stammer a bit and introduce them. It isn't a comfortable scenario. My whole game teeters, ready to collapse. So I apologize and mumble to my new friend that I'll have to catch up with her later.

Then I grab Amber's arm and take her into a little alley to talk privately. The poor girl from the restaurant is left alone, perplexed and unhappy. She declines to follow us.

Again, I've reacted without thinking. Here I am, pivoting from one girl to another and not in a good way.

"What the hell do you think you're doing here?" I ask Amber in a loud whisper. I feel like I have a secret to keep or else I'll be in big trouble, almost as if I'm a naughty child, as ridiculous as that sounds. I can't help it.

"Nice to see you too, Steven," she says.

"You shouldn't be here like this," I say.

"What's your problem? I can't go where I want? It's a free country. At least, it is here."

"I can't believe that you're dressed this way."

She looks amazing in a revealing bikini top with thin straps looping over smooth shoulders. Mirror sunglasses rest on the crown of her head, although they're useless except as a fashion item under this night sky. Her hairstyle looks a bit shorter than I remember, with her curly hair permed straight at the edges, perhaps shaded a touch darker. Her stomach and arms are lean and well-toned. I notice her nails, a bright lavender shade. I look down and see pink toenails too. She carries a small backpack, the kind that teenaged girls favor as purses, with name-brand logos displayed. In short, she's doing great. Without me.

All these observations cause me to wince from stabs of jealousy, knowing that a man must have brought her here. Anger boils within me, and it's too hot to repress. There's that, and it mingles with other feelings, those of deep desire. Pangs of regret hit me too. Why did we ever break up, and why did she move? Suddenly, my entire situation brims with involuntary emotions. On top of it all, I can add a self-directed anger and disappointment because I know that I'm not in control.

"Let's just get along," Amber says.

"I'm amazed to see you in a place like this. I thought you'd moved far away."

"I did move, but maybe not as far as you thought. Anyhow, I'm on vacation."

"You could have warned me you'd be here."

"Are you kidding me with this? I'm supposed to report to you on where I go? You're acting really creepy, Steven. It's not like I wanted to pull you away from your date. You seemed to be doing fine. Why don't you run and find that girl before it's too late? Then you can leave me alone."

"No, you're here now, and we need to talk. What are you doing with yourself?"

"I'm working as a model, in *Canton*," she says with a pretentious accent, "if you can believe it."

"A what?"

"A model."

"I, uh, heard you."

Taking a moment, I try to wrap my spinning brain around this detail. Is she serious?

Amber smiles in a confident, sexy way that I've never seen from her before. She shows an air of arrogance, as if really thinking that she's better than me. I can't stand it.

"A model," I say. "Really? You chose that from all the available jobs out there. I tried to get you into the trading firm, remember? But you weren't into it. Do you even know how the modeling business works on the mainland?"

"Lighten up! You're so judgmental."

"Amber, what happened to you?"

"Nothing, I'm exactly the same, but I'm doing well. That's the only difference. You should feel happy for me."

"You can't expect me to congratulate you. That's a seriously dirty business. You need to listen to me."

"What are you going on about? I just do some shoots for a few clothing lines. It's commercial fashion, nothing shady."

"Oh, right, *for now*. When will they start asking for favors?"

"Honestly, I have no idea what you're talking about."

"You know," I hiss, "sexual favors." I regret the words as soon as I say them, but can't take them back.

"Omigod! I still have no idea what the hell you mean by that."

Her anger simmers to the surface, but I have no choice. I'm compelled to say, "Model *slash* escort, that's the truth of it. Listen to me. I'm knowledgeable about these things."

"Shut up. Now."

"You know what, Amber? Maybe it does suit you to become a dumb model, but I never thought you'd be a slut."

Suddenly she lashes out, and a slap from her open hand smacks my face. Pain and shock arrive in an instant. I back away a step and see a look of serious hurt cloud her eyes.

"I'm sorry," I say. "I'm only trying to be helpful. If you'd just think about my point—"

"I'm leaving!" she yells.

Still jolted, I struggle to resist saying anything more. Amber strides away, quickly turns a corner, and I no longer see her. I make no effort to chase her.

Standing there, I don't know if I've made a deep impression and caused her to cry, or if she immediately will forget me and my impact on her life. Either way, I feel very alone.

Mere moments ago, there were two girls. One too many. Now there are none. The party was supposed to be fun. It nearly was. What just happened?

8
羊

"It's so weird! We're really here!"

I'm with a group of my friends. As our luggage transfers to a Thai Air Skybus, we're left to hang out at Hong Kong's epic airport. There are six of us, an even mix of boys and girls, including my good friend from my hometown, Derrick, one of his buddies, my two college roommates from Long Beach, and one of their boyfriends.

We flew from LAX, and for everybody except me, it was the longest flight ever. This is the farthest from home that my friends ever have gone. Landing at this airport marks the first time they've been abroad, meaning their first passport stamps and everything!

Now we're waiting for a connecting flight to Chiang Mai, Thailand. Then next week, we'll continue on to Bali, Indonesia. It's the big adventure that we've talked about all year, and finally we're doing it.

"A three-hour layover," Derrick says. "Is that enough time for us to leave the airport and check out the city?"

"Not really," I reply.

"You've been here before, right, Kyla?"

"That's right! I lived nearby for years."

"I guess that we'll all just have to listen as Kyla regales us with tales of her life in China," Derrick says sarcastically.

I've always suspected that he envies my years overseas. It was Derrick who originally suggested we should take a big trip together, but I'm the one who organized the details. For the longest time, it was just talk, and nobody thought we'd do it. But thanks to my encouragement, we all saved money for a few months, bought the cheapest tickets online, booked youth hostels, and now we've just gone and fucking done it. As I told them all, it's not that hard.

For the moment, we have nothing to do but wait, read, and wander. Probably the first part of our adventure should be to explore this airport. We're just passing through on the way to sunnier places, but it's a really nice airport, almost like a freshly opened giant shopping mall. Some places sure do keep their airports really clean-looking.

"I imagined China a lot differently," says Derrick.

"This isn't China," I say. "It's HKG."

"Look, I know you have a rule that walking around in an airport can't count as visiting a country, but let us have this. Technically, we're in Hong Kong right now."

"Yeah, but you don't get it. Technically, this still isn't mainland China."

"Kyla, don't be so obtuse."

"Geez, Derrick. What about the history, y'know? There's a reason why we don't need visas to land here and can leave the airport if we want. Because it's a... *whaddayacallit*..., a *Special Administrative Region*."

"What's that supposed to mean?"

"It means," I say, taking my time to decide exactly how to put it, "that Hong Kong used to be a British colony, and in 1997, it reverted to China, but the Chinese government had to promise to let the place have its own laws, economy, currency and stuff. Or else, like, there'd be a revolution here. Seriously, it's super different down here than on the mainland."

"Okay, Kyla. I get it already."

While I guess that I'm kinda our group leader, I still should be careful. I don't want to be a show-off or anything.

We go into a sushi restaurant in the airport. Everyone wants to exchange some money at a currency stand and take home a few Hong

Kong dollars as souvenirs, but I insist that I'll just pay with my credit card, and the guys can pay me back later. That seriously beats going for cash at those ripoff exchange places.

Right now I wish that I'd saved my own Hong Kong dollars. I definitely had some left from way back, but I have no idea where they went. They must be stuck in a box somewhere at Mom's place, I guess. Too bad!

"Do they have alcohol here?" one of the girls asks.

"I don't know," I say. Everyone's always asking me inane questions. "Look at the menu. Didn't most of you guys get drunk enough on the flight?"

"Yeah, but that was a different drunk. That was for sleeping. Now we want more like a partying drunk or at least a passing-the-time drunk."

"Heh," I giggle a little. "I know what you mean. Here, at least we can stand up and stretch. It's much more appropriate for chillin' and tipping back a few."

"Do you know what we're all really thinking?" Derrick says. He leans in close and speaks softly, but loudly enough so that we all hear, yet no one else in the restaurant does. Or at least he pretends like he's talking about something so private.

"We could use a certain remedy that's really good for passing the time," he says. "I mean, but damn, wouldn't it be cool to get some bud in here?"

"I could get some bud," I say at normal volume.

"No way."

"I could. Mind you, I'm not saying that I'd bring it to the airport or anything. But y'know, I seriously could leave the airport right now, buy some, get stoned, and come back to make the flight. I know exactly where I'd go."

"No fucking way," Derrick says. "That's too dangerous in a foreign country. I read that China has the death penalty for everything. It's communist, right?"

"But it's not quite so communist here in Hong Kong. Don't you get it? Anyway, I totally could get some herb, for serious."

"Are we even talking about Hong Kong?" Derrick's buddy asks. "What about the city next door. It's not semi-autonomous or whatever. What do you call it? Shen City or some damn thing?"

"First of all, dude, I could get bud even easier over there. But no, I'm just talking about here in Hong Kong. I'll tell you exactly how it'd go down. I'd travel from the airport to the Star Ferry terminal at Canton Road, near the big shopping mall with the boat. I'd just hang around, and the more touristy that I looked, the better. Then Muslim guys would start approaching me, talking about hash. Real good stuff too! You've never tried anything like it. Then we'd all go off to a nearby guesthouse, Peking Guesthouse or something. Pay for an hour, smoke it up quickly, and there you have it. It's that easy. The only hard part is getting cash in Hong Kong dollars."

"Omigod," Derrick spits out, blending three words into one. "Let's do it!"

"Yeah," says his buddy.

"For real!" chimes one of my roommates.

"I totally concur," chips in the other.

"You guys," I say, disappointed. "You really mean that?"

"Why not? What an adventure!"

"I hate to be a buzzkill. I really do. We'll have our adventures later. Only a few hours to go and then we're in Southeast Asia, yay." I say the "yay" very half-heartedly and lamely.

"Let's go now. If we hurry, we can make it!"

"Look, one day I'll take y'all to get high in China. I promise. But don't make such a big deal about it now. I've changed my mind. Sorry, it won't happen."

"So now the great Kyla backtracks. I knew that you weren't serious."

"I'll admit it. Maybe I kind of exaggerated a little. We'd probably miss our flight if we went all the way into Kowloon."

"All the way into where?"

"Kowloon. That's the name of, like, a peninsula part of Hong Kong."

"I bet she's making it all up, yo."

"Fine. Whatever. You guys got me."

We finish eating, still have time to kill and so keep trekking through the airport. Maybe some of my friends feel slightly angry at me for suggesting a bold plan and then chickening out on it. But come on, it was a stupid idea!

Taking our time, we look at advertisements, signs and stuff. Everything's bilingual, of course. I mean, any airport's bilingual, but this is Hong Kong so it's like *super* bilingual. Still, lots of Chinese characters as well as grammatically-perfect English.

Back when I studied Chinese, I proved especially poor at reading. My skills with Chinese characters are minimal, and all of these signs show that complicated kind of Chinese writing. What's it called? *Jianti zi.* Traditional.

As Derrick appreciates some beautiful calligraphy on a large billboard, he asks, "Kyla, what does that say?"

"I don't know," I answer.

"Can't you read Chinese?"

"No way! I never said that I could."

"Oh."

Someone suggests that we all go to freshen up by taking showers. With hours and hours yet until we make it to a youth hostel in Thailand, I must admit that I do feel gross, and a shower would be nice. One section of the airport offers those pay-for showers. We read the signs and follow. I'm asked how we'll pay, and so I mention that I still have my credit card.

Nobody really leads the way. We're all together as a herd, sort of, but somehow most of my friends tend to walk behind me. I'm not totally comfortable with that, but I make do. I'd better get used to it for the rest of our trip.

Actually, I'm pretty familiar with this airport. I used to come here twice a year. Well, I've spent a big fraction of my life on airplanes and in airports. I mean, every few months I'd take a trip, often with 12-hour flights, going to the airport two hours early, commuting, transferring, waiting, then returning and doing the whole thing over again. If I added up all of my time spent traveling and in transit, what would it total? Maybe I've spent, like, two per cent of my adult life that way. It's weird to consider.

Suddenly, I see a very familiar bus station, one that leads right into the city, if only I'd go. For me, this feels especially nostalgic, and I remember the route exactly. It's all right down that hallway... with the parking lot and those annoying sales ladies trying to convince you to use their minibus company. A person could go up to Lok Ma Chau, to Lo Wu, or to the bay.

I was joking around about going to Kowloon to buy hash. I really was, but as we pass a map of the MTR subway system, I can't resist looking at the route to reach that spot. The map shows how to get to Tsim Sha Tsui, Central, Happy Valley, the New Territories, and even to Disneyland. Or I could ride a ferry, go to Lamma Island, suntan on a small beach, or even rush all the way to Macau.

Why, if I wanted, I could even ditch this crew, travel on the MTR and transfer at Lai King onto the Tsuen Wan line, and then get a China visa at that guesthouse on Nathan Road. After hanging out with some young ESL teachers on visa runs, I could be back in the city where I used to live by tomorrow afternoon.

Then I could take a look at my old job and catch up with my ex-boyfriend. God, I wonder what he's up to now? Would he ever be surprised to see me! We had a few good times together. We really did, even if it soured at the end. We totally just weren't meant to stay together, that's all.

Those last few thoughts prompt me to tear-up a little. Why am I being so sappy?

"Cheer up, girl," I tell myself. It's nice to remember what helped make me the person I am today, but I don't want to dwell too much on the past. Gotta look to the future!

"Kyla," says Derrick. "Why are you just standing there? You need to show us the way."

"I'm coming!"

9
猴

It's a cool party. I can't deny that. But for the time being, it's not my thing. A lot of fuckin' temptation faces me these days. So I mostly keep to myself.

To avoid drinking, I sit in front of the ocean and watch the waves. I keep my notebook and cell phone handy for any bits of literary inspiration that come along. Not many do. Poetry may not be my thing either.

I came here with my girl. She's part of what I call "the Canton Contingent", a group of DJs and artists from the capital who help to organize events like this. I try my best to be supportive, and it's her first trip to Hong Kong, so I came along and here I am. Welcome to scenic Lamma Island, a place famous for its illegal raves and high-quality herb.

My girl gets quite excitable, and so I left her to party to her heart's content. I sincerely enjoy her company, but sometimes we all need a little break. I do trust her, most of the time, but I've learned that it's usually best to leave her alone when she gets too drunk.

Late into the night, a point comes when I need to rescue her. Hearing chatter about some hot girls skinny-dipping, I know just who I'll find there. I bring a towel and scare off the surrounding predators. We're all animals here. I make sure that she has a private moment so as to compose herself, but then things turn even worse.

An acquaintance of mine, a guy named Eric, also from Guangzhou and could be classified as part of our contingent, has some kind of a breakdown. Truthfully, I don't know if it's psychological or chemical in nature. When he washes ashore on the beach, in the nude and with foam running down his chin, it looks like the latter. From what I know about him, this may have been inevitable. Pretty much everyone knew he'd cross the line one day, and so here we are.

A dark part of me thinks: *I'm so lucky to be here on that day. Now I have something to write about.*

"Baby," I say to my girl. "Can I leave you alone? Will you be okay?"

"Whaaaat…?"

She sits on the ground, the towel enveloping her like a massive robe. I look around for someone trustworthy.

"Amber!" I call out. She's another acquaintance of the Canton variety, also drunk and disorderly, but appearing to know how to pace herself. Also part of the late-night naked swim, Amber's getting dressed. She doesn't make a big deal about Eric and laughs off her own embarrassment. It's dark, and I can't see much, but while looking towards her I kind of force myself not to peek. She approaches us, and I see that she's wearing a towel. Her shoulders remain bare. I have to admit it; there's more than a little curiosity about what's under that towel.

"Um, what's up?" she asks.

There's work to do, and I won't let myself be distracted. I take a deep breath, control my thoughts, and pass off my girlfriend. "Would you please take care of Ting Ting just for a little while? I have to go and check on something."

"Of course," she answers, leaning down and putting an arm around my girlfriend's shoulders.

"Just make sure that she's not, like, exposed or anything. You two get dressed. Rest up. Drink lots of water."

"Don't worry. We'll be fine."

Two nude women, absolutely beautiful, right in front of me, and I'm telling them to put on their clothes and be responsible. I might never forgive myself for this.

* * *

I thank Amber profusely, and when deeming it safe, I quickly ditch their scene. Nearby, the crowd that I'd shooed away from the girls has reappeared around the poor passed-out guy. About a dozen-odd people circle like vultures, ones too awkward to feed.

Eric, naked, has been pulled away from the water and lies on his side. It's funny how the vultures look right at him but avoid looking at his crotch. At least, they're not looking at it too obviously. Sand covers him almost like a second skin and seeps into his wet beard. I wonder how much went into his mouth.

Before, he'd screamed obscenities, but now he's eerily quiet. I can listen to what the others say. There's talk about something called "G", like the letter, pronounced "*Gee*", as in *Gee whiz*! I don't know that one, but it sounds like you shouldn't mix it with alcohol.

Look into his eyes, like foggy sunglasses over boiled water.

I keep listening as the bystanders narrate the whole situation. That's how people deal with stress. They just start stating the obvious, but it works to my advantage. The situation becomes clear. I learn that this isn't a drowning thing, and that someone with first-aid training has already induced vomiting. Luckily, Eric is breathing and his heart still beats. But mentally he's totally out of it. And maybe he pissed on himself.

Only a couple of guys, two white expatriates, are doing anything at all. I recognize them as party hands working for Pete. They even find Eric's shorts and compassionately put them back onto him. If I'd ever gotten alcohol poisoning back when I was at my worst, I'd be lucky if people like them would've helped me out.

Someone mentions contacting the police, and the expatriate who appears to be the most in charge loudly announces that won't be necessary. Now they're going to take Eric to a medical clinic in the main village. Suddenly it occurs to me that no police are present at this event, not even security guards.

So I volunteer to help. No one else does. After the announcement mentioning police, most of the people quickly disappear. Whether due to guilt, shame, or boredom, I don't know, but as the expatriates and I move Eric away, that section of beach empties and the dance floor fills. I hear a few people remark about how "fucked up" the situation is and send their condolences from afar. I assume that once we're out of sight, everything will return to what passes for normal.

Well, I sincerely hope that this mishap didn't ruin the party.

We're going. Each of Eric's limp arms circles a man's shoulders. At a few tricky moments, I need to lift his legs. We make determined progress. My notebook's in my back pocket, and I can't write anything until this part ends. We move in the direction of Yung Shue Wan. When carrying this guy, it's a very slow walk.

So we get to talking. I'm just making conversation. What else can I do? This isn't a formal interview, not yet. Just asking the guys where they're from and how long they've lived here. We introduce ourselves and talk about music.

They're surprisingly calm about all this. In the party business, maybe this counts as a normal event, something that happens all the time. I suppose it's professional to have contingency plans for such emergencies.

"Just pick up his right leg, would you, Terry?"

"Like this?"

"Yes, that's right. Let's move him along."

I imagine that these guys must deal with overdose situations about once a month. The confidence with which they drag an unconscious medical victim from the beach to the clinic amazes me. It's no big deal, all very matter-of-fact. Then again, maybe they just act like this to put on a show for me. Talk me down. Defend their territory. Do they know that I'm the media?

Or maybe they're also trying to convince themselves.

In any case, no one panics. After a long walk, I'm winded, but we make it back into the village. I recognize the Main Street, although it's dark with few streetlights. At this hour, almost everything's closed. Amid looming shadows, I make out the Tin Hau Temple. I'm told that we're approaching the North Lamma Clinic.

We struggle up a few steps and stop at a door with a red cross on it. The place looks much like it could be any humble little shop. Carefully, we set Eric down. Then the three of us still standing all knock, but the clinic's obviously closed.

There's a notice taped to the door. It's a shoddy piece of paper full of traditional Chinese, spattered with eight-digit numbers and with minimal English at the bottom. It looks so busy with complex characters stuffed into little squares on a faded photocopied sheet. I don't know how anyone could read it, especially in the darkness, but we only need the phone numbers.

I'm impressed when one of these white men calls the number and speaks fluent Cantonese. He pauses, says "*hai*" a few times, and disconnects.

I think he realizes that I don't speak the local lingo. "They're on the way," he tells me.

I nod. We wait.

"I take it that you don't speak Chinese?" I'm asked.

"Nah, man."

"Not even a bit of *Putonghua*?" he asks, switching to Mandarin.

"Maybe a bit," I say. "But not much."

"Oh."

"Appearances can be deceiving."

I'd guess that he grew up in Hong Kong and received a bilingual education. These days you meet a lot of *Putonghua* majors on the mainland, foreigners keen to learn the language of the "next big thing", and they tend to enjoy showing off whenever they can. But a white man who speaks Cantonese, that's rare.

"Want a cigarette?" the other guy asks me.

"Sure. Thanks."

Eric rests on a ledge, propped up against a concrete wall. Everyone smokes, except him. We make occasional coughing sounds, but mostly stay too silent for comfort. I can't wait until the doctor arrives.

"Tough job you guys do," I say.

"It's cool. We've dealt with worse."

I take out my notebook, look for any street signs nearby to help me describe the location, and begin writing a few sparse notes. Any impressions at all are worth scribbling down, like the name of the village or the doctor's hours. I also jot down a few questions that I want to ask later. They're just basic background: How long the doctor has practiced medicine, where he studied, and how often he gets awakened in the middle of the night to treat drug overdoses.

"So you're a writer?" I'm interrupted. "That's what I heard."

"Well," I say, "it's true what you heard."

"You must have collected a lot of material today."

"Maybe. We'll see."

"Just don't say anything too negative about the party, okay? We want press, but preferably good press, you know?"

"Don't worry," I assure him. "I'm interested mainly in Lamma's tourism industry. Basically, I'm a travel writer. That's how I pay the bills. But shit, I couldn't pass up this opportunity. Not to mention that I know Eric and sincerely do want to help."

"Yeah, thanks."

"No problem. Anyhow, for now I just hope to get some insight into the medical infrastructure and write something light. I'm certainly not keen on one of those fear pieces about drugs and misguided youth."

They don't look very reassured. But what can they do? I was kind enough to help out when they needed me, and it's not like they can support censorship. That wouldn't be very Hong Kong of them at all.

"You can trust me," I say. "Truly."

"If you say so."

"Anyway," I continue, "I'll save all the juicy parts for a novel."

Then three people arrive, one at a time. First it's a Filipina receptionist. She looks like she was abruptly awakened. Wearing raggedy clothes, without makeup and her hair a mess, she might've been dragged out of a war zone.

She unlocks the clinic's front door and explains that she's sorry, but she isn't allowed to do anything medical because of liability issues.

Inside, the clinic is small, cramped, and still in darkness. The two guys trip over each other getting Eric through the doorway. The patient remains silent, but at least has regained some level of consciousness.

Once we're all inside, the two guys seem to know their way around. They switch on the lights and carefully place Eric onto a small white cot. He lies silently, save for intermittent coughs.

The clinic consists of little more than a waiting room that doubles as an office with another space down a short hallway. From the waiting room, I can see the entire place. Around me are white walls, hanging charts, diplomas, and even some Chinese-medicine posters with yin, yang and all that.

Next a nurse arrives, followed by the doctor. They too look like they've been ravaged out of bed, but don't complain. The doctor thanks the receptionist for opening the door and then lets her go home. She writes something at the front desk before rushing away. Probably she lives the closest, and so for emergencies she simply needs to bring the keys and open the place. After that, the paperwork can wait until tomorrow's normal working hours.

The guys explain the situation. The doctor asks about drugs and directs the nurse. He tells her what to do in Cantonese. When speaking English, he's heavily accented but grammatically perfect.

The nurse takes a cloth and wipes at the sides of Eric's mouth, which drip with drool, and wipes his forehead too. I walk over and take a closer look at him. In the clear light, I see a film of sweat all over his skin, mingling with what remains of the sand.

After searching around in a cupboard, the doctor comes back with some small bottles and a needle. He loads a concoction, hands it to the nurse and starts writing on a prescription pad.

The nurse preps the inside of Eric's elbow, finds a vein, and then injects. The patient's coughs turn into moans.

The doctor says something in Cantonese I don't understand. Then in English he adds, "Who is this?"

I'm sure that he knows the other two guys, and they already explained Eric's situation, so the question must refer to me.

"I'm a friend," I say, "and a writer."

"A writer?"

Going closer, I wait for a moment until the doctor's hands are free. Then I introduce myself at length, and we shake hands.

"May I get a few statements?" I ask. "Purely on the record. You can choose your words carefully."

My query's intended for everybody.

The nurse says nothing, simply sitting at the desk in the waiting room, cupping her head in her hands like it's a huge struggle to stay awake.

The two expatriates reintroduce themselves and talk about the party, about Lamma's unique culture and about the rarity of such medical emergencies. They make sure to focus on the positive and how responsible they are in handling the situation. I write it all down.

As for the doctor, he doesn't say much, but tells me what I need to know. I'm thinking that this story will amount to about 1,000 words, which isn't as much as it sounds. A few times the doctor mentions some strange chemicals, and I ask him about spelling. I think that I'll have to take an anti-drug angle after all. It's kind of lame, right? I know, but I write what I must.

I learn a lot. With the clinic's limited resources, no one expects a full toxicology report, but between the rumors of certain drugs going around and the doctor's expert opinion, I'm assured that the problem arose from a dangerous mixture of GHB and alcohol. I also learn that mixing MDMA – that is, Ecstasy – with alcohol causes dehydration, but that's inconsistent with these symptoms. It's GHB that can cause loss of consciousness and vomiting, although the reactions vary. Since breathing isn't too suppressed, Eric's situation looks stable.

"Keep him warm, and get that winter blanket over here," the doctor tells the nurse in English so that we all understand. "Keep him on his side in the recovery position, and he must stay like this overnight."

I wonder how much this medical advice costs, but no one mentions a price.

Yup, I made a wise choice to stay sober at this party. Now I think that I should go back soon to check on my girlfriend.

I say thanks to everyone, wish them the best, and prepare to leave. Later I'll conduct research online, learn more about these drugs and their effects. I'll quote some statistics too. That's always good for fact-dropping. When I finish with a draft, I'll need to find somewhere to sell my story. Mainland publications won't touch it, expat-based or otherwise. This has little to do with the usual travel websites.

Sure, I want to write something entertaining, but I also hope that I'm at a stage in my career when I can write stories a bit deeper than the usual trite shit, something slightly important.

Just as I open the door to depart, I see a newspaper discarded on a tiny wooden table. It's the sole reading material in the waiting room. Somehow I didn't notice it before. This issue of the respected English-language *South China Morning Post* must be about a week old. I realize that much without even looking at its date. Last week's big news story about a political scandal dominates the front page.

I don't pick up the newspaper, but just seeing it makes a difference to me. Filing a mental note, I decide to buy a copy soon as I can, and make sure to highlight the submissions guidelines.

The clinic door is open, and I step outside. There, time flows as it always does. The blue light of morning approaches us all.

10
雞

I can get through this. I can do it. I'm a strong woman. I…

"AAAHH!"

My thoughts are interrupted by intense pain emanating from deep inside my belly. I knew this day would come. Now I must do this thing, and I'm alone.

For several weeks I've lived in this hotel room. It's clean and comfortable, but I'm bored and lonely.

My husband set up everything for me. He sent me luggage and strange plug adaptors. Earlier, he made sure that his company sponsored me with a business visa so that I can stay long enough in Hong Kong. He even prepared the documentation so that suspicious officials at the Hong Kong border would accept me in my pregnant state.

My family members helped me by scouting the hospital and the area nearby to make sure that the hotel would be convenient for going to the OB/GYN department. Then my husband arranged to hire an Indonesian maid. She comes here three times a week, brings me groceries, and even accompanies me for the weekly checkups and prenatal-care services.

My husband made so many arrangements all while working abroad. I'm grateful to him, but I haven't seen him for a month. He emails me sometimes and always asks about the child. Yes, he cares so much.

I'm not sure if I really miss him or not. In my heart, I know that I should miss him. I feel thankful to him for all that he has done. But I miss many other people a lot more, like my lovers from other times, old friends, and family members.

Most days I spend my time in the hotel watching television dramas. I wear loose maternity clothes and explore the neighborhood a little. I've tried many of the local restaurants. I find Hong Kong people to be very kind and helpful about my condition. It's amazing how they wait in line at a bus stop and stand aside when I walk past them. At a restaurant next door, the waitress gets to know me a little and asks about my husband, but I can say nothing.

I do little shopping. No more yoga classes. No driving lessons. I nap, watch television, get fat, and wait. On the weekends, my family visits me.

Today the pain began. It happened as I sat here on the sofa, barely awake and with crumpled candy wrappers on the floor, thinking about my life and considering another mid-day nap. Then a stomach ache rose up, and water dripped from my panties onto the cushion. This is the feeling of contractions.

"AHHH!"

So I struggle to the phone and call my maid. Today's one of her days off. She doesn't answer and just sends me an SMS message that I don't open. She's useless. Again, I'm alone.

Moving cautiously, I pull on loose-fitting pants, slip on my nearest shoes, and take my purse. No extra clothes, no paperback novel, just my ID card and some cash.

The ride down in the elevator is terrible, but at least it's just five floors. Furiously, I curse my husband. If he's such a smart man, then he should have thought clearly enough to find me a first-floor hotel room. That's the first of many curses.

As I moan in pain, people look at me. The hotel receptionist runs over and walks me outside. "Is there anything that you need, Miss?"

"I'm fine," I say. "I only want a taxi."

Fortunately, many taxis wait for passengers in front of the hotel. The receptionist opens a door to the first one for me. I still find it strange that the driver's side of the car is the opposite of what seems right. That's hard to get used to, but I'm not driving so I simply get into the rear seat and recline on my back.

"King George Hospital," I say.

"Miss, how is your health?" exclaims the suddenly anxious driver.

"I need to go now. Please hurry."

The driver doesn't even turn on the meter. He's kind and repeatedly asks about my comfort. Fuck all this kindness!

"Shall I go faster?" he asks me.

"Yes, go fast." Fuck!

"I'll be careful to avoid bumps on the road."

"Fine," I say and curse under my breath.

"My wife has two children," he says. "I know there's lots of pain, but that means you're healthy. Don't worry."

He knows nothing about women's pain. He still talks, but I don't want to listen. Instead, I focus on taking deep breaths. Sweat drips down my neck and it isn't elegant at all.

In one way, I don't want to go to a hospital at all. I wish that I lived in ancient times and that a midwife would rush to my home. Everything would be so much simpler then. I'd be a concubine, my husband would live in a grand estate, and although unfaithful, he'd stay nearby. We'd have no anxiety or confusion. Our roles would be clearly planned. It'd resemble one of those television dramas, a bit of a tragedy, but at least life would make sense.

No, maybe I don't really wish that. There's a reason why I value my freedom and independence. It's not because of a husband's faithfulness or lack of it. Nothing like that! Not because of my lover, nor even because of my own independent-mindedness. I need to live in this modern age because of the child.

I struggle to keep my thoughts on the child. This is all about her. People say that once the agony ends and you meet your child for the first time, then it's all worthwhile. Immediately the pain will be forgotten. I hope that's true this time.

After various twists, turns, and red lights, the taxi finally arrives. Speaking rapidly, the driver explains my dilemma to the guards in front of the building. They raise the gate and gesture for him to speed past. He pulls up to the hospital entrance and jumps out with the car's engine still running.

Opening the back door, he takes my hand. His grip feels firm, yet gentle with compassion. He pulls me out, slowly. Suddenly I'm lifted and carefully placed in a wheelchair. A nurse pushes me.

"Would you like to lie on your back?" the nurse asks.

"No," I say.

The taxi driver comes in with me, past the automatic doors. Everything happens so fast, and I'm rushed to the next place.

Doctors and nurses, the latter in white hats, surround me and begin taking notes.

"Where is your husband?" the driver asks. It's his last chance to speak before I must respond to all the medical people. "Is he alright? Do you have your mobile? You can use mine to call him."

"My husband is coming," I say.

The driver stops walking with me and vanishes from my sight as I speed down the hall. I'll never see him again. Although I imagine him waving behind me, I don't know. He never did charge me for the taxi ride.

Doctors and nurses ask me about medical issues, insurance, my identification, and any records about me that may exist at this hospital. I answer to the best of my ability. Nurses and aides write down everything.

Rooms transform into swirls of color as pain overwhelms me. I'm lying on my back again, this time in a hospital bed. From my purse, I take out my ID card and a credit card. Hospital records are printed, and I sign my name. I dream of the past and future, and I wonder if this really is happening. My memories of previous hospital visits overlap and bring fleeting images of bare white rooms. I think that maybe I'm given a shot. The pain recedes, and my confusion grows.

With effort, I stop moaning and try to relax. Suddenly, I'm wearing a hospital gown. The doctor, a woman with a pleasant voice, opens my legs to examine me and record the rate of contractions. Not feeling even the slightest sense of modesty, I let the medical people do what they do.

The doctor holds one of my hands, smiles, and asks questions about how I'm feeling. So I tell her that I feel like shit.

Thinking about doctors and hospitals, I decide that I've never liked these places, even going back to when I was a small child. But here in Hong Kong, it's all so different. This place resembles an alien planet compared to the hospitals of my memories. The people here even speak in a strange mixture of Yue language peppered with unpronounceable English words, although I hear some Mandarin too.

I'm told that my condition appears to be stable and that all we can do is to wait. That's my life alright. These things can take many hours. My mother always did warn me about that.

Feeling a bit less pain, I decide to call my mother, and we chat briefly. I tell her that my labor has begun. Immediately, she assures me that she's leaving for Hong Kong right now. As we talk, she excitedly declares that she's on her way. I know that it'll take several hours for her to arrive, followed by my father and then perhaps my aunt, uncle, and cousins. They'll all come when they can.

My mother reminds me about the *zuo yue zi*, the postpartum ritual by which I must stay in bed for the next month. She's so old-fashioned, saying that I must do this for my health or else face serious illness in the future. As much as I dread the pain of childbirth, I also dread the pending boredom of another month in that hotel room.

Still, I want my mother here. Right now! I need her, and so I ask her to hurry please.

She tells me that she'll call my husband and convince him to fly here tomorrow. Without hesitation, she'll spend her money calling him long-distance, but I know that they'll only quarrel. I don't expect my husband to arrive anytime soon, but I do expect him to make sure that all the bills are paid.

The hospital people check on me every few minutes and tell me to buzz them if the labor pains worsen. They come in, look me over, and then leave me alone while checking on other patients.

They show no antagonism to me, although I'm not from this city. They do their jobs, and that's their only concern. They clearly see from my ID card that I'm not a local. It's obvious. I've imagined this day for so long and expected a need to explain myself. I had a whole story planned. Yet no one minds me at all. They just do their jobs. I hear more Mandarin spoken in the direction of other rooms. I suppose Hong Kong hospitals must earn lots of money from us wealthy mainlanders.

The plan, of course, is for my child to be born with Hong Kong citizenship. It's not an original plan. These days it's a very popular one, and we must take full advantage while still able to get away with it.

All this pain and loneliness will be worth it because my daughter will grow up with so many opportunities that her mother never had. She'll never need to do the things her mother has done. She'll speak English, carry a Hong Kong passport, study abroad, and marry a foreigner. Her life will be glamorous and happy. She must travel far away from the sad land where her family lives, and merely reaching Hong Kong isn't nearly far enough. I hope that one day she won't be simply Chinese, but something more.

The pain comes, and my thoughts dissolve. I can focus only on the moment. It is all pain. I try my best to remember what this is all for. For the future. Don't forget. Pain is necessary. It brings new life.

11
狗

Bad luck today! Yes, very bad indeed.

"Here you are, sir," I say, handing over my little green booklet of nationhood. I try to keep my conversation to a minimum.

Luohu, Lo Wu and that Sham Chun River, or whatevers you call it. Simply goin' to the ordinary and routine border crossin' on a visa run, you know. I need to get that stamp, do some business in the HK with my homeboys and come right back home. What happens today so different than every other time?

Away I go. GZ East to the LH Zhan. Go to the foreigner line. Fill out the forms. A Chinese border officer open my passport. Guys like him always take a close look, but I do this many times before and always get through. Why not this time?

He turn the passport upside down. Squints. Scan it over that computer scanner thing, scan it again, and scan it one more time. It's no fakey. I know that he know that, and I'm sure he know that I know he know. If ya follow me! He just tryin' to sweat it out of me, to make me nervous, and he doin' a good job of it.

"*Nihao*," I say and smile widely. I want to act like that's the only word I know.

Look at all those white boys in the line over yonder. They go through like it's nothin'. A few of them stare at me, sneerin' and judgin'. Those people behind me in my line's gettin' impatient. All these old men in suits and the young-one backpackers, they think they better than me, but they'd buy from me on the streets all the same.

The passport-readin' guy still say nothin' and motion me with his hand. I hope I finally can go, but it's not that way. I crossed the yellow line, right true. There I stand in No Man's Land, right in the mid-section of one country and two systems. I want to get goin', but it's not goin'. No, not yet.

Three guards walk up to me. The white boy behind me in line breathe a loud sigh of relief. Then the line keep movin'. I grab my rollin' luggage, and we go somewhere else.

"Please come on with us," say one guard-boy with the worst accent.

"Yes, sir," I say.

I follow. Three of them, two guys and a woman, speakin' in the Mando, all talkin' about me. They think I don't understand, but I sure do. They talk about how they gotta be careful about the black man in their country, and they don't know why I been here so many year. They wanna ask me questions and see what I say. I listen close to hear if I have any troubles, if there any real law I broke or what. But they don't talk like that, about rule or law and such. They just spit and opine and opine.

Am I gonna be deported or what? What they plan to do with me? I don't know. For a minute, I truly feel shitty. I don't wanna be here.

Maybe this day had to happen eventually, but fuck, I don't like it.

I take a deep breath, and I'm not to show them my nervousness. It'll be fine, it have to. My luggage screechin' down the hallway.

Finally, they take me to some office and sit me down at a table. I've been to this border too many times and never seen these corridors. It's quite interesting, it is. I look around.

A secretary drink tea and play on a computer. All very relaxed. Two guys standin', and the lady-guard sit down across to me. I guess she speak the best English so they let her do the talkin'.

My passport there in the middle of the table, opened to my picture. The chair's comfortable. There's a window, and nobody lookin' at me but these guards hoverin' around. What the hell this supposed to be happenin'?

"Hello," she say. "Mr John?"

"Yes," I say.

"We just have questions."

"Please. I'm happy to answer your questions."

She flip through my book and look at the five Q visas stacked in a row. "I see you live here many years. How do you like China?"

"I like it very much."

"That's good."

"And what you are doing here?"

"Just traveling."

She open the passport again, her eyes lookin' at stamps years past and noddin' up to look at my eyes. "Just travel?"

"Yes, that's right, ma'am."

"Do you have job here?" she asks bluntly and tosses my passport on the table. "It's a long time to just travel here. We are wondering if you have job."

"No, I really do not," I say with the utmost conviction.

"How you afford to stay?"

"I'm spending my savings."

"Savings?" she asks.

"That's right, and some money that my family has given me. It's a nice thing in my country that family members help each other out."

"I see," she say, decidin' she can't interrogate me no more about that. "How about the registration please?"

"I have that right here for you," I say and unzip a compartment in my luggage to show my printout registration form with some false hotel address. She read it with intent. The other two look over her shoulder.

"You live in the capital city."

"That's right, as you can see here."

"Xiaobei?" she asks.

"No, it's another district."

"I hear about many jobs in Xiaobei, in clothing district."

"I wouldn't know about that," is all I say.

And I pretty sure that's all to it. That all they can ask, and I won't say nothin' else. There's nothing more to the situation. We covered everything. I'm not caught doin' anything wrong. Maybe they just want to show off or some shit. Really, they can't be serious with this thing.

In my head, I'm makin' plans for the rest of the day, countin' off all I must do. I'll be late to meet the boys down at the pier. Not that I would take any product with me. Ain't that stupid, but I thought to buy a bit of bulk and resell it at the big party we all been hearin' about. Guess the party go on without me. I'll do something else. Send a text and soon. Let 'em know I'm late.

Or I could be wrong in plannin' in my head like this. For all I know they may gonna' kick me out yet. Gotta plan for that eventuality too. Wouldn't be the most convenient, but I can deal.

So I make another plan in my head, and here it is: I'll call up some contacts, borrow cash, fly back home, visit my momma and family and it'll be a great trip. Surprise vacation, everybody appreciate that. Then I'll go to the Lagos office, pay off who need to be paid off, and get a new passport. Next go to the Chinese embassy, pay 'em off there too, and I'll come right back as I please. Should take me two weeks at most. My honey can take care of the pad for me. Boss won't like it, but circumstances happen, and we do what we do. He plenty happy if I keep my mouth shut, I'm sure. That's what truly important.

If it happen, it happen. Either way, I got a plan. I stick with my homeboys, and I do what I want. I ain't finished with this place. Not at all! I got things to do. And long as I got some plan, not let nobody gonna stop me, no way.

12
豬

I'm last. Almost everyone else is out riding on the ferry, going home, or already sleeping. The party's over.

Only I'm still up, eager for the new day, yet in no hurry to let the previous one go. I can't stop the feelings of optimism and love pouring out from my open heart. The smile on my face just won't go away.

I've hiked up Lamma Island's hills to see what I can see from here in the morning light. It's a good workout that makes me feel young, and the world looks new. Really I'm just in that altered state of consciousness that comes with getting fucked up and staying awake all night, but I still think that I'm onto something. I'm experiencing some little glimpse of a greater reality, like it's for the first time. And it's so damn beautiful up here.

The clouds loom big, soft and white as if I only need to jump a little higher to reach them with my hands. I imagine their feel and taste.

They'd be like the white cotton candy that I used to find in little carnivals and markets.

Other bright blue parts of the sky gleam like fresh paint. Everything smells clean and shines like CGI, as if the whole scene's a special effect just for my amusement.

I've walked uphill as high as the paved path can take me, even passing a lookout pavilion. Then I veer off the path to go even higher. Now I'm simply stepping on tall wild grass. With each step, I hear brief crumpling noises. There's a rhythm to them, almost like last night's music.

Turning around, I take it all in again. The path remains easily visible. I realize that walking on this tall grass holds me to a slow pace, but that's fine.

Several early-morning mountain bikers roll past. They wear vivid, clean colors, as if they'd glided off a computer screen. Their bikes are tough and muddy, but the helmets and spandex stay bright. The bikers vanish within moments, but at nearly the last instant I see one of them wave to me.

Hastily, I wave back and hope that some of them noticed. I wonder how they reached these lofty heights. It was hard enough for me to climb so high on foot. I admire these cyclists, and I hope at least it was a good wave. I hope at least one of them noticed.

I've passed all kinds of people on this hike. What a splendid diversity of humans, a perfect example of this post-globalist planet where we live.

I even saw a few local farmers, almost indistinguishable from those across the border in Guangdong Province. They're friendly and smile at me, but don't even try to communicate. According to what I've heard, many of the Chinese in Hong Kong working at lower-class jobs are immigrants from the mainland, and often illegal ones. I wonder about these people. If they grew up here before 1997, I suppose that they should speak at least a few words of my language, but then again, maybe not.

When a person stands at the heart of urban Hong Kong, everything's as modern as hell, and you easily get a sense that it's part of the First World. Clear differences exist from the Developing World, although they narrow each year. Yet when it comes to the poor service workers, farmers, or poverty-ridden peasants of either the rural villages or urban ghettos, there's not much difference after all.

This line of thought seems like a downer, and I don't want that kind of a mood. I'm simply observing this piece of China and thinking about how it compares to the other pieces. I do that all the time. We all do.

But don't stop there, I think. This island represents more than just China. Here, I could observe elements of the whole world as they pass before me. Along with the white Europeans and the First World Asians, there are those other immigrants, the poor women from the Philippines or Indonesia who work as maids, nannies, waitresses, and perhaps even nurses. All those feminine jobs. Is this much closer to the reality for most of the world's immigrating women?

Of course, I have my own experiences, but I'm a privileged expat, not an immigrant. My story is my own, and I cherish it, but really, it's naive. Most of the world doesn't live much like me, and I'll never truly see all the realities no matter how much that I travel. Most women going abroad don't become teachers and commercial models. They more closely resemble the woman seen socializing in parks or picnicking together on library staircases on Sundays. You pay them to clean your home and serve you drinks, and they do it with smiles, surviving at times in other ways that you never truly understand.

As my thoughts continue, I keep walking and climbing. Then large rocks line the landscape near me. I go even higher, and they get bigger, turning into boulders. This natural debris, silent and still, surrounds me.

Soon I'm overlooking a cliff. Silently, I step as close to the edge as I dare. Then I climb onto a huge rock and tip-toe as high as possible. Twisting around, looking down in a complete circle, I observe much of the island sprawled below me. From here, forests, even the banyan trees, look like grass. I see a brownish-blue sea, dotted in places by tiny boats, that appears to go on forever. In another direction, a few specks represent man-made structures, but nearby three huge smokestacks of industry rise from the power station. Elsewhere, the rocky coast of a beach zigzags in another direction. A fishing village, the periphery of Little Bay, the trees, the horizon.

Those sweet white clouds move, and the sun hits me from behind. Tomorrow my back will be sunburned, I know it. The thin straps of my top protect next to nothing, and my shorts cover little more. I can feel the skin on my shoulders and on the backs of my thighs slowly cooking and turning reddish-brown. But it's early, and the warmth on my person comforts me, at least for now.

As the heat slowly rises, my throat feels coarse. Maybe I can't ignore my thirst for much longer. Back down at sea level, I have several water jugs, along with my little backpack, my purse, my cell phone, and a change of clothes, all in my tent at the beach. Right now, I'm in no great hurry to see those things.

I don't want to descend, not yet. There are two reasons. For one thing, it's beautiful up here. For another, I don't want to hear bad news. Something terrible happened, and I'm reluctant to know the details. So I'll stay up here a little longer, and try to enjoy the day.

Something happened to Eric, but he has his own story, and I have mine. Whether or not his story has ended, for the time being it shouldn't overlap with mine. I'll leave him alone. We never were meant to be close. At times, our paths cross, but mostly we live in our own innately separate worlds. Our universes are totally different.

So many people down there live out separate stories that they narrate to themselves and sometimes to you. So many worlds of their own, you might say there's a whole unique universe for each person, for each life. Sure, they intersect all the time, but we never can know everything about how different or alike they truly are.

Steven definitely has his own universe, one where the girl called Amber is a slutty character. Inside his own tale, he knows best and is in the right while this flawed girl keeps making mistakes, and if only she'd let him save her. Who am I to disagree much with his perspective?

Ting Ting has her own universe too, where Amber's a proud and independent woman. Where we swim together and share wonderful experiences, where we're strong and life is positive and full of fun. Really and truly, that's a valid interpretation too. Good person or bad person, choose whichever version you prefer, and so will I…

I continue this line of thinking, about all the different lives scattered about with their own little eyes and souls. Endless stories told in endless voices, too numerous to comprehend. We can focus only on a few, maybe sense some patterns and try to grasp the basic idea.

Then Ting Ting's boyfriend comes to mind. What's his name again? Monkey? Terry? He's a storyteller of sorts and understands all this better than anyone. His work is to communicate what the world looks like from his own point of view, and I envy that ability. He's flawed, amazing, and sometimes crude. He can be loving or a drunk. As an individual, he can be so many things.

More distant from my own experiences, there's Mister Jones from the ferry, the guy who tagged along with us to the party. The worlds of business people like him rarely overlap much with mine. This archetypal American, who came here to kick ass and earn fistfuls of money, and then he becomes changed. He represents them all. Probably the lesson is that no one remains the same person for very long. We keep changing, and our stories get muddier.

Like the Chinese businessmen who reinvent themselves every day, and rapidly change the whole of their culture in the process. They're everywhere in this country; I've met those types time and time again. In fact, I met one last night, Mister Feng, another man just down the hill.

These thoughts carry me far beyond this vantage point, and I imagine other people elsewhere. An American girl, maybe even a teacher like me, probably passes through another outlying island, right now, ready to fly. She may travel the world, the surest way that we all try to change ourselves. Sometimes we succeed, and sometimes we fail. Maybe, I think, this girl once lived near here but left long ago. When returning to familiar places, we often hope that they'll look different, and they may, but usually just slightly. If we want change, we must do it from the inside out.

Across the sea in another direction, sometime in the near future, there is a mainland woman in a hospital. She's having a baby. Maybe she's still near her hometown, at least in a geographical sense, yet she's so far away. Her entire world is changing right there. Families try to be something solid, something that *exists*, but in the end it's as elusive as these clouds. In the end we are all alone in this. She could be one of the *nouveau riche* buying into Hong Kong citizenship, or at least doing so for future generations. That's okay too. It's a common story, and you can't blame her. If anything, she represents modern women worldwide, undergoing the ultimate reinvention, for the best of reasons.

There are sadder stories out there still. Maybe other men, less privileged, face discrimination from border officers or government officials. That's the story of Third Worlders trying harder than anyone else to better themselves. But if they can't even cross borders easily, what can they do? They struggle more than anyone in this race to the modern age, and sometimes they really do make it to the finish line. More than ever they are making it, and that is progress, it just has to be.

Meanwhile, ESL guys arrive in China, go wherever they want and no one stops them. In truth, this life-story's quite familiar to me. Led by school management directing their actions, they maneuver themselves through all the bureaucracies. They secure the chance to live in a new setting and earn money. That's a neat trick. It really is. I only hope that ultimately there's more to life than that.

These are a few of the lives that pass through in this one little head of mine, but I can't imagine or follow all of it. The invisible webs connecting all of us, stretching outwards infinitely in every direction. It is incomprehensible, except for those brief moments when you suspect you are getting a fleeting sense of it. Then the feeling vanishes, and you're back to your normal life, your normal, lonely experience.

Each and every one of us has an entire universe inside our heads, and it doesn't mean anything. We squander it, we try our best, and if we can fit just a little bit of love and wonder then I guess it's all worth it in the end. I guess it's all working out.

That's it, that's all I can handle. I'm thirsty, I have to pee, and I am so ready to get off this island. Time for life to go on.

Well, this is my universe, my voice, my perspective; it's for me, and at least that means I get to have the last word.

ACKNOWLEDGMENTS

I would like to thank a number of people for helping me in making this book a possibility. I wouldn't have made it all the way to China without help, and I particularly wouldn't have made it as a writer without support from these special people.

Firstly, thanks to Ariel Maayan for shipping me off to China in the first place. Thanks to the Guangzhou Open Mic and Shenzhen Writers Group for all the encouragement along the way.

Thanks to Adrian Cone for his friendship and care in my early years, and to Edward Derbes for the original push along the path of professional writing. Thanks to Kevin McGeary for those initial opportunities in Shenzhen. In no particular order, I would like to thank these friends for helpful editing and feedback during the different stages of my various manuscripts: Andrew Pang, Olivia Skwara, Joseph Simon Bleazard, Michele Chung, Natalie Ballard, Amanda Roberts, and Travis Lee.

Chinese Horoscopes by Debbie Burns (published by Landsdowne, 2007) was a very helpful book, being my primary source in researching the Chinese zodiac.

I will be forever grateful to Tom Carter for the final steps in the process of bringing this novel to fruition. Thanks to publisher Pete Spurrier as well.

Lastly, thanks to Bronwen Shelwell for her great support and for all the inspiration that is to come.

Ray Hecht
Shenzhen, 2015